PRAISE FOR SHAUN O. MCCOY AND EVEN HELL HAS KNIGHTS

"I read McCoy and enjoy him. If you have an ounce of imagination, so will you. He takes you places you can't go by yourself."
—McKendree Long, Author of Dog Soldier Moon

"McCoy has a queer ability to highlight the most delightfully horrific details imaginable. I grimace, suck air through my teeth and squeeze shut my eyes. Then I open just one so I can keep on reading."
—Fred Fields, Author

"In *Even Hell Has Knights*, McCoy depicts dark landscapes filled with fiery fury. His characters are soulful, at times wonderfully craven, surprising us with their humanity and evoking our laughter in unexpected ways."
—Chris Mathews, Author of GARGOYLES

"In preparing for this book, McCoy rampaged across three continents in an indiscriminant pillage of mythology, history and religion. The booty he gained has made for one of the most unique settings in the Fantasy Genre."
—Monet Jones, Author of Rehoboth

"McCoy's world-building is impeccable."
—Ginny Padgett, President of SCWW

"McCoy writes with a passion for action. He introduces us to graphic characters and takes us on a hair-raising journey through crumbling underground landscapes where battles rage to protect a magical child. This is a borderlands for where the quest for survival has never been so grueling."
—Bonnie Stanard, Author of Master of Westfall Plantation

OTHER WORKS BY SHAUN O. MCCOY

HELLSONG SERIES
Even Hell Has Knights
Knight of Gehenna
March till Death (May, 2014)

HELLSONG SERIES INFIDELS
Affliction (Coming Soon!)
The Eden of a Lesser God (Coming Soon!)

NOVELLAS
Electric Blues
Binary Jazz
Digital Muse (Coming Soon!)

Hellsong Series

BOOK I

Even Hell Has Knights

SHAUN O. McCOY

SISYPHEAN PUBLISHING

EVEN HELL HAS KNIGHTS

Editor-in-Chief: Gabrielle Olexa
Associate Editors: Justin Williams; Jody Wenzel; Brian "B-ri" Jeffcoat; James Mobley; Nichole Breton
Consulting Editors: Amanda Simays; Leigh Thomas

Title art: Thomas the Younger
Title Layout: Kirill Simin

A Sisyphean Publishing Book

www.ehhknovel.com

ISBN: 978-0615716541

First Edition October 2012

Printed in the United States of America

0 9 8 7

For Cory Wenzel

An Airman, Fighter, and Friend.

ACKNOWLEDGEMENTS

This book has many heroes, but my real life hero is my sister. She fights leukemia with more bravery than any fictional character I could imagine.

I appreciate the wonderful help of those who have made the exciting journey of writing this novel with me. In addition, I'm insanely thankful to my father for telling me his multi-epic "bedtime" stories from the moment I was old enough to comprehend the English language—and quite possibly before that; and to my mother for patiently reading to me countless young adult fantasy novels—although for some reason she waited until I was old enough to know what a sentence was before doing so.

Also, Professor Ben Greer, you happen to be the man, and there is very little in this novel which cannot somehow be attributed to your teachings. Mike Long and Bonnie Stanard have been marvelous mentors for me in the field of writing. Also in that regard, there is no one who can replace Walt Oliver—who gave me pink lemonade in my childhood and writing advice in my adulthood.

I can't fail to mention the Mason brothers, Scott and Jeremy, and their enthusiastic willingness to answer my firearm questions over plates full of General Tso's chicken. Narayan Boston, thank you for your support!

Lastly, I'd like to thank the *Sisyphean Publications* production team. The bevy of editors: Gabe, Justin, Jody, B-ri, James, Nichole, Amanda, and Leigh. Also, media arts moguls Kirill Simin and Erica Morgan. Without all these excellently talented people, life would be meaningless, and all would be lost. Enjoy!

EVEN HELL HAS KNIGHTS

— PROLOGUE —

Carlisle lay dying on the cold stones of Hell. He watched his black blood as it crept across the floor, a muddy river fed by the wellspring in his side. The half-congealed liquid was marked with his own footprints, his lifeblood depressed in the pattern of his treaded boots. On Earth, having suffered such a wound, a man could expect to die after an hour or so of slow bleeding. Here, in the labyrinth, the timing was less certain.

He could suffer for days.

It hadn't always been this way. He hadn't always been damned. He'd lain like this, once, in an Alabama cornfield, counting his blessings. For each of those blessings, his grandmother had taught him, there was an angel flying over his head. There had been so many angels then. They'd started to leave him, one by one, on the day he'd betrayed himself with Anna McNamara.

Certainly there were none above him now.

The Infidel was coming. The Infidel was going to kill him.

Rolling over was torture. He clutched at the floor with his blood covered hands, trying to drag himself forward. He failed. The grain of the stone felt slick beneath his fingertips.

He looked about for the Infidel, who he knew must be somewhere in this mile high chamber. With his sight fading, however, he could not find the man. He tried again to move farther forward but managed only to roll back over. Blood matted the hair on the right side of his head, soaking through his shirt at his shoulder and through his pants at his hip. He felt winded and struggled for air with each breath.

He heard his murderer's approach; the man's boots clopping at first against the stone floor and then slapping in the blood. Dark red droplets splattered into Carlisle's face.

"You'll fail," Carlisle said. "You'll see. I'm not the only one who protects the angel's get. We love that boy."

No answer.

The Infidel's expressionless face filled his vision.

"It's a liver wound," Carlisle whispered. "Christ, too, was stabbed in the side."

He was vaguely aware of the Infidel's hand as it came to rest on his shoulder. Carlisle might have found the gesture comforting had it come from someone else.

"You're lucky we didn't fight on Earth, Infidel." Carlisle's anger helped him find his breath. "God wouldn't have let you win. The angels, they would have helped me."

The Infidel remained impassive.

Carlisle wiped at the blood around his eyes. "You think I'm crazy, don't you? I'm telling you there were angels. Angels! You wouldn't have noticed. They wouldn't have come to you. They sang to me."

The hand on his shoulder pulled away, but the Infidel remained kneeling beside him.

The pain became intense for a moment, and Carlisle gritted his teeth, squeezing shut his eyes until it passed. "I hate you," he managed. "You think we're the same? We're nothing alike. Nothing."

Tears came to his eyes, summoned there from his agony. "You think because God damned us both we're equal? At least I tried. I tried!" Carlisle's body shook with his words, hurting him enough to make him sob, but he could not stop himself from speaking. "While you were up there, fucking, loving, gluttonizing, I was praying. I was fighting myself. I failed. But I tried. You just turned your back..."

Fatigue forced him to stop and catch his breath.

He noticed the Infidel was no longer kneeling. Carlisle attempted to look up at the man, but he couldn't focus. He settled for looking at the Infidel's booted feet. The feet began walking. At first Carlisle feared that he would be abandoned, but he was comforted when he saw that the Infidel was circling him.

"You think you're better than us?" Carlisle continued. "Because you didn't deal with demons? Maab had no choice. We had to."

He could no longer see the Infidel, but he could hear the man's footsteps in the blood behind him. Carlisle put a finger to his lips and tasted his own blood. It tasted rotten somehow, polluted—like he remembered menstrual blood tasting.

"I admit it, Infidel. Raping the women was wrong. Horribly wrong. We couldn't control ourselves. It was the demons. They made us do it. Listen. You're no better. Our people are good people. You should have helped us. Even Maab would have loved you. Pyle would have helped you."

The boots reappeared.

"I'm dying again, Infidel. My people need you. They're asking for you. Be our friend."

The Infidel turned and walked towards the wilds of Hell.

Carlisle reached out after him, but his hand touched nothing. "Don't leave me. Don't abandon me like you abandoned God."

The Infidel paused at the edge of his vision, looking at something, perhaps on one of the chamber's highest walls. Carlisle tried to see what the man was staring at, but his eyesight was too far gone. Slowly, surely, his world was shrinking in around him.

"It doesn't matter if I die. I'm not alone," he said.

Carlisle's eyesight dimmed further. The Infidel seemed like some distant shadow.

"I would have beaten you," Carlisle said. "On Earth I would have defeated you. God would have helped me kill you."

After a moment, the Infidel spoke. "God let His only Son be tortured and crucified. Why would He treat you any differently?"

Carlisle could no longer see the Infidel. He was sure the man was still out there, though, past the edge of his vision.

"Because God loves me!" Carlisle shouted as the black wings of damnation closed in around his soul. "God loves me!"

From Neostoicism: Philosophia

The Strong may choose Pacifism, the Weak are condemned to it.

—The Infidel

I climbed the highest mountain in hopes of finding a wise man, but when I reached its summit I found it empty. Tired from my travails, I paused to rest for a few moments—but no sooner had I sat down than I heard a noise behind me. I turned and saw another climber... he was asking me a question.

—Endymion

Part I
The Childe on the River

— 1 —

I wonder if Alice thinks I'm handsome.

The river his fathers Rick and Galen affectionately called the "Mighty Thames" was a slow and gentle stream, hardly worthy of a name, that meandered softly through the underground labyrinth of Hell without much of a fuss. Its waters were cool and crisp, and Arturus had grown up almost happily on its stone banks. In this chamber the Thames was so smooth that he had taken to using it as a mirror for his morning shaves. He would kneel on the dark red hellstone by its bank and gauge the stubble which covered his face's reflection in the flowing water. The air over the river was cooler than it was in his own room, and he always found the chill invigorating.

He was preparing to shave even now.

He felt the vibrations of the bone-handled straight razor as he drew the blade across his leather strop. He did so in short, even strokes, listening to the gentle flow of the water. In the next room the river narrowed slightly as its grade increased. It was there that the Thames powered their woodstone waterwheel. He sharpened his blade to the watery beat of the turning structure and then tested the razor on the hairs of his chin. Satisfied with the result, he laid the blade and strop down so he could wash his face.

The pristine water was cool on his skin. He could smell it, even.

With a steady hand he took to his ritual. A clean shave, Rick had told him, was a sign of a survivor. An unshaven and unkempt man, however, might well be weak, unpredictable or dangerous.

That wasn't why Arturus shaved, of course. He shaved because Alice had pointed out that his chin hairs were closer to peach fuzz than they were to a beard.

Arturus shaved down first, on his right side, with quick,

even strokes. Then he covered that same area with up-strokes. Galen had seen him do this once and called him a "brave lad."

For a moment Arturus paused, his razor held motionless above the water. He didn't want to place the blade into his reflection. It would feel almost as if he were stabbing himself. Instead he placed the razor in the water just a bit downstream. Above and around his own head, he saw the ceiling of this chamber. The whole of it was a soft, deep red. The stones interlocked in the arched roofing with a bricklike pattern. As a child, he had thought that those stones might fall down on him. The foolishness of his childhood fear brought a smile to his face. He watched the smile appear. After a few more minutes, he finished and inspected his work.

Not even a nick.

He decided that he must be handsome.

He hoped Alice thought so at any rate.

Again careful not to disturb his reflection, he washed off his blade, drying the razor on his pants before folding it into its bone handle. He stretched, yawned, and then walked back towards his dwelling. The hallways that led from the river room to his home were covered in gravel, and the loose rock crunched beneath his boots. Galen had laid down the stones so that the footsteps of an intruder could be heard more easily. He brushed through his door blanket to enter his sleeping chamber and placed his razor reverently next to the pile of blankets on which he slept.

The ritual finished, his face as smooth as a marble pillar, he wandered off to the battery room in hopes of finding a good breakfast, his eager footsteps crunching gravel as he went.

Galen had installed a small lip in the doorway of the battery room as a barrier to keep out the hallway's loose stones. Arturus stumbled over it in his haste, sending gravel scattering across the floor. He kicked some of the stones back over the lip, grimacing, knowing that he would probably be the one who would have to sweep it all up.

"Well, you're up early!" Rick hadn't yet shaved, and his brown stubble was almost as long as his close cropped hair. "I've not even started the plates."

Arturus shrugged. There were no time pieces here, save the one that Galen kept in his pack, so it could just as easily be that Rick had risen late.

"What's for breakfast?" Arturus asked him.

"Hound liver and flat bread."

"Sounds okay." Actually it sounded delicious, but Arturus knew that if he let his father know such a thing, the man might never get around to making his devilwheat wraps or dyitzu meat pies.

Rick began to hum to himself as he prepared some unleavened flatbread, his practiced fingers kneading the dough against the granite counter.

Arturus seated himself on one of the chairs that Rick had fashioned out of an old wooden barrel. Their table was made from a woodstone door that was now turned horizontal and propped up by four rectangular granite bricks. Arturus remembered playing with the hinges on it when he was younger. The hinges had eventually come off, but he could still see the depressions and the lighter colored woodstone where they had been attached.

"Do I have a purpose?" Arturus asked.

Rick flashed him a playful smile as he worked the dough. "What made you ask that?"

"Father Klein. He said that all of God's children were made to do a specific thing. But I'm not God's child, am I? Because I was born here?"

"No, Turi, I suppose you're not."

Arturus idly ran his finger over one of the door hinge depressions while he thought about this. "Does that make me evil, because I'm not God's child?"

Rick laughed. "No, doing evil things makes you evil."

There was the sound of stone grinding on stone as Rick switched on the battery. Julian of Harpsborough said that the battery wasn't really a battery at all since it didn't have any electricity. Julian had said it was just a big rock. But it was a *very* big rock, and the waterwheel would help lift it into the chamber's ceiling. Its descent was slow, but its weight would power any number of devices in the battery room through a series of gears, pulleys and belts. Rick had the battery connected to the heating plates, which were made of copper colored stones. As Arturus watched, they began to rub against each other. Soon they had developed enough heat to cook the food and toast the flatbread.

"Well, what's my purpose then, if God didn't give me one?" Arturus asked.

Rick tossed a cup of water onto the heating plates. "I guess you'll have to pick."

Arturus watched the steam rise to the ceiling. "You mean I get to decide?"

"You'd better. I don't know who else would. Sounds more fun than having someone else choose it, doesn't it?"

"But what if I pick the wrong one?"

Rick shrugged and went on humming.

"I think I'm going to make Harpsborough happy," Arturus said.

"Oh, are you?"

"Yes. Or maybe I'll rescue Alice from a devil!"

"I'm sure Alice will be glad to hear about that."

"Did Galen come in last night?" Arturus asked. Rick stopped humming and moved in front of the hound liver. Frown lines appeared on his forehead as he picked up a knife, and he started cutting with quick jerky motions.

"No," Rick said between cuts. "He didn't come in last night."

Arturus watched his father carefully. "He's late, isn't he?"

Rick looked towards a pile of devilwheat in one corner. Had Galen been home, it certainly would have been threshed and stored by now.

"Yes, Turi, he's late."

"What if he doesn't come back?"

Rick stopped cutting. "Then he doesn't come back."

"But then, how are we supposed to—"

"Don't talk about things like that. Whatever happens, we'll manage."

"Sorry," Arturus said.

"But if he's not back soon, I'll have to go hunting without him." Rick began cutting again. "That's a shame because we're low on shells, and I was hoping to get another barrel for one of our rifles in Harpsborough. I'll have to work hard today to get it all done."

Arturus nodded, but then he had an idea. If *he* were to go to Harpsborough, Rick wouldn't have so much to do today.

And I'd get to see Alice.

Arturus had never gotten permission to go to the city alone before, so he figured he had better start being as helpful as possible. Rick, unlike the more even mannered Galen, was much more likely to be lenient when he was in a good mood—and he certainly wasn't in a good mood now.

"Did you want any water?" Arturus offered.

"Yeah, and could you fill the pitcher too? We'll need it for the food."

Arturus grumbled to himself and picked up the huge clay urn they used to store drinking water.

He hadn't meant to be quite *that* helpful.

He dragged his feet in the gravel as he lugged the empty urn towards the Mighty Thames.

How am I going to ask this?

Arturus stopped downstream from the waterwheel where he filled the giant clay pitcher. He squatted low, and with a heave and a grunt, brought the thing back up on the bank. He figured he was just being paranoid, but he checked the urn to see if any of his shaved hairs were in there.

They weren't.

Maybe if I can get him to complain about hunting more.

He heard a noise across the river and looked up, hoping to

see Galen. . . but no one was there.

The sound had come from Rick separating the battery from the heating stones. The waterwheel spun slower now since its power was being diverted towards charging the battery—or raising the rock, as Julian would have called it.

He returned to the room, the urn sloshing in his arms, still unsure as to how he was going to broach the Harpsborough trip. If he wasn't careful, Rick might reject the idea outright.

"Water's cool today," he mentioned as he set down the clay pitcher.

Rick dropped the strips of hound liver onto the heating plates and gave them a toss of the water Arturus had just brought. Steam and the smell of food cooking filled the room.

Arturus' mouth watered.

"The water's cool every day," Rick told him, beginning to hum again.

Arturus nodded.

He watched the hound liver as it sizzled. He was glad Rick had turned off the hotplates before cooking the meal. If the heat dissipated fast enough, Rick wouldn't have a chance to burn the bread. Galen said Rick enjoyed burning the bread.

"Not many dyitzu about." Arturus tried hard to make his calculated remark sound like an offhand comment.

Rick paused before answering, busying himself by flipping the hound liver.

Does he know I'm trying to wheedle him into something?

Rick tossed more water onto the meal. "No, it might be difficult finding one to hunt."

Arturus watched the fresh steam dissipate into the air. There would always be water on the ceiling over the plates after meal times. Rick left the plates for a second and poked his head through the curtain which cordoned off their supply closet.

"Do you think I could go hunting with you?" Arturus asked.

"You know that you're only supposed to go with Galen," Rick called back over his shoulder. "I've got too many bad habits for you to pick up."

Arturus studied Rick for a moment as the man returned to the heating plates.

"Then let me go to Harpsborough!" he blurted out.

Rick looked up from his cooking. Arturus saw that he hadn't immediately rejected the idea.

"I know I've never been there by myself before," Arturus said quickly, "but you said that the dyitzu have been light. And I know how to handle myself just in case. Galen and I got in that firefight last month, you remember? Besides, I've got to start going there sometime."

Rick shook his head. "It's too dangerous. You might get

lost."

"I go there all the time, I know the way."

"There are dyitzu about. You could get attacked. Galen would *kill* me if he got home and found you hurt. Besides, you know you aren't allowed to travel that far on your own."

"I travel almost that far when I go to the Hungerleaf Grove. I do that all the time."

Rick's eyebrows narrowed. "Let me think about it."

"But—"

"Quiet, Turi. I said I'd think about it." He tested the liver with one of his knives, cutting into the center of it. "Get your plate."

Arturus walked over to the supply closet and picked out his favorite hellstone plate. It had a chip on one of its square edges from where he had dropped it years ago. The grain of the plate's rock swirled towards the center, making a dark spot which Arturus pretended was a girl sitting by a river. He offered it up to Rick, who delivered to him his portion of hound liver and flatbread.

Arturus' heart sank. Rick had managed to burn the bread. Arturus stayed quiet, not wanting to anger his father while he was in the middle of making such an important decision. He sat back down and waited.

Rick was frowning as he made his way to the table, deep in thought. Arturus watched him intently.

"Don't stare, Turi," Rick said as he took his seat.

Arturus looked at the hound liver. It was covering up the girl on the river. He wrapped it in the flatbread and started to eat it with his fingers. The liver was hot enough to burn his tongue a little.

He dared another glance at Rick.

"Can't let you go," his father said. "How would you make the trades?"

"I've watched Galen trade hundreds of times! I know who to speak to and how much to offer."

Rick took a bite of the flatbread and chewed it thoroughly. "They'll try and cheat you. They might think you are an easier mark than Galen."

"I'll be smart. Besides, I won't take much if you don't want me to."

"You wouldn't even know who to go to."

"Massan has shells, he always does, and he won't try and cheat me," Arturus insisted. "I can always trade at the Fore if he doesn't."

Rick sighed, putting down his flatbread. "There's a lot of trouble you can get into at the village. I don't know if I feel safe with you alone in Harpsborough."

"I'll just do the trades, I swear. Then I'll come right back.

Besides, if I get in any trouble, I'll go to a Citizen. They all know me."

"You could get lost on the way."

"I won't! I know how to get there. I can just head towards the Kingsriver until I get to the road."

Rick smiled and shook his head. "Perhaps you're right, Turi. I do need help today, and I suppose it's about time that you get some experience being out there on your own."

"Really?"

Rick laughed and nodded.

Arturus felt like hugging him. "Thank you! I'll do the trades right, I promise."

"Go get your bag. I'll help you pack. The barrel we need is for an AR-15, so you want to keep that part as private as possible. I don't need rumors of us using 5.56 spreading around Harpsborough."

"I'll be careful," Arturus said, his heart beating with excitement.

"And make sure you get a good deal, understand, or when Galen finds out he won't let you go to Harpsborough on your own again until you're old and sodden."

"But you said I can't get old!"

"Exactly the point, my boy, exactly the point."

Arturus hurried back to his room to gather his things.

— 2 —

"Stay alert," Rick told him as he left. "Don't forget to check the shadows twice before you enter every room."

"I will."

"I'm serious, Turi, we don't need a dyitzu getting a hold of you. And don't get lost. If you do, just find a river and wait for a hunter."

"I'll be careful!" Arturus said.

Rick gave him a serious look. "Keep your eyes peeled, and remember to announce yourself to the guards. People sometimes shoot first and look second."

"Of course I will."

"And don't spend too much time with that Alice girl. She's trouble for you—well, go on. And be careful!"

"I will," Arturus said as he crossed over the river's bridge, his feet thumping over the woodstone structure.

He stopped on the far side and turned around, suddenly unsure of himself. Rick had also paused. His father smiled sadly, waved goodbye, and then walked back into their home chambers.

I can do this.

Arturus steeled himself with a deep breath and left the red river room.

He's so paranoid sometimes.

Arturus began his journey, moving slowly and carefully through the labyrinth.

The next few sets of chambers were fashioned out of blue stone. Their ceilings, supported by a varied array of arches and pillars, soared above him. The light came from the floor of these rooms so that the walls darkened as they rose. The floor itself was an almost neon color, and it gave his clothing a cooler cast. He watched his own shadow march across the ceiling.

I better look where I'm going.

Dyitzu had been scarce, but that didn't mean he had to go

out of his way to make sure he'd get eaten by one. As he traveled through the labyrinth, he imagined one of those devils—black eyed, hunched over, long clawed—finding him while he was staring at his own shadow. It would rip him apart. Then he would be dead, his soul descending to a level of Hell even worse than the one he was on now, and Rick would be alone. For some reason leaving Rick abandoned scared him even more than his own death.

Just head towards the Kingsriver, you'll see the rustrock road.

He froze.

He'd heard the scuff of a shoe. It had sounded like it was coming from one of the dark corridors which led into this chamber. He moved to one corner of the room and crouched, peering intently into the blackness. Gingerly, as quietly as he could, he drew his pistol, shifting slightly as he did so.

He heard the sound again.

Wait, is that my own foot?

He jiggled his boot a little.

I'm an idiot.

He holstered his pistol and stood back up, feeling slightly relieved.

Have I been here before?

The stones of this room were frighteningly unfamiliar. Should he backtrack to another room that he knew? He had never seen a pillar like this before. Or had he? It was straight until its midpoint, where it began to lean off to one side until it melded into one of the walls.

But he had been through this chamber before, perhaps a thousand times. He remembered playing with Galen by that pillar as a child.

My mind is playing tricks on me. It's because I'm afraid.

If Rick had known how badly this trip was going to go, he probably would have forbid it. Arturus allowed his breathing to slow. It did not take long for his fear to play itself out, and when it was gone, he felt he was one step closer to the person that Galen had trained him to be.

He knew the way, so he pressed on towards the Kingsriver.

The rooms became smaller, and the stone dulled from the soft blues to a red which reminded Arturus of dried blood. Light ceased to come from the floor and took on its normal ethereal and sourceless quality.

After a few more minutes, he came to the road.

Halfway there!

The road was a series of rivets cut into the stone. Another type of rock, which Galen called rustrock, had been laid inside the grooves. It was a brown stone, almost black in color.

Arturus began to follow the road.

Galen had told him that if you spent the time to pry out

the rustrock, then the rivet would heal in a few decades. Arturus didn't like to think of stone healing. He had argued about this with Galen. Galen had taken him to a wall in his own chamber and made a chip in it with a few chisel strikes.

"Tell me boy, in three years' time, that I have lied to you."

Galen hadn't been lying.

Arturus adjusted the pack on his shoulders. It was almost completely full. He wished that Rick hadn't given him so much latitude in the trading, both because it was heavy and also because it gave him plenty of excess to be cheated with.

They don't have to know how much you have.

The riveted road forked, and a large violet stone, about two feet tall, was lying along one of the paths. Arturus thought that it might just be his imagination, but the air from that path felt cooler. Perhaps there was a river down that way. Violet stones such as this one had been placed by Rick, he knew, to warn travelers on the road not to take this fork. Paths marked by such stones led to the Carrion. Arturus knew better than to go near there. The place was thick with devils, and any man who survived in such a Hell was not likely to be friendly. Rick and the people of Harpsborough had spent many years barricading most of the main pathways that led to the Carrion, but Galen had warned him that there were still many more open.

"You cannot block out a whole region," Galen had told him. "Always there will be a hidden passage, perhaps a corridor or door which you missed. The enemy might go high or low or left or right, but they will find a way."

Arturus hurried past the fork, taking extra care to make sure that his footsteps were silent.

He felt much safer after he put a couple of turns and stone walls between himself and the Carrion path. In fact, the farther he traveled down the road, the more comfortable he felt altogether. It was secretly thrilling to be traveling the wilds of the labyrinth on his own. He imagined that this must be how Galen felt on his many long hunts.

His sweat was making his clothes stick to his body and his own movement through the air gave him a ghost of a chill, even in the temperate labyrinthine air. He stopped when he realized that the village's guards would be in the next chamber.

I made it!

He remembered that he needed to hail them before he entered. Arturus didn't think that they'd fire at him, but Rick had been pretty worried about it.

"It's Arturus, don't shoot," he said, his voice sounding high even to his own ears.

— 3 —

He rounded the bend and saw two Harpsborough guards leaning back against the stone wall that stood by the village chamber's entrance. Set against the wall beside them were two model 700 Remington rifles, which Arturus knew was the weapon used by most of the Harpsborough hunters. One of the two wore a hoodie, and the other had his arms folded.

"Well, look who just came out of the wilds beaming like a flashlight," the guard in the hoodie said.

"You broke your leash, boy?" asked the other. "Where's Rick and Galen?"

"I came by myself," he said proudly.

He had meant to say it in an offhand manner.

"Aren't you the adventurous one?" one guard laughed.

"Leave the boy alone, Avery. The wilds are dangerous."

"I wasn't scared," Arturus said.

"Then maybe you should have been."

Arturus felt childish and glum. He had meant to ask them about which traders were in, but he ducked his head instead and walked past the guards.

Why do they have to be like that?

Arturus pushed through into Harpsborough. He forgot his embarrassment almost immediately. Though he had been to Harpsborough many times, the fact that he was here alone gave the village a sense of freshness. The ceiling, vast, and made of the same arched and bricked pattern as the one over the Mighty Thames, hung nearly a hundred feet over his head. Most of the buildings were squat, barely five feet tall, and made of a mixture of stone and blankets. Life was as permanent here as could be found almost anywhere in the labyrinth, so many of Harpsborough's denizens had taken the time to add colored blankets, beads, or some other touch to personalize their homes.

There were two proper buildings which dwarfed the rest.

One was the church, whose twin, crucifix-topped steeples were nearly high enough to touch the bricked ceiling, and the other was the Fore.

The Fore was the supreme building of Harpsborough—a tremendous four story structure with its first few levels almost entirely intact. Only the fourth floor had devolved into the hodge-podge stone and blanketed mess which characterized the rest of the village's architecture. Harpsborough's most powerful people, called Citizens, lived in that building. Arturus longed to stand on one of its third story balconies and look down upon the town. To be a Citizen, to not have to hunt or work. . . it would be a dream. Then he could invite Alice to come dine with him, and they would eat as the Citizens did on those balconies. They would speak of petty things, like which vines grew the sweetest sinfruit, and which stones were the best for sculpting.

The town seemed deserted, and none of the traders Arturus was looking for had their wares on display.

They must either be out or sleeping. It's probably not morning yet.

He caught glimpses of some of the slumbering Harpsborough people through the cracks around their door blankets. Since light was a constant in the chamber, there was no mandated night or day, and people pretty much slept when they felt like it. Galen had told him that villagers tended to accidentally synchronize their sleep patterns.

"Be wary of the man who walks during the night in a good city," Galen had said, "and seek him out in an evil one."

Like I'd even get a chance to see another city.

Arturus spotted one man lying up against the Fore, his open eyes locked into a thousand mile stare.

"Excuse me, sir," Arturus asked him quietly so as to avoid waking anyone who might be sleeping inside the building, "is Massan in. . . do you know? I was looking for some shotgun shells. . ."

The man wasn't answering, and Arturus noticed that his eyes were so bloodshot that there wasn't any white around their irises.

Catatonic.

Galen had taught him that this happened to some people. They would become so depressed that they ceased to respond to anyone or anything. The villagers called it the stilling sickness. Galen had even related to him horror stories where such men were eviscerated by demons without even blinking. The stilling was a village thing, Arturus guessed. He had certainly never felt sad enough that he could have his bowels spilled without fighting back.

Arturus waved his hands in front of the man to make sure.

Yeah, he's gone alright.

Arturus remembered him vaguely. Galen had traded something to him for some wooden cups a few years back.

Arturus didn't remember him acting any differently than the other people here, which he found disconcerting.

What if this happens to Alice?

She would still be inside her hovel, he figured. He stopped to look at it on his way to Massan's tent. The cloth that covered the building's ceiling was blue and worn, and she hadn't beaten the dust out of it in some time. She'd hung an odd ornament from the stick archway which supported her door blanket. It looked like a spider web made of yarn, surrounded by a wooden circle. Caught within its strands were a few pebbles instead of people. She was probably inside that hovel, sleeping. He imagined her curled up on her side, her eyes closed.

Maybe someone else will tell her that I was here by myself. That I didn't need Galen or Rick or anybody.

He spotted Massan's tent and moved on towards it.

Or maybe she'll come out while I'm trading.

That thought excited him. He would look very grown up, he decided, haggling for shotgun shells all on his own.

"Oh, I'm just picking up some shells," he might tell her nonchalantly. "We've been running a bit low lately."

And then they would talk about something different entirely, and she would laugh at his jokes.

Arturus was startled by a noise from above him. When he looked up he saw a man standing on one of the Fore's third floor balconies.

It's Michael Baker. He's up early.

The First Citizen and leader of Harpsborough gave Arturus a slight nod and a smile before disappearing back into the Fore.

If he's awake, surely that must mean others will be getting up soon.

Arturus' pack seemed to get heavier as he came up to Massan's tent-house. He slapped his hands a few times against the door blanket which had been made out of dyitzu hide. Galen would have approved of the accoutrement. The man liked to make things out of the environment around him. He said everything else was cheating, since you could never be sure you could replace it.

Arturus noticed that his hands were shaking.

Why am I so nervous? Either I get the trades right, or I don't.

"Who is it?" a woman's voice answered.

That would be Kara, Arturus decided. She had been sleeping with Massan for a while now. Arturus had been a little surprised at the matchup since Massan seemed so ugly. Galen had told him that humor and riches could go a long way.

"Arturus, ma'am," he responded, speaking loudly enough to be heard through the door blanket, but softly enough—he hoped—to avoid waking any neighbors. "Is Massan here?"

"He went out to the river to get some water. He'll be back in just a minute."

"No problem. I'll try and meet him by the guards."

First Citizen Michael Baker eased himself down onto the Persian cushions which guarded his body from the brutal rigidity of his stone chair. After settling himself, he took a sip of his bloodwater. Across the Fore's parlor room was his sycophant, Davel Mancini, the brewer of the sharp, sweet concoction which he drank.

"Anybody awake out there?" the Brewer asked.

"Just a hermit trader. The village will be up soon, though."

The pair sat together in the Fore's parlor, located on the third story next to Michael's own sleeping chambers. The lavishly decorated room held more wealth than all of the rest of Harpsborough combined. The stone couch and two chairs which furnished the room were so finely sculpted that the people of Harpsborough believed it had been Hell's architect, not man, who had chiseled them. Each of the stone pieces was covered over in an assortment of earthen hued blankets and pillows. A set of shelves, full of rare and ancient guns, wine bottles and devil hides, adorned the wall across from Michael along with a full length mirror and a running water clock.

Michael regarded the ruby red bloodwater through his crystal glass. "Mancini, this is certainly smooth. Tart in a good way. The aftertaste. . . has something. . . odd. Sinfruit? You'd be able to trade this to the Pole."

"I might, when this famine passes," Mancini said after drinking from his own glass. "Which hermit is about?"

"Rick and Galen's boy."

Mancini stood up and walked across the dyitzu skin which carpeted the floor.

The room was illuminated by a pair of three foot tall stone spheres which could be covered by a varying number of blankets in order to control the level of light in the room. At the moment, a few thick blankets covered them to give the parlor a soft, homely glow. Mancini, who had despised light for as long as Michael had known him, added another pair of blankets for good measure.

Michael Baker stared at the draped spherical stones until the Brewer interrupted his thoughts.

"Hunters came home empty handed last night," Mancini said, sitting back down on the couch across from Michael.

Michael let his gaze return to one of the orbs. "Second night in a row. Not sure what it means."

"Maybe it means we should tell Aaron and his hunters to hunt up the Thames," Mancini said, "and tell Galen and Rick to hunt somewhere else."

"They've always hunted there."

"Hidalgo always hunted on the far side of the Kingsriver, and we demanded he hunt farther out."

Michael shook his head. "Well, that's different."

"Oh?"

"There's actually dyitzu on the Kingsriver."

Mancini paused before the parlor room's mirror long enough to pull a strand of his thick black hair behind his ear. "Galen and Rick never seem to be wanting."

"They're just one family. One devil for them is enough for a month. We'd go through that in half a day. Maybe Aaron's right. Maybe Hell is emptying out. Maybe we really should start sharing the Fore's food."

"Would have never happened when you were Lead Hunter, Mike. Let 'em starve."

Michael's gaze snapped back to Mancini. The after image of the orb blocked out the Brewer's face. He blinked a few times until he could see the man, but Mancini's expression revealed nothing.

Michael stood up from his chair, suddenly restless, and wandered across the carpets. He pushed through the door tapestry, making his way back onto the third floor balcony. He turned to see Mancini following, protecting his glass of bloodwater from the curtain with his forearm.

Michael Baker looked down from the balcony onto his sleeping city.

"What would Aaron know anyway?" Mancini asked.

"Nothing, but it doesn't matter. The hunters listen to him."

"They blame you for it, though, just because you're up here safe with us."

"I served my time," Michael said. "Has Aaron looked dead into the eyes of a Minotaur? Has he lain for twenty nights and twenty days upon the banks of Lethe, nursing the wounds made by its horns? I built bonds of blood with many of those hunters out there. I'm the one who trained Aaron. What's he done? Well, he's led the hunters through their leanest years yet and made sure there are fewer dyitzu month after month."

Mancini sipped his bloodwater thoughtfully. "They've forgotten you, Mike."

"Well, of course they have," Michael said. "Barely any of the hunters I used to lead are even alive anymore, and the rest of them have spent more time under him now than me."

"He says you're causing the problems. He says it's your restriction on how far they can go out that's starving Harpsborough. He even says that, if it were not for your direct orders, he might be willing to enter the Carrion to get food."

Michael gave a short laugh. "The fool would never do such a thing. The Carrion would eat him alive and he knows it."

"Perhaps that is in his mind, but that is not what's in his mouth."

"Where'd you hear that?"

"You know that the hunters gamble right by my room's walls. I can't help but hear quite a bit."

Michael took a large swallow of the bloodwater, trying to enjoy the taste and the burn he felt in his throat. "I wish he would go into the Carrion and get himself killed."

"Strip him of his Citizenship. No other hunter has a place in here."

Michael glanced over at the church. "That would be foolish. I hope this famine passes quickly."

Davel Mancini smiled wryly. "Doesn't matter to us. *We* don't have to worry about going hungry."

"Not yet. We may have to open up our stores, though. They're starving."

"At least consider sending our men up the Thames before we do something as drastic as that. Or better yet, let hunger take a few of them. That will balance everything out."

"We can't just let them die."

"Sooner or later, Mike, you're going to have to decide which side you're on."

For a moment, when he turned to Davel Mancini, he got a queer feeling about the Brewer. If Aaron were to perform a coup d'état, he wondered, how long would it be before Mancini managed to worm his way into the hunter's good graces.

The feeling lasted for only a moment. It had been Mancini, whom many expected to be the most stolid against Michael, who had grudgingly admitted the new First Citizen's merit. It had been Mancini who was the first to be brave enough to drop his bias and say that Michael would be a better leader than the man who'd lain dead at his feet.

"You're a good friend, Davel," Michael told him.

"And you're a good leader."

Arturus rubbed absently at his sore shoulder and thought about drifting off to sleep for a minute—but as soon as he considered closing his eyes, he heard the guards outside speaking. He perked up a bit when he recognized Massan's voice.

A moment later the trader came into the chamber.

Massan was a dark man of Middle-Eastern heritage. His hair and eyes were black, and his eyebrows, thick as they were, were actually thicker where they formed a unibrow over the bridge of his nose. Massan hoisted his water skin over one shoulder as he entered the chamber. Arturus could hear it sloshing. The skin was still wet from being filled in the river, and Massan left a small trail of water dripping behind him as he walked. Arturus recognized the skin, as it had been made by Galen and traded to the man for ammunition a few years ago. Galen had taught Arturus how to make such a skin from a dyitzu's hide and bladder.

"Jesus was a carpenter," Galen had told him then, "but there is not much wood in Hell. Better to be a mason or a tanner, if you were to pick."

Arturus didn't know too much about Jesus. Galen had told him it would have been different if he had been born back in the old world. He would know all about Jesus, and perhaps have had the right to hate him or love him.

"You cannot judge what you do not know," Galen had told him.

I hope he's safe.

Massan looked up and noticed Arturus as he began to head towards his tent.

"Lad!" Massan greeted him, leaning to one side so he could look at Arturus' pack. "Where are your parents? You stuff 'em in there?"

"They're not here," Arturus said, standing up.

"Surely you're no runaway?" Massan asked incredulously.

"No," Arturus said with a laugh, "I didn't run away. Galen's still out and Rick wanted to spend the day hunting, so I thought I'd come by and do some trading for them."

"Well, did you now?" Massan asked, flashing his crooked teeth with a smile. "What are you looking for?"

"Shells, 12 gauge. Some buck and ball if you've got any. And a barrel."

"Barrel for what?"

Arturus leaned in close, close enough that he could smell the man's sweat. They had been speaking softly already to be considerate to the sleeping villagers, but Arturus lowered his voice even further so that none could overhear.

"For an AR-15," he said.

"An AR-15?" Massan replied in kind. "That's a rare one. Don't see much ammunition for those about."

"Yeah," Arturus agreed.

"Well, come on by my tent, boy," the trader said in a normal voice. "I'll see what I can dig up."

— 4 —

Massan's water skin landed next to Kara, causing her to turn over and cover her head with a blanket. The trader began rummaging through the pile of packs where he kept his goods. Arturus glanced outside of Massan's door blanket and noticed that the nearby neighbors were stirring, perhaps awakened by the noise.

"Now why in the name of Christ Almighty do you want to get an AR-15 barrel?" Massan asked, his voice quiet once again.

"I don't know, maybe Galen found a stash of .223 while he was out on his last hunt." Arturus kept his voice fairly quiet.

"Could be... or he could have killed an Infidel Friend."

Arturus nodded slowly. If Galen had killed one of their kind, the others would surely want retribution. He felt his heart quicken, and he wished even more fervently that Galen would come home soon.

Arturus had never seen an Infidel Friend. To think of it, he didn't imagine that many in Harpsborough had either. Still, the Infidel's men were reputed to be an evil force, both deadly and amoral. And they used 5.56 millimeter rounds, the legends said.

You cannot judge what you do not know.

Massan's unibrow became even more pronounced as it furrowed. The man rummaged more ferociously through his packs. Arturus leaned over to look at what they contained.

There were a few shirts in there, and a wine bottle, the cork still wrapped. He also saw a collection of lighters, each plastic and painted with a unique design. There was a skull, too. Arturus breathed in when he saw it, and he moved a little closer.

"Hey!" Massan said suddenly, hiding the skull beneath the shirts. "Stay back."

"Sorry, sir."

The trader carefully held up the side of his pack, keeping Arturus from seeing his wares while he continued his search.

I wonder what that skull was from? Why wouldn't he want me to see it? Maybe he could have sold it to me.

Not looking up, Massan passed Arturus a box of 12 gauge shotgun shells. After a few moments, he produced a second box.

"Twelve gauge and slugs. That going to be enough shells?" Massan asked, his accent for some reason becoming more pronounced as he continued to shift through his things.

"Should be fine, sir."

Arturus opened the boxes. The boxes themselves were a bit banged up but the shells looked fine.

"Ah, what have we here?" Massan marveled as he pulled out a gun barrel from near the bottom of the stash. "Galen will be proud of you, son."

He has one!

"Where did you find it?"

"You may recall, a few years ago, that I got lost up near Macon's Bend. I found the barrel with an M-16, actually. The gun was hopelessly damaged, but I took the barrel just in case. I thought I might have to trade it to get someone to take me back to Harpsborough."

"You would have traded it to an Infidel Friend?"

"Son, I would have traded it to the Devil himself if he'd take me home." He looked past Arturus to the sleeping Kara. "You'd never know how a place you hate can mean so much to you, till it's gone."

Arturus had never been far from home.

Would I miss it?

"So, what have you got to trade?" Massan asked, suddenly all business.

"For the shells I was thinking a few pounds of dyitzu meat and some devilwheat."

"How about five pounds per box? It's been a bit rough finding shells lately. You can keep your devilwheat, we've enough of it here. Your friend Julian trades tons of that stuff to us."

"Five pounds! Galen never traded you more than one for shells."

"I charge everyone the same. I've made Galen pay that much in my day, when shells were scarce."

But shells aren't scarce right now, dyitzu are. I'm going to be cheated.

Galen had given him advice about trading. He had said that the truth was always best, so long as you only spoke part of it.

"Amazing that you are low on shells since there's hardly been any dyitzu to shoot at lately," Arturus said. "Look, I'm not stupid. I know that you are going to end up cheating me, and

I'm okay with that. But if you take advantage of me now, they won't send me back here. You'll be stuck driving hard bargains with Galen and Rick. But if you give me a good deal, then they will send me back, and you can fleece more off of me in the future."

Massan smiled. "Very well, boy. Dyitzu meat is rather hard to come by at the moment. And I'd play fetch with a hellhound before I'd eat another bundle of Julian's devilwheat." Massan's laugh was infectious. "Perhaps you will keep coming back, but I doubt I'll be able to cheat you much. Give me three pounds and I'll give you both boxes of shells. When you get home, tell Galen and Rick that you gave me an extra pound because food was so scarce. But for the barrel, you are going to have to do better than dyitzu meat."

Arturus pulled out what looked to be three or so pounds of smoked dyitzu and passed them over to Massan. Massan didn't bother to weigh them, which was a sign of great trust.

"Rick gave you a full pack, didn't he?" Massan asked.

"Yeah, I think he wanted you to be able to cheat me," Arturus said, and then he looked at Massan sternly. "He did not give me ten pounds of meat, though."

Massan laughed.

After a few more moments rifling through his pack, Arturus pulled out a nine millimeter pistol.

He offered it to the trader who partially disassembled the weapon to take stock of it.

"A fine gun. Normally I wouldn't trade it for a rifle barrel, but I don't suppose that anyone around here is going to have a need for an infidel's weapon."

"Is the rifling in it okay?" Arturus asked as he examined the item.

"I have no idea, Turi." Massan told him. "Never fired anything from it."

Arturus slid through the door blanket and held the barrel up to the light outside of Massan's tent-house. There didn't appear to be any carbon deposits on the inside of it. On the whole, the barrel looked pretty good.

He looked over to Alice's hovel then, hoping that she would be awake and moving about. She was not.

Galen and Rick always asked for information before they left. Galen only seemed to be curious about Harpsborough's leaders, particularly the First Citizen, Michael Baker. Rick asked for the gossip.

"Any rumors about where the dyitzu have gone?" Arturus asked Massan.

"A little quieter boy," Massan told him softly as he cast a glance at the sleeping Kara, "The others are still asleep, remember?"

"Sorry," Arturus apologized, smiling impishly.

Massan joined him outside of the tent.

"None that I believe. I'm almost worried about how few devils are about, though. Aaron says it's the calm before the storm. Like he'd know. He's been Lead Hunter for a few years, and all of a sudden he thinks that he's a prophet. Your friend Alice buys it, of course. You know how close those two have been lately."

Arturus shook his head and glanced over to Alice's hovel. He supposed it was empty. His chest felt a lot like that hovel.

"Oh, I wouldn't worry too much, lad. She's always been too old for you anyway."

"Why would you think I like her?" Arturus asked.

"Because you wear your emotions on your sleeve, like Rick. If you don't want people to know what you are thinking, then you should wear them on the inside, like Galen."

Arturus nodded.

"Sometimes I can tell you were born here," Massan said.

I wish everyone didn't think I was different.

"I better get going," Arturus said, "if I'm not back soon Rick will have two of us to worry about."

Massan nodded. "Goodbye, Turi. Don't keep him waiting."

The trader went back inside.

I really should go. I promised Rick I'd make the trades and that's it.

Besides, he had to ask Rick about the AR-15 barrel. If Galen had killed an Infidel Friend, Arturus would want to know. Maybe that's why the man hadn't returned. But just as he was moving to leave the city, he saw Alice coming out of her home. She yawned and stretched.

He imagined Alice to be a princess, like in one of Galen's stories. She was merely a common girl now, but she would be so much more when she met the man she was destined for. He watched her, a bit hypnotized, as she arranged her blue thigh length skirt. He could not understand how any man could look at her and not want to be with her. Massan must lie awake in his tent at night, dreaming of that fair maiden, cursing the fates that his age did not align with hers.

Arturus remembered to breathe.

I told Rick I'd go straight home.

When she looked his way he quickly averted his gaze and pretended that he was examining his pack. After a moment, he dared a few more clandestine glances. She was tying her blonde hair back into a ponytail with a blue hair tie. With her arms held high and back, her small breasts were pushed forward. The purple color of her bra showed through her white tank top. Arturus felt flushed, and looked away, embarrassed.

I should talk to her.

He couldn't imagine what to say, though. Anything he could think of was all about himself, and he had no idea why she would find his life interesting.

He considered leaving then, but the fact that he had come to the city all by himself made him bold. He approached her.

"How are you doing today?" he asked, his voice cracking only a little.

"Good," she replied, giving him a half-smile, "and yourself?"

"I guess I'm okay. I came in to trade for some things and got them. I'm sure Rick will be proud of me. I'm really worried about Galen, though. He's late."

Alice nodded politely. After a few heartbeats of uncomfortable silence, she started to move on.

"What's that?" Arturus asked her, pointing to the ornament that hung in front of her door blanket.

"It's a dreamcatcher." She turned back and reached out to touch one of the pebbles caught up in the yarn web. "It stops my nightmares from coming in, but lets the good dreams through."

"Does it work?" He looked at the dreamcatcher suspiciously.

Alice laughed. "It's just a symbol, silly."

Her words stung him slightly, but Galen had said that symbols were very real. Sometimes too real. Arturus knew that some men would die for a symbol.

Arturus took a closer look at the dreamcatcher. "Yeah, but does it?"

Her left cheek dimpled with her smile. "Almost. Keeps them all out but one. One always gets through."

"Must be broken. Bet you I could fix it."

The dreamcatcher's beads rattled as Arturus touched one of its strings.

Alice's ponytail swung back and forth as she shook her head. "I'd need to see your certifications."

"You can trust me," Arturus said, laughing. "I'm an expert."

"Oh are you?"

"Sure am. Hey, I was wondering if you—I brought some food with me to trade and I have a lot left. I'm sure Rick wouldn't mind it if you'd eat with me."

Actually, he'd probably be pretty angry.

Alice glanced up to one of the Fore's balconies. "Well, I can't. I'm meeting Molly at the church, but maybe we could eat together tomorrow?"

"Really?"

She nodded, smiling.

What if Rick doesn't let me come back?

"Wait, I don't know if I can make it to town," he said, thinking quickly, "but maybe we could meet at the Hungerleaf Grove?"

"Tomorrow, about this time?" she asked.

Their morning is just a little behind ours.

"Perfect," he said, and fought to keep himself from smiling too hard.

"I'll see you soon," she told him, and continued on towards the church.

"Wait," he said on impulse.

Alice stopped and turned back towards him.

"What's the nightmare, the one that always gets through?"

"Why do you want to know?"

"It's the same nightmare each time?"

"Yes, Turi. The same one each night."

"What is it? Maybe I can help?"

Alice smoothed some wrinkles out of her skirt with her hands. "You can't stop this one, Turi."

"Why not? What nightmare is it?"

"The one where I'm damned."

Arturus watched her as she continued walking. Before Alice had made it all the way to the church, though, she turned and looked at him. She looked sad, but she regained her half-smile briefly as their eyes met. She backed her way through the church's open double doors and disappeared into the building.

Galen had told him what he was supposed to do with a woman after he got her. Some of it sounded really unattractive. He almost felt like it would degrade her. But to kiss her? And hold her? That would be the most beautiful thing. He wondered how he could explain to her the feelings he had. How he could make her understand how well he would treat her since he cared so much for her. Galen would tell him what to say.

Maybe he's back already.

He walked out of Harpsborough and passed the two guards.

"Hey, Turi!" the sympathetic guard called after him.

"Yeah?"

"It's good to see you out on your own, you know."

Arturus grinned slyly. "It's nice not to have Galen and Rick around, slowing me down and all."

The guard gave out a surprised laugh. "Right!"

"See ya," Arturus said as he headed back into the wilds.

As Hell closed in around him, the rush of visiting Harpsborough rescinded and worry came up in its place.

Please let him be home.

— 5 —

If they recognize me, they'll kill me.

Pyle lay in the shadows, waiting, watching as the hermit boy made his way through the cavern. The young man was being careful, Pyle would give him that, but he was distracted and in a hurry. There was a pack slung over one of the boy's shoulders and a box of shells in what was probably his shooting hand.

He could be left handed. Still, he'd be an easy mark, and he's about the right age.

But even if this was the boy that Carlisle and the Infidel had been looking for, simply kidnapping him would not be enough. Would Maab remove the rustrock lined scars she had branded into the most intimate parts of his person in exchange for the lad's capture? Not likely.

The Infidel Friend had a saying: "Hell heals all wounds." Well, they had never met Maab. That woman knew how to make the wounds stick.

No, he was going to have to find out more than just who Carlisle was looking for. He needed to know why the Infidel himself had gone to such lengths to try and capture the youth in the first place. Then he might have enough information to make a deal with Maab.

Mancini can help me.

But to speak to Mancini he would have to get past the guards and into Harpsborough. And then what was he going to do? Just go traipsing around in there like they hadn't had him exiled? Some of the people he'd known had to have died off. It had been a couple of years, certainly. Still, some of the villagers would be left, and almost all of the Citizens.

If they recognize me, they'll kill me.

The young man exited the chamber. Pyle waited for one hundred breaths to make sure the boy did not return.

Then he stood up from the shadows.

They deserved it. Every drop of blood those devils took from Harpsborough was justified three times over.

Pyle drew out a long strip of cloth from his pack and began wrapping it about his face. He hadn't found any dyitzu near Harpsborough, but pretending that he had been burned by one was the best disguise he could think of.

With his head fully covered, he wrapped up his left hand as well.

I should go to the Kingsriver and check my wrappings in my reflection.

Pyle shook his head, rejecting the idea as one spawned by fear.

I need to be brave.

He moved towards Harpsborough instead, passing through the next few chambers in a daze. There was a time in Pyle's life when he had walked this very same path each day. He remembered Molly, sweet Molly, who he had kissed for the first time in the room ahead of this one.

Bitch left me.

He walked for another minute before stopping abruptly. Unless things had changed, two of Harpsborough's hunters would be in the next room, guarding the entrance.

If only I had an ally who could talk to Mancini for me.

But he had no one. Maab's men hated him almost as much as the people of Harpsborough did.

Poor little Pyle. He has no friends.

He could hear the sound of the village's guards echoing down the chamber. He closed his eyes and listened.

". . . never what I would have thought. I still don't believe it myself. Besides, these days we get so few lots it wouldn't even be worth it."

"They need to double us, at least."

"Triple, if they want to make it fair."

"Like that'd ever happen. Then Copperfield would have to lose a few pounds, and the Devil knows that'd be the end of Hell."

The men shared some laughter.

Pyle reached up and checked his bandages. He adjusted them carefully, trying to make the slit for his eyes as thin as possible. If they saw his un-burnt skin through the slit, they might begin to suspect him. He adjusted his belt, his right hand falling to his short barreled Remington coach gun. The walnut stock felt smooth to his touch. He flicked off its safety.

No. If they recognize me, I'll kill them.

Pyle squared his shoulders and entered the room. He was relieved to see that he didn't know either of them.

"Hand off the gun," one of the hunters ordered.

Pyle took his hand away from his Remington and placed it across his chest—that way it would be closer to the revolver he kept hidden over his heart. "I'm just here to trade." His voice sounded muffled through the cloth. He spread the wraps open around his lips with his free hand, being careful not to expose too much skin.

"Yeah?" the other hunter asked. "What do you have?"

"Some meat and a few torches." His voice sounded clearer now.

One of the hunters crossed his arms and sneered. "We've got torches."

"Meat would be nice, though." The other hunter licked his lips. "What kind? Dyitzu or hound?"

"Dyitzu," Pyle said. "The same one that took my face."

"Yeah?" said the cross-armed one. "Let me see the burns."

Damn.

Pyle shook his head. "My skin's healed into the cloth. It would hurt too much for me to take it off."

"Too damn bad." The hunter uncrossed his arms and let one of his hands rest on his sidearm. "No face, no entry. We're not kind to all hermits."

"You let the boy in," Pyle insisted.

"He had a face," the hunter said. "For all we know you're not burnt at all. You might be a corpse-eater. Could have the rot."

"But the rest of my body is fine," Pyle protested.

"No face, no entry."

This isn't working.

"Fine," Pyle said. "I'll let the burns heal a little more. I'll be back when I can get the wraps off."

"Good," said the other hunter, "don't eat all the meat."

Pyle wanted to gun them both down, but then he'd never get into Harpsborough. He left the chamber, took a turn and a dozen steps, then paused. The echoed voices of the guards came to him again.

"How'd he know about Turi?"

"Who cares? He had meat, Avery. We could have let him bribe his way in."

"Aaron would throw you through the Golden Door as soon as he found out."

"That's the point. He wouldn't find out."

"I think he would."

"Why?"

"Because my ass would tell him."

Pyle clenched his teeth and moved on, heading back into the wilds.

This isn't over.

The rooms passed by him in a blur.

That idiot hunter. Avery. I'm going to kill him.

There had to be a way in. He could come back during their

next shift, and the new guards might let him by. Or he could take the disguise off altogether and try to time it so that he entered Harpsborough while everyone was sleeping.

No. Someone would see me and gun me down.

He stopped when he heard the watery rush of the Kingsriver.

He entered the chamber slowly. There were very few devils around here, but it never hurt to be sure. It was empty.

I could shoot my way through the guards.

Pyle admitted to himself that such a thought was just a fantasy. He knew what he had to do.

He set his pack down by the river. The rush of the water helped sooth his nerves. He untied his bag's draw string and let it spill open. Slowly, he removed one of his torches. He held it aloft, still unlit.

I have to speak to Mancini. Hell heals all wounds.

He knelt by the bank and placed the torch reverently to his right. He met his own gaze in the water. His sister had always bragged about his good looks. About how all her friends had wanted to date him.

Ladykiller.

He fumbled through his pack until he found his firerock brick. The dark, heavy, almost metallic stone felt rough to his fingers. He struck it, hard, against the hellstone by the riverbank. Sparks flew from the brick, showering into the Kingsriver. A few settled on his hand. He let them burn out there. The pain was intense, but he knew it would be nothing compared to what was to come. He reached over with his free hand and picked up the torch. It took him two more strikes with the firerock before he had the thing lit.

The torchlight shone on the Kingsriver, adding its own ruddy glow to the room's ambient light. His hands were shaking, and the glow shook with it.

He held the torch up to the level of his eyes. The fire danced there before him. He looked away.

Hell heals all wounds. This is the way.

He couldn't hold the torch steady. He could feel the flame's heat on his cheek. The skin on the side of his face tingled with anticipation. The warmth was a good thing, he knew. The fire was his friend. The fire was going to get him into Harpsborough. The fire was going to let him know if that young man was indeed the one Carlisle had been looking for. The fire was going to help him control Maab. Help him get enough leverage to make that bitch restore to him those parts of his body she had taken. Clenching his jaw, he looked back towards the torch.

He leaned forward and immolated himself.

— 6 —

Arturus heard the sound of the Mighty Thames, and then, as he came closer, the splashes of the woodstone waterwheel as it turned. It spun quickly, so he knew that the battery had been charged.

"It's Arturus," he announced.

He crossed the bridge, his steps sounding off against the wooden structure. As he neared the doorway and the graveled floor, he smelled a bit of smoke in the air. That meant that the forge was on. That meant that Galen was home.

He ran across the gravel, passed the hallway that led to his room, and then turned into the forge. He felt the heat on his face when he entered. Galen's body armor and pack lay discarded by the room's entrance. The warrior was adding woodstone to the furnace. Arturus could see his father's face in profile. Even though Galen had been traveling for several weeks, his beard was as neatly trimmed as ever.

I'd swear his beard doesn't grow.

Galen rose up to his full height, his broad frame blocking the heat from the forge's furnace.

"Galen!" Arturus caught him up in an embrace as the man turned.

"Okay, boy," Galen told him, "enough."

Arturus ignored his father and held on.

"Enough, Turi, or this will turn into wrestling practice."

"You're home," Arturus said.

Arturus finally let go when Galen began extricating himself by force.

"I heard you had a big day today," Galen remarked.

"Wasn't so big," Arturus lied. "I went all the way to Harpsborough on my own, and made it back. I got shells and a rifle barrel, want to see?"

Arturus ignored the man's protests and rummaged through the pack. For a moment, Arturus saw Galen's eyes narrow when he produced the AR-15 barrel. "And all I traded was three pounds of dyitzu and a nine millimeter."

Galen nodded. "Not a bad deal at all. Well, bathe yourself, boy, and I'll see you for dinner. Did you run into anything on the road?"

"No, sir. Not many dyitzu about, and there usually aren't any corpses near the road anyways."

Galen looked back towards the forge's fire. "Run along, boy, let me finish my work before Rick gets hungry and eats without us."

Arturus ran his finger along the edge of the table, feeling one of the depressions on its edge. Rick had outdone himself with Galen's return meal. He had ground down hound meat, bone, and gristle, and baked it between crusts of honey covered flatbread to make a meat pie. The meat's juices filled his mouth with every bite, dribbling down his chin. The gristle caught between his teeth, but crunched satisfactorily as he chewed. They ate pickled knowledge fruit and salted devilwheat which had been soaked in dyitzu blood. Rick had wrapped up devilwheat seed in leaves from a hungerleaf tree, and then boiled and salted the wrap in hound's blood. He'd left spider eggs deep in the Thames for half the afternoon to keep them cool, and served them in small ornate stone bowls which Arturus had last seen during one of his birthday celebrations. He pretended he could feel the baby spiders crawling in his throat as he ate them. They drank cool water and warm hungerleaf tea, sweetened with honey. Arturus ate until he felt he might burst.

"We're eating like Citizens," he told Galen.

"Better," Galen said, "for Rick has a far fairer hand at exotics than Patrick the Foodsmith does."

"We should eat like this every night."

Rick gave Arturus a sharp look as he scooped out some more meat pie with two of his fingers. "I'd rather have my second death," Rick said, not at all joking. "And besides, you'd be a beggar within the week if we kept eating like this."

"But I'd be a fat beggar," Arturus said.

Galen laughed, and leaned back in his chair. There was plenty left on his plate. When he traveled for just a week, he would return as hungry as a hellhound. But sometimes, when he'd been gone too long, it would take him a few days to regain his appetite.

"Did you fight any devils?" Arturus asked.

Galen smiled, but it was Rick who spoke. "Galen tells you enough stories. You can't ask a man to make light of his own life and death."

"But Galen likes to tell me stories!" Arturus pressed on.

"Did you find anything on the road? A pack of hounds? A Nephilim?"

"Shush! Galen's trip was important." Rick pointed a hungerleaf wrap at him angrily before turning to the returned warrior. "Did you find the Minotaur? Any news?"

"So Turi can't have his story, but you want yours?" Galen asked with a smile.

"That's the way it works," Rick said.

Arturus took another bite of his meat pie to make sure that he didn't respond. Again the juices dribbled down his chin. He laughed and wiped them away with his sleeve.

Galen cleared his throat. "I traveled as far West as the Pole and circled back both North and South of Harpsborough until I came as far as the Carrion. I found nothing. The devils were light everywhere. You almost have to go looking for them to find them."

"It is a Minotaur, then?" Rick asked, worry in his eyes.

Galen shook his head and looked towards the spinning axle that came through the wall from the water wheel. He watched it turn for a few moments. "At first I thought so. I could practically smell a Bullman out there. Every place I looked was full of people and short of meat. But if there was a Minotaur drawing the devils to him, then the devils should have been going somewhere. There should have been a place near the Bullman where they were thickening. I asked around at the Pole, at Riverled and Macon's Bend to find where they had gone. I even went as far as Carlsbad. I heard nothing but silly rumors. It's as if all the dyitzu and hounds have just vanished."

Arturus munched quietly on his devilwheat seeds, and leaned forward.

"If I had just arrived here," Galen went on, "I'd have sworn this place had just been cleaned out by Infidel Friend."

"But aren't they evil?" Arturus asked around the seeds in his mouth.

"You cannot judge what you do not know," Galen told him.

"No Minotaur, then?" Rick asked.

"None that I could find."

"Then the devils' absence must be like a tide going out," Rick said. "You know it happens from time to time. The demons ebb and flow. We could be in for a time of great prosperity."

"Possibly," Galen said, nodding his head, "or perhaps there is a Bullman out there and it's just drawn the devils someplace where I don't know to look. Either way, we should enjoy the good times while we have them. In the labyrinth they don't come often, and don't last long."

There was a pause in the conversation while they ate.

"I was thinking I could gather the hungerleaves tomorrow," Arturus said, looking up from his plate to measure the reactions of both his parents.

"It'll be a heavy harvest," Galen said, "and that's pretty far out. You sure you want to volunteer?"

Arturus shrugged. "I made some mistakes when I was traveling to Harpsborough, because I was nervous. I wanted to work on them some. Traveling to the grove seems like the right way to do it."

Galen grunted his approval, and Rick was nodding.

Got it!

Arturus took another bite of a hungerleaf wrap to celebrate.

Galen pushed his plate, still half filled with food, towards the center of the table. "Which reminds me, Turi. Rick and I have been discussing you."

Arturus stopped mid-chew and looked back and forth between his fathers.

"Rick told me that he felt safe sending you to Harpsborough. I'm going to be very busy, as hunting for dyitzu is likely to take more time than usual, and the Devil knows I won't find a hellhound easily. I trust you won't mind going out with me on occasion?"

Arturus swallowed and nodded.

"And since you seem to be able to travel back and forth to Harpsborough," Galen continued, "I thought it might be nice to get you a job."

"A job?" Arturus asked, a little wary.

"Before I left, the First Citizen let me know that they were getting bored up there in the Fore. They wanted to commission some chess sets. As I will be too busy hunting, I thought I might have you make one."

Arturus frowned. "But I don't have the slightest idea how to make a chess set. I don't even know how to play the game."

Galen smiled, leaned forward in his chair, and scooped up a few spider eggs out of their stone bowl. He chewed them thoroughly before continuing.

"I'll show you how," Galen said. "I know you will be good at it. My only fear is the Harpsborough part."

"What do you mean?" Arturus asked.

"Well, the First Citizen is very particular about projects he commissions. After you finish each piece, you'll have to take it to Harpsborough to make sure he approves it. You'd end up going back and forth to Harpsborough nearly every day."

Arturus' heart leapt. "Every day?"

"Every day."

I'll get to see Alice. She might finally get to know who I am.

"Can you handle that, Arturus?" Rick asked him. "This is a big responsibility. We're asking a lot, more than just that you complete this simple job. We're asking you to take a serious step towards being an adult. After a few more jobs like this, after you are free to hunt on your own, you won't be our child anymore."

Suddenly Arturus was worried. "Would I have to leave?"

Galen laughed so loudly that Arturus looked towards the exit, afraid that there might be devils nearby their home which could hear.

"No," Rick said, glancing at Galen. "We'd be asking you to be our peer."

The young man nodded solemnly.

I'll go to Harpsborough every day.

"I'll do it!" he said.

"Now run to bed, Turi," Galen said. "Rick and I have a few things to discuss."

Arturus was so excited that he didn't even think to protest but instead ran quickly across the gravel hallway to his own room so that he could dream about his future trips.

She'll see me dealing with the First Citizen. Aaron won't be the only one who has connections to the Fore.

But in his haste, he had forgotten to relieve himself before lying down, and soon he was creeping back out of his chambers towards the river where he would give the Devil his water back.

He heard the echoed voices of Galen and Rick, who were still speaking in the battery room. From the way they were whispering he knew that this was a conversation he wasn't supposed to hear.

"You disapprove," Rick's hushed voice was saying.

"Yes."

Arturus looked longingly down the hallway. He needed to piss, certainly, but he wanted to hear the conversation too.

"He only spoke to Massan. Massan's a good man. He's not going to tell anyone. And if he did, the stigma would be on him as much as us."

"A 5.56 barrel isn't something I want Turi associated with," Galen said. *"You and me, that's one thing. But he's just a boy."*

Arturus crossed his arms over his abdomen and shifted from one foot to the other. That single crunch of gravel was enough to silence Galen.

Eavesdropping would be impossible now, so Arturus made a break for the river.

— 7 —

The chamber which contained the Hungerleaf Grove was filled with the Kingsriver's mist. Arturus loved the mists whenever they came. Galen said that they were caused by warm water, which had flowed through fires or been heated by the friction of settling stone. As far as Arturus was concerned, they meant that the water would be perfect for swimming.

The Harpsborough hunters, though, hated the mists. They liked to hunt along the Kingsriver because its chambers were so large—often miles long and hundreds of feet tall. A dyitzu was easy to spot in such a chamber and was little match for a man with a rifle at such a long range. But the haze would mean that a hunter wouldn't see any devils until they got close—close enough that the dyitzu's fire wouldn't be very easy to dodge.

Several land bridges connected to the Hungerleaf Grove, which grew out of a large natural island in the midst of one of the Kingsriver's oxbow lakes. Arturus felt very capable of protecting himself as he made his way across one of those bridges, his lightweight rifle strapped to his back, and his .38 pistol holstered at his side. The hungerleaf trees emerged from the fog as he approached, their long, spindly leaf covered branches reaching out, their scaly grey bark damp from the river's condensation.

He breathed in the warm air.

"Alice," he called.

He saw a shadow moving in the haze on the other side of the island.

"Declare yourself," he said.

He heard a girl's laugh. "You think I'm a corpse, Turi?" It was Alice's voice.

As she walked forward her distant grey silhouette slowly transformed into a beautiful blonde girl dressed in a blue skirt and white t-shirt. Her hair had been pulled back into a ponytail. While she tended to wear old world shoes in the village, she had on some dyitzu skin moccasins now. She had sewn them up beautifully but could stand to learn from Galen how to attach soles to them.

"You might be a corpse," Turi answered. "How should I know?"

She held up her hands before her and shambled forward. "Brains. Brains?" She clutched at his shoulders mockingly and began to pretend to eat his face. He felt her body as it brushed against his. She gave him a little shove, laughing.

Her laughter sounded beautiful in the mists.

He noticed she was almost exactly the same height as he. "What do you mean, brains?"

"Everyone knows corpses eat brains."

"No they don't," he said, puzzled.

She just laughed harder. "I can tell you were born here, sometimes. Did you bring the food?"

He unslung his backpack and held it up. "Yes."

"I brought something, too. It's not much, but it's wrong for friends not to share with each other. Follow me, we'll go get it."

Her blue skirt swished back and forth as she walked through the Hungerleaf Grove. One of the branches caught on her shoulder, and he had to duck to avoid it. Galen had been wrong, he noticed; there wasn't going to be much of a harvest. Many of the lower leaves had been taken already. It was possible that Rick had managed to get a run in recently, but it probably meant that the villagers were stealing from them.

They're so hungry in Harpsborough, I doubt Galen will even be mad.

She knelt down by a stump where she must have been waiting for him and picked up a satchel. It was definitely old world, and had a white kitten with a pink bow as decoration.

"What's in it?" he asked.

She opened the satchel a bit, and he leaned forward. She shut it suddenly. "You'll see."

"No! What is it?"

"Come on, where do you want to eat?"

He made a grab for the satchel, but she turned around and held it over her head.

"I was thinking here," he said. "Maybe we could go swimming."

He stopped suddenly, hearing something in the mist. Making sure to keep his body in front of Alice's, he drew his gun and looked out over the Kingsriver. A figure was standing at the far bank, looking at them from across the water. He couldn't make out the details of the thing, but it was almost too still to be a human.

"Declare yourself!" Arturus shouted.

No response.

"I'll get it," Alice said, stepping up beside him and drawing her pistol.

"Declare yourself!" Arturus tried again.

"It's dead, Turi."

Arturus gauged the distance. "That's a long shot for a pistol."

She took careful aim, and fired two rounds. Both hit, and the figure toppled back into the fog.

"Nice shooting," he said.

She nodded in satisfaction. "Well, maybe we shouldn't eat here. How about the Bordonelles?"

Arturus looked across the river, waiting to see if the corpse would get back up. "But the hunters won't go there.
Isn't it dangerous?"

"No! You're so young."

Arturus was crushed. "Am not."

"Maybe. Did your parents ever tell you not to go there?"

Arturus thought about this, eyeing her satchel in hopes of getting a clue as to what it contained. "No."

"That's because it's not dangerous at all. It's just a superstition from after your father killed the Icanitzu there. Martin's got them all afraid. Thinks he's seen a banshee."

"A banshee?"

"If Martin saw a banshee, he'd be dead."

He nodded. That was pretty good logic, actually. And besides, she had already said he seemed young. He didn't want to make *that* any worse. "Alright, let's go."

She flashed him a half-smile. "Follow me."

The Bordonelles were series of hollow cylindrical chambers which were connected to each other by narrow crawlways. Galen had shown him how to get to the Bordonelles, once, from the rustrock road. Alice led him in from a chamber off of the Kingsriver. He hadn't realized how close this part of the Kingsriver got to the road until now.

The crawlway she took him to was about three and a half feet tall.

"This way," she said, bending down and getting on her hands and knees.

Arturus did his best not to watch the effect this motion had on her skirt and followed after. "Do we need any light?"

"No, trust me."

She led him down a set of crawlways which he made sure to memorize. He didn't think that they would have any problems getting out, but it helped to make sure. The right side of the passage gave way to one of the cylindrical rooms, but she kept on moving, leading them farther into the darkness. After a quick turn, Arturus could no longer see.

"Almost there."

They entered into a room whose walls had collapsed. Light was streaming down from an opening near the ceiling. Unlike the smooth walls in the other Bordonelles chambers, these were now rugged and uneven. Much of the rock had fallen in and lay strewn about the floor.

The light streaming down from the ceiling illuminated a loose strand of Alice's blonde hair. "Pretty neat, huh?"

"Yeah, but why did you come here to begin with?" Arturus asked.

Alice walked over to the most damaged portion of the wall, found a handhold, and started to climb. "Well, I was thinking of the words of that famous American poet, Cynthia Lauper."

Arturus loved poetry. "What did she say?"

"Girls just want to have fun."

He looked at her, bemused, as she clung to the wall and laughed. Her laughter echoed in the small chamber.

He cinched his pack tightly to his shoulders while he mentally worked out a route. The climb looked like it would be pretty easy. He waited for her to get a little higher before beginning to make his way up. He caught up with her after just a moment and passed her quickly.

"Damn, Turi, where'd you learn to climb like that?"

"Galen, he teaches me everything. We headed to the light?"

"Yes, sir! I'm starving, so don't take your time or anything."

He made it to the top opening after another minute. The room's collapse had created a crack which led back into the Kingsriver chamber they had left. There was a small cubbyhole which looked down onto the river. This is where Alice must have meant for them to eat their lunch.

He had to admit that the view from the landing there was beautiful. He looked back down at her. "You want me to lower a rope?"

"Funny."

He helped her off of the wall and into the opening, again reveling in the closeness of her body. She walked into the cubbyhole and sat down. He watched her chest rise and fall. She wiped the sweat off of her brow and looked up.

"You're not tired?" she asked.

"No. Galen makes me climb like this all the time."

She nodded. "Sounds like something he'd do. What's for lunch?"

He took off his pack and opened it. He had some of the leftovers from Galen's return meal. He passed her a hungerleaf wrap and a cup of meat pie. She attacked the food. He'd never seen anyone so ravenous. All things considered, he was rather impressed that she had been able to wait so long to get here before starting to eat. He ate sparingly of his own portion, knowing that she would still be hungry when she had finished hers. It didn't take her long. She didn't offer any objection when he offered her his leftovers.

She drank his canteen dry after she had finished.

I should have brought more than just a snack. It was probably just enough to make her truly hungry.

"Been tough in the village," she apologized.

"I know."

She held up her satchel and opened the flap that had the white cat on it. "But look what I got."

Inside was a small clay jar, fired in Kylie's Kiln. She pulled out a knife and worked off the corking. Arturus leaned forward to see what was inside.

"Take a whiff," she said.

The smell burned his nose. "Bloodwater?"

She smiled.

"I've never had that before. Isn't it illegal for young people to drink that in the old world?"

She shook her head. "Turi, we're not in the old world anymore. Hell, you weren't ever in it. But Rick and Galen won't be mad. Hell heals all wounds, you know? No way you can get drain bramage."

"Drain bramage?"

She winked at him and took a sip. The clay jar was almost empty, but the stuff was probably worth as much as the food Arturus had shared.

She made sure to bring something that would be a fair trade. It couldn't have been easy for her. She's a good person.

She offered him the jar. Still somewhat dubious, he placed the jar to his lips and tilted it back. He had to tilt it farther than he expected, so that when he did get the bloodwater he got a mouthful instead of a sip. The liquid was bitter, sweet in an unpleasing way, and it burned in his mouth. He swallowed it quickly. The burning sensation went down his throat and disappeared into his stomach.

"Wow." He coughed a couple of times, his eyes watering.

She punched him in the shoulder. "Good boy, did you like it?"

"That was probably the most disgusting thing I've had in my life."

She smiled and licked her front teeth. "So you want some more then?"

"Sure."

The second swallow didn't taste any better, but he found the burn of the liquid pleasant for some reason.

Alice leaned back against the wall and looked out into the Kingsriver chamber. Arturus did likewise.

"Do you ever think you're better than us?" she asked.

"Because you weren't damned? You think you would have made it into heaven if you were on Earth?"

He thought for a moment. "You cannot judge what you do not know. I have no idea what people do to get sent here."

She nodded, and took a long swig of bloodwater. "Me neither. I'm betting I was sent here for my tattoo."

"You had a tattoo? Like Hidalgo?"

"Not like him!" she said, sitting up into a kneeling position. "It was right here."

She turned around and pulled up the bottom of her shirt. Arturus' heart picked up speed. She pointed to her lower back. "It was a tribal, except it had vines and flowers going all around it. It was my tramp stamp."

"Tramp stamp?"

"Sure was. Now it's gone though. Hell swallowed it up, so I'm not a tramp anymore." Her stomach rumbled audibly. "Sorry about that."

"No problem. I know it's been hard."

She pulled her shirt back down and turned back around.

"I don't have any more food," he said, "but I have some hungerleaves you can chew on if you want."

She accepted one. "Thanks, buddy. It'll help keep me awake too. I love hungerleaf, it's an optimistic plant."

"How do you figure?"

"It has three points, so it has to be. Sinfruit leaves, they have four points, so they're pessimistic. Watch, I'll show you."

She leaned up to the edge of the Kingsriver chamber. From their height, perhaps forty feet or so, the mist seemed to cover everything like a blanket. She ripped off one of the points of a dark green hunger leaf and tossed it. Arturus watched it fall into the mists below.

"Aaron loves me," she said, and ripped off another point. "Aaron loves me not." And another. "Aaron loves me. See, all out of leaves. With hungerleaf, all the men love you."

Does she really love Aaron?

Arturus felt his throat tighten. "All the men?"

"All the men."

"Even Mancini?"

"Eww!" Her eyes went wide. "I'd make sure to use a sinfruit leaf for him. So what's it like, Turi, growing up without a woman in your life."

He shrugged his shoulders. "Not sure really what to compare it to. What would I be missing?"

"Well, women can teach you things."

Now that could be interesting.

"Like what?" he asked.

"I don't know. A different perspective. Intuitive things."

"Galen says that female intuition is an oxymoron."

Alice's eyes narrowed. "Does he now?"

"Yes."

"We shall have to have a talk with him about that." She laughed and threw the remains of the hungerleaf at him.

He balled it up and put it in his mouth, letting the leaf's sourness wash away the ugly aftertaste of the bloodwater.

"It must be hard for you," she said. "There's no girls in the village your age. How are you going to find love?"

"You're my age," he said, looking down to the Kingsriver mists.

"Turi, I'm at least three years older than you."

He nodded. "Maybe, but I'll catch up."

Her laugh was delightful.

Those three years won't mean as much as time goes by, and then maybe you'll love me.

 — 8 — 

Davel Mancini marched up the Fore's stairs.

Finally, I have the Fore to myself.

Once a week Klein would hold a special service just for Citizens. The rest of the Citizens had agreed to stay late for a meeting about the lack of devils. Mancini didn't know what they could possibly have left to discuss. It wasn't like there was anything they could actually *do* about the problem. All that was left was to listen to Father Klein's drivel. The Father had been in Hell longer than him, sure, but Mancini was wise enough to know that when it came to things Klein didn't understand, he was full of bullshit.

And he sure as hell doesn't understand this.

Besides, Mancini knew they were discussing the wrong thing. Hell had its own rules, and no human knew what they were. Humans weren't made for this place. They were made for the old world. It was the devils that knew what was going on. If only a dyitzu was smart enough to speak, maybe they could ask one. It certainly couldn't come up with anything more cockamamie than the crap Father Klein was spewing.

He came to the third story landing.

Someone had left the parlor room pitch black, too dark even for his liking. Mancini, his arms held up before him, took ginger steps into the room. The door blankets that led to the balcony had been drawn so that they were perfectly flush with their stone frames.

Someone must have been sleeping in here.

He had to feel around with his feet to make sure he didn't run into the stone furniture.

He drew off a single blanket from around the first orb. The dyitzu skin felt soft to his touch. He let the blanket drop to his feet and stepped over it as the parlor was lit with the dimmest of illuminations. There was just barely enough light now for him to try and see. He moved towards the second orb, intending to take off another blanket.

He heard a click.

I'm not alone.

He saw a pale white face, disembodied in the darkness. Mancini froze, staring at it. He could not tell if it was human, or devil. It had no nose or lips to speak of, and its flesh seemed too swollen to be a person's. Tufts of black hair sprang up from its mostly bald head, disappearing into the blackness about it. In a few places the hair was as white as the skin on the face itself.

Mancini took a step back.

It wasn't too close to him, maybe thirty or so paces away.

That can't be right, there's a wall there. Is it in the wall?

He did his best to make sense of the room, trying not to lose sight of the face itself.

Don't move, maybe it won't kill you.

As Mancini's eyes began to adjust, he noticed that there was a shadow between the two of them.

Wait, it's not in the wall, that's the mirror.

He wasn't looking at the face at all. He was looking at the face's reflection. It could be anywhere in the room. If that was the mirror, then the shadow was himself. And that would mean that the face was right—

"Don't move, Davel," a voice whispered in his ear.

Mancini felt a gun being pressed into his back.

It knows my name.

His shoulders tensed so hard that they hurt.

"Don't shout for help," the voice ordered.

Mancini tried to nod, but his neck was so tight that he couldn't move it.

That voice.

Mancini saw his own eyes, their whites seemingly pale grey in the darkness, widening in the mirror.

"Pyle," Mancini said.

The Betrayer.

The gun pulled away from his back.

"Good, you recognize me."

How did he get in here? What happened to his face?

"Yes." Mancini whispered.

"Don't worry, Davel, I won't kill you. I'm a good man, and I remember all the fine wine you brewed me. I'm just here to ask you some questions."

Mancini's legs began shaking.

Control yourself.

"Why have you come back?" he asked Pyle.

"Questions, that's all. I just came in to ask you about the angel's get. That boy that Carlisle and the Infidel were looking for."

He needs something from me.

Mancini took his first quivering steps. His legs were shaky

and had no strength to speak of. Running wasn't going to be an option. The gun pressed again into his back.

"Where are you going, Mancini?"

He froze.

"The boy," Pyle demanded. "Tell me."

"That was before my time." Mancini's voice shook.

"It was, but I know you know the answer."

"What if I don't know anything?"

"Then you die."

He won't kill me. He needs to know what I know, doesn't he?

Mancini tried to read Pyle's face in the mirror. The room was too dark, and the scars hid any semblance of the man's expression. Mancini's neck cramped, and he jerked his head to one side in pain.

"Easy, Citizen Mancini. No quick moves."

Mancini felt Pyle's breath on the back of his cramped neck and tears began forming in his eyes. "I'll answer the best I can."

Pyle moved slowly around Mancini, coming face to face with him. The man was a mess of burns and boils. One of his eyes was milky white. When Pyle blinked, there was only half of an eyelid to cover that eye. "I don't really give a damn why Carlisle was looking for the boy. I knew Carlisle. All he wanted was to protect something holy. What I can't figure out is why the Infidel was looking for him too. But you're smart, Mancini. I know you must have it all worked out. Either that, or maybe Anna told you. You still have her locked up in your little brewery?"

The pain in Mancini's neck lessened a little, and he managed to swallow. "I'll tell you anything. Anything I can remember, but I didn't get it from her. Father Klein is the one who told me."

"Like I give a damn. Speak, Davel."

"The Infidel wanted him because there is some demon, like the Icanitzu, except it's immune to more than just bullets. Nothing in Hell can hurt it."

"And the Infidel thought the boy could?" Pyle asked.

"Yes."

"Because he's made from the stuff of an angel, not Hell or Earth?"

"Yes."

"But that's ridiculous."

Mancini shook his head helplessly.

"You must know something more," Pyle insisted. "The hermit, Turi I think his name is, could he be the one."

Mancini shook his head. "The Infidel killed Carlisle, remember. It's been well over a decade. That boy's in the hands of the Infidel by now."

"Damn."

That was desperation in his voice. He's not going to kill you. I've got to use this.

Mancini gathered himself.

This is the same man you used to work with. This is the same man who was your friend.

"I could pass a new law in the Fore." Mancini's voice was quivering with his fear, but he pressed on. "Make sure that no one with a scarred face is allowed in. Make sure that someone who could recognize you identifies each hermit as they enter."

Pyle moved across the carpet and sat down in Michael's favorite chair.

Had things gone a little differently, Pyle might be the one living here, and Michael would be skulking in the wilds.

"Was that a threat?" Pyle asked. "I might kill you now."

Mancini nodded, his neck stiff.

Pyle raised his shotgun.

Oh, God.

Mancini's legs almost gave out beneath him. "Kill me. Kill a Citizen. But hopefully no law will have to be passed, and you won't have to shoot me."

Surely Pyle wouldn't kill him. But this wasn't the same person that he'd known, Mancini realized. The wilds had changed the man somehow.

Is it possible he mutilated himself just to be able to get into Harpsborough?

Pyle shook his head and holstered his gun. "I'm listening."

Mancini brought his hand up to his neck and began massaging it. "I'm the only one in Harpsborough who will talk to you, Pyle. Father Klein would die before he gives you more information. But I'm sure he does know more. I'll grill him. I'll find out everything he knows about the boy, but. . ."

"But what?"

"First you have to do something for me."

— 9 —

"I saw you making eyes at that hermit boy," Aaron teased her.

"Turi? What was that, last week?" Alice laughed. "Please. He's too young."

"You shouldn't lead the poor guy on."

"I'm not! He's cooped up in that little room on the Thames with Rick and Galen. Doesn't even have a mother. He could use an older sister."

Aaron frowned.

"And an older brother, too," she said. "He might make a good hunter for you someday."

"Someday," he agreed.

"Besides, I saw you making eyes at Chelsea."

Aaron smirked and shook his head. "That's different."

Alice stood up from their dining table and took the two steps required to bring her to the edge of the third floor balcony. The whole village could see her from here.

So what if Chelsea sees me?

This was, perhaps, the finest place to dine in all of Harpsborough, not counting the First Citizen's private balcony.

Let her be jealous.

To her right was the church, and she was just below the level of one of its crucifix topped steeples. If she walked along the balcony's edge and peered around the corner of the Fore, she would be able to see Kylie's Kiln. She wondered what it would be like to be a Citizen, to be able to stand on this balcony every day, not as a guest, but as a person who belonged here.

This dream might all come true, she knew, if she accepted Aaron's advances.

And dropped in disgrace, if he decides he loves Chelsea more. Better listen to Molly and make sure he makes me a Citizen first.

There were other reasons for putting him off, of course. Ex-lovers seldom made for good friends, and enemies of Citizens did not have an easy time of it.

"I like it when we eat here," she said.

"And I like to treat you. What do you look at when you stand there?"

My house.

"Harpsborough looks different from up here," she answered.

"And so do you."

"You're just saying that 'cause you're lookin' at my caboose." she teased.

"No! I mean that up here you look like a princess."

"What do I look like down there then?"

He smiled. "An ugly-ass pauper."

"Aaron! I'm going to beat—"

She noticed the food arriving before she could finish. The bearer of the meal was John, who, at ten years old, was the youngest boy in the village. He wore loose sandals which clapped against the stone floor of the balcony as he walked.

"John," Aaron said as he helped the boy spread out the plates, "never compliment a woman. It's too dangerous."

John nodded solemnly.

"That's terrible!" Alice touched John's shoulder. "Don't listen to him, John. He's just not very good at it, is all. I'm sure you'd give wonderful compliments, wouldn't you?"

John nodded again.

The plates were made of polished granite and their silverware had been carved from woodstone. Each utensil had flowery designs whittled into their handle. When John removed the food's cover, Alice heard her stomach rumble. Her last good meal had been with Turi, and that had been at least five days ago. She used to be able to sew or patch clothes in exchange for food. These days people had so little that they were more likely to just wander around in ripped garments. Even the Citizens didn't seek her out anymore.

"You should practice," Aaron was saying to the boy. "Give Miss Alice a compliment. Tell her how pretty a pauper she makes."

"You have the most beautiful hair," John said, his face earnest.

Alice could not help but smile. Her cheeks felt a little warm too.

"You're adorable, John," she told the boy. "I'm sure you'll grow up to be quite the lady's man."

John scrunched up his face in disgust.

Alice returned to the table, laughing, and sat down across from Aaron.

The dyitzu meat looked especially succulent today, and it

was accompanied by an oatmeal-like porridge made from devilwheat. It reminded her of grits. The porridge was covered in a red powder that was either dried houndsblood or dyitzu. She could never tell the difference until she tasted it.

Aaron began carving up the dyitzu. She watched the juices and a bit of steam well up from the cut Aaron was making in the freshly cooked meat.

Alice's mouth watered, and her stomach growled again, this time audibly. Citizens tended to eat slowly, savoring each bite they took. Alice usually let her appetite get the better of her, but there were two other Citizens at the table on the far side of the balcony, and she didn't want to embarrass Aaron by eating like a villager.

She dug into her food as politely as possible. The porridge was closest at hand. She felt the warm devilwheat-meal slide down her throat. If anything, it made her more hungry.

"Can I get you something else, Citizen? Miss Alice?" John asked them.

She shook her head while swallowing her next bite. Alice could see why they kept him around. The boy was as polite as the butlers she remembered from old world television sitcoms. She made herself pause before dipping her spoon back into the porridge.

"Bloodwater, John. Some of Davel's new stuff, the darker kind." Aaron turned to Alice as John departed and spoke to her around the bit of dyitzu he was chewing. "You'll love this bloodwater. Davel's done something special to it this time. We can't get him to tell us what."

Alice frowned around her spoon at the thought of Mancini.

"Say what you like about his character," Aaron said as he placed a cut of dyitzu on her plate, "the man brews some mighty fine wine."

She glanced back at the two other Citizens on the balcony.

Don't do it girl, don't eat like a villager. Think about something else.

Aaron ate slower than she did, certainly, but faster than anyone else in the Fore. He was the only Citizen that still ranged the wilds—the only Citizen that still had to work to earn his keep. Maybe that was why she liked him more than the others.

He could stand to dress a little bit more like them, though.

Aaron was wearing a dark hoodie with some stains around the front pocket which she hoped weren't blood. While most people in the Fore wore more tight fitting—or perhaps even tailored—clothes, Aaron had on some baggy camouflaged pants. Except for the good repair of his garb, he could have been a simple hunter.

But he's not a hunter. He's a member of the Fore.

She watched him eat for a moment. She felt the porridge hitting her stomach. It almost hurt. The hunger inside her was building steadily.

Aaron can solve this. He can make it so you're never hungry again.

She fought to pause before she took another spoonful.

But he can die. He can keep you like a Citizen, hole you up in the Fore and fuck you silly for months. Then some demon can rip his throat out, and you'll end up right back in the village where you started.

The two other Citizens on the balcony, Herod the gunsmith and Copperfield the torch maker, got up to leave. Alice watched them go.

"Oh thank God!" She lifted up the dyitzu meat with her hands and tore into it with her teeth, not caring that the juices were burning her fingers.

"Whoa!" Aaron said, smiling. "Easy there."

Alice swallowed the meat having barely chewed it and bit off another chunk.

"You try starving in the village," she said, speaking with her mouth full, "and not eating all day."

John returned with the wine jar, which was a squat clay thing fired in Kylie's Kiln. Alice didn't bother slowing down for him.

Kid's ten. Who cares what he thinks?

"Thanks, bud." Aaron said. "We're good."

John nodded, almost like a little bow, and hurried away, his sandals clapping against the stone before going silent when they hit the dyitzu skin carpets of the parlor room.

Alice continued her feast, pleased that Aaron was polite enough to wait for her to sate her hunger before he said anything more. After she had wolfed down her half of the meat and another helping of porridge, she was able to lean back and relax. She used one of the Fore's cloth napkins to wipe the dyitzu grease off of her lips.

"Sorry," she said.

Aaron laughed. "No problem."

"I was impressed with John, though. He's getting very well-mannered."

Aaron opened the bloodwater's corking with his fingers. "Love that little man."

Jesus, he's strong.

Sometimes it was hard for her to remember that she was sitting across from the most famed warrior of Harpsborough. He was the Lead Hunter, able to run all day and all night. The best tracker and the best killer—but he wasn't very detail oriented...

"You forgot the cups," Alice chided him.

Aaron smiled, and stood up from his chair. "I'll get some

for us."

She used the moment he was gone to belch.

God, I feel better.

Aaron returned with two cups made of glass.

"Glass? Jesus, Aaron, what if I break one?"

"I'll say I did it. You won't have to pay."

She shook her head as he poured out the ruddy bloodwater.

She accepted the glass and took an experimental sip. It warmed her tongue and then her throat on the way down. There was some kind of aftertaste that she couldn't quite recognize.

"It is good," she admitted.

"Mancini's finest."

The conversation stalled for a moment. She watched him as he ate.

I've got to keep him interested. Maybe I should get him talking about his work or something.

"So, Molly says that Michael Baker is going to lead his own hunting party," Alice told him.

Aaron dropped his fork and looked up from his food.

Smooth, Alice. Smooth.

"What does Molly know?" he demanded.

Just enough to get me in trouble, apparently.

He took another bite and washed it down with a splash of the wine.

"Should you be drinking that before you go out?"

"It's fine," he said. "And you're right, Mike is thinking about going hunting. Not too bad an idea either, if you ask me."

"Molly says it's because he's threatened by you."

Aaron frowned before he responded, his eyebrows narrowing over his brown eyes. The expression didn't last long. Sadness rarely kept up with him, but he did seem more serious as he continued. "That's not true. And it's not because I'm doing a bad job either. There are barely any dyitzu out there. That's why my hunters are so hungry. We're fed by lot, and we get only one lot for each kill. I'm telling you, my hunters need special rations. The Citizens will be voting on it next week."

Alice was surprised to find herself slightly intoxicated. This new stuff Mancini had brewed hit hard and fast.

"Well, why do you think Michael's going out then?"

"The people are hungry, Alice. He's a good man. A good leader. I don't think he can sit idly by while his people are hungry."

Alice shrugged. "He could just feed people out of the Citizens' food."

I shouldn't have said that, either.

"He's actually mentioned that a couple of times." Aaron went on as if she had every right to speak out against the Fore.

"He can't, of course. There has to be some dream people can work toward, and the Citizens would probably kill him if he did it. But we've got to do something. He's a really good hunter. He taught me. He may be able to come up with a plan."

They ate in silence for a few moments after that.

Alice smiled. "I hope your vote goes well."

"It has to," he said between mouthfuls. "My hunters are starving to death. It's hard to hunt while you're hungry. They don't realize that we're ranging twice as far as we used to *and* we've still got to get back by third shift. Something's got to give. Either our restrictions have to be lifted so we can range farther than a day's travel, or we need more food."

Alice smiled at him as he prattled on about his hunting and served herself seconds. She had to make sure she ate everything she could while she had the chance. If tomorrow Aaron decided he wanted Chelsea, she might not ever find herself here again.

She studied his profile as he looked out over the city. His jaw line was particularly sharp, and she could see the muscles of his shoulders through his shirt.

He's so beefy.

Beefy was the kind of physique that Molly liked.

A beefcake. I could get used to that kind of thing. But Molly's right, I can't just give myself to him. No matter how much I like him, he's got to get me a Citizen nomination first.

When their meal was done they left the balcony together. Alice tried to sit down on one of the couches as they entered the parlor room, but Aaron shook his head.

"I've got to go out today. We've got to try and catch something. Thank God for Julian, eh?"

"Thank God," she mumbled, reluctantly passing by the cushioned divan.

He tried to kiss her at the bottom of the Fore's stairs. She dodged him, but he tried again in the waiting room. This time he caught her, and she let him go on for a moment until his hand reached up for her chest.

"Easy tiger," she teased him.

He shook his head. "I just don't get you."

"You wouldn't."

He rolled his eyes at that.

She leaned forward, pecked him on the lips, and pushed through the door curtain to exit the Fore. He adjusted his shirt and pants and came after, heading towards a group of his hunters. She spanked him on the butt as he started to walk away.

He jumped and gave a little yelp, obviously not expecting that.

His hunters laughed, and one called out to him. "You

alright there, sir?"

Aaron shook his head and smiled. "Great. Thanks for your concern."

"See you later, sweet-cheeks," she called after him, drawing more laughter from the hunters.

He's adorable when he smiles.

— 10 —

"There are sixty-four squares in a chess board," Galen had told him, "thirty-two light and thirty-two dark. On top of those squares you will find infinity."

Galen spoke of the game chess in the way that Father Klein talked about Jesus, but Arturus wasn't falling for it. Galen talked about *everything* like Father Klein talked about Jesus. It must be Galen's personal opinion, Arturus figured, that every activity contained within it some sort of transcendent, numinous, and all-encompassing wisdom.

It had been Arturus' suggestion to find several different types of stone for Michael Baker to pick from. It had seemed a sensible idea at the time. As he wandered the wilds of Hell in search of rare and beautiful types of Hell rock, he began to regret his decision.

The black marble with red veins was the hardest to find, and it was this kind of stone which he was gathering now. Even after he found a few patches, he still couldn't find a room where he could mine it safely. He finally settled on one, although he would have rejected it if the rock had been more common. The black marble was only on the back wall, so he had to view the entrance of the room out of the corner of his eye. The entrance itself was at the end of a long hallway, so he would have plenty of time to notice something if it started coming after him. He paused every few minutes to listen, just in case.

This part of Hell was dead quiet.

He continued chipping away and cursed when the brick he was working on broke in two.

I hope he doesn't like this kind.

He thought this, but quickly changed his mind. He had already decided that if he was going to be making a chess set over the next few months, then it was going to be the most beautiful chess set that had ever been created. Surely, the black marble with red veins would help make the most beautiful board.

He stopped after making some progress on the second brick.

There was some kind of noise, barely audible.

A distant rumble.

He put down his pick and placed both of his hands on the marble, feeling the sound as a vibration through the stone. He waited for a few moments and the sound died away.

Settling.

Galen had taught him that the force of the labyrinth's stones weighing down on themselves would cause them to shift from time to time. He waited for a moment and was about to start mining again when the settling returned.

Rick didn't call it settling. He called it thunder.

He heard a great crack, which was followed by the distant grinding and creaking of stone. The walls vibrated again, but this time more fiercely.

"They travel along fault lines," Galen had told him once. "You can tell when you're on one when you hear it getting closer and closer."

Arturus remembered being terrified of that. As a child it had been his pet fear.

He held his breath and listened further.

The sound came again, but it seemed farther away.

Good!

He let his breath go and waited even longer. He could feel his own heartbeat in his chest.

The next quake was so quiet that the only way he knew the thunder had come again at all was because of the slightest shaking of the wall.

The sound did not seem like it was returning.

It has passed me by.

Galen would undoubtedly go ranging to make sure that no chambers nearby had been damaged. He hoped all was well because he liked their home. He wouldn't want to have to find a new one. That, and they'd leave Alice behind.

"Don't make us leave," he begged the stone.

The half brick he'd mined already would be just fine, but Galen had taught him that he shouldn't make compromises after he had decided on how to do a thing. He paused at times to listen for more settling while he finished the new brick.

Nothing.

He placed the brick in his pack and shouldered it, anxious to return home.

There was a man in the shadows.

Arturus drew his pistol.

"Who are you?" he shouted.

The hallway that led into this room was long and dark. The

man had made it almost the entire distance without Arturus noticing.

I was too busy listening to use my eyes.

"Who are you?" he shouted again, and then remembered his training. "Declare yourself. I'm Arturus, a hermit near Harpsborough."

The man did not answer, but continued walking forward, slowly and deliberately.

"Declare yourself. If you do not answer, I will shoot."

He thumbed back the hammer, noticing that the barrel of his pistol was shaking. It never did that in shooting practice.

The man passed through the entryway. The rot smell hit Arturus at the same moment that the room's light illuminated the figure.

The corpse's face was grey, the eyes black with long since clotted blood. Its movements were smooth, but slow. It didn't seem to have the stiff legged walk of the corpses Arturus had seen in the past.

Arturus fired once. The report of the .38 was far louder than even the thunder had been.

Despite his nerves, the bullet had struck true. The thing's head snapped back, and it toppled over. The bullet had caved in the bones on the right side of its face, and its brains and clotted blood were leaking out onto the floor.

"You've got bigger things to worry about than the falling of the sky," Galen had said.

Is he ever wrong?

Arturus waited to see if the thing would move. He was pretty sure it wouldn't, but it didn't hurt to make sure. Then, slowly, keeping an eye on the stilled corpse, he stepped over it. He looked down the long hallway, his pistol still drawn and held at eye level. He took a breath and started walking. Devils were often drawn to gunshots, he knew.

But people are too.

The thumbed the hammer back down, as Galen had trained him, to make sure that he didn't shoot another human being. He searched the area thoroughly, but couldn't find any more corpses. He didn't holster his gun until he made it home.

The quake had driven the people of Harpsborough into the church. Alice was struggling to see in from where she stood outside the building's heavy double doors. Nearly all five hundred of the villagers were crammed within that structure's walls. The rest, save those on guard duty at the village's entrance, were gathered on the steps, peering over the shoulders of their compatriots and through the doors to try and catch a glimpse of the men inside. The only parts of the church that were not crowded were the first four pews, whose stone benches had been reserved for the Citizens.

She noticed Kara standing just ahead of her at the doorway.

"What's he saying?" Alice asked.

"That's Father Klein," Kara answered, "he's speaking now. You missed Baker. He says that there's nothing to worry about. Says it happened a few years ago. Says Hell trembles all the time."

"Hush," said another man on the steps, "I can't hear."

Kara wasn't the only person silenced by his words, and Alice found that she could now hear the Father speaking, though just barely.

"You have viewed this as a bad sign. As a bad omen. You feel that the hunger that has come upon us is a punishment. That times are bad and that we are in famine. I tell you that is a lie. We have. . ." the next few words were drowned out by a man's cough, "that quaking you heard, that glorious thunder, is the benevolence of God. He has turned His eye upon this part of Hell. We have been blessed, truly, for the great society that we have built. For those of us who have honored and feared God even in this distant realm of damnation, I call to you now—"

"Wish the windbag would speak louder," Kara muttered.

"Hush!" several people responded.

"The devils are few, and you lament. The devils are thick, and you lament. Take the fewer, it is your blessing. There is enough food to feed us. Few of us die on our ranges. Thank God for that! Surely, the weight of God's eye has driven out our enemies. It has bent the very stones of Hell. The wrath of God will not crush us, the Lord be praised, it will crush them! It will crush the men who follow in Maab's footsteps. It will crush the men who call the Infidel their man. But it will not crush us.

"Rather, let us turn to each other. It is a time of great need and great prosperity. Instead of fighting the devils, we must now find accord with ourselves. We must love ourselves. There is enough food to feed us. We must share it, and stop hoarding. We must—"

"Seems like the Citizens hoard the most!" a man called.

"Silence." That was Aaron, and his voice boomed loudly enough to be heard clearly outside the church. "You know full well that there's a vote to be had in the Fore about that."

"For your hunters, not for us."

Kara shifted back and forth, trying to see around one man's head. Alice swore she smelled Massan on her.

"My hunters hunt for you too," Aaron was saying. "Now I don't want that thunder to scare anyone. My men are working with a few of the hermits, Galen included, to search for the damage. Galen's pretty far out in the direction we think the quake came from, and he said there wasn't any cracking out their way. I'm told by Father Klein, who's been here longer than any of us, that if there's no cracking then there's no danger."

Alice shrugged her shoulders and wandered away from the church, leaving Kara behind. A few of the others followed her.

"You don't look worried," one of the men who had hushed Kara said to Alice.

She laughed and shook her head. She was worried, but she hadn't been waiting for the town meeting. No Citizen was going to tell the villagers what was really going on.

It was the truth she wanted, and she intended to get that from Aaron.

Arturus was still shaking in the battery room as he removed the black marble brick from his pack. One of his ears was ringing a little from the sound of his gunshot.

"Galen," the warrior declared his approach from outside the home.

Arturus could hear the crunching of the gravel beneath the man's feet.

"Arturus," he responded. "I'm home."

After a few more crunches, Galen entered the room and moved towards their provisions closet.

"I shot a corpse today," Arturus said.

Galen stopped rummaging long enough to turn back and flash a smile at him. "Well, good for you. Make sure you visit it again when it turns to dust. Mancini's brew could use it I'm sure."

"It almost surprised me. I was in a room on the end of a long hallway, working on the stone. It covered one hundred or so feet without me noticing it."

"That's not good," Galen said, his voice echoing out from the supply closet. "Why do you think it got so close to you before you noticed?"

"I was listening, really hard. I think I was scared by the settling."

Galen came out with two pieces of flatbread, some dried dyitzu meat, and a right angle leveler. "You didn't hear it?"

"It moved silently. Smoothly too."

"The old ones get like that. They start out stiff and uncoordinated, but give them long enough, and they move as smoothly as silk. Did it touch you?"

Galen was stuffing his food and the leveler into his pack.

"No, sir," Arturus answered.

"You should probably wash your clothes and weapons. And try not to die in the next couple of days, just in case."

Arturus laughed. "What are you getting ready for? Are you going out again?"

"Yes, but not far." Galen put his Heckler and Koch MP5

upon the marble counter and started to disassemble it. "I've been speaking with Harpsborough. I'm going to go out with some of their hunters and make sure there are no settling cracks."

"You know Rick hates it when you clean your guns on the cooking counter."

Galen nodded. "That's because he has to clean it up."

"Can I go with you?" Arturus asked suddenly.

"Not yet, you're probably a mite bit too young."

"Well, what do you want me to do?"

"Keep on making those squares, of course."

"Like nothing happened?"

Galen held up the disassembled barrel from his gun and peered along its sights. "What are you going to do, stop Hell from collapsing? Hidalgo, on the far side of Harpsborough didn't even hear it. And we're by the river. The settling's thunder travels well down the river. Like as not, we won't find a thing. If the settling keeps coming, *then* we have a problem."

Galen dipped a small piece of cloth in his homemade cleaning solution. He then threaded it through the end of his cleaning rod.

"Will it?" Arturus asked.

Galen looked up from his work. "Will it what?"

"Keep coming?"

"You cannot judge what you do not know. Let me know how you do with those sample squares."

"I'll show them to you when they're done."

Galen finished cleaning his rifle and reassembled it while Arturus watched. Arturus, who had been disassembling and reassembling weapons his entire life, could do so very quickly. He was even faster than Rick, but Galen was something else entirely. He put his rifle back together like most people breathed.

Packed and prepared, Galen pushed a clip into his gun and headed out of the battery room. He paused at the entrance to the gravel hallway. "A word with you boy."

"What is it?"

"You learned a lesson today, when the corpse got close to you. It's like in wrestling, when we talk about the principle of two weaknesses. You feared the danger of the settling, and didn't have enough presence of mind to defend against the corpse."

"I know. It scared me. I won't be as careless next time."

Galen nodded.

"But consider this also your first chess lesson."

"I don't even know how the pieces move."

"Maybe you will, if I ever have time to teach you. Chess players also use the theory of two weaknesses. You can defeat a novice if he doesn't know to protect both. You can defeat a master if he cannot protect both."

"I was a novice today," Arturus admitted.

"But don't be tomorrow. Rick cares for you a great deal, Turi. And I've put no small amount of investment into you either. Don't go dying on us."

Arturus nodded his head. "I won't."

He expected Galen to leave, but the warrior remained in the doorway.

"Promise me," Galen said.

"But you said not to promise things that are out of my control."

"Make an exception," Galen ordered.

"I promise. I won't die."

Galen nodded and left. Arturus listened to the crunch of the man's footsteps on the gravel. The crunches turned into thuds, letting Arturus know that he had made it to the bridge.

After that, nothing.

"I love you too," Arturus said.

— 11 —

"Alice, are you awake? It's Molly."

Alice gathered herself, sitting up from her bed of blankets and dyitzu hide. She could see Molly's eye peeking in around the door blanket.

"Yeah," she half-mumbled, "one sec."

She looked about her squat, dark, one roomed home and found her favorite shirt in the light let in from the crack between her ceiling's blanket and the wall. She had meant to fix that. She came up to a crouch, waited for the blood to return to her head, and struggled into her shirt. Then she pushed through the curtain to speak to Molly, jingling the beads that hung from her dreamcatcher as she did so.

"What were you dreaming about?" Molly said with a sly smile.

Alice wasn't sure what Molly was joking about. The woman's curly brown hair was tousled badly, so Alice figured she must have just come back from the wilds. Molly's grin revealed her one crooked front tooth.

"Huh?" Alice asked.

Molly raised her eyebrows, then reached out and touched one of Alice's nipples.

"Oh, Jesus Christ," Alice said, and bent back into her hovel to find a bra.

She only had two. She decided on the pink flowery one since she didn't have anyone to impress today—at least not until Aaron got back later on that night.

Is it still daytime? How long was I sleeping?

Molly was snickering outside, and Alice could feel the woman's gaze on her back.

Alice snapped the bra on around her waist and then pulled her shirt over it.

"A little maturity would be nice," she called back over her shoulder as she slid one arm back under the bra strap and into her sleeve.

"So would a little modesty," Molly said, holding open her door curtain. "I mean, it's not polite to point."

Alice finished getting the bra over her other shoulder, adjusted it and straightened her shirt. Molly was kind enough to hold open her door curtain as she re-emerged.

"Better?" Alice asked imperiously.

"I bet Aaron would have messed his pants if he saw what I've just seen," Molly said, and then, as if this had just crossed her mind and surely wasn't the entire purpose of her visit, she asked, "Speaking of, didn't you eat with him the other day?"

Alice nodded. "I'd almost forgotten with the settling."

"Settling schmettling. We'll be fine," Molly went on, touching Alice's shoulder. "So, how was the dinner?"

"It was perfect," Alice admitted, grinning.

"You're crushing hard," Molly placed her hand over her heart. "He's a good guy. Trust me, better than Baker. I'd know."

You would, slut.

"They eat so well up there. And the bloodwater and the meat. Makes me so sleepy."

Molly fingered the yarn web of the dreamcatcher. She ran her hands across a thread until she came to a pebble.

"So is this Aaron, trapped in your web?" she was trying to sound like she was still joking, but her tone had turned serious. "Or are you trapped in his?"

"Jesus, Molly."

"I just want to know if you slept with him. I happen to be an interested party."

Alice shook her head and began to run her hands through her hair to loosen the tangles it had gathered during her sleep. "I didn't fuck him."

Molly looked at her suspiciously.

"We just kissed," Alice said.

"Well, that's smart of you," Molly said. "You'll never get a nomination if you sleep with him too early. If I had known that a year ago, I'd be in the Fore and Chelsea would be out here bustin' her ass."

Maybe.

"I'll be smart about it," Alice assured her.

"How's he doing?"

Alice sat down against the outside wall of her hovel. Molly remained standing, toying with the dreamcatcher.

"He's worried about the food of his hunters," Alice said.

"Oh," Molly said, her face suddenly becoming a caricature of worry. "You better get in his ear about that soon. He's been letting his hunters eat some of the dyitzu they kill without reporting them."

"He wouldn't," Alice said.

God, I hope he wouldn't. The Fore would kill him. Or send

his ass through the Golden Door.

"That's one of the reasons we're so hungry," Molly went on. "Everyone knows there's enough food for all of us. And he's trying to get special rations for his people. The Fore will never go for it. By the time you get him, he may not even be a Citizen at all."

"They say there's enough food for everybody because the Citizens eat so much, Molly, not because there's enough dyitzu."

Molly shrugged her shoulders. "Thank God for Julian," she said, and then pointed to another stone in Alice's dreamcatcher. "And what about this stone, should we call it Turi?"

"That's ridiculous," Alice said. "He's just a boy."

"Sure." Molly feigned doe eyes. "But his shoulders are looking pretty broad these days. He's growing up fast."

"Whatever."

"Maybe I should check out his goods for you? I could let you know if they're any good."

Alice was assaulted by the image of big busted Molly riding the poor boy. "Leave him alone."

Molly sat down next to Alice and lowered her voice to a whisper. "I'm serious about Aaron stealing the dyitzu. The word is all over town. One of his hunters is talking. Or maybe that hunter's smuggling some of the meat and sharing it with his friends."

"Those are just rumors, Molly," Alice said. "Don't take that seriously. He would never do something so stupid."

"He could lose his position. And I mean it. They might even kill him."

"Rumors."

"Maybe you're right," Molly said. "Maybe I shouldn't believe all I hear. Aaron's not really a rebel, no matter what his reputation is. He wouldn't let his hunters steal any dyitzu."

Alice nodded.

"You hungry?" Molly asked her.

"Yeah, famished. I'm always famished the day after eating at the Fore."

Molly was usually stingy in the best of times, so Alice was grateful and a little surprised that the woman was in a giving mood.

"Tell me about it," Molly said, fishing about in her satchel. "I used to eat in the Fore every day when I was with Baker. It's like it expands your stomach or something. Loved it though, made my tits as big as trucks."

She held out her food offering.

"Here you go, Alice."

Alice felt a chill run down her spine.

Oh, Aaron.

In Molly's hand was a strip of dyitzu meat.

Rick and Galen had agreed to let him use up most of the battery for his project. Arturus intended to leave enough for a hot meal, though. He set his gun down on the cooking counter and used a thin charcoal pencil and a stone ruler to mark off the squares. He thought he'd start with the woodstone, because it was the easiest. The black marble, which was the hardest to gather, would be the last test square he made.

I could probably stand to find a better room to get it from, though.

He rummaged around the supply closet until he found a glass mask which would protect his eyes. Then he chipped away at the woodstone with his chisel, getting close to the charcoal markings. There was no point in getting the squares to be perfect yet, because he intended to use the battery powered grinder to touch them up.

He stopped working after he had shaped a square. His chisel mark had ruined the material beneath, but for right now, he had what he needed.

The grinder had three settings, run by three different gears, each using more of the battery's kinetic energy than the last. For woodstone, the softest rock in his bunch, he could use the lowest setting.

With a wide handled set of tongs he gripped the square and then wrapped some twine around the handles to keep it steady. He flipped the lever that switched the power of the battery to the grinder, and then let the battery run. The grinder spun into life and he began shaping the stone.

The piece snapped out from his tongs and went clattering across the floor.

"Damn," he said aloud, turning off the battery.

He checked the square for damage. Fortunately, it was fine.

He rummaged around further in the supply closet, but didn't find anything that would serve him any better. He wandered back through the gravel hallway and searched in the forge. There he found some tongs with a clamp on the end.

He returned to the battery room and clamped in the stone, using two pieces of Rick's cleaning cloth to keep the clamp from scuffing the piece. With his square hopefully secured, he turned the grinder back on. This time the stone did not escape him, and he was able to try and grind it into the correct shape. Woodstone sawdust sprayed all about him.

I'm going to have to sweep all that up.

He paused from time to time to inspect his work. After he'd finished, he looked critically at the piece.

"Well," he told himself, "it looks kind of okay."

And to think, woodstone is the easiest.

He moved back to his original set of bricks, took a section of white marble, and marked it off carefully with charcoal.

He heard the crunch of gravel.

He leapt for his pistol, his heart a wild thing in his chest, pumping as if powered by the battery. He grabbed the gun off of the counter and raised it.

I promise.

"Hello?" he heard a feminine voice call.

Alice?

"Hello?" The calling voice was high pitched, even for a girl. "Turi?"

Not Alice, but she knows my name.

"Declare yourself," Arturus shouted.

"Declare myself what?"

Galen would have had a fit at that answer.

"You're supposed to say your name," Arturus called out.

"Oh, Ellen."

"Okay, Ellen, you can come on..."

The girl, about Arturus' own age, entered the battery room and stared at the pistol which Arturus found himself pointing at her face. She held up two empty hands. Arturus looked at her belt, but she appeared unarmed.

"Rick sent me." She seemed a little terrified. "He said you'd be home. That you could get me some food."

Arturus took stock of the brunette girl who stood in front of him. She had no weapons, but her clothes were in excellent repair. She even had some make-up on her face. She was dressed as finely as a Citizen, with old world blue jeans, some new looking sneakers, and a thin cotton long-sleeved shirt that was soaked with sweat.

There was something suspicious about her.

"Sure," Arturus said, "what are you going to trade me for it?"

She burst into tears.

Arturus watched her collapse with a mortified sense of puzzlement.

What's wrong with her?

"Are you okay?" Arturus asked her.

"Jesus Christ!" she half shouted.

Arturus glanced towards the exit, afraid she might bring demons into their chamber with her noise.

Not like she's any louder than my grindstone.

"What did He do to you?" Arturus asked.

"What? No!" she shouted.

"It's okay, I'll get you some food." He hoped that the offer would stop her from crying.

It didn't.

"—and I don't even know where I am—" Ellen said through her tears, and then covered her mouth with her hands.

"Rick," his father's voice reported.

"Arturus," he shouted back, and since Ellen didn't seem to be about to declare herself he added, "and Ellen."

"—and how did I get here. . . was just walking. I was just walking—"

Rick entered the chamber and looked at the fallen Ellen. He gave Arturus an accusing look.

"I didn't do anything," Arturus insisted.

"What happened?"

"She just came in and asked for food," he held his hands out wide, and then realized he was still holding his pistol.

He holstered it quickly.

"I don't have anything to trade for it, alright?" Ellen shouted at him.

"She's just been damned," Rick told him.

"Oh."

No wonder she looks like a Citizen.

Arturus offered her his hand. "That's fine," he said with a smile. "Are you hungry?"

She nodded and stood after taking his hand, wiping snot and tears off of on her cotton shirtsleeve with her free arm.

"The flatbread first," Rick suggested. "It'll be the most familiar to her."

The church, Father Klein often insisted, was built by those same men who had designed the Fore. It was not, and of this he was most certain, designed by Hell's architect.

Its hallowed halls, made of slick blue marble, were large enough to hold all the Citizens and then nearly all of the villagers of Harpsborough. Its far wall, behind where Father Klein sat now, was marked with the dust and dirt of the villagers who prayed there. Above that line of pollution was a giant woodstone cross which hung down from the fifty foot ceiling. Along the church's east and west walls were tall Doric pillars, each supporting the high arch of the ceiling with its symmetrical sister. Between each supporting pillar was an ornamental one, which had once been topped with the pagan statues of strange gods and heroes.

Father Klein had made sure those statues were taken down, but even he was afraid to ruin them, and had stored them instead in the small room he called the catacombs. It was the same room where he stored the flatbread and bloodwater. He prayed over them nightly, begging that the body and blood of Christ would make some hopeless sojourn into the bowels of Hell to give the semblance of a communion to his damned flock. Backless stone benches were laid between the pillars, taking the place of pews. Forty-eight of the village's fifty Citizens sat in them now, not facing the pulpit as a congregation might, but arranged in a half circle, looking towards each other.

The Citizens had not always held their votes here. Even into the first year of Michael Baker's reign they had made their votes in the Fore's parlor. Now that there were fifty of them, the parlor's confines were too small. Father Klein had been only too happy to put them up in his church. It had been his suggestion, in fact.

First Citizen Michael Baker and Davel Mancini were the last two Citizens to enter the church, and the buzz of quiet conversation died down at their entrance. Mancini's booted feet could be heard clopping along the center aisle, echoing in the close stone confines of God's building.

Michael's footfalls, perhaps owing to his previous post of Lead Hunter, were much softer, and the room fell into silence as Mancini took his seat. Michael continued towards the pulpit. Unlike Father Klein, he did not dare stand behind it, lest his words be confused with God's.

Father Klein stood up from on one of the benches, and intoned the beginning of their meeting. "We came to Hell as Wolves. We denied our Lord God, in thought, word, and deed. In His magnificent judgment, He has damned us to Hell. We are contemptible men, deserving of our Fate. Though it is too late for our Salvation, let us leave Hell as Sheep, that we may do in Death what we failed to do in Life. Lord, if you see fit, guide us in our Damnation with Your Wisdom."

"Amen," came the Citizens' reply.

Mancini wasted no time in getting to business. "Alright, as you have undoubtedly noticed, the villagers aren't eating very well. Certainly you have seen the decline in our stores of meat. You have definitely resented the pressure we've given you to keep your villager's visits to the Fore at an absolute minimum."

He looked about the room at that, and received a few scattered laughs. "Particularly when a villager would eat a dyitzu whole if we let them." A few more laughs. "But I would argue that, by and large, this is actually a period of great prosperity. Times are tough in the village, sure, but there are more villagers than ever before. We may have had to cut down just a little in the Fore, but it hasn't been out of what we eat, it's been out of what we share. So long as we don't add any more Citizens, we'll be fine. I suggest then, that we keep today's business focused and not get sidetracked on the food issue."

Ben Staunten, the Master of Stores, stood up from his seat. "Davel must have been drinking too much of his own bloodwater," he said, his voice a resonant baritone. "We're eating through our dried foodstuffs. Keep on the way we're going and sooner or later we'll have to cut back."

"Devils haven't always been this scarce," Mancini responded. "We'd be foolish to expect them not to return."

Father Klein nodded. "I have been in Hell the longest of us, and I can agree with Mancini. I have never seen the devils as thin as they are now, but Hell definitely has a balance. That balance will be restored."

"I think we can all agree that we cannot feed the villagers from the Fore's storeroom," Ben Staunten chimed in.

"Of course," Michael said. "No villager would brave the wilds, looking for new sources of food, if he didn't think there was a Citizenship in it for him."

Chelsea, who had been playing with her long, red braid stood, letting it fall down one shoulder. "It's not just the meat. Our villagers are on the edge of starvation. Sure, there is enough to feed them now, but the produce of the wilds is not always constant."

She sat down quickly and resumed toying with her hair.

Aaron spoke next, "It's true. I mean, look at little Julian. He feeds over one hundred of our villagers with his devilwheat. What would happen without him?"

"He's a bright kid. He'll be fine," Copperfield, who made Harpsborough's torches, said loudly.

"He might stay alive or he might not." Mancini stood up from his bench and walked along his row towards the center of the Citizens. "Can we afford to lose him?"

Staunten shook his head.

"Then we should have him followed," Mancini suggested. "We should demand that he show us where he roams, and where he finds this devilwheat. If it is so important, then the Fore should control it."

"No!" shouted Michael. "I will not let it happen. We would break our trust with the villagers. They trust us to protect their right to their own findings. I will not have that compromised."

"And if he dies?" Copperfield asked.

"We know about where he ranges," Aaron said. "It's pretty close. Give my hunters a few days and we'd be able to find his stash."

"And if you can't?" Davel asked.

"Aaron's assurance is good enough for me," Michael said.

Chelsea stood again. "That's not the problem. The problem is that there are too many of us. Citizens never die. We keep the rule of one for every ten, but what happens if we start losing villagers to this famine? We Citizens grow our number when we can, but when we need to shrink, we can't. I know a thing or two about hunting from the old world. If you harvest an area too hard, you run out of game. Why can't you comprehend that this is happening here?"

"What are you suggesting?" Staunten snapped back. "That

we'll kill off all the devils in Hell?"

"Of course not. Just all the devils here. If we want them to return, we should stop hunting them for a while. Almost all the meat is being eaten in the Fore. The villagers don't eat hardly any. If we just eat as they do for a little while and let the wilds recover—"

"This is ludicrous!" Mancini shouted. "Hell is far too vast for us to deplete it. If we could, what kind of damnation would this be?"

"It does sound ridiculous," Michael told Chelsea, leaning back against the pulpit. "Aaron, is there any truth in your mind to what she says? It has been some time since I've been in the wilds."

"We're never going to run out of demons," Aaron answered. "But something does have to change. My men are ranging as far as they can within their restrictions. If you want us to pull in more meat, then you have to let us go out farther."

"Now who's the one drinking bloodwater?" Mancini joked with Staunten.

"It's true," Aaron said.

"I know your heart is in the right place," Michael said, "and I know you never saw the slaughter. I and my best hunters were out ranging when Pyle led the devils into Harpsborough. Father Klein and a few others were able to survive here, and most of the Citizens were holed up the Fore. You didn't see the corpses get into our food stores, or starve alongside us when the food rotted. If I had been there with my hunters, we would have been able to protect the villagers."

"That was the day he became First Citizen," Father Klein chimed in, "as most of you remember."

"And my first law was that no hunting group would be gone longer than a day. That way we would not be vulnerable for these night attacks."

"But we're still gone," Aaron said, his arms held wide in frustration. "It's not like they can't attack during the day."

"Well, of course they can," Mancini was walking down the aisle again, "but why leave ourselves more vulnerable than we have to? You say you want to expand the range? Let's do it. Maybe we should start ranging up along the Thames?"

"Galen and Rick are up that way," Aaron said. "And there are precious few dyitzu there, anyway."

"They never seem to be left wanting."

"Yeah, well Galen doesn't have to be back by bedtime."

"Enough," Michael cut in. "I will not have our men running all over the Thames. We have plenty of area to cover on the Kingsriver. Galen has proved himself an ally to Harpsborough and her Citizens. He saved my own life when we were afflicted with the Icanitzu. He has shown his worth again by guiding

Aaron to the place of the settling. Also, I know from my own experience that there's hardly anything to kill up there."

Copperfield shook his head. "We've taken in the ranges of almost all of our other hermits. Even Hidalgo has considered moving into the city. Why not them?"

"You want to add more mouths?" Aaron asked. "And my hunters are hungry. If we aren't allowed to travel for more than a day, then we need more rations."

A murmur of disagreement passed through the church.

"My men burn more calories than anyone else in the village," Aaron shouted, "or the Fore. To get any meat at all we have to run half the day out, and run half the day back, laden down by our kills—"

"Which have been precious few," Mancini cut in. "If Baker were still Lead Hunter, we wouldn't have this problem."

Aaron blanched. "Maybe not, but my men are fed only by lot. And with so few kills they eat less than ever. We need another system."

"I've heard they eat more than that," a Citizen shouted.

"What do you mean?" Aaron asked.

"Isn't it true that you let your men eat some of the kills?" Copperfield accused.

Aaron came to his feet. "No! I would never act against the Fore. I'm a Citizen, God damn it!"

Father Klein also leapt to his feet, and his voice overpowered all, even Michael Baker's.

"We are in God's house, and though He may never choose to visit it, should He wish to I would shudder for Him to have heard those words. You will *not* take His name in vain again in this house."

Aaron bowed his head. "Forgive me."

"Tell him what you found out, Staunten," Copperfield shouted across the hall to the Master of Stores.

"Your men are using more ammo than usual," Ben Staunten said. "So you expect us to believe that they are doing this while making fewer kills?"

"I do!" Aaron said. "I told you my men are starving. I did not say they were craven. We're soldiers, we obey orders. We are not eating the dyitzu we slay."

"I'm not disagreeing with you," Chelsea answered in a soft voice, "but how do you explain the extra ammo?"

Aaron reddened.

The answer to her question came from one of the Citizens who did not usually speak. He was called Patrick Foodsmith, and he had been made a Citizen as much for his wisdom as for the culinary skill which had given him his nickname.

"Aaron speaks the truth," Patrick said. "His soldiers have not been stealing kills. What they *have* been doing is reporting shots they have not made, and then bartering their Fore issued shells for devilwheat."

"And they should be punished!" Mancini said. "Maybe it's not eating meat illegally, but it's still robbing the Fore."

"They're starving!" Aaron said. "And they fight each day for you. If another attack comes, God prevent it, they will be the ones who defend the Fore. They deserve special rations."

No one spoke for a moment.

Michael cleared his throat. "I've heard enough, and I have made my decisions. Right now, with the weight being applied on the Fore, I can't authorize a vote which would assign extra rations to the hunters. . . yet. I don't want the punishment for those hunters who bartered their stolen shells to be severe, but make an example out of somebody. They can't be allowed to break our laws. Something does have to change. I am going to lead a grand hunt. I intend to take a few of the best hunters out with me. We'll go out a little farther than a day, as you suggested. I intend to return with a lot of meat and distribute that amongst the poor. I'll refill our stores, too. If it is as dead out there as you claim, Aaron, and there is little for me to hunt, then I will authorize your vote at the next meeting."

"First Citizen," Mancini said, returning to his seat. "I know that you and I have spoken of this before, but I must make my case again. We can't afford to lose your leadership at this time. Are you going on your own, or will you put this to a vote?"

Michael stood straight, ceasing to lean back upon the dais. "It will be voted upon."

"Then I fear I must vote against you." Mancini said.

"Why should we send you out?" The voice was Kylie's, Michael's mistress.

"Because we only have Aaron's word that the hunting is so bad," Staunten said. "And he leads a gang of criminals. There is far too much meat amongst the villagers, and I believe he and his men are robbing the Fore of their kills. We've earned Citizenship with our hard work, and his men are stealing it away."

"I don't feel quite so strongly, Aaron," Mancini said. "But at the least your soldiers are guilty of smuggling."

"This is not an issue of trust," Michael shouted. "This is an issue of skill. I know Aaron is trying as hard as he can. I trained him. I know him. You're foolish to doubt him. The reason why my hunt might succeed is because of skill. That is why you must vote me into the wilds. I will have no Citizen doubting Aaron. Staunten, tally the vote."

There were thirty abstentions, two against, and eighteen for, when all the votes were counted.

"Now this is one of those meetings," Michael said after the vote, "where things get a little uncomfortable at the Fore for a while. Remember the words your peers spoke were in haste, and made in the heat of the moment. Try not to take any of this home with you."

Chelsea caught Aaron's eyes and gave him a smile. He grimaced as a response.

"Take Ellen to your room, Arturus," Galen ordered as he returned home, "then come back out here."

Ellen's sobbing had stopped, but her face was still wet. Arturus had never seen anyone cry so much.

"Where am I going?" Ellen asked.

"It's a safe place," Arturus assured her. "Just don't touch anything. We're going to figure out. . ." *—what to do with you—* "how we can help you the most."

Arturus caught Rick's approving nod out of the corner of his eye. Rick always stressed how important word choice was. Arturus usually sided with Galen in thinking that a "silken tongue" was dishonest, but it seemed appropriate here.

He took Ellen by the arm and grimaced. She had wiped her phlegm on the sleeve he'd just grabbed.

"Come on," he said. "Come with me."

He led her back through the hallway towards his room. She scattered gravel everywhere, he noticed.

And guess who's going to have to sweep that up?

He pulled open the door blanket, holding it for her as she entered his room. She sat down on his bedding and began fiddling with his razor.

"Be careful with that," he told her.

She looked up at him. "Don't let them hurt me."

He shook his head. "Galen and Rick are very kind. You shouldn't have any fear."

"You don't understand, I'm not supposed to be here. I was good. I was a good person. How could He hate me?"

"Who hates you?"

"God."

"Did you ever meet Him?"

She issued another sob. "Of course I didn't meet Him."

"Then don't worry about it. You cannot judge what you do not know."

She lay back in his bedding, resting her head against the stone wall.

If only you were Alice.

"But He was supposed to meet me. To judge me. Only He's so glorious that if I saw Him, my soul would be destroyed. What did I do wrong?"

"They're very kind. You'll see. Don't worry. Galen and Rick, they'll make sure everything is alright."

"When you died? Did you see Him?"

"I was born here."

"Oh."

He was walking through his door blanket when she opened the razor.

"What happens if I die again?" she asked.

"It gets worse," he said, walking back into the room. "They say a man came back from there once, from the world beyond this one. They say it gets much, much worse."

He crouched beside her, reached over, and took the razor from her. He gently closed it.

Promise me you won't die.

"I don't believe you," she said.

I don't know if I believe me.

"Much worse," he repeated.

"How bad could it be?"

"If someone is wounded, mortally, and in excruciating pain, we feel the need to put them out of their misery. The men of Harpsborough will never do it. They say that whatever pain they feel is nothing compared to where your soul goes next. They'll watch them suffer, if they can, to be merciful."

She looked about the room, to the pistols and rifles that he kept there. Amongst them, Arturus realized, the razor was probably the least lethal.

Galen and Rick were seated around the table, so Arturus joined them.

"What's wrong with her?" Arturus asked. "I've never seen anyone cry so much."

Galen snorted.

"What's so funny?" Arturus asked him.

"You must not remember your early childhood. Where'd you find her, Rick?"

"Across the Thames, before the Kingsriver. She was still fighting through the initial stilling. It took her an hour or so before the weakness passed. Maybe another hour before she could walk."

"That's a pretty fast recovery," Galen said.

"She's got a strong heart."

It was Arturus' turn to snort.

"It's a rough transition," Rick said. "It's a bit of a shock, changing environments suddenly. Just be kind to her, and she'll pull it together eventually."

Arturus looked back towards the hallway which led to his room.

Rick leaned forward. "Well, Arturus, what do you think we should do with her?"

They're asking me?

Arturus pondered what would be best for the girl.

"Harpsborough. She needs Harpsborough."

"It'd have to be," Rick agreed. "It'd be easier for her to live as a hermit, these days, with barely any devils about, than it normally would. Even so, she still doesn't have the skills to survive. Keep her in Harpsborough for six months, then maybe she could learn the wilds."

"They might not take her," Galen said. "They're short of food in that town, burdened as they are by the Fore. I ran into one of their hunters today. Apparently it's so bad Michael Baker is thinking about leading an expedition."

Rick nodded and stood up from the table. "I see those hunters more and more," he said, pouring himself a cup of water out of the clay pitcher. "They're ranging a lot farther these days. I'm starting to worry that I might shoot one of them on accident."

Galen smiled and shook his head. "What do you think, Turi? How should we go about this?"

"They're hungry now, so there's no way Michael would push for her to join the villagers. If he's thinking about going out himself, they've got to be feeling the pinch."

"There's plenty of food. Just stop people in the Fore from eating like hogs," Rick said, sipping his water.

"If he fails," Arturus went on, "he definitely wouldn't want any more people. If he succeeds and gets some food, though, then maybe."

Galen raised his eyebrows and nodded his approval. "You okay with that Rick? Think we should wait for the right moment?"

Rick drained his cup. "Yeah, I'll go and find her a place pretty close, a little cubby chamber somewhere downstream. Turi, I might have you spend a few hours showing her how to navigate tonight. Maybe you can give her something to do so she doesn't go mad. You'll be going into town every day or so, right?"

Arturus nodded. "Almost, yes."

"Check around when you do. When you think the time is right, we'll bring her in and see if they'll take her."

"And if they won't?" he asked.

"Then she'd better learn to cry quietly," Galen said.

— 12 —

"Oh Jesus. Oh Jesus. *Oh Jesus.*"

The hunter Martin Warwick pulled on the binds that held his hand to the flat stone.

"Stop squirming," Aaron said. "You'll only make it worse."

The thirty-five hunters of Harpsborough gathered in a semi-circle around their comrade.

"Come on, sir," Avery said. "You know how hungry we've been. He was just doing what he needed to do to live."

Several amongst the circle nodded fiercely, but not everyone was on Martin's side. Aaron could only assume that the ones who remained stoic had some other source of food. Maybe they had a secret range that they gathered from when they were near home. Maybe they had a woman—or hell, even a man—they fucked for food.

"I don't give a damn how hungry you were," Aaron said, staring his men down. "I told you that I was going to fight for you in the Fore. Michael Baker himself is going to go rolling out into the wilds to see what hunting there is. Soon he'll know that there ain't shit out there. But did you guys back me up? Did you trust me? We have loyalty, as hunters. We watch each other's backs out there. Do you know what they accused me of today?"

His men shook their heads.

"They said we were stealing kills. They thought that because we were short on bullets we had been hiding the dyitzu away from them. Now is that having my back? Is that any way for a soldier to behave?"

Aaron motioned back towards Martin Warwick with his cleaver.

"Oh Jesus. Oh Jesus. Oh Jesus."

"Thank God Martin was retarded enough to smuggle his shells to a Citizen. That saved our asses in the Fore."

"Begging your pardon," said Avery, "but we could take the

Fore."

"You can beg for it, but you ain't getting it," Aaron said. "You want to murder now? When we're so close to getting better rations?"

"No, sir," Avery answered, crossing his arms. "I was just observing."

"Now I know almost all of you have been doing it, but it stops now. We can't have the Citizens thinking of us as criminals if we want to be fed."

"Oh fucking Jesus Christ. Oh fucking Jesus Christ."

"Martin, will you just shut up?" Avery said.

"Make him eat his hand!" a hunter shouted.

"Light the torch," Aaron ordered, "and be quick about cauterizing the wound."

"Don't take my hand, Aaron," Martin begged. "Please don't take my hand. Oh fucking Jesus don't take my hand. I won't be able to hunt. How am I going to eat?"

Aaron leaned down close to Martin, and whispered in his ear. "It'll grow back, you know. Hell heals all wounds."

He was close enough to Martin to smell the man's rancid breath.

"I don't have anybody, sir," Martin said. "Don't take my hand. Hunter's lot is all I get to eat."

"You know Julian has sinfruit too, right? Not just devilwheat?"

"Yeah."

"Well, I've made arrangements with him. He's been paid already. You'll be getting sinfruit and devilwheat for the next two months, okay? You'll just be able to relax and find yourself a woman."

"Oh fucking Jesus, thank you, Aaron. Thank you so much, Aaron. I knew you wouldn't let me down. I should have trusted you."

Aaron nodded.

"Oh fucking Jesus, don't make me eat it, please don't."

"Eat it?"

"My hand. You won't make me, will you?"

"No," Aaron said.

"Michael would have made me."

What the fuck were they doing before I got to Hell?

"I'm not Michael."

Martin Warwick nodded and closed his eyes.

He screeched when the cleaver took his hand.

Michael Baker placed a pair of blankets over the spheres to dim the room and eased down into his Persian pillows. Tossing back his head, he massaged the bridge of his nose with his thumb and forefinger. He closed his eyes and listened to the clinking of glasses.

"I hope like hell that you're pouring me some bloodwater," the First Citizen said.

"You bet," said Mancini.

Michael opened his eyes and accepted the offered glass. He took a sip and savored it before swallowing. "This is exactly what I needed."

Mancini sat down on the couch and drank from his own glass. "That went well."

"It went like shit. Did you hear them in there? Copperfield all but picked a fight with Aaron. Oh, how the villagers would laugh."

"He had every right to, though," Mancini said. "If Aaron had his way, every hunter would be a Citizen. They've got to fend for themselves, like all the other villagers. They're important for defense, sure, but Julian brings in more food. At times like this, when there isn't much we need to be defended from, well, they should have to tighten their belts."

"Maybe, but we still have to make sure they're happy. They are the ones with the guns."

Mancini shrugged his shoulders. "We're the ones with the ammo. People are creatures of habit. They're not going to attack the Fore. They're too used to taking orders from us."

"This isn't a God damned country, Davel," Michael said. "There aren't any endless walls of bureaucracy and process between the haves and the have-nots. There's no grey mass of government workers that can drag a man down and make him feel like he's been victimized by a faceless machine. They know us, Davel, and if we take advantage of them too badly, they'll know exactly where to find us. The only thing between us and a rioting pack of villagers is the walls of the Fore. And should those soldiers premeditate, and attack us while we're heading to the church on our way to a vote—well then, the only thing between us and that is Aaron."

Mancini leaned forward over their small table. "You're right, of course. This isn't a country. But we're not taking advantage of the people. We're protecting a system that works. We can't just throw it out every time we hit a bump in the road. We need tradition. We need there to be rewards. I only hope that the hunters that do feel like they've been taken advantage of haven't had their minds influenced by someone. I hope that Aaron hasn't been filling their heads with the nonsense that he's been trying to pass as law in the church. But you got what you wanted. You'll be leading a hunting expedition into the wilds."

"Indeed I will," Michael said. "I'm sorry, friend, I know you don't approve."

"Have you given any thought to who you're taking with

you?"

"Well, I was going to bring Martin," Michael said, "before Aaron chopped his God damned hand off."

"Do you think Aaron did that deliberately to weaken your expedition?"

"I think he did it because Martin was the only one he knew was guilty."

Mancini pursed his lips. "Who else could you take with you?"

"Avery, definitely. Maybe Fitch and Duncan."

"But Fitch and Duncan, they're two of the newest."

"Exactly." Michael looked hard at the bloodwater through its crystal glass. "Avery remembers serving under me, so he'll fall right in line. The other two are too new to disagree or point out any mistakes I make."

"There's so much to risk. What if you fail to catch anything? What if you get hurt? What if you're killed? Generals don't lead from the front anymore, Michael. That went out with the Roman Empire."

"I know. I know you're worried about me, my friend. I tell myself that it's because catching something will mean that there's no reason to go against the Fore. Even the hunters will be embarrassed to ask for more rations. They'll feel like they're doing a bad job."

"That's only if you succeed. If you fail—"

"If I fail, I'll have to give in to some of their demands."

Mancini stood up. "You can't be serious."

"Sit down. Sit down. Change isn't so bad. We'll make the right concessions, I assure you."

Mancini regained his seat, and shortly thereafter, his composure.

"I think that maybe there's another reason I want to go out there." Michael said. "Not to show Aaron that I'm still the better man. Not to quiet the resentment against the Fore. I just want to do it again, you know? See if I still have it. I miss the danger. I miss rush of shooting down a dyitzu that's charging at me, slinging fire and howling."

"Now I know you're insane," Mancini said.

Michael laughed. "Was there ever any real doubt?"

"I'd been hanging on to the last shreds."

Michael drained the last of his bloodwater.

"You want another glass?" Mancini asked.

"No. I've got a big day tomorrow."

"I'll save some for when you get back. Victoriously, of course."

"Victoriously."

— 13 —

Ellen followed the vein of blue hellstone as best she could. Turi had taught her last night that the colors of stones flowed like a river. It was darker here in the center of the vein, and if she traveled to either her left or right she knew the color would shift until she came to the strange neon blue rooms where the light streamed up from the floor.

I'll get lost if I go much farther.

The first chamber she remembered, the one where Rick had found her, had to be around here somewhere. She remembered the room having dark blue stones, darker than even the stone where she was now. It had seemed to her at the time that there were golden flecks in the stone as well. Surely Turi would be happy if she could lead him to the stone of that room. He might even pick it for that stupid chess set he was making.

She navigated through a few more chambers before she heard the sounds of a river.

Damn.

She had heard Rick mention other rivers—the Kingsriver, and Lethe. This one must be one of those. Turi had showed her how rivers had their own architecture and how their flow interrupted the patterns of Hell around them. She might not be able to find blue stone on the far side.

Besides, I don't think Rick and I crossed another river. We just came to the Thames and he sent me up it.

She entered the river room cautiously. Red bricks soared up along the walls, forming high arches. She knelt by the river and put her hand in the water.

Is it the Thames? I must have gotten turned around.

It took her a few moments, but she thought she recognized the room. It was between her home and Turi's.

If I travel downstream from here, I'll get home.

"Are you alone?" a voice asked.

Ellen stood up from the bank and faced the stranger. The man was kneeling in the back corner of the room. His short hair was half covered by a blue bandana. His face was swollen, blotched and strangely discolored in places. One of his eyes was milky white, covered over as if with a cataract. The stranger's jeans were ripped off at the knee and slit up the sides, perhaps to allow for greater mobility. He was armed with a shotgun which he had holstered at his right hip. The man's button up shirt hung open, revealing the bone-handled stock of a pistol.

"You're very young to be alone," the man remarked. "Perhaps you would like some protection?"

He began scratching at his jeans, which brought his hand suspiciously close to the shotgun he had at his side. Arturus had also threatened her with a weapon, but there was something about this stranger she did not trust.

Lie to him.

"I'm fine," Ellen answered. "But I am not alone. Take care, please. I don't want my friends to shoot you when they come through."

"Friends your age?" the man asked.

"No."

"What's your name, girl?"

"Ellen, and you?"

"Pyle."

He was leaning forward, aggressively. She felt like he could cross the twenty or so feet between them easily.

"I don't like the way you're looking at me." Ellen heard the quiver in her own voice.

Did he know I was lying about having friends?

The man scratched at his jeans even harder. Ellen didn't pay attention to his hand, but kept her eyes on the man's shotgun.

"I'm sorry," Pyle shook his head as he spoke, "it's just that you remind me so much of my sister. Seeing you makes me miss her very much."

Ellen felt a sudden tug on her feelings. Had she misjudged him? She had thought Rick was going to hurt her, too, after all.

"You had a sister?" she asked.

"A little sister. She's still alive, in the old world, I mean. She was the last person I saw up there, before I died. I think of her sometimes."

"Then I'm sure she thinks of you, too."

A smile appeared on his face, lasting for only a moment. "I'm sure she does. I was wondering if you could help me, girl."

Ellen chewed at her lip. Turi would have helped the man, she knew that, but she didn't want to.

"What is it?"

Maybe I'll have a good reason to leave him alone.

"I can't swim," Pyle told her. "I was hoping that you would get me across the river."

Ellen thought about the man clutching at her from behind while they were in the water.

"I'm very sorry, I want to help, but I can't. . ."

Ellen quit speaking. She felt like a terrible person for hating this man, for lying to him.

"It wouldn't take much." Pyle stepped closer as he spoke. "You could swim across to the far side. I would jump in a bit upstream, and you could just help me out of the water."

"Pyle, I'm sorry. I can't."

"Maybe your friends can help me when they get here?"

"Huh?"

Pyle's scratching was getting faster and faster. "You told me you had friends coming. You're alone, aren't you?"

"No."

A smile crept across his face. "You're too pretty to be a liar."

This time, when he stepped forward, she took a step back.

Ellen clutched at the gun Rick had given her. "Stay away from me."

He continued to move forward. Ellen drew her gun, keeping it pointed at the floor. She didn't dare provoke him. The gun in her hand shook furiously.

"Don't come closer."

Oh God. Where's the safety on this thing?

Pyle finally stopped moving forward. He raised both hands into the air, but not to surrender. He worked loose the blue cloth from around his head and began to re-tie it. A lock of long white hair escaped from where it was hidden by the bandana.

He might have a gun hidden there.

Now that Pyle was closer she could see the swelling on his face. It looked as if he had been badly burned. The skin had just begun to grow back in places.

"Tell me, the boy, the young one you were talking to yesterday. Was he born here?"

Ellen felt her hand grow steady. She knew this was the dangerous question, though she didn't know why. She certainly couldn't understand how the answer could even matter, but it was clear that to Pyle, for all his apparent nonchalance, this was important.

He's not here for me.

"No," she lied. "He was born in San Francisco. He died there when he was very young."

Pyle nodded, grimacing. "Run along, girl."

Ellen walked backwards to the room's entrance, never taking her eyes of the man. She found the stone wall behind her with her hand, and left the chamber. As soon as she put a couple of turns between herself and Pyle, she broke into a sprint.

Oh, Turi.

— 14 —

Arturus looked over the assorted stone squares he'd laid out on the table.

Michael better pick the right ones.

"They look fine," Rick assured him.

Galen frowned as he oiled his disassembled pistol. "I thought you were going to include blue hellstone as an option?"

"I was," Arturus said, nodding. "Ellen said she was going to find some that had golden flecks in them," he said. "We were going to go get a sample this morning, but she never came in. I didn't really like blue for a color anyway."

Galen ran his brush up through the trigger mechanism, shaking his head.

"I'm sure she's having trouble because she's new," Rick said.

"Turi?" that was Ellen's voice, coming in from outside.

"There she is now." Rick turned towards the room's exit.

"Turi," Galen joked, "you're outside."

"You're supposed to call your own name, dear," Rick called back to her.

Arturus listened to her footsteps as she came across the gravel. She entered into the battery room, stones skipping before her across the floor.

"You look tired." Rick told her.

"I didn't sleep hardly at all. I ran into a man last night, and I kept thinking he was following me."

"One of the Harpsborough guards?"

"No." Ellen sat down, a little out of breath. "Another hermit. He said his name was Pyle."

"Wow, that's a loaded name," Rick said, standing up and walking away from the table. "You want some water, Ellen?"

Ellen nodded.

"You think it could be Pyle the Betrayer?" Arturus asked.

"Doubt it." Rick pulled down a clay cup from the storage

closet. "He was exiled from the city years ago, before you'd ever even been to Harpsborough. Long before, Ellen, you were even here. That man is surely dead. What did he look like?"

"At first I thought he had short hair," she said, "but most of it was white and stringy."

"Can't be him, then." Rick filled the glass. "Pyle had dark hair. Don't worry, must be someone else with the same name."

Ellen nodded thoughtfully and accepted the cup. She drank from it noisily. "He asked me about you, Turi. He asked me if you were born here."

Galen's pistol thudded as he pushed it down on the table, still half disassembled. Arturus was surprised by his sudden movement.

Rick had gone quiet as well.

Ellen's hand shook as she placed her cup down.

"How did you answer?" Galen did not attempt in any way to hide the seriousness of his question.

Ellen swallowed. "I lied."

"What did you say?" Galen's stare was unblinking. "Tell me as accurately as you can."

"He seemed to think the question was really important, and I didn't like him, so I lied. I told him Turi was born in San Francisco."

Rick took two steps forward, but stopped when Galen raised his hand.

Arturus looked back and forth between his parents.

What's going on?

"Your instincts served you well," Galen said. "It is not often right to lie, so don't make a habit of it. Ellen, wait outside. Turi will be with you in a second."

"Sure." Her high pitched voice squeaked.

Arturus could hear her footsteps as she walked down the hallway. Rick sat back down at the table and looked towards Galen. The pistol lay forgotten on the table. The last of Ellen's footsteps faded away.

"Turi," Galen said.

"Yes, sir?"

"How long has it been since you saw Pyle?"

"About five years. I saw him once by the Hungerleaf Grove, maybe a year or so before he betrayed everyone. Maybe a year and a half before you took me to Harpsborough for the first time."

Galen ran one finger along the side of his closely trimmed beard. "You'd recognize him?"

"Yes, sir. I think I would, sir."

"Good. If you see him, kill him."

There was a table in the Fore's waiting room made out of

old world mahogany. Under the old First Citizen's rule it had become marred by scratches and watermarks. After Michael Baker had assumed the position, he'd ordered Copperfield to sand the thing down in order to remove the imperfections. Then he commissioned the hermit Galen to cover it with glass to help preserve it.

Arrayed before Michael on the table now were his body armor, rifle and pistol belt. Avery was watching him as he readied his equipment.

"How long since you've cleaned those weapons?" Avery asked.

"About two hours. But before that, maybe a year."

Michael picked up his bulletproof vest and began to strap it on. "Did you know that Kevlar shrinks when you don't wear it?"

Avery snorted.

Just outside of the door tapestry, Michael knew, the village was gathered about the Fore. They were waiting for him to lead the expedition.

"You sure this is a good idea, sir?" Avery asked. "I've been out there, and we aren't likely to even see devilsign, let alone get a shot at something."

"At the very least it will help me convince the Fore that there needs to be change. They've convinced themselves that Aaron's no good. If I fail, then we'll have proved that I'm not any better."

"Maybe he is no good," Avery said. "Maybe there's hordes of those devils hiding out there in the wilds. Not that it'll do us much good. Can't imagine running one down with your fat ass in tow."

He's testing me. He wants to know if he's going out with Michael the Hunter, or Michael the First Citizen.

Michael smiled to let Avery know the comment wasn't out of line. He buckled his pistol belt around his waist and picked up his rifle. It was a push fed Winchester Model 70, fitted for firing a high caliber round. He ran his hand along to the top of its barrel.

"Jesus, that's going to have a hell of a kick," Avery pointed out. "What's that fire, .416?"

".458."

"You expecting to find a Minotaur out there?"

"Just want to be prepared. Hell, for all I know the dyitzu have been getting as fat as I have."

"If only."

Michael walked past Avery and stopped for a moment before the door tapestry.

"They're all out there, waiting for you," Avery said.

"They always are."

Michael recognized the faces of several of the Citizens as he pushed his way through the crowd. Chelsea was there, along with Copperfield, Kylie and Mancini. Many of the others were looking down on him from the Fore's third story balconies and fourth floor. The hunters seemed strangely distant until Aaron came over and shook his hand.

"Good hunting," the Lead Hunter said.

Michael nodded. Only then did the rest of the hunters smile and wish him luck.

He spotted Fitch and Duncan on the far side of the mass. He recognized the faces of many of the common people as well. There was young Julian, his black face easy to spot against the Caucasian ones, his eyes wide with hero worship. He also saw Molly, that bitch, and Alice.

He could smell Massan as he neared the trader. The man smelled like sweat and rose petals. Undoubtedly he'd found some stash of old world perfume or cologne.

"We're hungry, Mike," Massan said.

"I know," he replied, "and I'm going to get you some food, one way or another."

Massan nodded solemnly.

"It means a lot to us," he heard Molly's voice, "that you're willing to risk your own skin for us."

I bet you're damn happy my skin is in danger.

"Get us some food, Mike!" someone shouted.

He nodded. He could feel the adulation from the crowd, the hope that he inspired. He could tell that they needed him. This was how it used to be, before he became the First Citizen. It was about time that these people remembered who he was.

You might die, though.

He spotted a man sitting against the Fore, disinterested. He thought to mark the man and remember him as a dissident, but then he recognized him. It was Benson, the fellow who had the stilling.

I should pass a law where we kick people like that out of the city.

"I wish I could go with you, Mike," he heard a voice behind him say.

He turned around to see Martin. He almost went to shake the man's hand before he remembered that it had been removed.

He reached out and clasped the hunter's shoulder instead. "Believe me, I was sore when I heard about your punishment. Not that it's not deserved, but you would have been one of my first choices."

"Thank you, sir."

Michael Baker pressed on and made it to the far side of the

villagers. He shook Fitch and Duncan's hands, making strong eye contact with the two of them. Fitch looked him straight in the eye, but Duncan looked down quickly.

"Like old times," Avery said as he emerged from the crowd.

If only this moment could last forever.

"I hope you brought some big packs, gentleman," Michael said. "It's been a while since I've been hunting, and I'm going to want to make up for it."

He could see the doubt on their faces, but it was quieted by Avery.

"You're about to see a legend in action, boys," Avery said. "You could stand to pick up a thing or two."

Michael looked back towards the crowd, and saw the hermit boy, Turi, coming through. He had a girl next to him whom Michael didn't recognize.

"Don't bother him, Turi," someone was saying.

Here it is, my reason to linger.

"Let him through," Michael said. "I have business with him."

For some reason Turi looked out into the crowd at those words, as if searching for someone. "I've brought some samples so you could pick which squares you like."

"Let me see them." Michael set his Winchester down against his side and held out his hands.

Turi fumbled with his pack, bringing out a few squares. "We could use woodstone and granite. Or hellstone. I'm going to make the pieces match whichever type of stone you want, though we'll make those out of glass."

Michael took the stones into his hands. "You made these, boy?"

"Yes, sir."

"Galen didn't?"

"No, sir, but he showed me how. This is my favorite here, the black marble. I thought if we mixed that with the white marble and glass that it would look the best."

Michael frowned. The black marble one looked a little crooked. Everyone was looking at him. He glanced about to measure their mood. Even the hunters seemed begrudgingly hopeful.

My legend still has some teeth.

"These are just the sample pieces," Turi was saying.

"I agree with you, Turi. I think the marble black and white would be the best. But the quality has to be high with what we're paying you."

"It will be, I promise."

Such an honest boy.

His own hunters were getting agitated.

"Don't worry folks," Michael said loudly to the crowd,

"we're going to take a long range, and since we might not be home by nightfall, we've decided to leave Aaron behind to protect you. These are hard times. I've got to go out into the wilds to see some things for myself. If we have to change the way hunting is done, we'll do it. If we have to change the way food distribution is done, we'll do it. I won't let you starve."

They were nodding solemnly, but there was no applause. Michael felt somewhat upset about that.

I should have ordered Mancini to start clapping as I left.

"Good hunting," Turi said.

Michael saw that he, like Julian, also had the look of hero worship in his eyes.

The First Citizen led his men past the entryway guards into the wilds.

"You'd think they'd never seen you go hunting before," Avery said.

"They're starving," Duncan replied. "They think we're going to bring something back."

"We are," Avery said.

"Maybe, but even if we kill a dyitzu, one devil won't solve anything. You'll just make it look like Aaron's an idiot. But he's not. There's nothing out here, Avery. If we succeed we'll just make things worse."

"Duncan," Michael said.

"Yes, Citizen?"

"Yes, sir," Michael corrected.

"Yes, sir?"

"Shut the hell up."

"Yes, sir."

"Who was that blonde girl?" Ellen asked as they were traveling down the rustrock road through a room full of waist high square blocks.

"Which one?"

"The one you were staring at, in the blue."

"Alice," Arturus said, "and I wasn't staring. She's just one of my friends. I wanted to say hello to her."

"Do you like her?"

"That's a silly question."

Arturus looked around the room for hiding dyitzu. Everything seemed safe—except for what Ellen was saying. The last thing he wanted was Ellen going into Harpsborough and telling everybody that he wanted Alice.

"I think you like her," she said.

Arturus shrugged. And of course, since he was the only person Ellen knew, she was bound to gossip about him to anyone she met. And if Alice were to hear...

But what if she likes me back?

"What was so important about that man leaving?" Ellen asked.

"He's their leader. It's been very hard for everyone to eat, so he's going to go out and try to get them some food."

"Oh."

"That's actually why we didn't ask him to take you in. If he gets food, or finds a way to make sure everyone isn't hungry, then we can see if you can join the village."

"But I don't want to join the village, Turi. I want to be a hermit like you."

"You said you liked the village."

"I do, but I can still visit as a hermit. Like you do."

"It's hard to live alone. If you don't stay in Harpsborough, you'll die."

"I don't mind," Ellen said.

Arturus stopped and looked at her. He wanted to shake some sense into her, to tell her that she must care, to tell her that if she didn't start caring she would be subjected to all manner of tortures. Then she would care, but it would be too late.

But the funny thing was he didn't have the slightest idea of what to say.

"I didn't mean it," she told him.

Yes you did.

"Okay," Arturus said. "Okay."

They walked a little farther into the wilds together while Arturus mulled over what she'd said. Soon enough he led them off of the rustrock road.

"Promise me you won't die," he said impulsively, not even thinking about the words.

"What?" she asked.

"Promise me you won't die," he repeated, this time more firmly. "Now."

"Okay."

"Say it."

"I promise."

"Say it all the way."

"Okay, Turi. I'll say it. I promise, I won't die."

He nodded satisfied.

"It's a stupid promise anyway," she said after a moment.

"Doesn't matter. You still made it."

— 15 —

People took their time going to bed that evening. Massan and Kara were speaking outside their hovel. Kara's eyes never strayed from Massan, though she moved about frequently. Her laughter often drowned out all of the other noises in the village. A few even hushed her. Father Klein could also be heard all across Harpsborough, his voice booming out from where he preached upon the church steps. A huddle of less faithful villagers gathered in one corner, betting what little food and ammo they had on the roll of some devilbone dice. Martin had played the game at times. They called it "Icatian Craps." Martin had called it "no craps" because he tended to lose all his food when he played it.

Late nights like this one would have normally annoyed him, as he was the man who, along with Avery, most often took the guard position during the night. It was hard to protect people, in his opinion, who were making enough noise to drown out the possible approach of a devil. His missing hand, however, had absolved him of this duty.

Martin wandered over to the kiln. Kylie was there, tending the woodstone torches which served as its fuel.

"Kylie, princess, I got to get me a pot."

"Martin, you always eat everything you're given. I thought for sure you kept a pot in your stomach."

She reached out and rubbed his belly.

As far as Martin Warwick was concerned, Kylie was the only worthwhile Citizen in the entire Fore, except for Aaron, of course.

"Well, babe, I've decided to start saving some food."

She nodded and glanced over towards the gamblers.

"Bad luck has also been my pot," he admitted, "but I've decided to stop gambling."

"Tired of 'no craps?'" she asked.

He laughed.

Lewd things were somehow more amusing when Kylie said them. Martin figured that Michael was a lucky man. Kylie wasn't the prettiest girl in the village, not by a long shot, but her hair was luxurious, her eyes were sparkly, her smile was wide—and she had a huge mouth.

As far as Martin Warwick was concerned, the mouth sealed the deal. "Losing my hand, it's kind of got me thinking, you know? I need to have some things stored up next time. That way, when things go bad, I can still eat right. I mean, what if I had a woman too? I wouldn't be able to feed her on what hunters get these days."

Kylie nodded. "Let me see that hand."

He held out his stump.

She ran her fingers across the growing hand, sending shivers of fiery pain to his brain and a similarly warm but more pleasant sensation to his heart and loins.

"Growing back fine," she said. "What do you think, a month or so?"

Martin beamed. "Maybe, if I'm quick about it. Could be two."

"Now about that pot. You know I'm not an old world kind of girl." Her tone was stern. "I don't do layaway."

"I've got devilwheat," he said defensively. "I'm not trying to be your charity case."

Kylie smiled. "Well, I might have made an exception for you, anyway."

Martin pulled out a bundle of devilwheat from his hoodie's front pocket.

"You want me to make you one fresh?" She asked. "I was thinking about firing another batch before I went to bed."

Martin looked at the few pots she had on display. One was short and squat. She'd covered it before its firing with mixtures of colored dust to paint a picture on the clay. Bands of darkening sandstone gave the impression of a beach. Dark blue hellstone made up the ocean. There were white marble dust seagulls and a single sail cresting the horizon. The sun was made from a red so light that it almost looked pink, and more of that dust adorned the crests of the waves where the sun's light hit the ocean.

The scene hit him hard for some reason. He spent most of his time ignoring his memories of the old world. Of the nine to five job he'd worked to pay for the Ford Taurus he'd driven. Of the Winsten Mill apartments he'd lived in with an old couch and some lawn furniture. Of the girl that lived in 111B who had asked him to come in and kill a spider for her. Of Caleb, the Lab/Boxer mix, who always shit on the carpet when he thought Martin had been gone too long.

"Can I have that one?" he asked.

"Martin!" she said. "I painted that one. You know that's worth a lot more than a bundle of devilwheat. I paid more to Kara for just gathering the marble dust."

"I know. I know. It just looks so beautiful. I guess I'll take the one next to it."

She started to pick it up, but changed her mind. "Just take it."

She shoved the squat painted pot at him.

"No, Kylie, I don't want to cheat you."

"Just remember you owe me one, alright. I'm just being sympathetic, you know. I wouldn't do this if you weren't injured."

"Are you sure?"

"Martin, I'm sure. Maybe it'll help you save up some food."

Martin nodded. "You're the best."

She hugged him, and then kissed him on the cheek.

"Alright," she said, "now run along, I've got to get this last batch out."

Grinning ear to ear, he held the squat clay urn to his chest as he wandered back across Harpsborough.

The late night was finally beginning to end. Kara was still laughing, but she was doing it from inside her hovel. Father Klein had retreated inside his church to speak with the last of the faithful. Only a few people were still moving about. A couple of men and women were walking in through the village entrance, having made their waste or gotten one last drink of water before they took to their beds.

Martin stopped beside the Fore, his cheek still burning from where Kylie had kissed it.

He wasn't ready for the day to end, he decided, but there wasn't really anyone for him to talk to.

He saw Benson. The stilling had taken most of the meat off of the man. His face was as gaunt as a holocaust victim's, his eyes as red as a hound's.

"Hey there, ole Bense," Martin Warwick said as he sat down next to the still man. "What did you see today?"

Benson said nothing, his face as pallid as a living man's face could be.

"Really?" Martin went on. "I got this pot."

The hunter held it up in front of his own eyes and looked at the beach. Some of the marble dust seagulls were smaller than others. He tried to perceive the depth which this represented in the painted urn.

"Did you ever get to go to the beach?" he asked Benson. "I never did, you know. I saw it on the Discovery Channel, and in a bunch of movies, but I never made it. Bet you it's for the best, though. If I saw the ocean, I'd probably turn straight into a pirate."

Benson said nothing.

"Arr, motherfucker," Martin told him, and laughed to himself.

He set his pot down between his legs and looked up to Harpsborough's ceiling. "I'm doing good these days, Benson. You're probably pretty proud of me. I got some steady food, you know. Better than hunting for the moment. I've got this pot. I'm going to save some of my food this time. I'll be ready for when I'm a hunter again."

He sighed before continuing. "Then I've got to worry about the woman situation. You know? Aaron told me I better find me one. And I'm not the kind of man who disobeys an order, am I fella'?"

Martin laughed at his own joke and uncapped his hunter's canteen. "Sure wish it could be Kylie. Woman's a Citizen, and a nice one to boot. Michael would probably have me killed, though. I'd be lucky if he sent me through the Golden Door."

Martin took a swig and recapped his canteen. "You know, I should get my hand cut off more often!"

He looked back towards his pot. To the ocean depicted upon it. He slowly spun it and watched the beach landscape change. The clay urn issued a grinding sound as its bottom scraped against the stone. "I know you took her death hard, Bense. No harm in that. We all did, you know? All us hunters. To see that girl lose her guts like that..."

Martin studied Benson's face. Not even a twitch. The man was very grey.

"I thought it was nice of you, what you tried to do. I wouldn't have done it. You did all you could."

It seemed like Benson was greyer closer to his mouth.

"Oh shit, man. You alive?"

Martin reached out to check for breathing.

He was relieved to feel just the faintest touch of air on his hand, but there was something else on the man's face. Some grey dust. "Motherfucker!" He lumbered to his feet.

The curse startled a young man out of his hovel. Martin had forgotten his name.

Martin drew his sidearm and reluctantly leveled it at Benson. "Go get Aaron and Father Klein," he shouted to the boy.

The young man stood still, confused.

Martin waved him on with his stump. "Some bastard's poured corpsedust all over ole Bense."

That sent him running

Martin bent down to inspect Benson as the boy ran off to the other side of the Fore.

"Fuckers," Martin told the still man. "And of course, they'd wait for Michael to leave before they did this to you."

"Not bad." Galen inspected the mold Arturus had made for the pawns. "Not bad at all."

Behind them, the forge burned steadily.

Arturus had never seen a chess set before, so Galen had made the appropriate drawings for him. The pawn had been the simplest, so Arturus had made one of those first. He had become a good whittler of woodstone, and the pictures were clear, so he felt confident he had made the piece and its mold correctly.

"I don't understand why there has to be so many of these," Arturus remarked.

Galen shrugged his shoulders.

"For every King there are eight pawns. For every Queen there are eight replacements. Just the way of the world."

Galen had made other demands of the pieces as well. For one, he insisted that the diameter of the base of the King was to be exactly half of its height.

"Why?" Arturus had asked. "Does Michael know that it's supposed to be this way?"

"No, but the ignorance of your fellows is no excuse for shoddy work."

Galen had agreed to work the bellows since Arturus had used the battery up on grinding sandstone. He had also made the sandstone mixture to Galen's exact specifications. For the black pawns, Arturus used nine parts ground sandstone, one part ground whetstone, and two parts ground pewter. For the white pawns he was going to use eleven parts sandstone and one part whetstone. He poured his black mixture into an obsidian cup. They used obsidian because it was the hellstone which was most resistant to heat. Galen held up the forge's grate, and Arturus used a pair of tongs to place the obsidian cup into the fire.

The heat was so intense that it was difficult for Arturus to stare into the fire for long, but he looked for as long as he could stand it, watching the sand melt together.

Donning a protective glove, he then used his tongs to grip a stirring rod. To make the piece perfect, he knew, the mixture had to be as even as possible.

Galen grunted his approval as Arturus began to stir.

"Why are we going to use whetstone dust in the white pawn's mixture? Won't it darken the glass?" Arturus' voice sounded weak, drowned out behind the forge's flames.

"You might have been right in the old world." Galen shook his head. "But for us it will just make the glass stronger. We don't want those men in the Fore knocking over the set and breaking the pieces."

"Why would they do that?" Arturus asked as he continued to stir.

"Chess can make people quite angry at times, boy. Make sure you are a gracious winner, should you play them."

Arturus laughed. Galen always assumed he would win at things.

He looked again at the mixture. It looked like dirty water. He stirred it just a little more.

"Do you have the syringes prepared?" Galen asked.

"I think they're ready."

The warrior nodded and opened the forge grate. Arturus reached in with the tongs and pulled out the cup of obsidian.

"Be careful with that, boy," Galen said. "That molten glass is hot enough to kill. Don't move fast, lest you stumble."

Arturus carried the cup away from the forge's fires. Galen gripped a funnel in his own tongs and held it above the closed mold. Arturus carefully poured the glass into the funnel. He stopped on instinct.

Galen looked down through the funnel, and then nodded. "Quickly, follow me to the river."

They hurried across the gravel hallways and entered the river room. The cool moist air was a relief to his face, which was hot and dry from being near the forge.

"You've got to get it just right," Galen said as Arturus dipped the mold into the river. "The outside of the piece has to be cooled enough to hold its shape, but the inside must still be liquid."

Arturus counted out a long sixty seconds as the river flowed by, and then took the steaming mold out and placed it on the bank.

"Quickly and carefully," Galen said.

Arturus used his knife to undo the buckles that held his mold together. To Arturus' relief, the pawn held together and did not melt as he removed the mold's top half.

"Pass me the syringes," Galen said.

Arturus pulled them out from his pack and handed them to the warrior.

"I'll only show you this once boy. The rest you must do on your own."

Arturus watched like a hawk as Galen punctured the pawn's thin crust of hardened glass with the first needle. He then inserted the same needle in a second spot and drew an imperceptible amount of molten glass into the syringe. He quickly emptied it into the river. Using the hole made by his first puncture, he put in the second needle. Galen injected just the smallest amount of the substance as he slowly withdrew the needle. He swirled the needle about as he did so, leaving a trail of red coloring inside the pawn. Arturus watched the substance as it touched the glass. The red hellstone seemed to flow within the pawn for just a second before stopping, leaving a trail of blood, frozen and hanging, within the pawn.

"Close the mold carefully."

Arturus did so, and placed it back into the river. "That's beautiful."

"Leave it in for another fifteen minutes," Galen said. "More won't hurt, but less might. Show it to me when you're done."

Arturus nodded numbly, staring into the river.

"And don't lose focus, boy," Galen said. "You're still in the wilds. Make sure you watch the exits."

Arturus nodded and shook his head clear.

He lost count a few times, but when he was sure fifteen minutes had passed, he took out the mold and looked at the piece.

The glass was dark, barely transparent in places, but in others he could see the red swirling of the hellstone. It was hypnotic.

Because it was made from a mold, there was excess glass at the base of the pawn that he would have to smooth off, but he was in no hurry to do that.

The red matches the red in the black marble.

He wandered back into his home to show Galen the pawn.

Galen grunted and nodded.

"Can we do the same thing with the white pieces?" Arturus asked. "Except maybe we'd swirl in some powdered white marble?"

Galen furrowed his brow.

"I had thought to make them clear, and perhaps glaze the outside. But this is your creation, boy, and if you decide to do so, I would support your decision."

"It will take more work," Arturus said.

Galen nodded.

Arturus thought about it. "I'll do it."

Galen grunted his approval.

Nearly the entire village had awakened and come to gawk by the time Aaron exited the Fore. Martin was waving the crowd back so that they wouldn't get too close to Benson. Aaron joined up with Father Klein and they made their way together through the villagers. They walked up to Martin, and the three squatted by the still man.

"Lookie here," Martin said. "Bastard's got it on his face a little, but check behind his teeth."

Benson issued no complaint when Aaron opened his jaw. Aaron tried not to get any of the saliva on him. He was amazed the fellow had any saliva left.

"See that?" Martin asked. "All down his throat."

Martin was right, the man had corpsedust coating the inside of his mouth.

"Jesus," Aaron said, giving a whistle. "Who would want to do that?"

Father Klein stood abruptly and shook his head.

Aaron looked about. Many of the Citizens had gone to the balconies and the fourth floor of the Fore. A few were coming out of the front entrance to see what was going on.

"Does anyone remember how long he's been still?" Aaron asked the crowd.

"About a month, maybe two," one villager answered.

Martin rubbed the skin at the base of his stump. "I agree, it's about that."

Aaron wiped his hands on his camouflaged pants.

"As soon as he dies, he'll rise," a voice warned from the crowd.

"He can't last much longer," another said.

"Father Klein, you've been here the longest," Aaron spoke out before the crowd could get too carried away. "How long can a stilling last before it takes a man?"

"It's not like the old world," the Father said. "There a man can sit still for three days and stand a decent chance of dying. Here it's different. I've seen the stilling last nearly a year."

"And how long does the corpsedust last?"

"Two months." That was Mancini's voice, Aaron realized. "After that it's not good for making bloodwater."

Aaron turned to face the Brewer. Mancini's beady black eyes were taking in the scene. Aaron wasn't used to seeing the man outside. He tended to either be in the still, the church, or the Fore.

"Well, what are we going to do about it?" a villager asked.

"We should kill him!" said another. "Otherwise he'll come and take one of us."

No one contradicted him. Many were even murmuring in agreement. A few women in the corner of Aaron's vision were nodding their heads in unison, no doubt imagining Benson as a corpse.

But Benson was so small, so frail. Aaron couldn't see how the man could do any harm, even if he were raised. He had to remind himself that these people didn't brave the wilds as deeply as he did. They weren't as used to the dangers.

I bet the Citizens are even more frightened.

"We're not killing him," Aaron said. "Michael Baker makes the decisions of life and death. The most we can do is keep watch over him. I'll post a hunter."

"I've got some handcuffs." That was Massan.

For some reason Kara hit him for making the suggestion. A few around them chuckled and the Middle-Eastern man looked away, abashed.

Oh Christ, come on people.

"Thank you," Aaron said.

"And we can wash him out in the river." That was Molly.

"Not a bad idea," Aaron admitted. "Davel, anything else we can do? Anything to make the corpsedust less potent?"

Davel's frown left wrinkles on his forehead. "We can feed him some sinfruit juice. Corpsedust tends to get caught up in that. We could flush him with it for a couple of days, but I don't know who's going to pay for it."

The villagers began to mutter.

"Well, you would," Aaron said.

Mancini shook his head. "I disagree. He should die. If he should kill another, they also would rise. Harpsborough is in great danger."

Coward.

But Aaron knew how to deal with cowards. "Mike decides matters of life or death."

"We could put him past the Golden Door," a villager suggested.

Neither Aaron nor Mancini responded to the man. As the two stared at each other, Father Klein stepped back into the crowd.

"If Mike wants to throw him through the Golden door, that's his decision," Aaron said. "Until then, we'll do no such thing."

"And if Benson should rise?" Mancini asked.

The crowd was starting to lean in the Brewer's direction. They didn't want to, Aaron could tell, but the man was speaking to their fears.

"Fine," Aaron said. "You want him dead, you kill him."

Aaron drew his sidearm and passed it over to the Brewer. "Kill him now."

Mancini took the gun as if he'd never touched one. Slowly, he turned it around in his hands so that the barrel was facing the right way.

You ever killed a man?

Aaron could see Mancini's hand shaking.

The Brewer held the gun out to Graham, one of Aaron's better hunters. "Shoot him."

Graham moved as if to take the weapon but looked to Aaron first.

"No," Aaron said. "At this I must draw the line. Death comes from the Fore. From the law of this city. Not from the village. Not even from a hunter. If you want him dead, you kill him."

The gun in Mancini's hand began to shake. He raised the weapon, and pointed it at Benson.

Coward.

"And remember to shoot twice," Aaron said.

The gun's shaking intensified. Mancini began to fumble for its safety. "Twice?"

"Twice," Aaron repeated. "The first time to kill him. And then again when he rises. Only be quick. It is said that men with the stilling rise quickly."

Mancini's aim looked now to be so poor that Aaron thought he might need to clear out the villagers for their safety. The wrinkles of worry on Mancini's face intensified. He seemed to be sweating. Finally he relented. "You're right. We should wait for the First Citizen."

Aaron breathed a sigh of relief. "Warwick, get a couple of hunters to dunk Benson in the river. Davel will get you some juice to feed him. Massan, you have those cuffs?"

Massan passed him the handcuffs.

Benson's wrists were so slight that Aaron figured it would be safest to put the cuffs around the still man's ankles. He rolled up Benson's pants to do so. The man's legs were thinner than Aaron's wrists.

He better not die now.

Aaron stood after having secured the man.

Martin had picked two hunters to help him. "Alright boys, let's get this guy to the river. Watch his teeth because if he dies on you, he's liable to be one hungry corpse." Then, more disturbingly, Martin started speaking directly to Benson. "You lucked out, ole Bense. I thought Mancini was going to shoot you for sure. Looks like you're going to live another day."

Aaron watched the hunters carry Benson towards the exit.

"Well, you've got your work cut out for you," Father Klein said.

"What? I can just have him guarded. No trouble there."

"Yes, but you've got to find out who did this, don't you? Whoever it was, it is not likely they are a villager."

Aaron nodded.

Yeah, well secrets are Davel's game. We'll let him play that one.

"His legs were so thin," Aaron murmured. "I couldn't believe it. Have you ever seen anyone survive the stilling sickness?"

Father Klein shook his head. "There's a first time for everything."

"You think we should have killed him?"

"No. No, you are a merciful man, Aaron. You wouldn't have fared any better than Davel."

Yeah, well maybe I'm a God damned coward too.

— 16 —

Aaron found Mancini in the parlor room. The Brewer had seated himself on the Persian pillow covered stone chair which Michael preferred. He had covered the light orbs with so many blankets that the room was nearly black. A thin line of light cut through the darkness, coming from an imperfectly drawn door blanket and stopping just inches in front of Aaron's feet. He almost tripped over a foot stool as he walked around the couch.

"You made a fool of me down there," Mancini said.

"Maybe."

"I don't have anything to say to you, hunter."

If he thinks I'm insulted because he forgot to call me Citizen. . .

Aaron took a seat on the edge of the couch. He reached over and removed one of the blankets from the light orb.

Mancini's forehead was still creased with lines of worry. "They'll be saying I never braved the wilds. I'll hear for weeks about how I can't even fire a gun."

"You can always try and pass it off as compassion," Aaron suggested.

"Why are you bothering me, hunter?"

Mancini was shielding his eyes from the light with his hand. Aaron picked the blanket back up and threw it over the light orb.

"I'm here because I need your help," Aaron admitted.

He saw the shadow that was Davel Mancini lean forward at his words. "You want to make some kind of peace, is that it?"

Aaron tried to make out Mancini's features in the dark. It was taking a while for his eyes to adjust.

"Somebody put that corpsedust in Benson's mouth, Davel. I don't know who or how. Maybe it's just some villager gone flat crazy. Maybe it was somebody's sick idea of a joke. I mean, I figure we're all in Hell for a reason, right? Even if it is just a joke, even if there isn't anybody like Maab or the Infidel's men trying to get us, we still need to find out who it is."

Aaron still couldn't see Mancini's facial features, but he noticed the man straighten.

He's probably wondering why he wasn't thinking about that. He was so busy being the fool he forgot to worry about his own skin.

"Okay," Mancini said, his head bobbing in the dark, "you're right. We need to find out who did it."

"I can't imagine it's any of us. The Harpsborough people, I mean. We would just be endangering ourselves."

"What hermits have been in the city lately?" Mancini asked.

"Hidalgo. Turi and some new girl, but they were here just for Michael's leaving. Someone would have seen them if they did it. There was the man with the burnt face and a couple of visitors from the Pole a few days ago."

"Hidalgo is crazy, but he's the wrong kind of crazy for this. Kara came to me to trade corpsedust, though. I have too much already, so I turned her away. We should check to make sure she still has it."

"That's a good point," Aaron said. "I'll ask around to find out who had any corpsedust during the last few days. Did you say you had too much?"

"It's the new brew," Mancini said. "It's made smoother. And while the devils have been thinning out, the corpses are just as thick."

Aaron nodded.

"Has anyone else tried to sell you corpsedust recently?"

"Ryan and Julian. I can't imagine Julian would do a thing like this."

"He wouldn't—"

Aaron was about to say more when he was interrupted by some shouting outside.

"The guards," he said, leaping up from his chair, banging his foot against a table in the dark.

Mancini swept the blankets off of one of the light orbs and the pair rushed out onto the balcony.

Aaron could hear the shouts more clearly now. "Wait. They're celebrating."

"He's back! He's back!"

For the second time that night, the villagers exited their hovels and the Citizens lined the roof of the Fore.

Michael Baker had come home. Slung over his shoulder like a log was a hairy, six-foot section of a giant spider's leg.

He's been wounded.

But the wound must not have been great, or Michael wouldn't have been strutting so. Duncan, Fitch, and Avery came in after him. Their packs were full, and they also carried sections of giant spider leg.

"Sorry I'm late," Aaron heard Michael Baker say. *"If we'd brought an entire hunting party, we'd have been back in time. Too much to carry. We'll have to get some hunters and villagers together to go get the rest. There are enough spider eggs to fill a hovel. My friends, we'll be eating for weeks. This food isn't for the Fore. It's for you."*

The villagers were cheering, some were even jumping up and down. Aaron knew how starved they were and how much this would mean to them. He saw many of his hunters down there, looking up at him. They had expected Michael to fail. They had expected to get better rations.

That son of a bitch.

"Turi! Turi!" Ellen's voice came from outside his sleeping chambers. "It's Ellen. Are Rick or Galen here?"

Arturus reached for his pistol as he sat up from his sheets.

"No, they're hunting."

If you thought they were here, why didn't you call them?

"Turi, I need your help."

Begrudgingly, Arturus stood up and pulled on a shirt. "I'll be right—" He almost shot her as she burst into his room. "out."

"There's a corpse by the knowledge fruit. I was trying to gather them, but it's wandering around in there."

Arturus wiped some of the sleep out of his eyes. "Well, did you shoot it?"

"No."

"Why the hell not?"

"Galen said that if I was in any trouble I should come straight here."

She seemed very distraught.

I'm not sure Galen would classify this as trouble.

"Was it armed?"

"No, I don't think so."

Arturus gave her a flat look.

"Will you come kill it for me?" she asked.

"You need to learn to handle these things yourself."

"Please?" She was in earnest.

"Alright. Take me to the thing."

He kicked some of the gravel she'd brought in his room back into the hallway and followed after her.

"Hold on," Arturus told her as he stopped by the battery room. "I've got to let Rick and Galen know where I'm going."

He found a woodstone block and carved Ellen's name into it. He placed it by the entrance on their way out.

She led him down the river, past the sloshing of the woodstone water wheel, and through the chambers which led to where she slept. He saw the warning stone Rick had placed to advise visitors from Harpsborough that someone lived here. The stone was a red cube about one foot in height. Arturus had been this way many times to gather the knowledge fruit, so he took the lead.

Ellen followed behind him.

His sense of danger overpowered his tiredness. He checked each room carefully before he entered, not wanting to be caught unawares.

"How can you be so calm?" she asked him.

Do I look calm? How can you be so noisy?

"You sure it's not armed?"

"Pretty sure," she said.

Arturus smelled it before he saw it. He stopped Ellen, and they waited patiently by the entrance to the next room.

It shambled into their chamber.

This one was particularly horrific. Some hound had taken its face off, leaving only rotted muscle and bone behind. Whoever had become this corpse had almost certainly died by being mauled. There was a knife on its belt. A lot of the corpses never even drew their weapons. Galen warned that he should never count on them failing to. Who knew what instincts their bodies kept after death?

For some reason he was suddenly struck with the idea that this had been another human being. That this person's soul was in a deeper level of Hell, facing an even more terrifying world than this one.

It's because of her. She's seeing everything for the first time, so I am seeing it with her.

It took a step closer.

"Is this what will happen to me, when I die?" Ellen asked.

"Sometimes. If another one's touched you. Or if you ate something polluted with it."

"Is there any way to stop it?"

"If you burn someone, they won't come back like this."

Arturus raised his gun and pointed it at the corpse.

"Will you burn me when I die?" She asked.

"You're not going to die."

"Promise me."

"Okay, I'll burn you."

"Promise me all the way," she said.

"Okay. I promise. If you die, I'll burn you. Now cover your ears. Gunshots are loud."

She did so, and he fired.

His aim was perfect.

— 17 —

Mancini sat down upon his mattress and leaned back against the wall. His bed smelled of his own sweat, though the aroma was too familiar to be off-putting. His room was dark, kept so by a thick window tapestry. It didn't help as much as he'd like.

In his hands he held a colorless Rubik's cube. The person who gave it to him had said it was an old world joke, an "idiot's cube," because no matter which way someone turned it, the puzzle had still been solved. At first Mancini had meant to add colors to it, to make it a proper cube, but in the end he found something much more challenging.

He'd imagine the colors.

He painted one side red with his mind, the others orange, green, yellow, white and blue. He'd twist the cube around and try to remember which colors went where. Then he'd reverse his motions and try to align the colors together. After a year of this, he no longer even needed the cube itself. He loved it when he'd forgotten which moves he'd made to tangle the colors up, yet was still somehow able to solve it again.

But now he was having trouble keeping the colors straight in his head. Now his thoughts were interrupted by the startling image of Benson's bloodshot eyes. Now the jubilant shouts of the villagers, who were celebrating the First Citizen's victory, were distracting him.

What are the odds that Michael would find a spider? What are the odds he'd survive?

Mancini closed his eyes and ran one hand through his thick, black hair.

What are the odds that Aaron would come to me for help with Benson?

His room was on the first story of the Fore, and the hunters often leaned upon his wall to speak and gamble. Mancini guessed they had no idea how often it was that he eavesdropped.

It was Martin and Duncan who were speaking now.

Mancini tossed the cube across his bed and listened.

"He was amazing," Duncan was saying. *"We were just out, wandering like normal down some corridors I hadn't been down in months."*

"Which ones?"

"By the Canyon, all the way out to the Pole road."

"That place has been dry for months," Martin said.

"I know, right? At first I thought he was crazy. Admittedly, he hadn't been out in the wilds for years or whatnot. About midway through the day he must have smelled something. Heard something. Sensed something. I don't know what, but he knew it was bad. He motioned us back, told us to keep a good distance. Avery was worried, but he remembered how good Michael was. We didn't know. We'd never seen him hunt. He found this crawlway that went down. I don't know how the hell he spotted it. Even Aaron wouldn't have seen that shit.

"He goes down, and then there's some gunfire. It's a good thing he brought that monster Winchester. Avery goes rushing in. Fitch didn't want to go, but I couldn't let them be down there all alone. Shouldn't have worried. By the time we got there it was all over. Spider guts everywhere, man. Michael had to take a dip in the river to get that shit off of him."

"How much food is there?"

"That's the crazy part. That spider was huge. Michael's not exaggerating when he said that the eggs could fill a hovel. More than that. The spider's body itself could fill a hovel. It was hell carrying that leg back. Its leg hairs kept getting caught in my hair. Juices dripping down the back of my pants leg.

"I'm telling you, Martin, there's a reason Michael's First Citizen. He didn't get it just sitting on his ass, that's for sure. That man can hunt."

Mancini opened his eyes and cleared his mind.

None of the plans he'd devised to help deal with Michael's failure would be particularly appropriate now.

We'll all be happy. The villagers are fed, the Citizens won't have pressure to give up the Fore's stores.

He heard girls laughing outside. One was calling Martin's name.

It can't last. It won't take long for the village to eat through the spider.

Michael had only postponed things, he decided. Hell was still disturbingly empty of devils. There still wasn't enough to feed the Citizens and the villagers.

He'd just have to wait.

Arturus watched as fresh steam soared up from the hotplates. Rick was using one of Galen's masonry chisels to tenderize the dyitzu flank he was preparing.

"Those knights are looking good," Rick said as he pounded out the meat. "You make them today?"

"Been working on this one all morning. I had a couple of missteps. I'm going to have to go out and gather some more sandstone to grind at this rate."

"Can't argue with the final result though."

"Wait till I make the black ones."

Rick smiled and poured another cup of water on the plates. "I think you're turning out to be a fine artist, Turi. Have you seen Galen yet this morning?"

"No."

"He was down at Harpsborough earlier today. Can you get him up for breakfast? I think he's napping."

Arturus grumbled to himself and got up from his chair.

"And can you fill the urn?" Rick added, "I'm almost out of water."

Arturus paced back across the battery room, grabbed the urn, and went out into the hallway. He wandered over to Galen's door tapestry.

"Galen," he called.

"Yes." Galen's voice was alert.

Arturus had a pet theory that, along with his beard never needing to be trimmed, Galen didn't need to sleep. "Rick asked me to tell you that he's making breakfast."

Galen's head peeked out from around the tapestry, sniffing the air. "Is that dyitzu he's cooking?"

"Sure is. And he's using one of your chisels on the meat."

"Then he must fall," Galen said.

Arturus laughed and headed out for the river.

"Turi," Galen said.

"Yeah?"

"The gravel's starting to heal itself together, will you make sure to rake it sometime today?"

Everybody has something for me to do.

Rick's cooking wasn't done by the time Arturus returned with the water, so he went to the closet to get the gravel rake. Galen was standing at the counter, cutting up some knowledge fruit. Arturus watched, hypnotized by his father's motion as the man diced the fruit into small cubes and then dropped them into the boiling devilwheat-meal.

"Not yet, Turi," Galen said to him as he reached for the rake.

Arturus didn't need to be told twice.

"I was in Harpsborough today," Galen said.

"Anything new?" Arturus asked.

"Michael came back a day or so ago. Killed a spider."

Rick whistled. "Well, good for him. I knew he had it in him."

Arturus had never seen a spider. He'd only eaten their eggs. He hoped those creatures didn't hold grudges.

Galen nodded. "Michael did well. They've got expeditions going back and forth between the village and wherever it made its web. Probably going to feed Harpsborough for a month."

"That's great," Arturus said. "Makes it easier to trade."

"Are you going to the village today?" Galen asked.

Arturus felt very adult answering this question. The fact that Galen asked it meant that it was Arturus' decision about whether or not he'd go.

"Yeah, I wanted to get his okay on the knights. I'm going to try and make the black one in a little bit. If Rick leaves any of the battery left for me."

Rick shot him a squint-eyed glance as he stirred the near boiling devilwheat-meal.

Galen laughed. "You should take Ellen with you. This food boom has their spirits up. You might be able to get Michael to take her as a villager."

"I hope so. Did you know she came over to have me kill a corpse for her the other day?"

"Did she really?" Rick said with a laugh.

Arturus nodded, watching as Galen began preparing another knowledge fruit.

"She gathered these for us," Galen said. "Said it was thanks for helping her out. Was the corpse much trouble?"

"No," Arturus answered. "She said it was wandering in the knowledge fruit, though."

Galen stopped cutting and looked at the fruit suspiciously.

"Hey," Rick said, "if it doesn't kill you, it makes you stronger, right?"

Aaron nodded to the hunters on morning watch and hurried out towards the river. He caught up with Molly before she made it to the river room.

"Molly, wait!" he called.

Molly turned around, smiling. "Hey, boy! Why are you chasing me down all alone in a place like this?"

"I need to know, Molly. What's going on with Benson?"

Her smile disappeared. "I wouldn't know."

"Don't joke with me, Molly. I don't need to know names. I just need to know if it's Maab, or something like that. If it's just one of us then..."

Molly pulled her brown hair over one of her shoulders and started working out the tangles. "Well, come protect me while I pee. Then maybe I'll tell you."

"This is serious."

"So is being attacked in the river room."

Aaron rolled his eyes and followed her. They waited for a girl there to gather her water in one of Kylie's urns. When they were alone, Molly pulled up her skirt and squatted by the river.

Aaron looked away.

"Why look away?" Molly teased. "Not like you haven't seen what I've got."

"I'm not the slightest bit interested."

"I bet not." He could hear the tinkle of her piss in the river as she spoke. "I probably bruised your ego pretty badly, huh? Still disappointed that your extra forearm wasn't enough for me?"

"That's not how I remember it."

"Oh, how do you remember it? Do *tell* me."

"Can we be serious for a second?"

"I am being serious. You're probably also feeling a little insecure about how well Michael did on the hunt."

The tinkling continued.

"I'm happy he found the food, Molly. We're all hungry."

"I bet."

He heard her stand. He turned around, a little too quickly.

She was about how he remembered her. A little skinnier, perhaps, probably from being deprived of the fruits of the Fore.

"Enjoy the show?" she asked him.

"It was great," Aaron said. "Now tell me what's going on."

She laughed and adjusted her skirt. "What, you're not attracted to me anymore?" Her eyes mimicked tragic disappointment.

"Not even remotely."

"I bet you're just afraid I'd tell Alice."

Aaron nodded. "And the rest of the village. Now what's going on, Molly. Or if you don't know, just admit it."

"You and Davel have been banging your heads against the wall about that one, haven't you?"

"Basically."

"It's not your fault you can't figure out why someone would do it, Aaron. You don't think like a scoundrel. Dusting Benson, just leaving him there, it wouldn't do anyone any good. Distractions are only useful if you can control them. You know, make them start when you need them to."

"That's just the thing," Aaron said. "Who knows when he'll die?"

Molly shook her head and pursed her lips. She bent down to the river, dipped a hand in the water, and used it to clean herself.

"Jesus," Aaron said, looking away again.

"See, I told you, you're too good a man. Whoever was using him as a distraction would only have to kill him to set him off."

“Okay. Distraction for what?”

“There’s only one thing in that village worth raiding.”

“Staunten’s storeroom?” He looked back at her.

Molly nodded. “You got it, cowboy.”

“But that wouldn’t make any sense,” Aaron protested. “After the fighting was done, people would be running out of the Fore to see what was going on. It’d be almost impossible to sneak in with everyone running out.”

“Sure would. If you were a villager. A Citizen, on the other hand, might find himself suddenly alone. Of course, with all the new spider guts in town, I’m sure you won’t have to worry about any attempt to get at the Fore’s food. So long as those eggs last, who would want to risk it? So long as they last.”

Don’t forget that this woman is usually full of bullshit.

But it was hard to ignore her words. They certainly made more sense than anything he had come up with.

“If I find out you’re lying to me...”

“You’ll what?”

“People could die, Molly.”

“It’s okay,” she told him as she walked by, “Michael couldn’t handle me either.”

She left Aaron alone in the room.

“I hate that bitch,” he told the river.

— 18 —

"Where are Rick and Galen?" Ellen asked Arturus.

"They should be here in just a bit. We'll head on down to Harpsborough as soon as they're back."

"I went exploring today," she told him.

Arturus grunted. It reminded him of the grunt that Galen would give when he was pleased with something. Sometimes it surprised him how much he took after his fathers.

"Be careful not to get lost," he warned, "but I like that you're doing it."

"I'm careful. I go a little farther each day. I mean to shoot the next corpse I see. Make you proud. Of course, you say it's because you want me to be able to take care of myself," she broke into a grin, "but really you're just too lazy to come and kill them for me."

Arturus laughed at that.

Ellen leaned over the table and saw the knights he had been working on. "What's this?"

She held one of the white knights up first, and Arturus could see her eye through the clear portions of the milky glass. Next she held up a black knight. Arturus was proudest of the black ones, of the ashen colored glass with the trails of crimson running through it.

She placed the knights between them. Arturus' fingers ran over the depression on the table's edge.

"This is you," she said, smiling, and pointing to the clearer piece. "My white knight."

"The black one looks better," Arturus said.

She brought her head down to the level of the table, looking at the darker piece. "Well," she said, resting her nose on the woodstone, "I guess you were damned. I suppose you'd be the black one."

Her nose twitched as she sat back up.

"I wasn't damned, remember?" Arturus told her. "I was

born here."

"Yeah, sorry, I forgot about that."

Ellen sat even farther back in her chair, looking shocked. The wooden legs scraped against the stone floor. "But then you never had a chance to go to heaven! That's not fair."

Arturus shrugged. "What's so nice about heaven?"

"This is horribly wrong," Ellen's face was mask of worry. "I mean, what if you lead the good life down here? You'll always be damned. Maybe you don't have a soul. . . I don't know where you would have gotten one."

"I'm pretty sure I have a soul," Arturus said flatly.

She seemed deep in thought. "I guess it's not so odd. I mean, everybody born in Iran goes to Hell too."

"Why's that? What's wrong with Iran?"

"Turi, they don't believe in Jesus."

"Believing in Jesus is what gets you to heaven?" Arturus asked her.

"Of course it is, silly."

"Did you believe in Jesus, in the old world?"

"Yes, but look, I wasn't perfect, you know. Let's talk about something else."

Arturus shrugged his shoulders.

He heard a voice from outside. "Galen."

And then another. "Rick. We're coming in."

"Ellen and Turi," she reported for them in her high voice.

She stood up to leave. "I'll wait outside."

Arturus nodded.

She passed him the white knight. "And I'll have you know," she said, rubbing the hair on his head while she looked directly into his eyes, "that's a very fine looking white knight."

She left, smiling at him as she walked by the entering Galen.

"Well, what was that about?" Rick asked after they could hear her footsteps on the bridge.

"She just likes the knight, is all," Arturus could feel a bit of flush coming to his cheeks.

"I don't think so. I think she likes you."

"Maybe. Doesn't matter, though. I like Alice."

"That's usually the way of things." Rick set his pack down by the table. "But you should consider her, at least."

Arturus stood up. "I can't think of anyone other than Alice. Ellen, she just doesn't get along very well."

"Not yet," Galen observed.

Rick gave Galen a long look. "You're not helping."

"The boy can like who he wants," Galen said, but then turned to Arturus. "Be careful, though. Ellen may joke about the knight on that table, but Alice really wants one. Beware of ambitious women."

Rick had wandered behind the stone counter and was rummaging through the supply closet. “Can we not fill his head with misogynistic bullshit, please?” he called out over his shoulder. “It’s hard enough, the boy not having a mother. You don’t want him to grow up and hate women.”

“He seems to like them just fine,” Galen said. “But be careful nonetheless. Alice wants something. She wants to be placed on a pedestal.”

“She belongs on one,” Arturus said.

“No one deserves that, Turi, man or woman. A pedestal and a tower are very similar.” Galen looked to the knights on the table before continuing. “And there’s precious little difference between a knight and a dragon.”

The guards waved them into Harpsborough with little more than a customary greeting, although Avery gave Arturus an approving nod that he thought had to do with Ellen. He hoped the cross-armed guard wouldn’t go speaking to Alice about this.

He had never seen Harpsborough this crowded. Her citizens lounged about, many spooning bulbous green and black masses of spider guts into their mouths with their fingers. One man had chunks of the stuff running down his beard. Smoke rose from the kiln and from the stones above the still. Other woodstone fires burned at random intervals throughout the village. Some villagers were boiling their spider eggs, Arturus presumed, to make sure that they wouldn’t hatch. Here and there, jars of Mancini’s bloodwater lay about, their corking undone. The people were joking and laughing. He saw one couple feeding each other. Father Klein was walking amongst the fires, blessing the food, speaking with those he passed.

Arturus pulled the wide eyed Ellen through the mass of celebrating villagers.

“I didn’t know there were so many people here,” she said.

“I didn’t either.” Arturus was only half joking. “I guess since everyone’s fed, no one is gathering in the wilds.”

“It smells like. . .”

“Spider guts,” Arturus finished for her.

At least, he hoped that’s what the smell was.

He stopped by the kiln where he found Kylie working. The kiln was full of pots, and she had another batch ready to go.

“You look busy,” Arturus noted.

Kylie gave him a wide smile.

“People all of a sudden have food to store, and food to pay with. It’ll be a busy holiday for me. Who’s the girl?”

“I’m Ellen.” Ellen held out her hand.

“Citizen Kylie. Why Arturus, she’s such a pretty little thing.”

“Nice to meet you,” Ellen said.

The smell of the baking clay, Arturus noticed, was far preferable to the smell of boiling spider eggs. "Is Michael in?"

Kylie's smile became even wider. "Our hero is certainly in residence. I think he's drunk as a skunk, up in the Fore."

"Thanks!" Ellen told her as they walked away.

Massan waved to Arturus as they moved to the Fore.

Ellen pinched her nose. "How can they stand it?"

"Better than being hungry."

He spotted Alice and Molly by Alice's hovel. He wished for a moment that Ellen wasn't following quite so closely. He moved a little faster, hoping that a little distance would let Alice know that they weren't together.

Arturus batted at the door tapestry which hung from the Fore, but no one answered. He could hear raucous laughter from inside.

"Can't we go in?" Ellen asked.

"No, only Citizens are allowed in the Fore without special permission."

After a minute or so, John, a boy just slightly younger than Arturus, opened the tapestry. "Turi, may I help you?"

Ever since John had become the de facto servant for the Fore, he had started talking funny. Arturus tried to ignore it. "Yes, John, I've got a meeting with Michael."

"I'll see if he's ready for you, Turi."

Behind them a great shout came up from a group of hunters. One man was shaking his fist in the air while another was kissing his devilbone dice.

Ellen smiled. "They all look so happy."

"See," Arturus said, "Hell's not all that bad. Though it's not usually quite this nice. . ."

John returned. "You can come on up, Turi."

They started to enter.

"Not you," John said to Ellen.

"Don't worry," Arturus told her. "I'll be right back."

She gave him a fake smile.

Ellen waited at the door to the Fore and did her best to look like she belonged. She couldn't help but fidget with her hair, though she stopped herself whenever she noticed she was doing it.

She didn't appreciate the predatory looks she was getting.

Now why doesn't Turi see me like that?

She looked over towards Alice, accidently making eye contact. She did her best not to give the girl a hard look. Who knew what Turi saw in her?

She's not even that pretty.

As she looked away, she got an eyeful of an approaching man. He had a bit of a pot belly and, shocking her slightly, a missing hand.

"Hey, princess, whatchya waitin' for?"

"Turi."

"Turi?" The man seemed to have trouble focusing his eyes. "He's not likely to come out of there."

"I don't see why not," she said. "That's where he went in."

He nodded seriously for a moment, as if considering some deep philosophical thought. To her disgust, he rubbed what appeared to be a small fingernail growing out of the stub that was his hand.

She felt nauseous and looked down the side of the Fore to avoid looking at his deformity.

"You're a fine sight. God was a fool to send you here, I'd say."

He's drunk.

She gave him a disapproving frown, but she doubted he even noticed.

He looked at her queerly. "You been here before?"

"Once. Turi is trying to get me to become a citizen."

"A Citizen, hah! Lucky if you get to be a villager."

"Whatever."

He reached out with his stump hand and placed it on her shoulder. She did her best to avoid retching and looked him in the eye. She didn't want to seem like a victim.

"Well, if you ever need anything, remember that I'm here to support you."

"I didn't bring my Elektra complex to town today."

She had meant that to be some sort of stinging insult.

The man stared at her dumbly. "Ele-who? Look. Can I show you something?"

Oh, God.

"I'll be right back," he said.

Turi, I don't even want to live in this stupid town. You get your butt back down here.

She watched the drunken one-handed man hurry off, but her fear transitioned quickly to bemusement when he returned. He had a clay urn cradled against his chest.

He handed it to her. "Look. Isn't it pretty?"

She studied the beach scene, which was painted with colored dust.

"It goes all the way around, see? Isn't the sky beautiful? 'Cause it's grey I pretend the top is the clouds. And do you see how the sun is on the water there? Turn it, it goes all the way around."

She looked at the urn, slowly rotating it.

Simple, but beautiful.

"I never got to see the beach, you know," he was saying.

She looked back towards him. He had seated himself while

she was studying the urn and was leaning his back up against the Fore. She handed the clay pot back to him and placed a hand on his shoulder.

"Well, you got to see it now," she said.

He nodded glumly.

"Sometimes I think that I'd rather be just like ole Bense. Just sit here and stare at the urn. Nothing really so pressing, you know? It's all going to happen to you sooner or later. Why not take it early, I say."

Ole Bense?

"We used to eat the best, you know. Better than the villagers. But Hell dried up. We eat worse now. But we do all this hard work. That was going to change. Sure, we got spider eggs now. That's why I'm saving up, you know. Aaron says it's the calm before the storm. Something's coming, something big. Hell's going through changes, you know. It does that sometimes, when too many people are dying."

"How long have you been here?"

"About four years. I used to hunt under Michael."

"Only four years?"

"For some, that's a long time, princess."

She nodded. "Have you seen Hell change before?"

"No."

What was it Turi had told her when they first met? It had stuck in her head for some reason.

You cannot judge what you do not know.

She stared at the strange, sad man who sat beside her and marveled at the attention that he paid the urn. It was as if it had him hypnotized.

Maybe living here wouldn't be so bad.

"My favorite is the seagulls," he said. "You see how they get smaller as they go back? It gives the thing. . ."

"Perspective?"

"Perspective. Yeah. That's it. That's what every pot needs."

The man was snoring gently by the time Turi came back out of the Fore. Turi had a sour look on his face.

"He didn't want me, did he?"

Turi shook his head. "No. No he didn't. I'm sorry. I tried."

"Turi, it's okay. I didn't want to live here anyway."

"It's safer here."

She touched his arm. "I know. But I'll be fine. I know you'll protect me."

— 19 —

Aaron found Michael sitting in his favorite chair in the parlor room. The Lead Hunter took a seat on the couch.

"You're pissed at me, aren't you?" Michael was holding a small piece of glass in his hands.

"You know I've always idolized you," Aaron said. "Do I feel belittled because you went out and did something I can't do? Yeah. It's true. But it gives me faith, too. Father Klein warned me to be humble. I forgot how good you were, Mike. I stopped getting better as a hunter because I thought I was better than you."

Michael smiled. "So tell me how you really feel."

"What do you have there?"

Michael handed the glass pieces to Aaron.

"Chess pieces?" Aaron asked.

"Yeah, I've got Turi making them. Give us something more constructive to do in the Fore. Hell, maybe it'll keep Davel's damn mouth shut. Who knows?"

"I very seriously doubt a game could do that."

Aaron stopped for a moment to consider the two knights Arturus had left behind. One was made of clear glass with streams of white caught up in it somehow. The other, made of a murky, dark glass, had streams of blood running through it. He wondered how they had been made. Next to such craftsmanship even some of Kylie's creations would seem like the products of an amateur.

"So did you come to make peace, or is there business?" Michael interrupted Aaron's thoughts.

Aaron handed him back the knights. "Both. You know some bastard poured corpsedust down Benson's throat?"

"Jesus," Mike leaned forward and began rubbing the back of his head.

"No one's told you yet? I had Benson washed in the river. Mancini is funneling sinfruit juice down his throat. Fortunately we haven't noticed the man's piss smell because of all the spider guts."

"Aaron, why didn't you just shoot him?"

Aaron thought about that.

Did I save Benson just to disagree with Mancini?

"Might have been best," he said. "Would've taken two bullets, though. One to kill him, and another to keep him down. Besides, Father Klein said that the stilling can last almost a year. That would probably outlast the corpsedust."

"What if it doesn't?"

"I've got a man on it, and I shackled Benson's feet together. But I'm more worried about why someone would do it."

"Oh?"

"Molly seems to think it was a plot against the Fore. She says they wanted to get into Staunten's storeroom."

"Did you believe her?"

"The villagers were hungry, Mike. Very hungry. And they had to sit down there starving in their homes while they could look up at us stuffing our faces on the Fore's balcony. She also seemed to think that a Citizen might be in on it, too."

Michael sighed and began brooding.

"Did you enjoy it?" Aaron asked him. "Being out in the wilds again?"

Michael's eyes came alive. "It's insane. Aaron, a few years ago I would have done anything to get out of Hell. Showing you the ropes was almost more than I could bear. But now? I want it back. I want that torture. I feel like I'm cheating God's justice by holing myself up where the devils can't reach me."

"You should feel grateful for what you've earned. The people in the village, they'd kill for what you have."

"They would indeed," Michael said. "I approve of how you handled Benson. You followed the law when it was easier not to. You're a good man, Aaron."

Or a coward.

"And yet," Michael continued, "you want to change the law of the hunters' rations."

"I will follow the current law until it is changed. Those are the rules I agreed to follow when I swore into Harpsborough as a villager."

"Jesus, you really are a good man. But it doesn't look like that law will change now."

"Maybe. The hunters are happy. They're eating fine. The pressure is off of us. I understand the Fore wants us to go back to hunting full time, but until you say otherwise I'm letting them have a bit of a break. The food will run out, though. Unless you can go catch another spider, we'll be right back where we were. I'm a patient man. Sooner or later, Mike, you're going to have to change one of the rules, or the hunters won't be any good to you."

"Unless the devils come back."

"Unless," Aaron agreed.

Aaron stayed seated, but Michael didn't appear to have anything more to say.

"If we split the food evenly, we wouldn't have to pray for the devils to return," Aaron said as he stood.

"Fair," Michael said, "but people don't work like that. This system works because we're selfish. If we weren't, we'd be in heaven, no?"

Aaron bit his lip and headed for the door.

"You are right, though," Michael said, stopping the Lead Hunter in his tracks.

Aaron turned around.

Michael stood up and walked to the door tapestry that led to the dining balcony. He looked out through the crack between the curtain and the doorway.

"About what?" Aaron asked.

"About this being the calm before the storm. I thought that I'd feel it in my bones, if it were true. The settling, the missing dyitzu. . . it's the dyitzu that bother me. They can sense the changes in Hell. That's what I learned while I was Lead Hunter. We were designed by God, Aaron. We weren't built for this place. But they, they belong here. They can smell it coming. They can feel it in their bones, and they're running like rats leaving a sinking ship. Hell is changing."

"We can run too, Mike. We can move the village. It's not too late."

Michael nodded, but said nothing.

Finally, Aaron left the parlor room.

He won't run.

— 20 —

"These are the bishops," Galen had told Turi as he was leaving to show Michael the new pieces he'd made. "In most situations they are slightly more powerful than a knight. They were called camels and elephants as well, in parts of the old world. Each king starts with two of them. The pair of them can be very important to preserve."

"I still don't know how to play," Arturus had replied.

It was almost liberating to return to Harpsborough alone. The last couple of times he'd had Ellen in tow. This time he didn't have to worry about the noise that she made when walking. Still, he did miss having someone to talk to. She was kind of funny, too, in her own way.

I think I just like protecting her.

But couldn't he be making himself her crutch? Was he stopping her from being able to survive on her own?

She won't learn too well dead, will she?

Michael would like the bishops. He was sure of it. The rooks would be easy to make, too. It was the Queen he was worried about. Galen had showed him the drawings, but Arturus felt that she should be something more impressive. He wanted to actually carve a woman and put her on the board. She would be regal, strong, the kind of woman that Galen would approve of.

The next turn would bring him to the Harpsborough guards.

I'm getting close.

"It's Turi, don't shoot."

"Sure as hell won't." The call came back.

Arturus approached the entrance corridor. He could smell Harpsborough from out here. It smelled like sweat, piss, and warm spider guts. He recognized the hunters by face only.

"It's daytime in there?"

"Sure as hell is, Turi," one said. "If you're here to see

Michael, you better hurry on through. He's going to be making a speech in the church in just a little bit."

"I hope he doesn't say anything too important," the second one added, "since we're not going to hear it."

The first hunter shrugged. "He'll just be talking about rationing the spider eggs. You know that's what's coming. He wants it to last, of course. We've been gluttons. I can hear Father Klein preaching in my head each time I take a bite."

Arturus walked past them.

The smell of the city hit him full in the face.

He threw up a little in his mouth. It was an act of will to swallow it down and hold in his dinner.

I bet a hound could smell this place a mile away.

The entire village had been feasting rather than leaving during the day. Everyone was home. Everyone was sweating and breathing the same air. The city seemed hot, perhaps for that reason.

It was smoky, too, he realized, from the fires at the kiln and the fires at the still. He moved carefully through the crowd, heading to the Fore. Then he found himself face to face with Alice. His heart skipped a beat.

"Hi," he managed.

"Hey Turi," she said, flashing him a half smile. "Where's your girlfriend?"

"Girlfriend? Oh, yeah. Ellen. She's just a friend, but she's good. Galen and Rick have been showing her how to survive and stuff. They gave her a gun. I've been showing her how to get here."

Arturus noticed her pink bra strap had fallen off of one of her shoulders and then quickly looked away in embarrassment.

Did she see me looking? Who cares? She's probably used to it by now.

"You've been spending a lot of time in the Fore, lately," she was saying.

"Yeah. I've been making a chess set for the Citizens. Want to see?"

She nodded.

He showed her the two bishops, one clear with white streamers, the other dark with red. "I'm going to make the Queen next. That's the best piece, so it has to look the best. I'm going to make the white one look like you." He saw the worry in her blue eyes. She wasn't comfortable with him speaking honestly about his feelings towards her, but he had expected that, and kept on speaking. "I'll make the black Queen look like Chelsea."

He watched his joke touch her face. At first she just seemed relieved that he hadn't meant the words as a hopeless compliment. Then she laughed, without any hint of falsity, at the humor.

See, I'll change your mind, one little bit at time. I'll grow stronger, and you'll get over Aaron. You'll see.

"I better hurry on," he told her. "I don't want to interrupt the First Citizen's speech."

She nodded and waved goodbye.

He walked on, wondering if her eyes were on him. He imagined they were.

When he made it to the door tapestry he glanced back.

She was looking at him.

His heart skipped a few more beats.

I can do this.

"I can't hear him," Molly said to Alice. "Why'd he take so long to get here, anyway?"

"He was dealing with Turi."

Alice could hear Michael's drone echoing out of the church, though she couldn't understand what he was saying. It couldn't have been too important, otherwise the people inside would be making more noise.

One of the hunters picked little Julian up and placed him on his shoulders. Julian was short for his age and wouldn't have been able to see otherwise.

"Fuck it," Molly said. "We'll just ask someone else later."

"Just wait for Aaron," Alice whispered.

"Oh, we'll hear his big mouth, that's for sure."

Alice watched Molly try to stay patient for a few moments. The woman began chewing her lower lip while shifting back and forth.

"Jesus," she said finally, "if the God damned Citizens didn't take up four whole rows for themselves, there'd be room for all of us in the church."

The statement struck Alice as some sort of particularly profound analogy, if somewhat blasphemous. There would be food enough for all of Harpsborough if the Citizens didn't hoard and gluttonize. Even more, if they actually worked. They would have been able to take in Turi's new little friend as a villager. They would be able to feed the villagers and hunters. She wouldn't have to be so damn hungry all the time. If it wasn't for Julian, she probably would have starved to death by now.

"Thank God for Julian," she mumbled under her breath.

"What?"

"Don't say things like that, Molly. People can hear you."

"Well, at least somebody can hear somebody—"

She was cut off by the hunter carrying Julian.

"Quiet, Aaron's almost up," he said.

When Aaron spoke, Alice could hear him clearly. She snickered fondly.

You and your big mouth.

"For our part," Aaron was saying, *"the hunters are going to resume hunting schedules tomorrow. We've given Hell a little time to recover, so maybe she'll have some dyitzu for us. We'll try and extend the time that we have left with our new rations of spider food. Besides, I think we're all getting a little sick of those eggs anyway—"*

"Speak for yourself!" a man yelled loudly enough for Alice to hear.

The congregation laughed.

"At any rate," Aaron went on, laughter in his own voice, *"in case anyone else is sick of eating spider and is ready to trade the Fore for some meat, we'll be back hunting."*

Someone asked Aaron a question, but Alice couldn't make out the words. His response was clear though.

"No. That is true. We've been on extra long routes lately because we've been catching very little. We're only returning to our old routes for as long as the stores last. So don't worry, I won't be working them like dogs yet."

There was some more laughter.

Aaron stopped and his firm voice was replaced by the distant echoed thrum of Father Klein's.

"Don't forget to be thankful. It is not every day that..."

"What's the ration?" Molly asked those around her.

"I think it's supposed to be a pound, measured out by Staunten," the hunter carrying Julian said.

Molly looked at him suspiciously. "Did you hear it from Baker, or are you just guessing."

"That's what Citizen Mayse said before they started."

"Did anyone hear?"

The villagers on the church steps didn't know.

They had to wait for the service to end before they got their answer. A quarter pound of spider guts and a half pound of spider eggs, picked up from Father Klein at the church each morning.

"That's a good thing," Molly said. "Klein will give you two servings and never know it. Staunten would probably write your name down."

Alice was surprised to see Arturus come out of the church with the last of the villagers and the first group of citizens. He was talking with Michael Baker. Michael was laughing.

Arturus looked at her and smiled.

That little twerp. I don't know how he does it.

"Oh, yeah. Like Turi needed to hear," Molly said. "He doesn't even live here. This shit is so unfair."

If Turi thinks I'm going to fall all over him because he's found a way to get Michael Baker's ear, he's in for some disappointment.

Arturus awoke to Ellen's voice. He could hear her footsteps on the gravel.

"Turi," she sounded frantic.

Not again.

"I'm awake," he said.

"Turi, I really need you this time."

He grabbed his gun belt, checked to make sure the boots he'd slept in were tied, and hurried out across the gravel hallway.

"What's going on?" he asked.

He hadn't seen Ellen looking so upset since the first day he met her. She glanced frequently over her shoulder. Not as if someone was chasing her, but as if she had left something behind.

"Someone's dying. I helped him out of the river. I don't know if he's going to make it."

Arturus ran back into his room. He checked his pack to make sure that he had his bandages. He found the woodstone board which had Ellen's name on it and tossed it by the entrance so that Galen or Rick would see it.

"Ready," he told her.

Ellen led him, running at times, along the river.

There was a smear of blood and water at the entrance of her room.

"He was right here," she said.

Arturus could tell that the wounded person had dragged themselves away from the riverbank and into Ellen's room.

Smart. And if they were strong enough to do that, they probably aren't going to die.

Arturus and Ellen followed the trail of blood and water. Ellen stayed just slightly behind him but was close enough to peer over his shoulder.

He entered the room and took stock of the figure. He immediately put out a hand to keep Ellen back.

The man who lay before him was unfamiliar. He had scratches along his armored vest, as if it had been clawed by dyitzu. A bullet had struck him on his unarmored shoulder, apparently of small caliber. It looked like the bullet was still in him. His right leg was a bloody mess, sporting two different sets of lacerations. Arturus figured those were probably hound bites. But for all his wounds, the man was well groomed. His face was clean shaven and his hair was short and neatly cut. Even his fingernails were trimmed. He was well armed, too, with an M-16 rifle slung at his side and a pistol holstered at his hip. Arturus approached the wounded stranger carefully, making sure that the man's eyes were closed and that his breathing was regular. He reached out and touched the stranger's right hand, checking the palm.

Scarring. Hard to do in Hell, Arturus knew. One had to treat a wound with rustrock to keep it from healing properly. The scar that had been cut into his palm was a symbol, a triangle within a trapezoid which had two lines running through it.

Arturus drew his gun. The end of it was shaking. He tried to keep control of it and his breathing while he reached for the man's rifle. As carefully as he could, he removed the straps from the gun and pulled it aside. Then he stole the man's sidearm out of his holster.

Arturus looked at Ellen.

"Go to Harpsborough." Arturus' voice was hoarse.

"What?" Ellen sounded frightened.

"Go to Harpsborough, now."

"I don't know the way."

"Then find it. Get the guards. As fast as you can. Tell them you've found an infidel."

Part II
The Squire of Harpsborough

From the Book of the Infidels, Gehennic Law: Fisher of Men

The Little Boy Jesus came to the Sea of Galilee with His nets. He thought that fishing was rather hard work, so He decided that He'd play His flute in order to entice the fish onto the bank. He played then such a beautiful song that the birds silenced their chatter just to hear Him.

But the fish could not hear Him, so they did not come onto the shore and swam instead in the muddy sea.

Angered, but still unwilling to cast His nets, Jesus played another song. This time the song was so beautiful that the trees bent in close, and the breeze itself stopped to listen.

But still the fish did not come onto the bank.

Jesus' anger grew, and He resolved to play a song more beautiful than had ever been heard on Earth or in the Heavens. Its beauty was so great that the angels came down from clouds, and the sun and moon stopped their fighting, instead sharing the sky, that they might hear the melody.

But still the fish did not come onto the bank.

Enraged, Jesus leapt to His feet and opened His nets. He cast them into the sea, and when He had captured the fish He tossed them on the earth. He watched the fish flop about as He prepared to gut them.

"Well," He said, "there's no use dancing now."

From Neostoicism: Philosophia

"Free will was the greatest gift God gave to Man. Is it any wonder that this was the first thing He wanted back?"
—Ares

"Wisdom is such a tricky thing. I speak often to wise men. They are always telling me that, when they were raised, things were done this *way. They also tell me, that had things been done* that *way when they were little, they would have been chastised and beaten. I always wait for their argument, but it seldom comes. It seems sufficient to them that they should think as their mothers did—as if other people didn't have mothers who disagreed."*
—Endymion

Benson saw a figure running through the cavern.

Is he real, or a figment?

Whatever it was, it stopped in indecision.

He's real.

"Wait, wait!" Benson shouted. "Carlisle? Is that you? It's Benson."

Don't forget. Don't forget. The caverns that look like the belly of a giant worm. The twin pillars that stand there like guards. Don't forget. Don't forget.

"Carlisle, stop. You can't go running here. It's not the same. You'll never find your way back."

Carlisle turned, his chest heaving as he tried to catch his breath. He bent over as he spoke, placing his hands on his knees. "I can't. He's after me. He's shot me already. In the side. Like Christ."

"Who, Carlisle? Who's shot you?"

"The Infi—"

"Don't say his name!" Benson screeched.

The fool. Doesn't he know how many people the Infidel's touched? How many minds he's imprinted himself upon?

Carlisle looked horribly lost. Benson tried to remember how long ago it had been since he'd seen him. It was before Harpsborough. Before the Citizens.

Don't forget. Don't forget. The caverns that look like the belly of a giant worm. The twin pillars that stand there like guards. Don't forget. Don't forget.

Carlisle looked to be regaining his energy. He stood, placing his hands on his hips. Sweat dripped from his brow and splattered against the cavern floor. "He's been here. I can feel him. The walls remember him. He's after him. The boy. He's after the boy."

"What boy? Carlisle—"

"The *angel's get!*" Carlisle shouted. "The Infidel can't be allowed to have him."

"Angel's get? Jesus Christ, Carlisle, that was over ten years ago. You heard La'Ferve. That boy was human. Human, Carlisle. His mother was fed human blood. You know that."

Can he even hear me?

Carlisle turned and ran, his bare feet slapping against the cavern's stone. Benson chased after him. They passed through a room that had a floor made all of gold and then through an archway whose natural rock formation looked like the mouth of a dragon.

Don't forget. Don't forget. The caverns that look like the belly of a giant worm. The twin pillars that stand there like guards. The mouth of the dragon. The floor of gold. Don't forget. Don't forget. You'll make it back to the cold room. And then you'll remember. Somehow you'll remember. It may take years but something will spark your memory and you'll know the way.

He reached out and grabbed Carlisle's arm. The man turned, looking about the chamber, unsure of where he was.

"Carlisle stop. You can't keep running."

"The boy," Carlisle insisted.

"We're dead, Carlisle. We've gone further down, to another level of Hell. You fool. You can't go running. Hell here only stays the same if you remember it. You can't find the boy. The Infidel can't catch you. You're dead again. Do you get me?"

Carlisle's eyes widened.

The only chance a man here had for happiness was to find another who could help ground him. Someone who could project a shared reality into the Hell about. But it was so easy to lose that person. Particularly when one slept.

Benson doubted Carlisle could ever help root him.

He's mad. Don't forget. Don't forget. The caverns that look like the belly of a giant worm. The twin pillars that stand there like guards. The mouth of the dragon. The floor of gold. Don't forget. Don't forget.

Carlisle's face tightened in fear. "No. I have to find him."

"It's over, Carlisle."

The man ran again, and Benson chased after him.

They ran through a chamber of stalagmites and into a mist covered river that was only a few feet deep but nearly a hundred feet wide. Benson tried to keep up with him, stepping into the water. The water clung to his feet, slowing each step as he sloshed after the running Carlisle.

Don't forget. Don't forget. The caverns that look like the belly of a giant worm. The twin pillars that stand there like guards. The mouth of the dragon. The floor of gold. The room of stalagmites. The knee deep river. Don't forget. Don't forget.

"Carlisle, you can't get anywhere."

Benson understood. He knew that the farther out you got from whatever center this Hell had, the less real everything became. The rooms would disappear as soon as you blinked. Once you got this far out, it was almost impossible to get back. You could get lost sleeping and be forced to remember your dreams to try and figure out how and where you traveled. And the rooms were just like that, dreams. You could remember them, just barely, if you tried hard enough. Sometimes you knew the room was there, you could feel it, but the harder you tried to remember its details the more it slipped away.

"I can," Carlisle shouted, turning about in the river. "I can make it back. Don't you remember what the Infidel taught? Hell is infinite. Its end is also its beginning. If I go down far enough, I'll find the boy."

Don't forget. Don't forget. The caverns that look like the belly of a giant worm. The twin pillars that stand there like guards. The floor of gold. The room of stalagmites. The knee deep river. Don't forget. Don't forget.

A cold shiver rippled up Benson's spine.

I forgot something. What? What did I miss?

"Carlisle!"

The man was receding into the river's mists.

"Carlisle!"

You'll remember. It was just one room. You'll remember it. And then you'll get back to the cold room. And you'll remember how to get to the silver falls. And you'll remember all the way back to Harpsborough.

He dreamed about the village sometimes. He dreamed of sitting against the Fore and watching through blurry eyes as people walked by. But each day those dreams grew dimmer.

"Carlisle!"

The man was gone.

— 21 —

Julian moved quickly through Harpsborough, passing Kylie's Kiln on his way to the side of the village that was the furthest from Father Klein's church. Mancini's Still was the only underground room in Harpsborough, save for Ben Staunten's storeroom under the Fore. Smoke seeped up through the cracks in the hatchway, and the heat blasted him as he opened it.

Julian closed the hatch behind him and crept carefully down into the still's stairway. Smoke poured up along the slanted ceiling above him like an upside-down waterfall. Julian let his fingers trail along the inside wall to keep himself steady as he descended away from the light. The tight confines didn't bother him at all, though he always wondered how some of the others, like Copperfield and Ben Staunten, were able to come down the stairs. The heat increased at each turn in the stairwell, and he began to cough a bit.

"It's Julian."

"I know," Mancini answered.

The last few stairs were lit by the fires below. Julian was sweating profusely by the time he entered the still.

Mancini was standing by his quicksilver thermometer. The man kept a careful eye on it while Julian tried to wait patiently. He watched the smoke pouring up the stairs. Then he watched the copper tubes on the ceiling and pretended he could see the bloodwater flowing down them and into the collection barrels.

Mancini, apparently satisfied, turned and spoke. "Got the feathers?"

"Yes."

"You didn't let them touch anything, did you?"

Julian shook his head.

With Mancini, he knew, the fewer words you spoke, the better off you were. He dug around in his pack until he found the old world plastic bag that he kept the dirty brown harpy feathers in. He produced it, and passed it to the Brewer.

"Julian," Mancini said harshly, "the bag's not tied twice."

Julian nodded, trying to look as sorry as he could.

"This isn't like corpsedust, kid. A bit of this gets in Staunten's stores, and you'd take out half our food supply."

Julian looked to his shoes.

"Promise me you'll bathe in the river after you leave here."

"Yes, Citizen."

Mancini seemed satisfied and went to the back of the room where he kept his stock. He gathered three jars of his new brew, a box of shells, and what Julian longed for the most, some honey from the Pole.

Julian could feel himself smile as soon as he saw the honey.

"You were safe, as always?"

Julian nodded, thinking for a second that Mancini was concerned about him. That seemed a little odd.

"No chance of the harpies following you?"

Julian shook his head glumly. He hadn't really thought that Mancini was concerned about him as a person, but it would have been a nice gesture for the man to at least pretend he cared. Mancini was still staring at him, so Julian figured he would need to speak a little.

"I never see the harpies. The feathers fall down through a grate. I gather them very carefully, like you say. I have too, because I can't let them spoil the devilwheat."

"Good enough," Mancini said, "but if you ever feel like there's danger, just stop, okay? This new brew is helping me out. I practically own the Fore by now, but there's no sense in bringing harpies down upon us, okay? Okay?"

But Julian had been followed.

Even if Mancini doesn't care about me, he cares about getting the feathers. He'll stop the burnt man, if he can.

"I have been followed, Citizen," Julian said, "just not by harpies."

"Who, then?" Mancini asked.

"A man with no face. He's quiet, quieter than the hunters. He moves faster too, and knows the labyrinth well on the far side of the Kingsriver."

Mancini nodded slowly, pursing his lips. At long last, he spoke. "Don't worry about him, Julian. That man is of no danger to you. He is an old friend of mine. Has he discovered where the devilwheat is?"

"I don't think so."

"Good. Even if he does, don't worry. He'll not harm you, or take your share." Mancini passed him the bloodwater, shells, and honey. "Now run along."

Julian did, clutching his loot to his chest and running up the stairs as fast as he could. He felt safer in the wilds than he did in the still.

He put a little distance between himself and Mancini before he finally sat down. He pulled out his jar and eagerly worked at the corking with his knife. The seal was stubborn, so he had to work at it a bit longer than he liked. Finally there was a little pop, and the jar opened. He put a finger into the honey, closed his eyes, and then sucked on it. The sticky sweetness clung to his tongue, and he pushed it toward the roof of his mouth.

He sighed as the honey dripped down his throat.

"You doing alright there, Julian?" a hunter asked.

"Yes, sir," he said.

The hunter laughed.

There was some shouting, and then a gunshot from the entrance. A young girl was screaming.

Julian quickly sealed the honey.

"God damn it, Huang, keep that weapon safetied," one of the guards from the entrance shouted. "You damn near shot her."

The guard, who tuned out to be Fitch, poked his head in. "It's okay, everything's okay."

But Julian wasn't listening to him. He was listening to the girl.

"An infidel. Turi sent me for help. We found an infidel wounded on the river."

"What?" Fitch shouted back.

"An infidel!"

"God damn. Get Aaron."

Arturus finished bandaging the man's leg, and as quickly as he could, redrew his pistol. Normally he would have done a tourniquet on that limb, but it had stopped bleeding already. There were some burn marks there, too, which must have helped cauterize the wound. The burns were too sporadic to have been carefully applied. They appeared to have been caused by dyitzu fire.

Could this be deliberate? Could he have meant to burn these wounds closed?

He leaned back against the wall of Ellen's chamber. She had chalked something into the hellstone. It read: "Remember."

Don't look away.

The Infidel Friend was breathing deeply, as if sleeping.

"I know you're awake," Arturus tried.

If the Infidel Friend wasn't unconscious, he was calling Arturus' bluff.

Arturus had left his safety on. Galen had taught him to do that so he wouldn't accidentally take another person's life, but he didn't know if that applied to an infidel.

It would only be a little longer. If he could just hold on

until Ellen returned. What if she hadn't made it? What if she'd been killed on the way? What if she'd gotten so lost that he'd never see her again?

The man took a sudden breath, and his eyes shot open.

Arturus jumped, his left hand flying to the safety.

The Infidel Friend's head lolled over towards Arturus. One of his eyes was as bloodshot as a still man's. The other was clear. His voice was hardly a whisper.

"Safe?"

Arturus nodded.

The man's eyes closed again. Arturus waited, but he showed no more signs of life.

Come on, Ellen, don't leave me alone in here.

She'd only been to Harpsborough a couple of times, but surely she would have run into the road. Maybe not at the right spot, but she would have run into it.

Arturus jumped again when he heard voices from the river room outside. One of them was Galen's. The rest seemed like they were Harpsborough hunters.

He must have seen my note.

"Turi, you in there?" Aaron shouted.

The shouting didn't seem to disturb the Infidel Friend.

"Yes, everything's fine," Arturus reported.

They came in with weapons raised anyway, except for Ellen, whose gun was holstered. Aaron sent his two hunters to the corners of the room. They trained their rifles at the wounded man as Galen and Aaron moved towards him.

Arturus showed them the mark on the man's palm.

"Should we kill him?" One hunter asked.

Aaron shook his head. "Death comes from the Fore."

"You dressed the wounds well, Turi," Galen commented, looking at the bandages. "Is that a bullet wound in his shoulder?"

"Yes."

"Did you remove the bullet?"

"No."

"Do so now." Galen turned to the hunters. "He's stable enough not to die."

Arturus went back into his pack. He had no forceps, but he found some large tweezers in his kit.

Well, this isn't going to be easy.

"The other infidels wouldn't know we killed him," one hunter pointed out. "Maybe we should finish him off now."

"Maybe," Galen answered. "How many in Harpsborough know of this?"

Aaron looked at Ellen. "She shouted it in front of the entire city. No way we'd keep it a secret from the hermits and traders."

Galen nodded.

"I'm sorry," Ellen said.

"You did nothing wrong," Galen assured her.

Galen knelt by the Infidel Friend while Arturus removed the bandage around the man's shoulder. Arturus pushed at the wound with the tweezers, finding the bullet quickly. He was able to work the bullet out with surprising ease, and began to re-apply the bandage.

"You're good at that, Turi," Aaron said.

"Galen makes me practice getting the bullets out of dyitzu."

"Smart."

The Infidel Friend's eyes opened.

Galen bent over him, getting closer than any other dared. "Easy, we're healing you."

"Ares?" the man asked, "is that you?"

"You've mistaken me for someone else, friend," Galen replied. "You are in the lands of Harpsborough, and your kind are not welcome here."

"Harm me not."

Aaron bent down to meet the man's gaze. "You will be treated fairly."

The infidel's head lolled again.

Arturus finished the bandage and quickly checked the man's pulse. It was harder to find than normal, and slow, but it was still there. "He's lost consciousness again."

Galen and Aaron stood up together.

"We can't leave him here," Aaron said.

"Undoubtedly, but moving him might be dangerous. Best not to get him killed unless we mean to."

"I want him in Harpsborough," Aaron said.

Galen nodded. "Agreed. We'll need a stretcher to take him there."

Aaron looked over to the two guards. "Go back to Harpsborough. Talk to Chelsea and get something to carry him on. Be back as soon as you can."

The hunters nodded and left.

"What's he doing all the way out here?" Aaron asked.

Galen shrugged and moved to the man's equipment.

"Ellen found him in the river," Arturus said. "Who knows how far upstream he fell in."

Galen grunted. "It's not like one of them to get caught in an ambush. It happens, but not often. There must be some conglomeration of devils upstream."

"Should we check it out?" Aaron asked.

"You may find more devils, surely, and if your city is starving, it might be worth it. But you may come back with more than you bargained for. Infidel Friend often move in packs."

"Can we afford just to sit by?"

Galen shook his head. "When he awakens we need to find out what he knows. He may just be ranging. He could be lost. But he could also be a scout. He might know where the devils have gone."

Arturus heard Aaron's swallow.

He looked at the Infidel Friend. It was hard not to sympathize with this figure.

He's barely human. A monster. You can't nurse a dyitzu to health and expect its thanks.

"Will we kill him?" Arturus asked.

"I don't know, Turi," Aaron said. "I just don't know."

The hunters returned with a flat piece of woodstone. It was barely wide enough to hold the infidel. Galen grabbed the man's shoulders and Aaron held his feet. They moved him as carefully as they could onto the stretcher. The man awoke again at being lifted but didn't stay conscious for long.

It's the pain, it wakes him. But he doesn't show it, even from sleep.

"We move, guns drawn," Aaron ordered. "There could be other infidels about. Stay sharp."

Arturus complied, drawing his pistol. He wished he had brought his rifle, but he figured there wouldn't be too many rooms between here and Harpsborough where he'd need to worry about having any range. He felt unarmed somehow, as if the bulk of the weapon would add some protection.

He watched the corridors as they headed towards Harpsborough. Galen moved amongst them, taking his customary care in looking down passages. He seemed remarkably unconcerned. Arturus envied him. It seemed an attitude impossible to emulate. Simpler for him to master was Aaron's manner. Aaron was also alert, on edge, even. Unlike his men, however, he didn't appear fearful. More hunter than prey.

Arturus thought there were shadows in the corridors, some of them even appeared to move, but when he focused he never saw anything. His heart beat so loudly and quickly in his chest that he feared the others might hear it.

If there are any hounds around, they will smell my fear.

"I need a break, Aaron," one of the hunters said. "I can't carry this shit anymore."

"Spell him, Turi," Galen ordered.

Arturus dutifully holstered his gun and took up one end of the stretcher. He looked at the fallen man's boots. They were still wet from the river.

It must be safe since Galen's willing to put me here.

But he didn't know if Galen would make a decision like that for his own safety. Would Galen be more concerned for the group as a whole? Did his father make the decision simply to help these men?

I'm the least experienced gun here. He can afford to lose me.

But that didn't seem right. There was another reason Galen might assign him to the stretcher. Arturus was much less likely to drop the infidel.

He can tell I care.

The Harpsborough man obviously didn't. He kept looking back over his shoulder, as if worried that the Infidel Friend would rise up and strike at him. Each time he did so Arturus had to struggle to keep the stretcher steady.

"If it's easier, I'll take the lead," Arturus offered.

The hunter gratefully accepted.

Galen grunted.

He's proud of me.

— 22 —

"Good timing? Davel, you're insane." Michael fumed as he paced about the parlor. "No one's going out into the wilds. Aaron's got his hunters working half shifts. All of Harpsborough is going to explode with gossip. They'll want his head."

"Don't we?" Mancini asked. "There have been troubles in Harpsborough. Unrest. We need a common enemy to pull us together, and the devils have been doing a poor job of it lately. Let the Infidel Friend take their place."

Michael moved to the balcony curtain, looking through its crack onto his city. "I don't want this to be some kind of lynch mob justice."

"Aaron helped you out with that," Mancini said. "Your Lead Hunter dragged the man all the way back here for judgment."

"And what, I summarily kill him?"

"Why not, Mike? You summarily killed Charlie to take the Fore, and this is something that came with it. You've ordered hermits slaughtered before for less grievous crimes."

"But that's just it, they did something. We're going to kill this poor bastard for who he is."

Mancini shook his head. "I don't see the difference."

"The difference is that the others did bad things."

"Mike, they did bad things because they were bad people. This Infidel Friend is a bad person. Besides, what else are you going to do to him? Let him go? He'll be back with more of them. Those things are monsters. You've heard Father Klein's stories."

"Just stories. If Molly said—"

"Molly's a whore, Mike. This is Father Klein. He has no reason to lie."

"We'll have his trial in the church."

Mancini shook his head again. "I don't think that this is necessary."

"You're the one who wanted a common enemy. What good

would he be if we didn't prop him up in front of everybody?"

"Ask Klein about it. They're all trained in sophistry. You let that man heal and represent himself, and he'll talk circles around you."

"I doubt that, Davel."

"He'll appeal to the baser amongst us. The villagers may not be smart enough to see their way through his arguments."

"Just the Citizens, then. They'll vote him guilty or not guilty. I'll decide the punishment."

Finally Mancini nodded. "Okay. Just the Citizens, but—"

He stopped as he heard footsteps coming up the stairs. Young John's face appeared through the tapestry. "Aaron would like to see you, sir."

Michael nodded. "Bring him up."

Michael could hear the unrest of his city while he waited for Aaron to appear. So many people were talking that it sounded as if Harpsborough itself were a hive of angry bees.

"Smart," Michael lauded Aaron as the man entered the room. "You made the right decision in bringing the Infidel Friend here."

"I appreciate that, First Citizen."

Mancini snorted. "'First Citizen?' You're being awfully polite. You must want something."

Aaron laughed. "I posted two hunters at the church."

"And?" Michael asked.

"I don't think they'll be enough."

Michael pushed through the tapestry and walked out onto the balcony. He moved to the edge, leaned against the railing and looked out towards the church. Half of the villagers, perhaps, were gathered around the steps.

"Fine, post more. No, better yet, get Klein to kick them off his steps."

"We better get him to trial fast," Mancini said.

"He must heal first. You know what? Even better. Aaron, move him to the Fore. Give him to Staunten. The villagers go into the church all the time. They never go into the Fore. Then your two guards will be enough."

"Sir," Aaron said, "if they raid the Fore..."

"He's right, Mike," Mancini said, "we'd be forced to shoot at villagers."

"They're more curious than anything else. He'll have to wake up before they get angry. Aaron, do it."

"Yes, sir."

Arturus sat on the church steps watching Galen help move the Infidel Friend into the Fore. He marveled at how easily his father fit in amongst the hunters.

He helps them a lot. Maybe I can help them someday.

The rest of the villagers began to mill about. A few moved towards the Fore, standing outside the man's new resting place.

Behind him, the church doors opened.

"Arturus," Father Klein greeted him as he fastened one of the great double doors to the wall. "How nice of you to visit. Have you come to pray?"

"But you say that God can't hear."

"Of course he can't. God cannot look on sin, and we are in Hell. But prayer is a powerful thing. You cannot discount it just because there is no one there to answer. How much can you learn about a person by listening to his wants?"

"A lot, I guess."

"Then think how much you could learn about yourself from your own wants?"

Arturus mulled this over. "But I'm me, shouldn't I know me anyway?"

"You should indeed," Klein said. "But sometimes it helps to talk these things out. Sometimes we lie to ourselves, and praying helps you find out. Besides, imagine how God might think of your requests. He would frown upon you if you wished harm on someone, so through prayer you can try and put things into perspective."

"Okay," Arturus said. "I'll try."

He followed Father Klein up the steps and walked through the one open double door. The inside of the church was lit by windows set high in the walls. The ceiling itself was over four stories tall, and Arturus gazed up at it. All around the top edge, and in the windows themselves, were woodstone crosses. They were irregularly sized, and cast shadows of themselves across the marble stone floor and woodstone pews.

Klein walked all the way up to the steps before the pulpit and knelt. Arturus did likewise, closed his eyes, and prayed.

Can you hear me, God?

He listened for a reply. He could hear the soft whispers of Klein's own murmured prayer. He could hear the angry buzz of the village outside. He could hear his own breathing, but nothing else.

I've never prayed to You before. I wish You could hear me.

Wait. This is stupid. God can't hear me. I'm talking to myself. I should try, though.

I'll pretend You can hear me.

If I had been born on Earth, maybe then we could have really spoken. You and I. You could have watched me grow up. I was pretty bad when I was younger. Hopefully You would have found that funny. We could have been friends. Maybe You could have helped me. You could have made sure I was safe on my way to Harpsborough the first time I went alone. You could have protected me during my first firefight. You could have stopped me from killing that man who surprised me when I was eight. Galen beat me for that. Maybe You could have helped me through that, too.

I guess what I want to pray for is that infidel. I don't want him to be hurt, God. I want him to be okay. Will you make it so he's okay? I don't want him to hurt anyone else, but I want him to be fine, too.

His eyes fluttered open.

"Who's Ares?" he asked Father Klein on an impulse.

The world seemed brighter somehow, and he had to adjust to the light. He felt a great sadness in his heart. He imagined it was from the prayer.

Father Klein also opened his eyes.

He swallowed, and Arturus watched the man's Adam's apple move up and down.

"In the old world," Klein said, "Ares was a false god. His symbols were the hound and the vulture. He was a God of war."

Arturus knew all that. Galen had told him stories of the Greek gods.

"In Hell," Father Klein went on, "there's a man with that same name. He's a follower of the Infidel. One of the most vicious and feared in all of the labyrinth, next to Archades, Kent, Endymion, Past and Present."

"Why is he so feared?"

"They say he wields a sword of bone, carved from the femur of a man he's slain. They say he wears armor made of men's ribcages, and a helmet like might be worn by an ancient Greek knight—a hoplite helm. He doesn't use bullets, preferring to feel the blood of his victims. Of all the Infidel's men, he is perhaps the most godless. He is a monarch to those who serve him and slays those who question him. Where did you hear of him?"

"The Infidel Friend we captured. He was coming in and out of consciousness. He spoke the name."

Father Klein swallowed again. "Let us hope that he simply knows Ares in passing. If this Infidel Friend that we have is under Ares' command, then we are surely in grave danger."

"Do you think he'd come for us?"

"Turi, you may be afraid of shadows."

There are better things to worry about than the falling of the sky.

The young man nodded. "Are all the Infidel Friend evil?"

"They are all godless. They go through Hell making wolves of men. We came to Hell because we were evil, Turi. It's hard for you to understand that, since they say you were born here. We were ordered to be sheep, to be obedient and follow the Lord's will. Instead we wandered. Some of us, those who are mature enough to admit our mistakes, try and continue to follow His teachings. The Infidel's men think differently. They are angry at God and blame Him for their damnation. They refuse to take any responsibility for their failures on Earth. They continue to ignore His teachings. By ignoring those teachings they hurt people. They are inglorious murderers who take no pleasure in helping humankind. It is difficult to tell them apart from the devils."

Arturus imagined the wounded man he'd found in Ellen's chamber. How weak and powerless he had seemed. He'd been laid low.

If one can be hurt, then they all can be hurt. Even Ares.

Father Klein smiled and placed a heavy hand on Arturus' shoulder. "And your prayers, how did they make you feel?"

"Sad, Father. They made me feel sad."

"That's the separation from God that you are feeling. Our souls were not meant to be taken away from Him. That's the worst part of Hell, Turi. To be separated from the Father of all."

"I never got a chance to meet Him," Arturus said.

"Nor did I, young man," Father Klein said, looking sadly to the largest cross which hung behind the pulpit. "Nor did I."

Aaron tapped gently on the door blanket next to the dreamcatcher. Some of the stones, caught as if nightmares in its yarn, rattled as he did so. "Alice, are you there?"

"One second," she replied.

Aaron wiped the sweat from his face and tried to arrange his hair while he waited for her. After a few moments, she emerged from her home. He could see the lacey edge of her pink bra peeking up from beneath her blue v-neck shirt.

"Yeah, Aaron, what's up?" she said. "Are you okay? You look worried."

"I'm fine, I guess. Hey, I know this is kind of a funny time, but it's been a while since we ate together. Would you like to eat in the Fore with me tomorrow?"

She smiled. "Of course." And then she wrinkled her nose. "You'll have to bathe first, though. Don't much care for skunks."

Aaron laughed. "No problem. I have a trip to the river planned in my very near future."

"Fine," she said, "it's a date, Mr. *Le Pew*."

Aaron had no idea why the word "date" made him feel so excited. He thought about leaning in and kissing her, but remembered that he wasn't smelling very good at the moment.

Aw, what the hell.

He brushed one of her loose strands of hair away from her face and kissed her. She pushed him back after a second, her cheeks turning red.

"Easy tiger," she said, grinning, but then her expression turned serious. "God, you are worried. What's going on?"

Aaron hadn't realized that his emotions were so transparent. "It was weird. Protecting that Infidel Friend, I mean. On the way back I was afraid I was going to die. Like the

Infidel himself was going to spring out of the shadows and kill me."

Alice shuddered visibly, and looked away.

"I wondered, then," he went on, "what you might have thought about me if I died."

"Why are you saying this?" Alice asked. "I don't like thinking about that."

"I just thought you should know, you know? That I. . . well, I figured that if I thought of you when I was afraid then. . . well, then I knew I liked you."

Alice shook her head. "It shouldn't take almost dying to help you realize something like that, Aaron."

"I know but. . . well, it made me understand how much."

"That's sweet," Alice said.

Aaron nodded, and started to leave.

"Wait."

He turned around.

"That Infidel Friend, should we even be keeping him here? He might be dangerous."

"I'm not worried about that," Aaron said. "We keep talking about what we're going to do when he heals up. The man might not even live. It's amazing he's survived this long."

"But you *are* worried, Aaron, about something. What is it?"

"That man came here for a reason, Alice."

"But what could he want?"

I don't know, that's what I'm worried about. Who could trick him into talking?

"Where's Molly?" Aaron asked.

"Why would you want to talk to her?"

"Because if anyone can drag secrets out of an Infidel Friend, she can."

"I think she's by the river."

— 23 —

"Sir," Avery said, "he's awake."

Aaron started, sitting up from his bed. Chelsea stirred beside him, groaning and covering her eyes with his blanket.

"Who let you in the Fore?" Aaron asked.

"You did, sir. You assigned me to guard the Infidel Friend."

Aaron shook his head, and rubbed his eyes. "Well, feed him."

"No, sir."

Aaron cast a blurry glance towards Avery. He had drawn his shutters to help Chelsea sleep, so the only light entering the room came from behind Avery. The brightness was enough to make Aaron close one eye. "Excuse me?"

"I didn't want that no good motherfucker here, sir. I'll be damned if he eats meat from my table."

"Your table?"

"Figuratively speaking, sir."

"Alright, I'll be up in a second. I'll bring him his food."

Ben Staunten had opted to give up his own room rather than let the Infidel Friend stay with the stores. Michael had agreed to it since Staunten's room was one of the few in the Fore that actually had a door and the only one other than the storeroom that had a lock on it. Staunten had taken his mattress with him, so the infidel lay against the naked stone. The man had propped his head up with his shirt which he had balled into a makeshift pillow. His bandages had been soaked through with blood that had since dried. He had gone so far as to remove two of them.

"I've brought you some food," Aaron said to the infidel.

The man moved only slightly, as if he had been awake when Aaron had entered the room. Whether this was simply the case, or whether the Infidel Friend just made it seem so, was beyond him.

"Then I give you thanks," the infidel replied.

Aaron had decided to bring spider guts, though he knew it would anger the villagers if they found out.

The Infidel Friend began to eat the meal slowly. Aaron hadn't provided any silverware, forcing the infidel to eat his food by dipping two fingers into the green and black guts and spoon it into his mouth. From his proficiency of eating in such a manner, Aaron guessed he must do it often.

"Did you kill the spider?" the Infidel Friend asked him.

Fucker knows how to piss people off from the first sentence, doesn't he?

"No. Michael did."

"He must be a strong warrior."

Aaron nodded.

"Do you mind if I keep the bowl?" the Infidel Friend asked him.

"Yes."

"Then I shall attempt to finish. I would appreciate it greatly if you gave me some of your patience. I have been deeply wounded."

Aaron nodded, and sat down in one of Staunten's chairs. "Take your God damned time." He'd meant to present a more upstanding example of himself to his enemy. "I'm sorry," Aaron apologized.

"For what?" the infidel asked.

"I didn't mean to say the Lord's name in vain. Kind of stupid to apologize to you about it, though."

"You didn't take the Lord's name in vain."

"I said 'God damn.'"

The infidel shook his head seriously. "Yahweh. You're not allowed to say Yahweh. They used to kill men for saying it. 'God damn' isn't at all what the ancients had in mind. That's something uneducated Christians came up with later."

Aaron shifted in his chair. For some reason the way that the Infidel Friend was eating angered him. "You could sit on one of the chairs, you know. Would be softer."

"I am a guest here. I'd not bleed on my host's furniture."

"You're no guest. You're a prisoner."

If this was a revelation to the man, he showed no sign of it. After a few more measured bites he answered. "Then I shall probably take a seat."

Aaron drew his gun when the man began to stand.

"Are you drawing your gun as a precaution? Or is it that you would rather me not bloody the chair?"

"You have no idea how badly I want to kill you."

"Maybe. But you're not exactly hiding that intention."

Aaron watched the infidel stand up. He chose to do so in an odd manner. He lifted his body up with his right hand and left leg, and then swung his right leg out to get his feet under him. Aaron figured this must have been the only way he could stand without aggravating his wounds. Slowly, the Infidel Friend moved to a chair and sat down. Only then did he continue eating.

"I have eaten half," the infidel said. "If this food is allotted to more men than me, please tell me now."

"Just finish the damn bowl, okay."

"I appreciate your generosity."

"You know damn well that's a pittance. As a man recovering from a wound, you should be getting far more than that."

The infidel shrugged. "Then, having recognized this indemnity, would you not request more food on my behalf?"

"No."

The Infidel Friend took another bite. He swallowed slowly and breathed deeply.

Aaron shook his head. "Hurry up. I've got some water for you when you are through."

Another bite. "Pardon my speculation, but I feel it unlikely that your hostility stems from my actions."

Unfailingly polite. The fucker doesn't even speak with his mouth full. Even the way he eats. It's schooled.

"Well, you're dead wrong."

"I think you're mad at the way I've been treated. I think you're mad that your man didn't bring me the food himself. You're mad because you didn't kill the spider that I eat."

"I think you're a liar."

"Then I trust you will ask me no questions."

"I didn't say I thought you were a good one," Aaron muttered.

The infidel laughed. It was a shallow laugh, as the man was obviously trying not to disturb his wounds, but it seemed genuine.

Aaron let the tension flow out of the room, and laughed too, shaking his head helplessly.

Don't trust him, he's trying to get on your good side.

Another bite.

As before, the Infidel Friend finished chewing and swallowing before speaking. "I know that you are supposed to provide a stern front with me, but you have no need to keep up such pretension. I know that if it was up to you, you'd free me."

"You *are* a liar," Aaron said.

"You are a good man. You have empathy. You wonder, what has this man done that could be so bad. Can we kill him, just for the symbol cut into his palm? What kind of leaders do I serve, that will kill this man no matter what he says? How would I feel in his shoes?"

"I've thought none of these things," Aaron said. "I know you're just trying to turn me against my people. I know you're trying like hell to save yourself the only way you know how. This place has mercy, Infidel Friend. Your fate is not forgone. You will have a trial, and if you deserve it, you will be spared."

The man stood up, causing Aaron to tighten his grip on his gun.

The Infidel Friend offered him the empty bowl. He had eaten every speck. "Now it is you who is the liar."

Aaron took the bowl and looked again into the man's eyes. "I'll recommend that you be allowed to recover before your trial."

He can see my guilt.

The infidel nodded. "You're a good man."

Or a coward.

Aaron felt shaken as he left the room. He closed the door behind him and twisted the lock.

Avery stood in the hallway, arms crossed, a sneer on his face. "I can't believe you fed him."

Aaron pulled him away from the door. "He makes me feel uneasy."

"No shit, sir."

"I don't want anyone going in there alone, unless they're unarmed."

"I ain't letting anyone in there without a weapon, sir."

"Then send them in pairs. No one alone is to be armed. Understood?"

"Yes, sir."

"Besides, if you do send someone in alone, that infidel doesn't have to know that the gun isn't loaded. I'd rather him have a hostage than a weapon, okay?"

"As far as I'm concerned, it's law, sir."

"Good. And that especially goes for Molly."

Avery was so surprised that he uncrossed his arms. "Molly?"

"I'm going to get her now. I want her to interrogate the Infidel Friend first. She can't have any loaded guns, got me?"

"I've frisked worse," Avery said, grinning.

Aaron rolled his eyes.

Arturus had finished smoothing the last of the long marble rectangles he would use for squares. Galen had suggested that he glue them together into a board shape first, alternating light and dark. Then he could cut them across and flip over every other one. That way each square wouldn't have to be quite so perfect, and it would make his board look less crooked. Soon he would have to go out and trade for some knowledge fruit to help make the glue that would hold the tiles together. If he had used white marble tiles for the white squares, the job would be easier, but he had elected for clear glass tiles instead. They would appear white because the entire board was set on a clean white marble slate.

Ellen was watching him work, which was something that she said she liked to do. He figured she was just afraid to be alone.

"It looks good," she said.

It does look good.

He felt a bit of pride when he looked at the unfinished board. After this, he would only have to carve out the King, make the King's mold, and cast those last two pieces in order to finish. "Thank you."

"Did you want to go to Harpsborough today?" she asked.

"Not today, probably. I thought I might go tomorrow when I have the entire set done. Michael will love it."

"Is that all you can think about?" she accused.

He looked at her, confused. "It's all I've been thinking about for the last couple of hours, yeah. Why did you want to go to Harpsborough?"

"Fitch came by my place today," she said. "He says the Infidel Friend is awake. Turi, I have to see him."

"They're probably going to kill him."

"No! Why?"

"Infidel Friend are bad men, Ellen. They kill people. They have no respect for things here. They hate God."

"Well, maybe they ought to. They were damned. It only seems fair."

I wish Father Klein had heard that.

Arturus smiled. "Don't go saying that in Harpsborough, okay?"

"I didn't mean it." She shook her head. "It's just. . . well, I went through all the effort to drag him out of the river. I'd hate to think that they'd just kill him. I have to see him."

She feels guilty. If it hadn't been for her he wouldn't be imprisoned. Then again, he'd probably have drowned.

"Alright. Let's wait for Galen to come back. He might want to go too. He might not, though."

"Why?"

"One of the things he taught me was not to go out of my way to witness human suffering."

"What if we can make a difference?"

"You mean, like, convince Harpsborough to save him?"

"Or ease his last moments. You know? What if he looks at all those hateful people, and sees us, loving him. I have to at least talk to him."

Arturus looked at her sharply. "Are you sure you belong here?"

"Huh?"

"You're awfully nice to be in Hell."

She laughed and blushed. Then she pulled a knowledge fruit out of her sack.

Aha! I need that little sucker.

"Anything I can trade you for the fruit?"

She smiled, and held it behind her back. "You can give me a kiss."

Ridiculous.

"Forget it. I'll get some from Julian."

She threw the fruit at him and stormed out of the room.

He watched her run in surprise, rubbing his shoulder from where the knowledge fruit had impacted.

What the hell?

He heard the gravel scattering as she ran down the hallway.

And guess who's going to clean that up.

"We should not wait long before we have the trial," Mancini said. "The whole town wants his blood."

Michael Baker shrugged. "I'm going to do the right thing, Davel."

"No problem. Just remember the right thing also includes the four hundred and change Harpsborough villagers who will be camped out in front of the Fore, armed to the teeth, and chanting for his blood."

"Come on, Davel. It won't be as bad as all that."

"Maybe. Maybe they'll just want him imprisoned forever. Who knows what villagers want? But, after what he did to Molly—"

"Molly? What'd he do to Molly?"

"No one knows. Aaron let her in to speak with the guy. I guess he wanted her to find out what the Infidel Friend was coming here for. She left in tears. Won't tell anyone what went on in there."

Michael chuckled. "He probably wouldn't sleep with her."

"That'd be a first," Mancini said.

"Well, if he doesn't tell me why he's here when I ask him, he really will be killed. Have you spoken with Father Klein about the possibilities of retribution?"

Mancini nodded and tossed some blankets on the light orbs. He then sat down on the end of the couch closest to Michael's favorite chair. "He says that he doubts anyone right now is a spy. He's worried, though. By making this whole thing public, it'd be easy for some trader or hermit to find out about it. Infidel Friend don't go missing very often, Mike. If he does, the others will ask questions. The infidels have been known to slaughter whole villages in order to get revenge."

"Surely not the size of Harpsborough."

"No. Klein says the village he heard of only had about thirty people or so. But they killed everyone in it."

"Brutal."

"Mike, Klein said there were only three of the Infidel Friend who did it."

The First Citizen looked up into Mancini's dark eyes. "Only three? Killed thirty?"

"That's what he said, and he didn't give me the impression that this was one of his exaggerations. Only a couple of the villagers lived. They were apparently with the old village, the ones that stayed behind when Charlie brought us to Harpsborough."

"Well, maybe the Infidel Friend won't be so angry if we just exile him."

"Maybe, but then you'll have the villagers to explain your mercy to. Besides, maybe the Citizens won't even vote him guilty."

"You must be joking."

Mancini smiled. "I was."

"How's our food holding out, do you know?"

"You should ask Klein, but when I spoke with him last we were right on schedule. Better take this Infidel Friend to trial soon. He can talk already. Aaron says he can move, sort of."

"I will not have a man who can hardly stand face judgment."

"Well, don't wait too long. He's sleeping in our house, and I don't want to be caught up in a lynching."

Arturus thought it would be wrong to use the fruit he hadn't paid for, so he worked on making the King's mold until Galen and Rick came home.

"Turi," Rick said, "there's gravel all over the place."

Rick passed where he was working and went to the storage closet.

"Ellen," Arturus replied, whittling away.

"What got into her?"

"She told me I had to kiss her for a knowledge fruit. I told her no, so she threw it at me and ran."

Rick popped his head out of the closet.

"Did you run after her?"

"No."

"Well, why not?"

"Why would I? It's obvious that she wanted to be away from me. Why would I chase her down?"

Galen covered his mouth as he sat down at the table, attempting to stifle a laugh.

Arturus felt vaguely insulted, but when Rick gave the man a stern look, he realized that the joke wasn't on him after all.

"Turi," Rick said, "when Ellen runs, she expects you to chase after her."

"That's ridiculous," Arturus said, "if she wanted to keep speaking with me, why wouldn't she stay and try to come to an understanding?"

"Yeah, Rick," Galen chimed in, "why?"

Rick ignored Galen. "Turi, it's a different communication style than you're used to. Ellen's upset, so her running expresses that efficiently. By chasing after her you show her that you care."

Galen snorted.

Rick gave him a sharp glance. "We agreed that I would be the one to teach him about these things."

Galen stood up from his stool and examined the work of the model King. "You carved the base to the right dimension. Looks great. As long as you form the mold right I think your Kings will be perfect."

"So what should I do?" Arturus asked Rick.

"Go after her," Rick answered.

"Chase her down," Galen agreed. "By all means, indulge her churlish behavior."

Arturus shrugged and grabbed the knowledge fruit. Rick was right about the gravel, he noticed as he was leaving. She had managed to kick it into nearly every room.

She must do that deliberately.

He trotted along the river, and soon he spied the red marker stone that was by her home.

"Ellen," he called in through her hallway, "It's Turi. You home?"

"Fuck off," her voice replied.

He entered.

She was sitting Indian style on the floor, dicing a knowledge fruit into very small pieces.

"What do you want?" she asked coldly.

He held up the fruit she had tossed at him earlier. "I felt guilty taking this without paying."

She didn't say anything, so he bent down and kissed her on the forehead.

"Oh," she said.

She stood up like a fresh corpse, and hugged him. She hugged him for a long time.

"You still want to go to town today?" he asked.

"Yeah. Yeah, that'd be nice."

— 24 —

Alice looked particularly beautiful today.

Aaron's eyes followed the single braided lock of her hair as it draped down her shoulder. She leaned forward to eat some of her devilwheat. He could see a bit down her white v-neck t-shirt. She was wearing the purple bra, he noticed. The right shoulder of her shirt had been repaired with black thread. Chelsea would never have made such an off-colored repair, but Alice, even though she did a lot of the village's sewing, wasn't always able to collect the correct thread.

Molly maintained that you could tell the difference between the two seamstresses work, never mind the color, by just looking at the quality of the stitching.

I hate that useless bitch.

Some of Copperfield's incense burned on the table next to them, filling the air with a soft scent that did a passable job of disguising the spider gut and sweat smell that Harpsborough had begun to reek of.

The blonde braid fell over her shoulder as she turned her head to look out at the village. The end of it caught on the lip of her v-neck. She had bound the braid with a black rubber band, just like Chelsea did. Her profile struck him as beautiful. He imagined kissing her chin.

"You're gorgeous," he told her.

"I know," she said, turning back to her meal. "My mirror tells me that every day."

She was eating slowly, like a Citizen.

Maybe she's had more practice.

He watched her eat a spoonful of devilwheat porridge with disinterest.

Maybe it's just that she's had enough to eat, for once.

He wondered then about how odd it was that the villagers and hunters were usually starving.

"Hey," she said.

"Huh?"

"Eyes up here, bucko."

Aaron smiled. "I was lost in thought."

"Funny, it looked like you were lost somewhere else."

Well, I suppose this is as good a time as any other.

"Will you be my girl?" he asked.

"Will you make me a Citizen?" she shot back.

What?

Aaron looked down at his food dismally. "I wish I could, but I can't. You know I've already spoken about this with Michael, right?"

"You have?" She leaned forward.

"I thought there had to be some way, some thing, I could do. But we can't even add villagers now, Alice. Surely you've noticed that the Fore's grown too big."

"But when the devils come again—"

"Then we'll add you, I promise."

Alice's smile turned into a sneer. "You won't like me by then. You'll be tired of me. Then you'll take some other girl, and leave me out in the village like you left Molly."

Her anger spent, her sneer faded into a frown.

"What happened to Molly is Molly's fault," Aaron said. "Even Father Klein said so. There's no one else I could imagine myself being with. Surely there's nobody else here for you?"

Alice turned again to look out over Harpsborough, towards the entryway and the wilds.

"There's no reason for us to just stay here and be lonely," he said.

She wouldn't look at him.

"Alice. Alice?"

"It wasn't her fault!" she said suddenly, with enough emotion to send Aaron back in his chair. "You all made her what she is. She wasn't a slut until you used her up. Then you threw her into the lion's den with that fucking Infidel Friend. What did you expect? For her to just fucking get all his information and report? She's hurting now."

"Is this why you won't be my girl?" Aaron came to his feet. He knew that the Citizens in the parlor room would be able to hear him, but he didn't care. "Because Molly flipped her shit and won't talk to you?"

Alice also stood and pointed a finger towards his chest. "No. I won't be your girl because I won't let you use me like you used her."

"I never used her."

She turned away from him. "Bullshit."

Aaron wiped his hands on his camouflaged pants and looked around. Some villagers had stopped below and were looking up at him.

Great.

"Well, I don't know," Aaron said after a while. "That's just how I feel."

"Molly feels differently."

"This isn't about Molly, this is about you and me. And don't pretend it's about the Citizenship thing either. I know you like me for more than just that."

"You're wrong." Her eyes were stubborn. "You're dead wrong. I'm not going to let you just toss me aside—"

"Toss you aside? Don't lie to me, Alice. I've seen you when I kiss you. I *know* you like me. You'd like me if I was just a villager. You'd like me if I was a fucking dyitzu."

"I fucking hate you."

"Shut up." Aaron waved his hand while he spoke, knocking over one of the glasses. It rolled over and shattered on the stone floor of the balcony. "You want to lie to me, fine. Some couple we'd make, huh? How are we supposed to make it if you won't even tell me the truth? Well fuck you. You can go sleep with Turi for all I care."

"And you can go sleep with Chelsea." She shot back.

Aaron froze.

Oh shit.

Alice was furious, her face was red and her nostrils were flaring. "You think I don't know? Everybody knows, Aaron. Everybody. There's no secrets in Harpsborough."

A voice came over Aaron's shoulder.

"Aaron." It was Avery.

Avery? The hell? Right, the Infidel Friend.

Alice walked past him.

"Alice," he said. "Alice, wait."

She left without speaking, barging by Avery.

"God damn it," Aaron muttered.

Avery leaned back against the Fore wall and watched Alice leave. "Don't let Father Klein hear you say that, sir. Taking the Almighty's name in vain is against a commandment."

"That's not what it means anyway."

"Sir?"

"Taking the Lord's name in vain. . . never mind. Is it the Infidel Friend?"

"You're the one who had to feed the bastard. Now he's asking for a bucket, and Staunten won't hear of him shitting in his room." Avery crossed his arms and looked out across the village. "Seems different from up here, sir."

Did this have to be an issue now?

Aaron massaged the bridge of his nose. "What, Staunten wants us to take him to the river?"

Avery shook his head. "He wants him out of his room. But other than that, the river, yeah."

"Can the infidel even make it that far?"

"If we're lucky, he'll bleed to death on the way."

"Like the other infidels will believe that," Aaron said. "Get some men together, good shots. We'll make him do his business in the center of the river room. We don't want him trying to escape."

"I'm not going anywhere with that man."

"Fine, I'll get the men. Will you go tell Alice I'm sorry?"

Avery grunted noncommittally and left the balcony.

Fuck.

Aaron followed Avery through the parlor room and passed him on his way down the stairs. Duncan was still on duty outside of Staunten's door.

"Go get the soldiers who helped bring this bastard here," Aaron ordered. "We're going for a walk."

"Can't we just take it up with Michael?" Duncan asked. "Get him a chamber pot or something?"

"Trust me, we'll end up doing the same thing. I'll take over here."

Duncan rushed out of the Fore. Aaron leaned back against the door which guarded the infidel's prison.

"We should never have brought him here," he muttered to himself.

"Damn right," he heard the Infidel Friend say from the other side of the door.

Martin felt like a new man. Bored, certainly, perhaps more bored than he had imagined possible, but bored and *full*. It was being bored and hungry that irked him. He hummed to himself as he sat down outside of his hovel and set his beach-sunset pot down between his legs. Julian was still dutifully delivering shares of devilwheat to him, and since Martin didn't mind living on spider guts and eggs, he was able to save every last grain.

The sinfruit, on the other hand, he ended up eating right away. He had meant to save it, he really had, but some temptations were just too much. Martin was okay with that, though, since he'd never been as rich as he was now.

Not in Hell at least.

Harpsborough was having another busy day. Some people had returned to the wilds, even though Father Klein assured them there were plenty of rations left. Martin understood their feelings of restlessness, and it was true, he supposed, that the devils were so few and far between that the villagers weren't very likely to die out there. Still, he couldn't imagine himself being *that* restless.

Some of the hunters were also out, but Aaron had them running on shorter routes. Martin wouldn't mind a short route so much, like the ones he used to do when Michael Baker was still Lead Hunter. He flexed the stub fingers on his regrowing hand. The stub thumb almost had a full nail growing out of it.

My fingers look like a baby's toes.

Moving those fingers hurt, but in a way that felt good to him. It reminded him of working out, sort of, or like the pain his gums had felt on Earth after flossing.

"Whatch'ya waitin' fer, hunter?" a girl said.

Martin would recognize Kylie's voice anywhere. "Julian, he's bringing me some wheat."

She smelled like the smoke from her kiln. Martin watched her shadow approach.

"Yeah, I was supposed to meet him yesterday for some pot supplies," she said. "Missed him, though. Say, that's a mighty fine looking pot you got there."

Martin grinned up at her from where he sat. "What?" He lifted the pot. "This old thing?"

He held it up between his hands. The grainy touch of the pottery felt abrasive on his new hand.

No calluses. I'll have to rebuild those.

"How's that baby arm coming along?" Kylie asked, as if reading his mind.

He placed the pot down between his legs. He didn't mind it when Kylie teased him about his hand for some reason. "I can give a thumbs up, if I felt like it. Or if you were Molly, I could flick you off."

Kylie's full smile split her face. That smile always sent a thrill down Martin's spine.

"Now why would you. . ." Kylie broke off mid-sentence, her head jerking towards the Fore.

The Infidel Friend walked through the door curtain.

Jesus.

Martin scrambled to get to his feet, bumping the pot as he did so. He grabbed at his pistol, forgetting in his fear that his fingers hadn't finished growing. Pain lanced up his arm and he sucked air in through his teeth. He fumbled for his gun with his left hand.

Duncan and Fitch walked out after the infidel, their rifles raised.

The infidel looked around Harpsborough. His nostrils flared, as if he was catching the scent of the village for the first time. Martin could see the disdain on his face.

So it stinks. So what? It's not always this bad in here.

The man had paused in front of the Fore. Duncan and Fitch came up behind him.

"Don't get too close," he heard Aaron say. "Stay back and keep your rifles trained on his head."

Martin didn't like the look of the man. He seemed too arrogant, and the way he regarded his guards was troubling.

Martin couldn't quite put his finger on why, though. It wasn't like the infidel viewed them as his own personal escort. It certainly wasn't that he acted like they weren't there. The man seemed to be paying careful attention to them when he wasn't checking out the village.

"Aaron," the Infidel Friend was saying.

The Lead Hunter exited the Fore. "What is it?"

"The one on my right, his safety is off, if it bothers you."

"It doesn't."

"Then the one on my left's safety is on. I assume there must be some protocol here."

"Shut the hell up." Aaron was visibly frustrated. "Duncan, safety your fucking weapon."

Martin realized what it was that bothered him about the infidel's manner.

He thinks he deserves the guards.

Martin nodded. That's what it was, to be sure. It was ridiculous to have two armed men watching over one prisoner so wounded that he could barely walk, but the Infidel Friend thought this was necessary. As if he, even while unarmed and after having nearly died such a short time ago, was that dangerous.

So much pride.

The despicable man started forward, and the people of Harpsborough, sprawled about the village as they were, scrambled to get out of his way.

Not me, he's going to have to walk around me.

He noticed Kylie was now behind his right shoulder. He took a deep breath, and made sure to keep himself interposed between her and the Infidel Friend.

He has no right to see a Citizen.

The infidel moved with a limp but managed to make it look almost like a strut.

He's staring at me.

Martin flinched away from his gaze and glanced down.

I don't need to be afraid of you.

He looked back up, trying to lock eyes with the infidel, but the man was already looking past him.

"Faster, infidel," Duncan said.

"Cris," the man responded.

"What?"

"My name is Cris."

Martin felt the blood tingling in his bad hand. His blood was up.

I won't let him think I'm some kind of pussy. I ain't moving out of his way.

"He doesn't care what your name is," Martin spoke up, "unless it's Speedy Fucking Gonzales. The man said faster."

The Infidel Friend turned towards him. The tingling in his

right hand gave way to a burning sensation. His left hand inched across his belly towards his pistol, which he had never managed to draw. He felt keenly the empty place between his shoulder blades where he strapped his rifle during hunts. He wished he had put it on before he left his hovel this morning.

The infidel did not seem angry, but curiously intense. The man's gaze was hypnotizing.

"I am wounded, soldier," the infidel said.

He can tell. He can see that I'm a hunter. He knows, somehow.

Martin nodded, not saying anything.

"Perhaps," the infidel went on, "if you want me to go faster, you would be so kind as to help me walk."

The request stunned Martin. He took a step back. The infidel was still staring, and he had no idea whether this was an honest plea for help, or some kind of challenge. He looked around. The whole village was watching.

Martin nodded, undid his pistol belt, and held it out to Kylie. "Hold this."

"Don't help him," she whispered in his ear.

"He's still a man, Kylie. God damned all of us, remember?"

Martin walked forward and took the infidel's right arm over his shoulder. Aaron seemed to be leading them towards the exit of Harpsborough.

It's silent.

No one was speaking. They were all just staring. Kara even forgot to get out of the way until the last second, when Massan had to reach out and grab her so that they didn't run her over.

They're judging me.

Some of those eyes were angry. How dare he help the enemy? Others seemed ambivalent, as if they had expected him to help. Others were nodding. Father Klein even gave him a grim smile.

Let them judge.

He saw Molly, but the girl's eyes were only for the Infidel Friend. She seemed sad and terrified all at the same time.

He could feel the infidel's warmth on his side. He was supporting the man with his right arm, which he had hooked under the Infidel Friend's shoulder and around his back since he couldn't grab with that hand. The friction of the cloth against his regrowing skin was killing him, but he refused to show it. He wasn't sure why he had to fight back tears. Were they coming from his own pain, or from the empathy he felt for the man he helped support?

Halfway to the entranceway, and he hasn't killed me yet.

He could feel the eyes of his friends on his back. He could sense their fear and hatred. It was the same fear and hatred that he had felt, but it was almost impossible to hate a man you were helping.

Maybe when the other infidels come and slaughter us all, he'll let them know that I was kind.

He saw the hunters at the entranceway. Their rifles were ready, but at least the weapons weren't pointed straight at them. Martin hoped Duncan had safetied his weapon. A stray round in his back would be a terrible way to die.

The weight of the Infidel Friend lessened.

"Thank you, soldier," the man said.

Martin nodded.

Without aid, the Infidel Friend walked through the entranceway, his two guards and Aaron in tow.

He's still a man.

Aaron followed his hunters and the infidel into the river room. The sounds of the water usually calmed him, but not now. Not with the devil himself standing before them.

"We give our water over there," Duncan said, pointing.

The bed the river flowed through was about ten feet wide and ten feet deep. The chamber's side walls closed over the top of the river, which Michael Baker swore meant that no devil would come floating downstream. Aaron had his doubts about that, but he'd never seen anything come out of these clear waters so far.

He wondered if the Infidel Friend knew if that were true or not.

"No," Aaron ordered. "You piss in the center of the room. We don't want you jumping in and trying to escape downriver. Not that it will do you any good, mind you. You'd drown long before the next chamber."

"So you say," the infidel said.

Does he know I'm lying? What is downstream from here?

The infidel let his pants drop away and walked, half nude, towards the river.

"Have you no shame?" Aaron was disgusted.

His initial instinct was to look away, but he could not. The man could escape if he wasn't careful. He looked to Duncan and Fitch. Both were still on their guard.

The Infidel Friend squatted down on his left knee, kicking his wounded right leg out straight, supporting himself with his right arm. He tucked his penis between his legs so that his piss would join with the river.

When he was finished, he sat up, leaned back and shat.

Aaron had never watched a human defecate before. It wasn't too dissimilar to watching a dog do it, except that the infidel was so brazen that Aaron figured a dog might actually have been more abashed.

Blood began to seep through the man's shirt at his

shoulder. Aaron looked at the wound on the infidel's leg. Someone, maybe the Infidel Friend himself, had re-bandaged it. The dressing didn't cover all of the burns, however. They were fresh, and sported pus-filled sores around their edges.

The man stood in that odd way of his, using his right arm as support to help get his right leg beneath him. "I would bathe, if you would be so kind as to allow me. My treatment, as fine as it has been, has given me no opportunity to lance my boils or wash off my dried blood."

"He could swim off," Fitch warned.

"You could shoot him," Aaron shot back.

"If it is of any help to you," the infidel said, "I could remain right by this edge. I will not stray from the stone."

Duncan shot Aaron a worried glance.

"Go ahead," Aaron said, and then turned to his men. "If he lets go of the edge, shoot him."

The Infidel Friend took off his shirt, again shamelessly. The wounds were horrid. Aaron shook his head, but kept his eyes on the man. Blood was seeping from the bullet hole in the infidel's shoulder. Purple bruises lined the man's torso. Aaron knew that kind of bruise, having had them himself. They were from taking a bullet while wearing body armor.

Aaron wandered over to the river to make sure he would have a good shot in case the infidel decided to try and swim for freedom.

The infidel did not enter the water immediately, but instead unwound his bandages; first the one on his shoulder, then the one around his chest, and finally the one about his leg.

Aaron, despite his best effort, did look away as the last of the man's wounds were revealed. The infidel had been bitten mid-thigh, and the jaws of whatever beast had gotten to him had ripped through the muscle there. The burns covered the bite thoroughly, and the skin had healed over the lacerations in loose, scabbing chunks.

Resolutely, Aaron looked back. "Was it a hound that got you?"

"There, yes," the man replied, pointing to his leg. "A big one, nearly five feet tall."

Duncan whistled.

"Rare to find beasts that big, even when the devils are thick," Aaron said.

"I'm a lucky man."

"You are," Aaron said. "You should have bled to death, it's a blessing that you got burnt in the same place."

"Dyitzu fire. And again, I'm a lucky man."

He dipped the bandages into the stream and kneaded them with his hands. The blood colored the water just slightly, before becoming invisible in the light current. He did the same with his pants and shirt before wringing them out and laying them across the stone floor to dry. Only then did he descend into the water.

Aaron wondered if it hurt him to feel the cold water on his wounds.

"It's Turi," the boy's voice came from the hallway behind him.

Aaron jumped. Duncan's gun went off, and water shot up from behind the infidel.

"Damn it," Aaron shouted. "Duncan, I told you to safety that rifle."

Duncan did so.

"Everything's fine," Aaron shouted. "You can come in."

"Martin told us you had the infidel here," Turi's voice was getting closer as he spoke, "and Ellen wanted to talk to him."

"What on Earth for?"

Turi and a young girl entered.

Ellen.

"I'm the one who saved him," Ellen said, "so I need to talk to him."

Turi began to whisper in her ear.

"She's new," Aaron explained to Duncan. "And keep your rifle trained on him."

Duncan, who had let his rifle dip, brought it back up.

The infidel had settled into the water and was keeping himself afloat by resting his crossed arms on the shore.

The bloody trails coming from his body took longer to disappear into the river than did those that came from his bandages. Aaron shook his head. Somehow it seemed wrong to imprison someone injured so badly.

If he were healthy, he'd have killed you already.

"I do remember you, miss," the infidel said to her. "I am fortunate that you were there to pull me from the river."

Though the words seemed sincere to Aaron, they struck her like a blow.

"I need to talk to him," the girl pleaded. "Can I speak with him in private?"

Duncan's eyes widened in alarm.

"No," Aaron said. "Say your peace, and leave quickly. You shouldn't have been let in here."

She rushed forward, pushing off of Turi and running to the infidel. She knelt on the bank next to him.

Duncan flipped off his safety.

"Jesus," Aaron shouted, grabbing Duncan's barrel and forcing it upwards.

"I'm sorry," Ellen was saying to the Infidel Friend, nearly in tears. "I didn't know. I went to get help. I didn't know they were going to kill you. I'm so sorry. I wouldn't have told them. I would have kept you secret."

Aaron grabbed her by the arm and pulled her away from the bank. "Jesus, girl! Don't you get it?"

She caught her balance as he let her go and looked at him. She rubbed at her shoulder where he'd grabbed her, looking like a beaten innocent.

"This man is a killer," Aaron said. "A killer. We aren't keeping him prisoner because we feel like it. We're keeping him because if we don't, he'll hurt people. People like you. You can't get that close to him. He can use you against us."

Aaron noticed Duncan's rifle was still pointed towards the girl.

"Duncan."

"Yes, sir?"

"Eyes and gun on the infidel."

Duncan snapped his rifle back in line.

"There's a story, miss," the infidel said, "about a scorpion and a turtle. Have you heard it?"

Turi stepped back, his mouth open.

What? Why is he surprised?

Ellen shook her head.

"The scorpion comes to the turtle and says, 'Can you take me across the river.' The turtle says, 'No, why would I? You'll sting me.' 'Of course I won't,' says the scorpion, 'If I do we'll both drown.' Satisfied, the turtle carries the scorpion across the river. Midway through, the scorpion stings the turtle. The turtle feels its body numb as the poison enters its blood, and asks, 'Why? Why would you kill us both?' The scorpion replies, 'It's my nature.'"

"Is it?" Ellen asked. "Is it your nature?"

"Not mine."

The Infidel Friend pulled himself out of the water and came to his feet. Ellen gasped, and stepped back.

"You're beautiful," she said.

Damn, I forgot.

Even in the presence of a lady, the man showed no shame.

"Ellen," Aaron told her, "you should avert your eyes."

She blushed and did so.

Aaron turned back to the Infidel Friend. "Get your clothes on."

"They're wet," the infidel pointed out.

"Now."

The Infidel Friend wrapped his bandages with laborious care, tying them off expertly with his teeth as if he had done this a thousand times before.

"Where'd you hear that story?" Arturus asked.

"Why, have you heard it?" the prisoner asked as he gingerly pulled on his pants.

"No." There was a catch in the boy's voice.

"You want to know if the Infidel told it to me, don't you, boy? You wonder if I'm just quoting some ancient Sanskrit tablet, or if it's one of the stories from the book of Gehennic Law."

"Is it?"

"No, I saw it on an episode of *Star Trek*."

Ellen burst out laughing.

"We go now." Aaron said, not amused.

Michael Baker ascended the church steps. He felt as if he was carrying a pack full of lead. He tugged at the huge church door, which opened easily on greased hinges.

Dyitzu fat. The doors to the house of God are greased with the fat of devils.

He walked into the church.

Father Klein was sitting in one of the pews.

"Are you always praying?" Michael asked.

Klein stirred and stood. "No, I just sleep with my hands like that," he said, cracking a smile, "makes me look more pious."

Michael snorted. "Funny."

"So, First Citizen, leader of Harpsborough and protector of her people, it has been some time since we have talked, just the two of us."

"I came for advice," Michael admitted. "I need to know what to do with the Infidel Friend."

"You've already spoken with Mancini about this?"

Michael nodded and took a seat on the front pew.

Father Klein sat back down beside him. "And what did he say?"

"Kill him."

"Sounds like Mancini. Well, you wouldn't be here if you had no doubts about doing so."

Michael shook his head and looked up at the pillars. One of the church's crosses cast its shadow upon him, covering his face as he looked up. "Tell me, Father, what would you do?"

"Mercy is a beautiful thing, Mike. The way we treat our prisoners speaks volumes about us. Remember though, that mercy is by definition the suspension of justice. It would not be just of us to let him go that he might terrorize or kill other people."

"Does it even matter? I mean, we're all damned anyway."

"That's an excuse and you know it. We have all been good at times, not because we wanted to, but because we knew God was watching. God could tell, Mike. That's why we're here. Maybe it's nothing. Maybe it's just a spit in the cosmic bucket, but I want to be a good man. I may not be able to be redeemed in Hell, but I want to try. Part of that trying is minimizing suffering. The sooner we die here, the sooner we suffer. So yes, it matters."

"So he dies?"

"I can't give you a good answer, Mike. Maybe this one's different than the rest of the Infidel Friend, but it's a gamble you take if you set him free. I wish we could afford to keep him locked up forever somewhere. Somewhere where he couldn't hurt anyone.

"Now this shouldn't change your decision, and I'm sure Davel told you this, but I feel I must too. If you kill one, the rest may come. Our old village was taken, Mike, after we left the Carrion, and you and the others had gone upriver to live. It was taken by three people, they slaughtered almost the entire village. Just three Infidel Friend."

"There may not be any others."

Father Klein closed his eyes, and dug at his eyes with his fingers. "Remember Benson?"

"Yeah," Mike answered, "Corpsedust. . ."

"I know you thought that it was someone in the Fore, maybe in conjunction with someone in the village. Someone intent on stealing from you, perhaps. But that isn't the only possibility, Mike. Even the Infidel Friend would have a hard time attacking this place. There's only one entrance. It would be hard to break through. They'd need a distraction."

Mike leaned back in the pew and looked up to the large cross on the far wall. "I hadn't thought of that. But that was before we found the infidel."

"You're assuming he wasn't here to scout us out. They might be coming anyway, Mike, no matter what you do."

The infidel moved more quickly, enlivened, perhaps, by his brief immersion in the river. Aaron could hear the ruckus just a few turns away from the entryway chamber. The buzz of the village had an anxious tone.

The guards had worried expressions on their faces.

"Johnny," Aaron said to one of the hunters. "What's going on?"

"Julian is missing."

Damn.

Aaron drew his pistol and leveled it at the infidel. "Are your people responsible for this?"

"Can't be." The infidel shook his head. "I'll not say others aren't coming, but they aren't here yet."

Can I trust anything he says?

"You're in this village too, now," Aaron told him. "If we starve, you starve."

"I swear it, on the Infidel himself. I came this far south to check on the settling. I was scouting on my own."

Jesus.

"Turi," Aaron asked, "do you know if Galen's home?"

"He should be."

"Good, we're going to need his help."

— 25 —

Arturus found it odd to see Aaron sitting in their home. He felt that the Lead Hunter's presence signified something important. Rick had pulled up an extra barrel for Aaron to sit on and was nice enough to provide everyone with wooden cups—whose water, of course, Arturus had been asked to fetch. He had been in such a hurry to hear the conversation that he had almost pulled himself into the Thames while he was filling the urn. He was still panting a little bit, even now, which seemed unbecoming at the dinner table. Fortunately, none of the adults seemed to notice or care.

"How much food does Julian pull in for you?" Rick was asking.

"That gets right to it, doesn't it?" Aaron said. "It's true, we are worried about the food. Michael's orders to me are that this mission can be finished without Julian, but it can't be finished without finding his devilwheat cache. There's no urgency for the food since Harpsborough is fat on spider eggs right now, and I didn't jog all the way here because I thought the devilwheat was going to go somewhere. I'm after Julian. I couldn't give a rat's ass about anything else right now, no matter what Michael ordered me to do."

Arturus watched as Rick nodded and drank deeply from his cup.

The still man, he was the one who traded us these cups.

"No shame in those orders," Galen said. "Your people need to eat. That's Michael's responsibility."

Aaron nodded. "This mission won't stop until we find where he was getting his devilwheat, that's true. But Galen, I'm not asking your help for that. I want your help finding the boy. We'll be looking for the wheat, sure, but only because we think that'll help find Julian."

Arturus chewed on his lip. He didn't like the idea that Julian wasn't more important than the food he provided. The idea of a rescue sounded so much more noble than a hunt for resources.

Because you're fed. Because you're not like those villagers in Harpsborough who will die if this devilwheat isn't found.

"It's going to be tough, though," Aaron said, gazing at the curious machinery connected to the battery.

"How long has he been missing?" Rick asked.

"Maybe two days, by now. Things have been so busy in the village with the spider food that we didn't really notice. But that's not why I say it's going to be tough."

"Why then?" Arturus broke in.

He almost clapped his hands over his mouth. This wasn't his conversation to speak in. He was an outsider, a child lucky enough to overhear important information at his parents' table. Aaron, however, answered his question without a pause.

"We've looked for it before, while Julian was in the village. Michael Baker wanted me to do it. It wasn't a very complete search, but we tried it a couple times. Didn't get any leads. You can't go telling anyone in the village this. The villagers wouldn't like to hear that the Fore wants to know where everyone's stashes are. Even a lot of the Citizens don't know."

"But you know," Galen stated, leaning his elbows on the table.

"Of course, I was the one who went looking. We weren't going to take any of it away from him. He pretty much taxes himself by giving everything to the Citizens for cheap. It's just that he brings in so much food that Michael felt we had to know. Particularly now that the devils have all but abandoned this place."

"I'll help you. How big is the boy's range? Do you know?"

Aaron nodded. "It's on the Harpsborough side of the Kingsriver, east of the road fork. I know almost exactly where he goes. I followed him as far as the fork once, and he came back within a couple of hours. Area's small but tricky. Lots of tall and short rooms full of stone blocks. Lots of uneven ceilings. Plenty of places where there could be hidden passages that go up or down."

Galen pushed his cheek out with his tongue and used his thumb to scratch that part of his beard. "I know the place."

"So you'll help us?" Aaron asked.

"Yeah. I'll want to bring Turi, though."

Arturus almost choked on his water. Carefully, he placed the cup down and cleared his throat. "I'd love to help."

Do I want to help? I could get shot. This is a job for hunters, not little boys.

Aaron raised his eyebrows.

"Boy's got a keen eye," Galen said. "And he's just small enough that he'll be able to scoot down tight passages that we'd have trouble with."

Aaron nodded in agreement.

Galen thinks I should go.

The thought filled him with pride.

"Wait outside," Galen told Aaron. "Turi and I will gather our things."

Aaron got up and walked out of the room.

But what if I do get shot? What if I make too much noise and bring the devils down on us. Galen won't ever let me do this again. He might not let me go to Harpsborough.

"Your rifle clean?" Rick asked Arturus.

"Of course it is," Galen answered for him. "Turi's old enough to keep his rifle clean."

I could say no. I could say I'm not ready. Galen wouldn't call me a coward.

But he'd be disappointed, Arturus knew. And there were other reasons he wanted to go besides just being an adult.

Julian's one of us.

They met Aaron's hunters at the fork. He had chosen five of his favorite men for the rescue. Duncan and Fitch were there, who Arturus knew had become famous lately from the spider expedition, along with Avery and Johnny Huang. Arturus recognized the face of the other guard, but didn't know his name. He wondered if he should have.

"Why's the kid coming?" Avery asked within seconds of Arturus' entrance.

"He's got good eyes," Aaron said.

"It's not like there's any devils around, Avery." The fifth guard's voice was strangely familiar to him.

Patrick. Patrick is his name. Molly used to say his voice was sexy.

"Through there?" Galen asked, pointing down the fork marked with a purple stone.

The thought of heading near the Carrion sent Arturus' heart rushing.

"Nope, this way." Aaron motioned down the other corridor.

Arturus breathed a silent sigh of relief.

"Keep your eyes peeled," Aaron went on. "We're going to break up into two groups, so keep your weapons safetied. That means you too, Duncan."

"Funny."

"He's been missing for two days or so. We're probably not going to find him alive. Hopefully we will. Maybe he just took a vacation, I don't know. Julian's a little guy, so check the corners of the ceilings and the floor. I've been through here a few times myself, and I've never seen any devilwheat stash. Not even a little one, let alone one big enough to feed us. My guess is he found a chute which leads up or down. Michael says we had better find it before the spider food runs out, or he won't have a vote about our different food rations. Maybe we can convince him that we should get ten percent of Julian's stash rather than the Fore."

"Good," Patrick said. "If that's true, I'll shoot the little fucker on sight."

Arturus disliked him already. He looked towards Galen, but the warrior didn't seem to care.

Not that I'd be able to tell if he did.

"Galen, myself, Patrick and Avery will check on the far side. Duncan, Fitch, Johnny, and Turi, check near Harpsborough. Two shots if you find him or the wheat. Anything more or less, and we'll assume you need some help. And remember, safeties on."

Aaron stared Duncan down.

"Who'd care if I fucked up and shot an infidel?" Duncan asked. "Huh? Who'd care?"

"If I tell you to do something, I expect you to do it."

"And if you were Michael Baker, I'd expect I'd do it, too."

Fitch sucked air through his teeth. Avery crossed his arms.

"Look—" Avery began.

"And, if I were Michael Baker," Aaron responded over Avery, "I'd have the kid already home, found a second store of devilwheat, and fucked Kylie twice by now." The men laughed at that. "So unfortunately we're going to have to get a bit sweaty. You good?"

Duncan nodded. "I'm good."

Aaron knows what he's doing.

But then he thought of Aaron and Alice, spending time together. He imagined them kissing. Usually he felt for Alice in his chest. Now he felt for her in his throat.

Jealousy.

"Jealousy is God's sin. Pride, the Devil's," Galen had told him. "We're humans, so we're lucky enough to have both."

They divided into their separate groups of four and began their search.

Huang was the quietest as they marched through the endless winding corridors, earning Arturus' respect immediately.

"Should we call out for him?" Arturus asked the group.

"No, boy," Fitch said.

"There's a reason Julian didn't come back," Duncan whispered, "and we have no idea what that was. Maybe he's lost. Maybe he broke his leg. But maybe something got him. You know, an Icanitzu, a Minotaur, maybe even a Nephilim. You want to call those things down on our heads?"

Arturus shook his head.

Soon they paused at Duncan's direction. The room they stopped in was red, dim, and had uneven brick walls interspersed with jutting formations of natural rock.

"Let's check this place," Duncan said. "Wouldn't be surprised to find a tunnel here."

Arturus ran his fingers along the stone as he searched the uneven wall. He noticed Huang standing next to him.

"How do I say your name?" he asked the hunter.

Arturus' hand glowed, colored with a fiendish cast as he ran it over the red stone. He looked for disruptions in the light. This was the best way, Galen had taught him, to search for passages in illuminated rock.

"Johnny," the man answered.

Arturus laughed as softly as he could. "Not that name."

"Whowang."

"But that's not how everyone else says it."

Johnny shrugged. "They mistook me for my cousin."

"Did not."

"Sure did. His name was Johnny Wang. It's just they couldn't tell because we all look alike."

Arturus laughed again.

"God made everyone unique and special, Turi. He just got tired when he got to China."

"Quiet," Fitch ordered.

"Found something," Duncan reported.

He had climbed up nearly to the ceiling on one of the sections of natural rock. The right half of his face was lit up from the light of the wall.

"Looks like someone can crawl through here."

At first it was hard to see the small opening, but as Arturus neared it and held a hand up before his eyes to block out the glare of the red rock, he could see the passageway. It was a small one. A dyitzu would have to struggle to fit in there.

"Can you check it out, Turi?" Johnny asked.

I have to be brave.

Duncan and Fitch helped him climb up the stone.

It's tighter than I thought.

He looked into the hole. The red light of the stone slowly faded away as the passage continued. He passed his pack back to Johnny, and after eyeballing the passageway a little more, handed his rifle to the hunter as well.

Arturus stood on Fitch's back, drew his pistol, and crawled in.

"I may need a torch," he said back over his shoulder.

His voice sounded muffled in the passageway.

"Let us know," Fitch answered, his head framed by the square entrance. "I've got a couple. I'll pass one to you."

The crawlway was so small that Arturus found it difficult to use his legs to propel himself forward. His knees simply could not bend far enough. His pants were pulled tight by the friction, restricting his movement. The air was warm, and seemed empty. He couldn't get enough of it.

He placed his pistol down in front of him and started pushing it ahead of himself.

Is it getting tighter?

Johnny's voice echoed down the crawlway, but it was too soft for Arturus to make out. He couldn't turn his head back to look. He seemed to have been talking to Duncan or Fitch.

What if they're attacked?

He was struck suddenly by a fear of them dying. Of a dyitzu crawling after him down the corridor. Of its clawed hands grabbing at his feet. Of its mouth tearing at his Achilles tendon.

Could I point the gun back in time?

Arturus tried to figure out how he could fire behind himself. Perhaps he could get his arm back from out in front of him, and then shoot along his leg down the corridor. He tried to wiggle his arm towards his hip, but his elbow kept running into the stone. Finally, he pinned his elbow against the corner and squeezed his arm beneath his body.

He issued a sigh of relief. It was possible. He tried to look behind himself, but bumped his head against the rock.

I won't be able to aim.

He was sweating badly, he realized, and his breathing was heavy. He tried to move forward, but with his arm now caught against the stone, he couldn't budge. He tried to move back. No luck.

I'm stuck.

His heart beat faster. He could feel his blood pounding in his ears. He could smell his own warm breath as he was forced to breathe it in again.

Help me.

He thought about shouting. About how long it might take for them to try and excavate him out of so much stone. Would his air last long enough?

This reminded him suddenly of his wrestling sessions with Galen. His arm was trapped, and he was stuck in a tight place under immense pressure.

"Stay calm," Galen would assure him. "Assess the damage you are taking. Find a plan. Seize any opportunity. Little advantages can turn into big ones if you fight hard enough."

My arm.

He flattened his hand and moved it back up along his body, propping his elbow in the same corner he had used before. When his hand was in front of his face, he was able to corkscrew his arm forward again.

He could breathe.

He could move.

I can do this. Julian needs me.

He crawled farther forward. Ahead the tunnel got dimmer, but using a torch would be useless, he realized. First of all, he'd have to crawl all the way out just to get the torch in front of himself. Secondly, even if he did all that, the torch would burn up all of his air in a hurry should he run into a dead end.

Just a few feet in front of him, hardly visible in the faint light, was a bend. The crawlway took a ninety degree turn to the right. He closed his eyes for a moment and felt the stone with his fingers.

He remembered a way that Galen had taught him to turn around at such a bend.

It won't work here. Not enough room.

He took the turn slowly, having to wriggle his body to squeeze through. The stone was cooler here, and he couldn't see at all. His gun hit a wall.

"Oh thank God," he muttered.

The passageway dead ended. He inspected the dead end carefully to make sure that this wasn't a false wall.

If it was, he figured, it was a damn impressive one.

And now I have to go back.

Arturus emerged, feet first, hot and sweaty, his hands shaking from spent adrenaline, his chest heaving, out of the crawlway.

"You alright?" Johnny Huang asked, lifting Arturus to his feet.

Arturus nodded, his vision swimming.

"Dead end," he reported between breaths.

Fitch looked down it, and shook his head. "Man, imagine if you were running from the devils and tried to hide down that passage. You'd dead end, and they'd tear you to pieces."

Duncan and Johnny nodded.

"Simon died that way," Duncan reported. "His body and face were fine, but they'd torn all the flesh off his legs."

There were more passages. Many more. Most were not as small, but a few were. In the larger tunnels, one of the hunters would travel along with him. It usually ended up being Johnny. Arturus didn't mind this. He actually preferred the man's company.

Finding the tunnels was a difficult task in and of itself, and Arturus found himself wondering how many passages they were missing between the ones that they found.

No one said this was going to be easy.

"Hey." Duncan's voice was a harsh whisper.

As careless as the footfalls of the hunters could be, they knew how to keep quiet after a warning.

Duncan's figure was a dull red, lit only by the light from another tunnel. The hunter's dim hand beckoned them forward. Beyond Duncan there was only blackness. Arturus feared that he might be standing on the edge of a cliff.

Duncan stepped forward into the dark, fading away into the blackness. Fitch followed him, unslinging his rifle.

"Torch please." Duncan's voice came from the emptiness beyond.

Fitch complied, kneeling at the edge of the light, and pulled out a woodstone torch. It had a thin wrapping of cloth along the top, marking it as one of Copperfield's.

Fitch's lighter had long since run out of butane, so it took him a while to get a spark to catch.

The torch caught fire in a rush, and the black room beyond was suddenly alight.

"There," Duncan said, "on the wall."

The wall itself was made of Hellstone, so Arturus was unsure as to why the chamber was so dark. Usually light flowed through hellstone rather well, but this oddity was not what had captured Duncan's attention. Deep grooves had been cut into the stone at almost head height.

"Is that hound sign?" asked Johnny Huang.

The four of them gathered around the grooves.

"Can't be, too tall." Duncan said.

"No, it is." Fitch said. "It's just a really big fucking hound."

Duncan shook his head. "Impossible. It would be *huge.* It would have left deeper marks."

"It did," Arturus said, touching the stone. "Look at the spurs in the grain here, you can see where the stone is healing over. This sign is very old. Maybe ten or eleven years."

Johnny nodded. "Boy's no fool."

Arturus smiled.

"The Infidel Friend said he was bit by one that big," Duncan said. "I didn't believe him though."

They followed the grooves along the wall, none of them willing to stray too far from the light.

"I'll hold the torch in the middle," Fitch said, stepping into the center of the room. "That way you can spread out."

They found hound sign along the walls.

"It could be Beast," Fitch said.

"Who's that?" Arturus asked.

"We used to see him around Harpsborough when Mike was still Lead Hunter. Biggest hound you've ever seen. Klein said it followed the founders here. Mike says he shot it about three times. They thought they killed it once, but no one was sure. No one's seen him since. Well, no one I believe at any rate. Martin says he sees him every couple of months."

These are very old.

Arturus traced the marks with his fingers. He could feel the small spurs of stone shooting up from the wounds. Hounds' teeth never stopped growing, so they would grind them down against stone. After months of doing this they would create these grooves. The younger ones preferred woodstone.

"These could be his, then," Arturus said.

"Maybe he came back," Duncan wondered aloud. "Maybe he got Julian."

"If so, we should see his blood," Fitch was saying.

Arturus looked down one of the hallways.

This is it.

Hounds would dig out sleeping holes for themselves in woodstone. You could always find their chamber because they wouldn't mark the walls leading up to it.

But there's no woodstone here.

The passage also dead ended.

"Bring the torch," Arturus called.

Fitch walked over his way.

Towards the back was a burrow, cut straight into the hellstone.

"Damn," Duncan said as he walked up behind them, "that was one tough hound. A burrow in rock? Good eye, boy."

The heat from the torch was uncomfortably close to Arturus' face. He moved in to inspect the burrow. Its edges had healed in quite a bit, making the burrow smaller now than it must have once been. There was a blanket there, and four backpacks. He opened one, and found it to be full of devilwheat.

Fitch whistled. "Well, he *was* here. Any blood?"

Arturus shook his head. "It looks like he slept here sometimes. Maybe to get away from the village."

"He may have had more than one place like this," Fitch said. "We'll keep our eyes sharp. He's more likely to be around one of these hideaways."

Ellen uncrossed her legs and sat like a man. She leaned forward and let her arms fall by her crotch. She looked across the table to where the discarded mold of Arturus' knight lay.

"How can you stand this?" she asked Rick.

Rick shrugged, and looked up from his whittling work. "I whittle."

"What are you making?"

"A type of flute."

"Why?"

"To give you something to do while you wait and worry."

"I've never been much good at musical instruments. You

may regret it."

Rick laughed and lay his knife down amidst the excess woodstone. "I might. But I'm sure if you practice long enough you will get very good at it."

"Isn't it dangerous, though, making so much noise?"

"Yes, it is indeed. You shouldn't practice unless you are here."

"When I'm good, I'm going to learn to play the saddest song."

Rick nodded.

She looked at his serious face, which was frowning. "And when I play it, you're going to look exactly like you do now."

"It's something, isn't it," Rick said. "To be able to express your emotions. I always have this feeling, right here." He pointed to his stomach. "A tightness. I'm used to worrying for Galen. He's gone often. But now I feel for Turi, too. I think I would like to play a song as well. Maybe feeling it will get it out of my damn belly."

"Do you play?"

"Yeah. I was a music teacher, in the old world. I taught band."

"I bet you were wonderful at it."

"I was a monster!"

"No!"

"I was indeed. I would work those kids so hard. I thought that was the way to teach them, you know."

"You don't seem that way at all now."

He picked up the unfinished flute and pointed it at her. "I haven't started to teach you yet. Just you wait."

Ellen giggled. "You'll be nice. I know."

"You're right, I teach differently now."

"You've taught people in Hell?"

"Turi."

"Why do you teach differently?"

"Galen. Galen changes the way you do lots of things. He asked me to teach Turi an instrument, because he thinks that's very important. I was teaching Turi how I always had. Showed him how to read music, chastised him for even the slightest errors. He became an excellent machine."

"And then?"

"Well, I was teaching him to play music in the same way that Galen was teaching him to wrestle and to hunt. Turi was getting very stressed. Galen suggested I change how I taught him. I told him that I knew what I was doing, thank you very much, and that if he wanted Turi to learn how to play anything worth a damn, this was the way to do it. Then I went too far."

"Oh?"

"Yeah. Then I told him he could teach Turi to play his

damn self."

Ellen leaned forward over the table. "What did Galen do?"

"He took over Turi's lessons. He asked Turi to write him a song."

"That's it?"

"I was horribly embarrassed. Turi had no ability to write anything at all. He could play the music I had written down for him as well as a record. He knew chord progressions and enough theory to make him a prodigy in the old world, but he couldn't write a damn thing. I told Galen that was something that couldn't be taught.

"I feel bad about that sometimes. Not just for Turi, but for all the children I ever taught. For every child that was ever taught that way. I wonder why we figured it was right method? Maybe it came from military training, or something. Passed down from some weird totalitarian past.

"Anyway, Galen agreed to take over the lessons. He just told Arturus to go to his room and write him a song. Turi would do this for the entire time that he would have normally practiced. He had all this emotion, all this passion pent up from Galen's teachings, the boy was just dying to release it. That's when I learned that Turi was an artist. I was destroying that in him. I'd destroyed that in so many people. From that moment on, Turi wanted to play. He learned little tricks, and some bad habits too, mind you, but little things I had never taught him. And they were his. All this time, I'd been teaching music, without having the first God damned clue of what music was about."

"So can Turi still play?"

"Of course. And make sure that's a lesson to you. Never challenge Galen."

"Oh, I would never be that stupid."

She could almost see the sad feeling return to Rick. She knew what he meant about it being in his stomach. About waiting for someone to return. "I think I love your son."

"I know you do, sweetheart. We all do."

"He doesn't love me. He wants Alice."

"Boys are dumb sometimes. He may never turn around, or he might. It's hard to say."

"The saddest song."

The worst of the crawlways was one made of blue crystal. It tore Arturus' shirt in a couple of places and gave him cuts all along his arms. That passage had been particularly complicated. Each crawlway seemed different, but they all had one thing in common.

They led nowhere.

The main passageways had the same problem. They would

dead end at random places, usually into Carrion barriers. At first Turi feared running into those barriers, but they were cooler, and he had to admit that the air was refreshing. Even Fitch got turned around, leading them into the same barrier a few times. After the third time, Duncan demanded they take a break and sat down on the purple stone marker.

Fitch tossed his pack next to the barrier and leaned against the wall. Johnny collapsed into a corner.

"This is the worst area Julian could have got lost in," Fitch said.

"At least it's small," Duncan said, pulling out some devilwheat meal.

The hunter poured the meal into the cap of his canteen and then mixed water into it. He swirled it around in his hand for a moment and then drank it. The other hunters followed suit.

Arturus pulled out some smoked dyitzu. The meat was tough, but he enjoyed it a hell of a lot more than he would have enjoyed the devilwheat meal.

"That's some fine looking jerky you got there," Johnny remarked rather suggestively.

Arturus smiled and shared it with the hunters.

"Whew. Anything but spider guts," Fitch said. "Amazing how quickly you can get sick of that shit."

"I started off being sick of it," Johnny said. "You guys are just catching up."

"Why?" Arturus asked him.

"Michael's not the first one to kill a giant spider," Johnny answered. "I was swallowed by one before I made it to Harpsborough. I was so hungry, I ate my way out."

Arturus fought to keep his laugh quiet.

"No one thinks you're funny, Johnny." Fitch said.

"Turi does."

They ate some more in silence. Arturus' legs began to cramp, so he stood up and stretched.

Duncan must have felt similarly, because he began pacing. "I don't know where this kid could be. We've been down all these passages."

Fitch just shrugged his shoulders.

"He's got to be up or down a level," Duncan said.

Johnny's head followed the pacing hunter. "Thank God we're right up next to the Carrion. Otherwise we'd have a lot more to search."

Duncan ignored him. "He's got to be somewhere. It didn't feel like we were missing any big. . ." He trailed off.

Fitch put a finger to his lips. "Did you hear that?"

Arturus cocked his head to the side and listened. He heard voices.

Aaron. That's Aaron's voice.

"Turi," he announced himself.

"Galen."

Galen, Aaron, Avery and Patrick came around the bend.

"You find anything?" Aaron asked.

Fitch nodded. "We didn't find any leads, but we did find a few packs of devilwheat Julian had left in an old hound burrow. We can take 'em back to town when we're done, maybe get a hunter's lot of the wheat. We figured Julian was sleeping there. The burrow was dug into the hellstone, just so you know."

"That would be a dangerous hound," Galen said. "Any sign of it?"

"No. Must have left years ago. No blood either, so we don't think it got Julian. We'll take you there."

Fitch moved to stand up but stopped when Aaron raised his hand.

"In a minute," Aaron said. "We haven't rested yet. We might as well join you."

Arturus watched the hunters fan out. He dropped down to his haunches while Galen sat beside him.

"How are you holding up?" his father asked.

"Well, sir."

"Did you find anything else? Anything in any of the passages?"

Turi shook his head. He watched Aaron pull out a canteen and mix in his own devilwheat meal.

Alice likes him more than me.

"Some of them were very small." Galen said.

"I almost got stuck," Arturus admitted.

"Don't do it. Would be hard to get you out. You keeping up with the hunters?"

It was an odd question. The hunters from Harpsborough were fairly noisy, and their sense of direction seemed poor.

I was born here. And Galen's been teaching me. If they had been born here, and Galen had taught them, they'd be as good as me. They're better fighters, I know.

"Yes, sir."

But I'm a better scout!

"You look a bit cut up."

"The crystal passage. Very sharp."

Galen grunted.

"Where could he be?" Arturus asked, surprised to hear the concern in his own voice. "We can't find a trace."

Galen shrugged and nodded towards Aaron.

Arturus listened in on the Lead Hunter's conversation with Duncan.

"Nothing. Absolutely nothing. I'm not sure how many passageways we've got left."

"We should go home," Duncan said, "maybe try another day."

"Not for some time yet," Aaron said. "And it wouldn't help us anyway. You know Mike wants us in these tunnels until we find that devilwheat store."

"But how? He had so much wheat. How could we not find it?"

"Probably—"

"Shh!" Galen quieted them harshly.

The conversation died away, and Arturus tried to listen to what Galen may have heard. Galen could pick out one noise from another with an ease that amazed him, but if all was quiet, Arturus knew he could hear the fainter sounds.

He heard Johnny shifting from foot to foot. He heard one of Avery's knuckles crack as the man gripped his holstered pistol. Arturus even heard his own breathing, which he struggled to keep soft.

Nothing.

Galen heard it. Maybe it's gone, or maybe I'm just listening to the wrong thing.

He tried to ignore the hunters. To ignore himself. He cocked his head to one side and closed his eyes.

A girl's voice? Am I imagining it?

It was so faint that Arturus had no idea if the voice was real, or if it was just the musings of his own mind. Whenever he tried to concentrate on her tone, the sound seemed to disappear. Even worse, at times it seemed to meld into whatever sound he thought it might become. If he imagined the pitch higher, it would become higher. If he thought it might be lower, it became lower.

Is she singing?

He tried his best to clear his mind, to not guess what her next sound would be. He tried to listen without expectation. It was one of the hardest things he had ever attempted to do in his life.

Galen stood slowly, so slowly, as if he were afraid that any noise would scare the sound away. He waved them back. As quietly and as quickly as he dared, Arturus obeyed. Step by step, he made his way back down the corridor.

He could hear her voice clearly now, a long, lonely single note.

The hunters followed suit, their eyes fixed on Galen's statue still figure. With the greatest of care they retreated down the corridor, moving past Arturus. Galen raised a hand and stopped them. He knelt, as quietly and as slowly as he had stood, and opened his pack. Arturus watched Galen while the man reached in and pulled out a small piece of folded cloth. He unfolded it and produced a single pure white feather.

Galen stood again and moved next to the barrier.

He held the feather in the air, stepping to one side. Gingerly, he let the feather go. At first it descended gently, swaying back and forth in the still air—but then it took flight, swirling about in the corridor, dancing.

Wind.

Arturus watched, hypnotized with the rest of the hunters, as the feather finally alighted to the floor.

Her voice is the wind.

Arturus and the hunters came forward quickly. Galen ran his fingers along the barrier, grasping at the stones, the feather lying abandoned on the floor. He found the passageway near the base of the barrier. A rock there, which seemed as secure as the rest, gave some when Galen pulled on it. It was shaped like a flagstone, large but flat. Galen kept tugging, and the rock came out from the barrier like a door, hinged on one side. Now that Arturus knew what to look for, he could see where it had scraped along the floor. Another hint was on the purple marker stone. The flagstone had run into it several times, and was marked with an indentation where it had collided with the other rock's corner.

Behind the flagstone was another crawlway, but this one was hollowed out not by Hell's architect, but by the careful and diligent work of a human being. The barrier had been breached.

"He wouldn't have," Aaron said aloud.

"He did," Galen whispered. "Julian found a way into the Carrion."

— 26 —

"God damn!" Michael lost his temper.

He swung his arms about, scattering chess pieces across the table. Some bounced off of the carpet and onto the floor. Aaron stepped back. Even when hunting in the wilds, he had never seen Michael lose his temper.

"Did he have any idea how much effort it took to build those walls?" Michael asked, "How many men we lost?"

Aaron looked behind him towards the exit. He didn't like the prospect of being alone with this man. Then his stomach growled. "We need the food, sir. Julian fed almost one hundred of our people. Without it, you'll have to change things. A lot."

"Fuck food. Can't you keep your head on straight for a second? Food is nothing, Aaron. Nothing. Do you understand me? You weren't here when Pyle led the demons to us. You weren't with us before we fled the Carrion and settled down. We used to scurry from room to room like roaches. When the Minotaur came we had to leave. There was no village, you get me? No home. You never lived with that kind of fear over your head."

Aaron waited for the man to calm. Michael's eyes were wide, his nostrils flared. His breath came in heavy gasps. He swung out again as his rage boiled over, knocking the blankets off of one of the light orbs. Rarely were all the blankets removed. The light was harsh, so bright that Aaron had to shy away from it. He could see every pore in the First Citizen's face.

Molly had warned him that Baker got like this. She said that he had never really recovered from the Minotaur, from when he'd been gored by the Kingsriver. She had claimed that he came too close to death. That he had seen a bit of the world beyond and that it had lodged in his soul.

She also said that he would go mad and beat her. But who the hell would listen to Molly? The Michael Baker he had known would never do such a thing, but who knew what the man in front of him now was capable of.

"Aaron. Aaron," the First Citizen was mumbling.

Post Trauma. Like a soldier having returned from one of the old world's wars.

"Michael. No devils have come through. Julian went through that door regularly for the last year."

"This isn't how Hell is supposed to be. You get me? We're not supposed to be holed up all safe and sound behind these stone walls. We built this village to hide from our damnation, Aaron. We built it because we couldn't stand Hell. Before this, before we walled off the Carrion, it really *was* Hell. Your every moment was filled with fear. We can't go back to that. I know Harpsborough seems safe to you. Maybe it is. But you have no idea what's in that place. You have no idea what devils we left alive behind those walls."

He doesn't want us to go through.

"You're right about one thing, sir," Aaron said. "This is Hell. We are damned, and there's no way around it. Julian tapped a resource that was feeding nearly one in five people in Harpsborough. Shit's different now. It's a different Hell than the one you knew. We need to go in there, sir. We've got to find that devilwheat. You've got everyone in this place riding on your shoulders, so you better fucking face this."

Michael picked up some of the blankets and covered the orb. The light dimmed to normal. "Send in Mancini." He collapsed into his chair. "I'll consider what you said. Send him in."

Michael took the steps to the church three at a time. He ripped open the right of the church's huge double doors and entered. He stopped between the back pews, his feet spread apart, his hands clenched into fists at his sides.

Father Klein looked up from where he sat near the front of the church. The three women he had been speaking to were staring at the First Citizen.

"I need to talk to you," Michael said.

Klein stood. The women didn't move.

"Alone," Michael clarified.

"Go on," Klein told the women. "We'll speak of this later."

Michael did not move until the last woman left and then it was only to slam the door. The thud of woodstone on hellstone echoed through the church.

"You know why I'm here?" Michael all but shouted.

Father Klein nodded and walked towards the pulpit. He had a stone chalice in his hands. The man had been giving communion, Michael realized. It was an empty ritual here, where Christ's body and blood could not be.

"Aaron told me," Klein said.

"Aaron wants to go in after him," Michael said, staring at the Father.

Klein picked up a white cloth from the pulpit and used it to clean around the mouth of the stone chalice. Then he drank its remaining contents.

"It's an empty ritual, Father," Michael told him.

"It's not. It's comforting."

"It was comforting on Earth. Here it's blasphemy. Pretending God would send his essence into Hell to bless Mancini's bloodwater. It's an empty ritual. And if it wasn't, what right have you to pull Christ back into Hell?"

"He was here for three days, Mike. He may come again."

"Fool."

"So what if I am? So what if I preach false hope? Who cares if I just make it up? No one has a full copy of the Bible down here. No one knows. What's wrong with giving someone just an inch of hope? Huh, Michael? Or is that your job."

Michael bit his lip. "Lies, Father. You're sinning."

"We've already sinned. It's done for us. We're just shadows, waiting to be swallowed by darkness as the last of God's light fades around us. Who gives a damn if this fucking cup has no blood in it?"

They stayed silent awhile. It was Klein who finally broke it. "Besides, even if it is an empty ritual, the cup still has Mancini's brew in it. That'd make almost anyone feel better."

Michael shook his head and forced himself to laugh.

Klein nodded and sat down in a pew. Michael followed suit, sitting beside the Father.

"I won't let them go back in there," Michael said. "Aaron is an idiot. He's never been in the Carrion."

"Mike, at this point, very few of the Citizens ever have. All those people are dead. Hell's been picking us off, one by one."

Michael frowned, and looked up to the cross that hung on the far wall, then above the crucifix to the church's ceiling. He imagined looking even higher than that. Through the millions of tons of stone that separated him from Earth. And then through all that air between Earth and Heaven. He thought he would look all the way up until he saw God.

"I don't deserve this, Father."

"Of course you deserve it," Klein whispered. "Never doubt that. Never start doubting that. It's a terrible place to let your mind go. It comes with pride, Mike. I don't know what you did in your life. I can't tell you. But I do deserve this. I did something so despicable, well, I would have sent myself here. I don't know how I tricked myself into thinking I wouldn't be damned. I told myself that I had asked for forgiveness and that that had to be enough. But I do deserve this. God's a fair God, Mike. He's the ultimate Justice. And if He judged that we belong here, then here we belong. Don't let pride tell you otherwise. Self-delusion is what got us here. The one thing we can do is use this last chance at existence to accomplish this second time what we were supposed to do in the first."

Michael looked to the Father. His eyes were closed, tightly, as if he was engaged in his own terrible battle inside his own head. And of course he was. The Carrion brought that to people. It was their shared past. The Egypt of their own exodus.

"They should listen to me, Father. They never were in the Carrion. All they know is the hunger of the villagers. They think I don't know that, too? Why can't they listen to me since I've been through it?"

"Skepticism. It's rampant on Earth. It sends us here. They'll have to see it for themselves. It's a useful weapon against the Devil but too often we use it against ourselves. That's what makes the infidels, Mike. They take it one step further. They use skepticism against God. But they're fools. This place is death incarnate. By the time they learn that they're wrong, it'll already be too late."

Michael could feel the weight of the stone above him. It was blocking his sight. There was just too much Hell between himself and God.

"What should I do?" Michael asked.

"Follow your heart," Klein said. "It's the only thing here that wasn't made by Satan."

"My heart is a mystery."

"There's no Holy Spirit to guide it here. You'll have to make this decision on your own. We're in a place with no shepherds. Some of the sheep have to lead."

"What would the villagers do, if Julian's food stopped coming."

"They'd starve."

"Would they come after us, in the Fore?"

"Yes. You'd have to do something terrible. Fight them off. Send some of them away. Grant them food from your stores. The balance of power would never be the same. Even I can't protect you from that, Mike. I can preach to them all day long, but they won't be able to hear me when they're hungry."

Mike grabbed Klein around the wrist and locked eyes with the Father. "If you tell me, I'll do it. You were in the Carrion. You know what it was like. You know far better than I. You were the slave of that blonde haired bitch woman who lived there. I never was. I never even saw her. If you tell me that the food is worth it, I'll send them."

Klein didn't blink. "I can't Mike. I just can't. No one can make that decision for you. This is a devil you must wrestle yourself."

Aaron watched his door blanket fall closed behind Chelsea. She was wearing a red robe, the same color as the braid of her hair whose end she was fiddling with. Her eyes were on him, astonishingly blue, interested—and anything but vulnerable.

"Who'd you tell?" Aaron asked.

Chelsea cocked her head, unfazed. "No one. Believe me—"

"Well somebody told her."

"Aaron, sweetheart, this is the Fore. There aren't any secrets."

"You think I wanted this? You knew for months that I wanted Alice, and you kept fucking me!" Aaron pointed a finger towards her chest. "I didn't want this relationship, but you kept pushing it—"

Chelsea stepped forward, forcing him to pull his finger back to avoid touching her. "Aaron, baby, hold out your hands."

"What?"

"Hold out your hands."

The hell is this about?

But he held out his hands anyway, palms up.

She took another step forward and put her hands in his. "Now look into my eyes."

Aaron looked away.

"Look, Aaron."

Her blue eyes were almost entirely drowned out by her black pupils. A sad smile came to her lips. He could not help but imagine kissing them. For some reason, the fact that he was about to deny her made her charms all the more powerful.

She chewed her lip thoughtfully. Then she whispered, "Aaron, I know that you are used to fighting when you break it off with a girl. It's natural. I'm sure it helps enforce a separation you and that girl might sorely need. But we can't separate. We're stuck here together in the Fore. I like you. You're a wonderful man, and you're a really great fuck, but I don't love you. Not like Alice loves you, and not like you love her. I'm still your friend, and I'd be a shitty one if I didn't step out of the way. It's okay, Aaron. You don't have to fight with me. We can just stop sleeping together."

"Oh no you don't. You can't just pretend we did nothing wrong."

"We didn't."

"Yeah? Well you may not understand this, but there's something sacred about the relationship between a man and a woman, and we abused it, Chelsea. We did."

"Nothing's sacred in Hell."

"Don't spit blaspheme—"

"Who made it sacred?"

"It doesn't matter. It's still a sacred thing. We weren't—"

She would not relent. "Who made it sacred, Aaron?"

"God did. But it's still a sacred thing. We can't. . ."

Her gaze was too much. Aaron looked down. But she did not let him, reaching out and touching his chin. "Who makes it sacred now?"

"I don't know." Aaron wanted to shake her.

"Who?"

He couldn't believe that she could stay so calm. "We do."

She stepped even closer to him, chest to chest. He felt her small, soft breasts pushing into him. She tilted her head up ever so slightly. "Are you going to hurt me, Aaron, to avoid offending a God who isn't even here?"

Aaron's lips parted, but he couldn't think of anything to say.

"Are you?"

"No."

"This is damnation, Aaron, dearest of my friends. You and I, we strangled some happiness out of it, all for ourselves. You and Alice are going to strangle out even more. You have no reason to feel shame. We did nothing wrong."

Aaron could not believe how beautiful she looked. "I wish that were true. We could have brought a child into this Hell. No one deserves to be born into such a place."

"You aren't going to sleep with Alice then? And I know my cycle. It's not like on earth. You know we don't sleep together when—"

"That one time—"

"Then that one time was the mistake, not what you did with me. Now I'm your friend, so I'm going to talk to Alice for you. I'm going to tell her how you love her. I'm going to tell her how you came to me to end us."

Aaron was surprised at how hard he was breathing. "Really? You'd do that for me?"

"Of course." Her finger left his chin, and ran slowly down his chest. Aaron was surprised by how much his body was responding to her. She looked down, noticed, and smiled. "And I can't say I'll miss sleeping on your ridiculously hard mattress."

Aaron laughed. "Thank you for talking some sense into me."

She winked at him. "I'm not going to lie, it's going to be hard to replace you. Only, can I ask you one more thing?"

"Of course. Anything."

Chelsea's hand dropped to her side, moving her robe a little and outlining her figure. "Kiss me goodbye."

She was right there, only inches away from him. Her eyes looked so sad.

Aaron nodded. "Of course."

He leaned forward, and their lips touched. Suddenly her hands were all over him. Aaron could not remember her ever being so passionate.

She wanted a goodbye something, but it sure as hell wasn't a kiss.

The door curtain opened without anyone having knocked on it. Chelsea shot up from the sheets, shouting. Aaron rolled over to his side, reaching for his gun.

Michael stood in the doorway.

"Sir?" Aaron asked.

"You're going."

"Sir?"

"To the Carrion. Gather your men. You're going."

"Thank you, sir! Thank you! The villagers need this."

But Michael hadn't waited to hear the praise. The door curtain fell shut. In the quiet of the Harpsborough night, Aaron could hear the man's heavy footsteps on the stairs.

"No," Chelsea said. "Baby, don't go there. You can say no."

He realized then, for the first time, what exactly it was that he was trying to do. A chill passed down Aaron's spine.

Oh fucking God. I'm going into the Carrion.

— 27 —

"No!" Rick shouted. "Why? Why would you want him to go with you?"

Arturus cringed in his room. Rick and Galen had been arguing about something, but now their voices were loud enough to carry through the home.

"It's his decision," Galen responded.

"Is it? Should it be? What good can he do you in there? He's hardly more than a boy. Don't you feel anything?"

"La'Ferve will be out there, Rick. I can't fight him with a horde of Maab's men nipping at my heels. I'll die without help. I need a gun I can trust out there. Plus, I'll have the hunters in tow. There's too many of them for me to take care of."

"Then I'll go with you."

"He's already better than you. You know that."

"In a crisis? Are you sure about that? Is this a rational decision? When you come back with Turi dead, what are you going to say?"

"We don't have all the time in the world, Rick. An Infidel Friend came down the Thames the other day, remember? Pyle's back, sniffing around. We can't hide here forever. I'm going to make sure he's ready for when the time comes."

"Or you'll make him dead."

"Or dead," Galen agreed.

Arturus didn't feel guilty for overhearing this conversation. Their voices had become so raised that he couldn't have helped it. Their words sent his mind spinning.

At first he felt pride.

Galen wants me to come.

But Arturus was confused as well. Why would he be of any help in the Carrion? Why would Galen say he was better than Rick? Could that be true? What were they getting him ready for?

But one question stuck in his mind, drowning the others

out.

Who is La'Ferve?

"You're leaving," the Infidel Friend told Aaron.

Now how in the Hell did he know that?

The man accepted his bowl of spider guts and eggs with two hands. He was sitting cross-legged in a corner. The man's posture reminded Aaron of the way Japanese people sat in old samurai movies. "You're too kind."

Aaron watched the man eat with his fingers in that practiced way of his. The Infidel Friend ate slowly, as he had the last time Aaron had watched him.

Like a Citizen, not like a villager.

"I am," Aaron admitted. "I'm going to a very dangerous place."

"For a purpose?"

"Rescue."

"The boy, Julian." The infidel intuited. "The one you were afraid my people had captured."

Aaron rubbed his eyes. He hadn't slept much last night, so he was surprised to find sleep in them.

Don't forget, he's dangerous.

Aaron let his hand fall to his side, closer to his pistol. The infidel took no notice.

"That's right," Aaron told the man. "Julian. I'm going after him."

The Infidel Friend stared straight into his eyes. Aaron didn't let himself back down from the gaze.

"Dangerous. Like near the Pole?" the infidel asked.

Aaron shook his head.

"The Carrion then."

Aaron nodded and swallowed the lump that had formed in his throat.

"That is dangerous," the Infidel Friend said. "And perhaps only slightly less so, with the demons being so thin. Even an infidel takes care when entering that place."

"But you do go?"

"Not often, but my people have been there. Perhaps I could make you a deal. I'll escort you through the Carrion and help you find this boy. If I find Julian, then set me free."

"Never."

"There is a saying in the East, and it goes like this: 'It's okay to hold hands with a devil for a mile, when crossing a bridge.' And to boot, I'm not even a devil."

"You're close enough. What can you tell me of that place?"

The Infidel Friend stood up from the floor in that funny way of his, and then sat down in Staunten's chair. "It's dark. You'll need to bring torches. Huge veins of whetstone run through that place. Light can't flow through whetstone, and you'll find even skystone without illumination. The ancients, who knew the secrets of mining the substance, used to live there long before the Carrion's current devils showed up. You'll find their signs, their words of warning written in Latin. You won't know what it means, of course, but you'll wish you did.

Hell's architect was busy there. There are many traps. Stone floors that fall away into pits. Ceilings that fall to crush you. And worse."

"I think you're trying to scare me so that I will take you."

"I have no need, Aaron. You're terrified already."

"I'm not afraid."

"A hound can smell fear, you know. Not that it matters very much. They'll try to kill you even if you smell like a daisy, but you can tell they know. Except for the angle, a hound's eyes are so much like a human's."

"I'm not afraid of hounds."

Fitch said the hound sign was almost five feet high.

The Infidel Friend leaned back in his chair. He was healing a little too quickly for Aaron's taste. His movements were more fluid now. He didn't seem as stiff, or as fearful of pain.

"You're healing well." Aaron said aloud.

"I am. Your village has been kind to me, considering that you hold me to be your foe. I have appreciated your rations very much."

"You're only getting half of what the villagers are."

"And they, only half of what you get."

"Not everyone deserves the same treatment," Aaron said.

"I cannot help but agree with you. But it is important to note that many men have given their lives fighting against that principle."

"You're just saying that because we've got you locked up."

"I am."

Aaron laughed. "I hope the Citizens are merciful to you in your trial."

"You and I are in agreement there."

The infidel chewed thoughtfully before handing Aaron his empty bowl.

"Why are you here?" Aaron asked suddenly.

"Endymion, one of our leaders, sent me scouting. I came farther when I heard the settling, and stayed longer, because I noticed there were so few devils."

"I'm afraid we've killed them all."

"I'd considered that as a possibility."

"What's he like, the Infidel?" Aaron asked on impulse.

The Infidel Friend leaned forward, and put his elbows on his knees. He looked down to the stone floor. Aaron could see a clean space on the stone, where Staunten's mattress used to be.

Every night I sleep on bedding. He sleeps on stone.

"Have you met him?" Aaron asked.

Soon enough, if we can't find Julian quickly, I might be sleeping as you.

"I have," the infidel responded, his eyes still downcast. "That's a good question. Not all of us have. I fought with him at the Well. It's difficult to describe the man."

"I've told you enough. You should give back a little."

"Reciprocation comes between friends, not between guards and prisoners."

"Maybe, but it looks to me like you need all the friends you can get."

"Do you even remember my name?"

"No. But you can tell me if you like."

"Cris Caledon."

"Can I call you Cris?"

"You're the one with the gun. You can call me Susan for all it matters to me."

As always, Aaron found himself disarmed by the man's sense of humor.

"We infidels worship nothing but humanity. Did you know that? We consider people and their wants to be more important than God's or Satan's—"

"You're not answering the question."

"I am, be patient. We call ourselves infidels because Hell was made by some devil. We don't accept morality by fiat. The Creator of the universe doesn't decide what it is. As soon as there is sentience outside of a God's, then morality becomes an opinion. That the consequences of this universe are dictated by Satan is merely an accident of power."

"I'm not here for preaching. I'd go to Father Klein if I wanted that."

"Very well. The Infidel is a hero. Like Achilles when he slew the river, except not blinded by rage or put off by jealousy. He's like Wotan, standing against Fenris and the tides of Frost Giants as they assault Valhalla. He's like Aeneas marching forward to slay Turnus. He's like your David, facing Goliath, except that he would never send a man to die that he might have his woman.

"I fought for him in the Well. That's when I met him. The Icanitzu kept coming down like rain, and we had to fight them from the walls of the cliff. I despaired. I broke, inside, like people do sometimes. When the devils were gone and defeated I was still broken. When the Infidel came to me I lied to him. I told him my lover had fallen in that battle. I couldn't bear the thought of being so weak in front of him."

Aaron felt as if he was paralyzed by the man's words. He had never imagined that he would ever be face to face with an infidel, let alone that he would be receiving war stories from one.

"He told me his lover had fallen, too," the infidel was saying. "I was lying, you see, to try and express the truth. I was trying to express to him how much I was hurting. My boulder was more than I could bear, and I should have told him that rather than make up some fantasy. I admitted my lie to him, then, so that I could say that I told the truth.

"You lovers of God, you claim that unconditional love is some great virtue that you aspire to. But it's useless. Even your own God doesn't practice it. Look at us down here, tortured. Taking the pain of this universe and turning it inwards towards ourselves. Imagine what it would be like if God or Satan really loved us. If they actually had our best interests at heart. If they cared about our achievement or self-actualization. If they wanted to help you attain greatness rather than claim it for their own. That's how the Infidel loves people, Aaron."

Something about the infidel's words made Aaron unnaturally angry. His ears felt hot. "Who are you, to judge God?"

"Who would I be, not to?"

"How could you look at our failures, and attribute them to Him? Are you not willing to take any responsibility for your actions on earth? We're here because we failed."

"At what?"

"Loving Him."

"Why on Earth would we have wanted to love Him?"

Aaron shook his head, clenching his fists at his side. "You fool! He sacrificed His Son for us."

"Well not us, per se. We're in Hell. But I must admit, even on Earth, I was a bit bemused by the Crucifixion. He absolved me of a crime, Original Sin, which I did not commit by means of a sacrifice I didn't make, and then creates some big ado over the whole thing. But hey, I thought at the time, if ole Yahweh wants to sacrifice Himself to Himself to save us from Himself, bully for Him—so long as He does so responsibly and without hurting anyone. Looking back at it now, He probably didn't deserve the benefit of the doubt."

"He loved you, Cris."

"He did not! He didn't love you either. He sent us to an eternity of punishment for a finite crime. At least if we sent Him to an indefinite punishment, He'd deserve such a thing for having inflicted it."

Aaron's rage boiled over. "You'd damn God?"

"I doubt it, actually. I consider myself to be a good man."

"God is good. He is the source of all that is good. You cannot claim that he is evil since he is the one who defines what evil is."

The Infidel Friend laughed. “Perhaps he is good, but he would send people here while I would not. Which is more likely, do you think? That I am more merciful than an all loving God, or that you are somehow mistaken about his nature?”

Aaron had never before heard such blasphemy. His gun flew from his holster into his hand. The infidel was on him before he could look up, gripping his wrist with both hands. The world spun as he was forced down to the ground. He felt his elbow pop and he shouted as the gun fell out of his hands.

He shook his head, not sure how he had been dazed. Sweat dripped down along the side of his face.

Not sweat. Blood.

He stood dizzily, flexing his arm. His elbow was sore, but didn’t seem to be seriously damaged. He heard the sound of his own gun being cocked. The infidel stood before him, pointing the pistol at his head. Outside he could hear the guards shouting.

He incited me. He used my anger against me. These men are devils.

“Well,” Aaron said, “I guess you can call me Susan now.”

“Sadly. I cannot,” the infidel replied. “For you, in your prudence, neglected to load your weapon.”

Thank God I follow my own orders.

The infidel reversed his grip on the gun and offered it to Aaron.

Aaron accepted the weapon. Then he slammed it into the man’s head. “I was just starting to like you, too.”

The infidel had fallen into the corner, bleeding from his brow line where the gun’s sighting had hit him.

“Everything okay in there?” Aaron recognized Patrick’s deep voice.

“Fucking great. Thanks for asking.”

Aaron touched a finger to his own brow. The cut didn’t seem bad. “I’m sure you’ll miss me.”

The man stirred, rolling over and touching the wrappings on his thigh. “In all honesty, I will.”

“Oh?”

“When you’re gone, Duncan feeds me.”

“I wish I could go with them,” Martin lied to ole Bense.

Martin was leaning back against the stone wall of the Fore. It was shaping up to be another busy Harpsborough day, and that made Benson an even better companion than usual. The still man’s eternal, unblinking stare and perfect silence had a tendency to put people off. Privacy, in these times, was a gift Martin would take gladly. Ole Bense also didn’t have anything to say, which made him a perfect listener.

He saw two people, Aleck and Sarah, chasing each other.

Aleck had somehow gotten a hold of her hair tie and was attempting to keep it away. They ran through the village, jumping over other people, disturbing belongings and tearing down door curtains.

"Even with all these people, it's kind of quiet. Except for them," Martin observed.

Benson's stare did not follow the pair as they ran by.

"Because of the expedition, you know. They're all waiting to see them off. Probably no big deal, though. I mean, how far into the Carrion could Julian have gone? He's probably right on the other side of the barrier, sleeping on a pillow of devilwheat."

Smoke began billowing up from the stone floor above the still. Martin watched it swirl upwards towards the Harpsborough ceiling.

"That's good news for us, eh? Mancini's a brewin'. People will be sad tonight, with the hunters gone. He'll be making us some comfort. We'll have to get comforted ourselves."

It was definitely quieter than it should have been, Martin decided. People were waking up later and later as well. All their routines had been changed. Usually, the villagers would try and head out into the wilds in the morning, traveling to whatever secret caches they had to gather a living. Afterwards they would keep searching, hoping to stumble upon another find. Perhaps, if they were lucky, they'd discover one like Julian's. Martin had always hated that rat race. He had done it himself, before he became a Hunter. Once he had found a hungerleaf tree growing in a cavern by the Kingsriver. It had been enough to keep him fed for a while. He hadn't claimed it with the Fore though, and he hadn't the will to shoot the poor girl who had found it after him. She swore she'd found it first.

Hell, maybe she was right.

A man named Dooley saw to it now. The girl had gone missing a couple of years ago.

"It'd be like the old days, Bense. Like when Baker was still Lead Hunter. I miss camping out in the wilds. Dangerous as shit, you know, but the camaraderie. . . We don't have that anymore. That's what's wrong with hunters these days. We don't camp out in the wilds, so we turn against each other. I think Kyle would probably shoot somebody for the killer's lot. Hardly enough for us to eat, anymore."

The smoke was beginning to coalesce on the ceiling. If Mancini was making a particularly big batch, the smoke would become thick enough to look like clouds. Martin would pretend that there was no stone above him, just the empty sky, stretched out forever above the haze.

"Going to be cloudy, Bense. This is the first time I've been mad about the hand thing, you know. I don't mind when the girls look at it funny, they look at me funny anyway. And the food's been great. But my fellow hunters are going out into the Carrion without me. I wish I could go. I ain't afraid of that place. Why would I be?"

Benson's eyes seemed to glaze over.

It was just from the smoke, Martin realized.

He looked above him to the clouds. The smoke on the far edge of the chamber began to descend upon the church. It was as if he could see the air behind the steeple.

"It'll be a damn good brew."

The smoky fog increased in thickness until all the villagers of Harpsborough looked like two dimensional cut outs, moving amidst the haze.

"Hunting's probably real thick in the Carrion. It ain't devoid of devils like we are here, that's for sure. Probably a ton of food in there. I can't believe I ain't going, Bense. I should be out there with them. All because I was smuggling shells. Shit, everybody was doing it. I'm just the only one who got caught, you know?"

He coughed a little, but the smoke was starting to lessen. "I'll share some with you, Bense, though God only knows why. You get all that sinfruit juice for free. You're a damn lucky man, Bense, a damn lucky man."

The village came alive as Aaron exited the Fore, clustering around him and the men who followed. The Lead Hunter seemed angry, and had a cut on his brow.

"Look at him! He's all business," he told Benson. "Wouldn't want to get on his bad side today."

The last of the hunters Aaron had chosen came out of the Fore.

"He would have chosen me, Benson. You know he would have."

Duncan and Fitch were there, of course. They were an inseparable pair now, and famous for backing up Michael on his hunt. Avery had been chosen, too. They'd assigned him the AK-47. They'd picked Kyle, their best shot, who had his M-24 strapped across his back. Kyle was slow to aim, but if you gave the man enough time, he would not miss. Patrick and Johnny Huang had also been invited.

"I wouldn't have chosen them. They were probably picked just because they were out looking for Julian earlier. And they didn't take Graham. I'd have taken Graham."

Wistan and Mabe were the last to leave the Fore. They were great runners, and Mabe had a peculiarly good sense of direction.

The group had all assembled. Martin could not help but feel a sense of pride while looking at his fellow hunters.

"Those are some bad motherfuckers," Martin told Benson. "The Carrion better watch itself. They're going to fuck that place up. Just you wait, Bense. And Galen's coming too. Whew! Be lucky if a demon is left alive in there."

He heard some announcements at the entranceway. It was hard to make out their figures through the smoke, but Martin could recognize them as they came closer.

He saw Galen, Rick, Arturus, and that mouthy girl he had met in front of the Fore.

Water was dripping down Benson's cheek.

"You okay there?"

It was the smoke, Martin realized. It had irritated Benson's eyes until the water in them had turned into tears.

"I feel you, Bense. I feel you. I'm scared for them, too. Don't you worry. Our boys will come back. You'll see."

He saw Galen and Arturus join the group of hunters. They began shaking hands in greeting. The villagers' voices began to pick up, making Harpsborough sound like it was humming. Citizens began to appear on the street as well, coming out of the Fore to help see off the hunters.

"You'll see."

The villagers surrounded Aaron on all sides. His men were being showered with goodbyes and good lucks.

Is this how Michael felt, when he went out to hunt?

As the leader, he was afforded a special kind of consideration. It was as if people believed that his survival was assured.

"Take care of Mabe for me? Okay? Make sure he comes back?"

"Don't let the Carrion take Julian."

"Keep their heads on straight, out there."

He nodded seriously to each person's requests. Their hands reached out to touch him as they spoke.

"Let's start heading towards the entranceway," Aaron ordered his hunters.

Together the hunters tried to move. Each step was a battle. The villagers' hands clung to him, holding him back. Their wishes weighed on him. Each person he was told to safeguard served only to further his worry about their death. The hunters' movement ceased. One of his men near the front had stopped to speak to someone. A loved one, perhaps.

He found himself looking through the throng for a single face.

Alice.

She came to him, pushing through the masses.

"Alice!"

She smiled and put her arms around him. "Come back soon. Don't let them take you."

Finally. Someone cares about me.

"I will. I promise. If we're even able to live through this."

She smiled sweetly. He could smell her when she was this close. She leaned forward and kissed him deeply. "Go get Julian," she whispered into his ear. "Be a good tiger and get him."

There was something very right about her telling him this. He closed his eyes.

I'm her warrior. I have to fight for her.

He opened his eyes and looked ahead. No one was moving yet. He caught sight of Duncan, shaking hands with Copperfield. He saw Fitch and Michael, shouting into each other's ears. Galen seemed to be enjoying it all, smiling and shaking people's hands. His actions reminded Aaron of a politician. Arturus was beset as well. He had that young girl, Ellen, from the wilds. She was kissing him on the cheek.

"He's not going, is he?" Alice said suddenly.

"Who?"

"Turi? You're taking Turi into the Carrion?"

"It was Galen's decision."

"Why? You can't let him go! He'll get killed out there. Aaron, you have to put your foot down. You can't let this happen."

Her blue eyes narrowed, focusing on the boy. Aaron admired her profile, her sharp nose and angular jaw.

"He's our tunnel rat. We have to have someone small enough to go where Julian goes."

"He's nearly full grown."

"Would you rather we take someone younger?"

She shook her head. Then she reached into her pocket and produced a thin braid of hair. "It's supposed to bring you luck. Massan told me that this is what people used to do."

Aaron nodded. He was sure he'd heard of that in one story or another.

He saw Chelsea out of the corner of his eye. He suddenly felt dizzy.

I'm sorry, Chelsea. This is the woman I love.

"Let's keep it moving," Aaron shouted to his hunters, doing his best to avoid making eye contact with Chelsea. "Julian's out there and he needs our help."

Slowly, the hunters began to walk again. The people's hopes and prayers melded together into one congruous hum.

It's only a place. We'll be fine.

The villagers were worried, Aaron realized. Without this food they would starve. He was their hope. The Citizens didn't care nearly as much, but he figured they should. If the people got too hungry, they wouldn't go into the wilds of Hell to gather. Why would they, when there was plenty right there in the Fore?

It's only a place in Hell.

Finally, they made it to the entranceway, and the hunters entered into the wilds. Aaron looked behind him. The people were there, waiting. Graham and a couple of the remaining hunters began moving them back into the village. They didn't touch Alice, though.

She'll watch us till we're gone.

He saw Chelsea, too. The guards wouldn't harass her either, as she was a Citizen. The last image of Harpsborough Aaron saw before he left was that of Chelsea and Alice holding hands.

Arturus moved with the hunters and their silent procession. His pack was heavier than usual. He had brought with him some woodstone torches of the type that Rick made because they lasted longer than Copperfield's. He had also brought enough food and water for three days along with a medical kit. Galen had said his razor could double as a knife, so he kept that in his pocket. He thought bringing all of this was a bit much, but he had been warned that they might not be able to return from the Carrion at will.

He counted the missing rivets of rustrock as they followed along the old road.

One day, I could repair this road. There is a quarry of rustrock towards the Pole. I could dig out some and put the rivets back in.

He wondered if that had been done already. Maybe if he studied the rustrock road markers he could find subtle differences between those made by the builders of the road, and those who repaired it.

Who were the people who built this road, anyway? Was it the King on the River who had ordered it built? Someone else? Someone older?

They moved off of the road when they made it to the fork.

He recognized other landmarks here as well. The crawlway made of crystal. The dark room with the hound sign. Kyle, Wistan, and Mabe, who hadn't been with the original group, shuddered when Aaron showed them the hound's burrow.

"Beast?" Kyle asked.

"Might have been," Aaron answered. "But he was dead before I even got to Hell."

The words were comforting, but Arturus remembered Fitch's tale. Fitch believed that the great hound's body had never been found.

He heard the woman's singing as they approached the barrier. As before, the notes she sang were only the ones he expected. If he emptied his mind and only listened, he could tell it was just the whistle of the wind.

The chill air brought goose bumps up on Arturus' flesh.

The hunters stopped at the Carrion barrier.

"Julian's been waiting for three days," Aaron said. "He may not have much longer. He may already be dead. The Carrion is a place from our nightmares, from the history of Harpsborough. I don't need to tell you all about the journey Michael and Klein took to bring our people out of this damn place. I don't need to tell you how much they fear it. But we're men, the same as they. We'll survive it, the same as they. Little Julian went in here almost every day for the last year. It simply cannot be that dangerous. We're to rescue the boy, if we can. We're to find the food, if we can. We have to make sure that it's safe to keep getting the food, too.

"That means that we may have to stick around in the Carrion even after we've found what we're looking for. If it's too dangerous, we'll have to find some other way of getting wheat. No matter what happens, no matter how dangerous it gets, we are not to lead the devils back to Harpsborough. We cannot let them find that there is a door in one of the walls which protect us. If we do not return in five days, Michael will have the door filled up behind us. We'll be stuck in that foul place forever then, so let's not do it.

"Any questions?"

The hunters held their weapons at the ready. Arturus heard the clicks of rounds being pulled into chambers.

Aaron opened the door, the stone grinding along. It hit the Carrion marker stone. The crawlway was small, dark, and deep.

A cool breeze came through. He felt Galen's hand on his shoulder.

"Alright, Turi," Aaron said. "You're our tunnel rat, so you go first."

— 28 —

Arturus emerged, pushing his body out of the crawlway. The Carrion air was cool on his skin. He found himself on a narrow shelf in a dark room. There was light, certainly, but barely enough to make out the walls. Huge portions of this chamber were covered in shadow.

The passage is not hidden on this side.

Any demon that happened upon this place might easily find its way out of the Carrion.

Julian, what were you thinking?

Arturus knew that he could not call the rest of his group in unless he made sure there were no devils here. He lowered himself down from the shelf. The fall was longer than he was tall, so he had to drop the last few feet.

He unslung his rifle and waited for his eyes to adjust.

Slowly, shapes appeared in the shadows of the room. They were mounds of loose stones, perhaps graves. He moved across the chamber as quietly as he could and checked the two exits. The exits themselves were archways, designed by Hell's architect to have huge central keystones made out of violet hellstone. He could see no enemies beyond. He moved back to the mounds. They had been laid out some time ago, by human hands perhaps—or a devil's. The stones themselves were healing together, and some had already completely fused. Arturus guessed they were at least a decade old. The stone had healed enough that, should there be corpses within, he doubted they could escape without a long and careful effort.

Twelve of them, and one unfinished.

He inspected the mounds just long enough to make sure they were safe and then began to make his way back to the shelf. He moved, walking backwards, as quickly as he dared. A loose stone skittered away from one of his footfalls.

Arturus dropped into a crouch, shouldering his rifle.

The exits seemed clear. He listened as hard as he could.

His heart was an engine in his chest, powering him like Rick's battery powered their stone grinder. The woman's song was clear now, loud in his ears and beautiful.

But he could hear nothing else.

He stood and continued backing up. Not daring to look away, he stretched out his hand behind him. It touched rock.

Arturus leapt up, using one arm to hold himself up on the ledge. He ran his rifle butt into the stone by the crawlway twice to signal the hunters. Then he let himself drop back down to the floor and re-shouldered his rifle.

Their crawling seemed loud to his ears now but so too did the song.

Aaron was the first one through. Arturus offered his hand to guide him and his knee to support him. The Lead Hunter came down gracefully from the shelf. The man quickly drew his weapon and moved to one of the exits.

Just like Galen would do.

Galen was the next through, jumping down as silently as a hound to the stone below. He immediately covered the other exit.

The hunter called Wistan was next, and he gratefully accepted Arturus' hand and knee. The rest of the hunters followed suit, spreading out into the room. Johnny Huang was last.

Aaron moved back from his exit and pointed first at Wistan and then to Mabe. The two stepped forward. At Aaron's direction they slung back their rifles and drew pistols.

Silencers. They'll be able to kill, and as long as we don't have to shoot, we won't call other devils towards us.

It might be difficult to gauge when he should open fire and when he shouldn't. He wouldn't want to allow anyone to die, certainly, but he wouldn't want to shoot too early, either. Galen would be furious with him for embarrassing himself in front of the Harpsborough hunters.

I'm still a child.

Galen would be mad? That was what he was worried about? He bit his lip solidly to try and wake himself from his dream world.

If I fail, we'll all be dead.

Mabe and Wistan moved shoulder to shoulder towards the right exit. The rest of the hunters followed as silently as they could. Arturus could feel his legs shaking as he walked. Only then did he admit to himself that he was terrified.

They traveled carefully through the Carrion wilds. Every joint that popped, every hushed curse, every time someone's rifle butt brushed against the stone, Arturus cringed. The sounds assaulted his ears, even more so when they were from his own missteps. But though he tried, he could never make himself watch his footfalls.

The Carrion was a place of darkness. There was almost always enough light to see but never much more than that. Most of the rooms had black pools and pits of shadow, created by rock walls or outcroppings that blocked the sources of the low illumination. The features of this place were unfamiliar to him. Stone blocks were usually formed into brick patterns, and in several places he found more of the gravel funeral mounds. Most of the arches that framed the exits and entryways of the chambers had the same overlarge violet keystones he had seen in the first room.

As they progressed deeper into the Carrion, the hellstone itself deepened into a purple so dark it was difficult to distinguish from black. Occasionally bright violet veins would run through it, casting light onto the nearest of objects and shadows upon the farther.

Hell's architect had left odd stone stairways, sometimes leading up to other levels, sometimes leading down. A few led straight into the ceiling or stopped in the middle of a chamber without any landing whatsoever.

The Carrion's chill air became even colder as they moved on.

The chill must be coming from some water.

After a few more rooms he could hear the river. Wistan and Mabe steered for it. They led the hunters into a room only six feet tall and lined by wide sandstone pillars. The exit was four feet tall, so they had to duck to make their way through.

Arturus noticed the landscape was changing again.

It's always different by the water. The river keeps its own house.

The river chamber was huge, perhaps a few hundred yards across, and he could not see how long. He could make out the far walls in only a few places. The river was lower than they were now, running through the center room. It was the one thing Arturus could see clearly. A skystone vein ran through the hellstone that made the bed of the river. Normally skystone shined out a very bright blue light, almost neon. But here, the vein was so muted that the blue was a far deeper hue. Its light was the only source for the chamber. The air chilled further as Arturus ducked through the entryway.

He shivered, the hair on his arms standing on end.

There was a walkway on a ledge which led down along the wall towards the water. Mabe and Wistan were slowly edging along it, and after checking to make sure that Aaron and Galen were still behind him, Arturus followed.

Stone banks and hills cast long shadows across the chamber. The rush of the water affected the skystone's light, causing it to wave back and forth along the ceiling and walls. This caused the shadows to move too, often making Arturus start.

As they crept along the walkway, he could see his own shadow, along with Wistan and Mabe's, sliding across the wall on the far side of the river.

His heart skipped a beat.

There's no light behind me.

Wistan and Mabe froze.

Arturus quickly held up a hand to warn the hunters behind him. A few hadn't even made it into the chamber yet.

His eyes focused on the shadows.

Other silhouettes appeared as the first few faded out of view. Most of them moved on two feet. A few were so hunched over that they used their arms to help walk. Even though their shadows rippled along the wall, distorted by the river's light, Arturus could make out their stub wings.

Dyitzu.

The shadows kept disappearing, but more were taking their places.

There might be over a hundred.

He looked behind him. Aaron's eyes were wide, hypnotized by the procession.

Patrick's breathing quickened.

Arturus' eyes shot back to the dyitzu shadows. He studied them intently, watching for any sign that they might be able to hear Patrick.

The man's breaths became gasps.

He's hyperventilating.

Arturus tore his gaze away from the shadows and looked pleadingly towards Galen.

The warrior had already moved back in line and was whispering into Patrick's ear. The hunter was nodding, his facial features obscured by the low light.

Galen and Aaron shared a glance, and the Lead Hunter waved them back out of the room. Arturus moved forward and tapped Wistan on the shoulder. He too was breathing heavily, but at least he was doing it quietly.

Wistan looked back, and Arturus pointed him towards the exit. Mabe followed them as they crept quietly back the way they had come. They left the low ceilinged pillar chamber behind them too, without a word.

Aaron grabbed Arturus by the wrist and brought him together with Mabe and Wistan. He spoke in the softest of whispers.

"How many?"

Tears were coming down Mabe's cheeks. He didn't look sad at all, just overwhelmed.

"Hundreds," came Arturus' hushed reply. "There could be hundreds."

The hand on his wrist was shaking. Arturus looked down at it. Aaron withdrew the hand, and looked towards his men.

He's afraid, too.

"Should we go back?" Johnny asked the inevitable question.

No one thought to call him a coward.

"Soon," Aaron whispered. "Very soon. We certainly aren't going any farther. With so many devils I'm sure Julian couldn't have been coming out this far. We should look closer to the Carrion barrier."

Galen shook his head. "Julian's devilwheat had been watered."

"You're not seriously suggesting we go back in there?" Johnny's whisper was just a bit louder than Arturus was comfortable with.

Galen shook his head, and placed a finger to his lips to quiet the man. "Along the river would be too dangerous. Below it though, that's where we should look."

"There was a stairway down a few rooms back," Arturus remembered.

"Yeah, by a pile of stones," Mabe agreed.

Aaron nodded. Arturus wondered if the low light made him look more or less worried than he actually was.

"Alright," Aaron said finally. "Take us back."

Mabe and Wistan led them, their pistols drawn, down the staircase. Johnny slipped on a stair and fell, landing on his ass with a clatter.

"Jesus," Aaron whispered.

They huddled in silence on the stairwell, Wistan and Mabe looking down while Duncan and Fitch looked behind them. After a few minutes, Aaron ordered them to continue with a wave of his hand.

The stairway ended on a sandstone landing. They moved slowly through another archway into the maze of corridors below.

It wasn't long before Mabe admitted he was disoriented. He pointed down two passages alternately and then held his hands up, miming indecision. Aaron and Galen huddled. Arturus found he could overhear their whispers if he held his breath.

"But the ceiling there is made of hellstone," Aaron was saying, "if water was seeping through there it would have healed already."

"Trust me," Galen responded. "That way is beneath the river."

"But if it was, that devilwheat wouldn't have been watered

for very long. Maybe only since the settling. I don't like our chances."

"Humor me."

"This isn't the time for hunches."

"I think I can smell it."

Aaron thought about this for a moment and glanced back down the passageway they had come down. His frown seemed more serious in the darkness. He caught Mabe's attention and motioned him towards the passage Galen had counseled.

If we're under the river, then those dyitzu are right above us.

The next room had twelve passageways leading out. Mabe threw up his hands in frustration.

Galen walked up to a ledge, leapt up upon it, and placed his hand against the stone above him. He shook his head, waving them on.

What's he doing? Can he feel the vibrations of the river?"

In the next room Aaron knelt down, offering to be Galen's stepping stone. He did so again in the room after.

In the fourth room Galen nodded.

The chill. He can feel that the stone is cooler beneath the river.

"The river is right above us," Galen said. "Turi, Wistan, Mabe, did you all see any hounds while you were up there?"

They glanced at each other and all shook their heads.

Galen nodded. "Follow me."

They stopped from time to time while Galen checked the ceiling. He felt it with the back of his hand, and occasionally touched the floor as well. Arturus, though, doubted this was necessary. The area beneath the river had its own distinct look. The river kept its own house *and* basement, he figured.

The rooms were wide and spacious, making their ceilings seem low and ominous. The larger rooms were all pitch black, but their spin off corridors and cubbyholes were lit with a bright yellow luminescence, casting long paths of light through the rooms they traveled.

Galen stopped them in one of the long dark rooms with a raised hand. The shadow of that hand moved along the far wall, almost causing Arturus to draw his gun.

He listened.

Drip. Drip. Drip...

There was a long pause. The hunters began to shift back and forth on their feet. Avery unslung his AK.

Drip. Drip. Drip...

This time Arturus thought he knew where the dripping was coming from. He couldn't say for certain, of course, because of the way the echoes of the chamber distorted the sound, but he believed it was coming through a particularly narrow archway. Like so many other of the Carrion arches, it was marked with a large violet keystone. Galen must have agreed with him, because he led the hunters through the arch.

The next room was long and black, similar to the others. It was lit only by one cubbyhole, maybe a hundred yards or so away.

Drip. Drip. Drip...

They moved towards the sound.

Arturus thought to try and check the ceiling for cracks, but it was too dark to see any. He could barely distinguish the hunters from the shadows about him, even when they were only a few feet away. He saw a mound, though, oddly circular, lit by the barest hint of light. Just beyond that he could see the falling water droplets.

Drip. Drip. Drip...

A glint of light passed through each droplet as it fell, though it was too dark for him to make out what crack it might be dripping from or even the pool it was falling into.

A hunter's shadow darted by him. They were making him edgy.

Drip. Drip. The distant cubbyhole illuminated the head of a dyitzu as it came under the dripping water. *Splat...*

Arturus' eyes went wide. He looked about to see how many of the shadows around him were devils and how many were his own men. Dyitzu fire sprang into existence, illuminating the room. The fireball was headed straight at him.

Wistan and Mabe came alive, their silenced pistol muzzles flashing. Arturus dropped to one knee, and leveled his rifle at the nearest of them. The fire passed over his right shoulder. He felt the heat stinging his cheek.

Don't shoot too soon.

But he was ready. His finger on the trigger, his safety off. The dyitzu in his sights dropped, felled by three quickly fired bullets from Mabe's gun.

The room became silent. Arturus looked about to make sure none of the enemies were moving.

Drip. Drip. Drip...

Galen moved amongst the devil corpses, making sure they were dead. For him, this involved slitting the dyitzu's throats. Galen wouldn't bother to check if they were alive or not beforehand, Arturus knew.

"Good shooting," Aaron said.

Arturus nodded in agreement.

Dyitzu fire, having missed the hunters, clung to the walls, slowly burning away and keeping the room lit. Avery and Johnny Huang moved about the chamber, looking for more devils.

"I think we got them," Johnny reported.

"Quietly, too," Galen said. "We may be okay."

He moved up to the pool where the water was collecting.

Drip. Drip. Drip...

The pool itself looked bloody. Arturus wondered if it was from the fiery lighting, or if a dyitzu had actually bled in there.

"I'll be damned, Galen," Aaron said. "You were right. A crack, right there in the hellstone."

"Not from the settling, I don't think," Galen said. "It runs sideways. I'd think the cracks from the settling would be more likely to run with the grain."

"What are you saying, that this crack is deliberate? Caused by someone?"

Galen shrugged. "Let's spiral out from here. We may be close."

"No way." Avery crossed his arms. "If Julian had to come all this way each time he gathered our food, he'd be dead."

Johnny Huang nodded.

"Not necessarily," Galen said. "The boy was quick and quiet. I always wondered how he had become so adept. I think he may have been tested here, in the Carrion. Still, there is something to what you say. It's not impossible that we are in the wrong place."

Mabe and Wistan pushed more rounds into the clips of their pistols. The other hunters turned their safeties back on, but no one reslung their rifles.

They moved in steady circles, walking from room to room beneath the Carrion river. This time it was Arturus who stopped them. He heard the woman's song again. That meant there was wind.

Julian would have heard it, too. I'm sure that's how he found the weakness in the Carrion barrier.

There was a crawlway, nearly ten feet high, on one of the walls.

"If we had come through here," Arturus said, pointing to the crawlway, "I doubt the dyitzu would have noticed us."

Galen found a few handholds in the stone, and climbed up into the passage. He tossed down a rope, gripped it with both hands, and set his feet against the stone to help support it.

"Turi, first," he said.

The hunters crawled up the rope, one by one. The crawlway was fairly wide and tall enough so that Arturus could stand up so long as he hunched his shoulders. There was no light in it whatsoever, though.

"Hand on each other's backs," Aaron ordered. "I want to make sure that everyone's together."

Arturus felt Galen grip him around his belt.

“Easy, son,” his father said. “Slowly forward.”

Arturus led them into the pitch black passage. His steps were short, both because Galen had him by the belt and because he couldn’t see where he was going. He ran the fingertips of his right hand along the stone. He reached out with his left periodically as well to make sure that he didn’t miss any branches.

I hope there’s no pit.

Galen did have his belt, however, and might be able to catch him should he fall.

Might.

The blackness was so complete that he could close his eyes and not notice much of a difference. He became aware of a blue splotch in his vision where he had first focused on a dyitzu fireball, and that was all he saw. At times he almost thought it something more than just an afterimage floating in front of him as the light seemed to dance, moving this way and that as he turned his head.

I’m getting tired. I need to rest.

His back and shoulders were sore from leading them all in this crouched position.

And I’m the short one. It must be worse for the others.

Her song became louder and louder before quieting suddenly. Then he saw a dim grey light coming from the end of the passageway.

“I see something,” he whispered back to Galen.

“Good,” Galen answered.

As Arturus moved forward he felt something crunch under his feet. He stopped the hunters and knelt to inspect it.

He held up what he had found into the dim light.

“Devilwheat,” Galen said.

Arturus smiled and then led them quickly down the tunnel, feeling Galen’s hand tugging at his belt every few steps. He could smell the wheat when he came to the tunnel’s edge.

The passageway became a high shelf in a dark grey room. The room itself wasn’t too large, maybe just a little more than fifty yards across, but it had more devilwheat growing in it than Arturus had ever seen before.

— 29 —

"Well, I guess this was the only place it could be," Aaron said. "Close enough to the barrier, under the river. Good job, Galen."

The shelf was nearly twenty feet tall, so Galen lowered a rope to help them down and braced himself by setting his feet against the stone. "This place might have been a harpy trap once." He grunted as Arturus began going down the rope. "The wheat would attract people, and the harpies could have come in through here to kill them."

Arturus slipped down the rest of the rope easily and regarded the devilwheat. It grew up from a raised woodstone floor in five foot tall stalks. The wheat was thick enough that it would be hard to walk through. Except for the outermost four or five feet of the room, it covered the entire floor. Huge cracks ran along the ceiling, water dripping from them in places.

Much of the devilwheat had been harvested already, leaving several almost bare patches of woodstone.

"This place is well tended to," Galen said after he had climbed down, "and by more than Julian."

Arturus and the Hunters began to walk around the field.

"Well, he sure as hell isn't in here," Aaron said.

"Could this place feed Harpsborough?" Avery asked, leaning against one wall.

"All of it, about," Aaron answered. "If this is the place, then surely Julian was killed trying to make it here. Pressed his luck one too many times."

"Likely," Galen agreed.

"Johnny, what's up with that exit?" Aaron called.

"Locked, sir. Steel door. We ain't getting through there. Whoever else runs this place must have the key."

Aaron nodded. "We shouldn't stay here long, we may run into them."

"Oh my," Fitch said. "Julian may already have. Come look

at this."

They walked around the field to where Fitch was kneeling. There were a few splotches of dried blood.

"I'd bet it's human," Galen said. "Devil blood clots differently. Still, it's hard to tell after it's dried completely."

"Can we be sure it's Julian's?"

Arturus looked at the wheat. It had been harvested on this side as well, but far less efficiently than elsewhere. Someone had taken care to only remove every third stalk or so. Other stalks were broken here, making a path towards the center of the room. He followed through the wheat and found a bed of the flattened crop.

"Someone could have been waiting here, and ambushed him," Arturus said.

Aaron came through the devilwheat after him. "Good eye, boy."

Arturus looked to Galen. His father was also nodding. "I see no bullet scores. He may well have been taken alive."

"Fuck him," Patrick said. "Let's get the hell out of here. This place is busted already."

"Maybe." Galen scratched his well trimmed beard. "That might be the wisest course of action. Julian is, after all, a boy who is quick of thought and loyal to Harpsborough. But I do not think that whoever owned this place is happy that we were taking their food. Perhaps their failure to kill him was an act of mercy. If that were the case then we should be safe returning to Harpsborough. But that is not the only possibility."

"You think they'll want revenge," Aaron said.

"I left the Carrion with your First Citizen and Priest," Galen went on, "and I can tell you that the men here are often a vengeful lot. Your village founders were wise to have left this place."

"Vengeance would be a dangerous thing for them to pursue," Aaron said. "They are surrounded by enemies. This place is crawling with devils. I'm amazed they can even survive."

"Yet survive they can." Galen stood up and looked towards the steel door. "And largely thanks to a place like this. They have no more precious resource."

What does Galen want? Are his arguments real, or does he just want to convince them to save Julian.

"So now what?" Aaron asked, biting at his thumb nail. "We kill them and take back the boy?"

"No," the word came unbidden from Arturus' lips.

"No?" Johnny asked.

"We can't kill them. We've stolen from them. That's the extent of it. They've protected what's theirs. We'd just escalate things."

Galen grunted.

He approves.

"Look little man," Fitch said, "this isn't the time to occupy the moral high ground. They've got Julian. They've got this food. We need this food."

"The hell we do," Johnny said, "If the Citizens didn't gorge themselves on meat the whole damn day—"

"Enough," Aaron said. "We won't fight against ourselves. Not here, at any rate. There's time enough for that when we get home."

"Alright." Johnny held up his hands as if to keep Aaron from coming closer to him. "Fine. No problem. What's the plan, sir? We ain't going to last too much longer in here."

Aaron crouched down by the wheat.

"Sir?"

"I'm thinking. Jesus Christ."

Arturus moved over to Galen and tugged on his sleeve.

"What is it?" Galen whispered.

"I think I know the answer."

"Then say it boy. Tell them all."

Arturus nodded, and bit his lip.

They've always listened to me so far. But what if they think my idea's stupid?

"We should trade for him," Arturus suggested.

Fitch snorted. "Naïve little bastard, aren't you?"

"Fresh eyes, fresh ideas," Galen said. "The idea of working with a group out of the Carrion seems foreign to me, too. After all, I remember what these people were like. But if we offer them an easy way to get everything they want, they may capitulate."

"And they're not using all of their food, either," Arturus said. "We could get Julian back and work out some agreement. We could trade them shells or something for devilwheat."

"He's got a point, Fitch," Aaron said. "We should at least try to reason with them. What kind of people would we be if we didn't?"

"Alive kind of people," Fitch answered.

"You want to skip straight to the fighting? We can die there, too."

"But then they don't know we're coming, sir."

"Your points are valid, Fitch," Galen said. "Now Aaron must weigh them."

Aaron sat back on his haunches, covering his mouth with his hand.

I said it, and they didn't think I was stupid.

Arturus bit his lip again.

It's not about me, it's about my idea. We need to do the right thing.

"It's clear to me what Father Klein would say," Aaron said finally.

"Who gives a fuck about that windbag?" Fitch all but shouted, stopping himself before continuing in a lower voice. "He wants us to appease God, but God's not even here. Our souls are still at stake, Aaron, but they're not up for judgment. Not anymore. If we die here it only gets worse. There's no point in dying for a moral."

Aaron looked at him fiercely. "That's blasphemy, friend. Have you been feeding the Infidel Friend lately?"

"Aaron, you're right that what he says seems godless," Galen broke in. "But you have to admit that Fitch's argument is pragmatic."

"You agree with him?"

"No, but his words are correct and need to be weighed. We can't just call them blasphemy and ignore them. It's our lives, our souls, that are on the line here."

Fitch nodded. "But you disagree with me, nonetheless."

"Nonetheless."

"Why?"

Galen glanced at Arturus before speaking, and gave him a smile. "We've forgot what we're fighting, I think. We've had it so good for so long that we think the devils are the enemy. Or that the men of the Carrion are the enemy. Hell wants us to be evil. Its every stone has been laid to make us lose our way as human beings. Your founders, Michael and Klein, are from here. They remember it. It's Hell that we are fighting, more so than anything else."

Fitch wrinkled his nose. "Alright, let's meet these guys."

Aaron nodded.

"Then we kill them," Fitch said.

Aaron snorted. "Should we wait for them here?"

"If they come through that door, I know they'll shoot us," Avery said.

Aaron looked to Galen. "Can you take us back around, to the other side of this door?"

"I can."

"They must be close, the Carrion people."

"They must."

"Take us round."

Galen walked back towards the crawlway and was preparing himself to climb up it when he stopped suddenly. He ran his fingers over a symbol that had been carved there in the rock. "Well, lad," Galen whispered to Arturus, "no one can tell you that your heart was in the wrong place."

Galen found finger holds in the stone which no normal man could ever use, pulled himself upwards along the wall, and then climbed into the crawlway. Then he dropped the rope down.

Arturus grabbed it and looked at the symbol.

It had been carved by humans, certainly. It was in the shape of a bull's head.

Galen knows what that means.

Galen's words were an itch in Arturus' mind as they climbed back out of the crawlway. His father dropped down behind them last, coiling the rope quickly.

Galen had come from the Carrion, Arturus knew. He had survived that time like only a few in Harpsborough had. Could it be that Galen knew what tribe used that symbol? Did he know that they wouldn't be willing to trade for Julian? But Galen couldn't be certain of this, or he would have told the group that Fitch was right after all.

Of course he can't know for sure.

Harpsborough had a new leader now and an almost entirely different set of villagers. The Carrion was so dangerous that people here would probably live shorter, not longer, than those in Harpsborough. It was very possible that this tribe, perhaps once unfriendly, might now be benevolent.

Maybe.

But how long ago was that? How many years since then? Ten years? Twenty?

Did I come from the Carrion?

They moved back through the dark underbelly of the river. Arturus made sure not to look at the bright cubbyholes in order to keep as much of his dark vision as possible.

Drip. Drip. Drip...

The thoughts stirred up other curiosities in his mind. Questions which he had begged Rick to tell him without ever having received satisfactory answers.

Where was I born? Are either of you my blood father? Who was my mother?

The answers had all been non-answers. He had been born in Hell. Both Rick and Galen were his fathers. The only questions Rick had tried to answer at all were the ones about his mother. "She was a wonderful and beautiful woman," Rick had told him. "You are lucky to be related to such a lady."

Drip. Drip. Drip...

But Rick would say no more, and he had only said that much, Arturus knew, because he had wanted to answer those questions so very badly.

Soon I will be their peer. I will demand they tell me.

Galen shouldered his rifle and fired without waiting for Wistan or Mabe's silencers. The report of the rifle shocked Arturus. The flash from Galen's muzzle illuminated the reasons why he'd loosed a bullet. In what little of the next room was visible through the hallway, Arturus could see a mass of dyitzu—perhaps even outnumbering the group they'd seen by the river.

Walls of dyitzu fire came tumbling in through the passageway. Arturus dropped into a crouch behind a grave mound for cover, drawing his pistol and firing twice down the corridor as he did so.

Some of the fireballs were disturbed by his bullets. The fluid centers of the fire splattered across the wall, burning in the hallway and slowly dripping down to the floor.

The rest of the hunters followed Arturus' lead, jumping for cover. Johnny and Kyle landed behind the same mound that Arturus had. For a moment both the hunters and dyitzu sat quietly. The low sound of the flames left over from the dyitzu's first volley was all Arturus could hear. Kyle pulled out his M-24 and set it on the mound. He looked carefully along the sights.

The silence was broken by his shot.

In the other room a dyitzu screamed. Arturus heard the sound of Kyle's shell casing skittering across the stone floor.

"Fuck 'em up, Kyle!" Johnny shouted.

Another wave of fire came through the corridor, impacting against their stone mound and sending droplets of burning fluid splashing over them. One landed on Kyle's shoulder. The man didn't blink. Arturus doused the fire with his shirt sleeve as the hunter took aim.

Drip. Drip. Drip. . .

Kyle fired again. Another dyitzu screeched in pain.

"Good one," Aaron called. "You got his fucking hand."

A shadow amongst the dyitzu moved towards the corridor.

Kyle fired again. Arturus' ears were ringing from the gunshots.

"You missed!" Avery shouted.

Kyle shook his head. "No I didn't."

"Icanitzu," Galen warned. "Two of them. Don't waste your bullets trying to shoot them."

"Fuck," Aaron said. "We should have brought that damn infidel."

Kyle fired again and was rewarded with another shout.

Johnny fired too, and was joined by a few of the other hunters. No hits.

"Save your bullets!" Aaron warned. "Shoot only if you know you've got them. And don't worry about the Icanitzu. Galen and I will handle them if they come."

More fire swarmed through, and Arturus ducked low behind the mound. The fluid was catching across from him and had seeped into the cracks between the stones. Kyle had to stand up to aim over the flames, only allowing himself to cough after he had fired and knelt back down.

Drip. Drip. Drip. . .

The funeral mound was getting warm.

Arturus stared between the twin flames that were coming up from inside his stone cover. He couldn't get a good shot at any of the dyitzu. He could see the tip of one's stub wing, but he didn't think he could hit it.

Then one peeked out of its cubbyhole. It cocked its arm to throw, a fireball forming in its hand. Arturus shot it in the throat. The fireball spun uselessly in the air, suspended in place as the thing dropped. Beside him, Kyle shot as well. The stub wing Arturus had passed over erupted, spewing out a geyser of blood.

"Fuck 'em up boys!" Fitch shouted.

The dyitzu responded. Arturus ducked down. A wave of fire swarmed over his head. The room was lit now with the dying fireballs. The corridor between them and their enemies was entirely aflame.

Another wave.

Arturus dared to look over his cover after the fire swarm had passed.

Drip. Drip. Drip. . .

The Icanitzu were already in the corridor. They were as immune to the fire as they were to Kyle's bullets. Arturus had never seen one before.

They were far more human than the dyitzu. On their own, their facial features could have passed for a person's. Their skin tone was too grey, however, and Arturus couldn't tell if they were tinged with red, or if that tint was caused by the illumination of the corridor's flames. Their eyes were the same glossy, obsidian black pupil-full orbs that the dyitzu had. Arturus noticed, as the first came through snarling, that all of their teeth were canines. Their bodies were masculine in form but devoid of any genitalia. Five fingered hands ended in claws, their human ankles were attached to demonic three toed feet—two talons in front, one towards the back. They had wings as well. Long black bat-like wings which they kept folded behind them.

Fitch was the closest to the corridor and stood up behind his mound to face them. One Icanitzu leapt upon the mound, its talons digging in with enough force to knock some of the stones loose, its wings spread to help its balance. The thing swung out with one claw. The blow caught Fitch across his face, sending him spinning back to his hands and knees.

"Fitch!" Duncan shouted.

The claw had ripped open Fitch's cheek from the corner of his mouth to the back of his jaw. He held his hand to his face to try and stop the bleeding. The Icanitzu kicked out, its talons finding purchase in Fitch's side. It pulled its leg backwards, ripping cloth, flesh and muscle away from Fitch's abdomen. It leapt down from the mound, mouth open, and bit into his neck.

Drip.

The second Icanitzu came over the mound at full speed—and ran straight into Galen's haymaker. Blood fountained from its nose as it stumbled away from the corridor and into one corner.

Drip.

The first Icanitzu stood up from the mess of blood and flesh that it had made of Fitch. Galen had dropped low, like a wrestler, and shot in towards the beast. Arturus had experienced in practice the force of the man. One might as well try and resist a ton of stone.

Galen got in under the devil easily and powered his way up. The Icanitzu struggled to claw at him, but the warrior shoved it away, transferring his body's momentum to the beast. It slammed into the far wall.

Drip...

"Keep shooting!" Aaron said, dashing past the corridor's entrance to face the Icanitzu.

"Keep the dyitzu out," Galen ordered.

The Icanitzu Galen was fighting swung at him. He moved back quickly, but the devil was able to rake its claws against his side. The blow did little more than tear the cloth that covered his body armor.

Arturus turned back towards the corridor in time to see the next wave of fire.

"Duck!" he shouted as he took cover.

The hunters followed his example and dropped behind their stone mounds. When Arturus stood again he saw some of the dyitzu had made it into the corridor. They had ducked low and were covering their faces as they charged. Unlike the Icanitzu, they were not immune to their own fire—nor to Arturus' bullets.

He let loose several rounds with the rest of the hunters, their efforts mowing down the devils as they neared Fitch's bleeding body.

"Keep them off me!" Duncan screamed, getting up and running towards his fallen friend.

Arturus glanced towards Galen and Aaron. Aaron was bleeding from his shoulder and had been backed into a corner. Galen had locked up one arm of his Icanitzu and had his other hand on the back of the devil's head, pushing it down. He forced the thing into the wall. At first it tried to strike out with its free claw, but as Galen began throwing knees at its head, the devil brought its arm to its face to defend itself.

Everything he taught me works.

Arturus tore his gaze away from his mentor and ran around his mound, firing as he did so. He tried to keep in front of Duncan as the man ran for Fitch's body. Avery and Johnny

Huang came out firing as well. Duncan grabbed Fitch by the shoulders as Arturus ducked a fireball. Arturus cast another glance behind him when he heard Fitch's body drop. Duncan was running back for cover. Arturus could see why. Fitch was beyond hope. So much of his blood pooled about him, gushing out from his neck, that it had spread into some of the dyitzu fire. There the blood bubbled as it evaporated.

Arturus took two running steps and dove back over his flaming funeral mound. Johnny Huang did likewise as Kyle let off another shot. Arturus did not doubt that the marksman had felled another one.

Drip.

Arturus focused on another shadow in the room beyond and brought it down with a well aimed bullet. The dyitzu corpses in the corridor were burning. He could smell their fat as they were incinerated.

Drip.

"Turi!" Galen's voice immediately called his attention. "Choke!"

Drip...

The Icanitzu Galen faced was a mess of blood. One of its obsidian colored eyeballs dangled from its empty eye socket, having been forced out of its head by the fierceness of Galen's knees. Its skull had been fractured and was not in entirely the correct shape. Had the thing been a human, Arturus had no doubt it would be dead. The devil was still pushing back. Galen let it off the wall and stepped half out of its way. He tugged at the Icanitzu's arms and tripped it to the floor. It landed on its knees. Arturus ran towards it. He jumped on the devil's back and wrapped his legs around its waist as if he was going to ride it piggyback. He slid one arm around its throat and the other behind its head.

The thing reached up with its claws, ready to rip at Arturus' arms.

"Flatten it out boy!"

Arturus had no idea whether the voice was Galen's in reality, or if he was just remembering his lessons. He pushed the weakened creature's legs back with his feet. The Icanitzu went face first into the stone, crushing its own eyeball between the floor and its cheekbone.

It got one of its claws on Arturus' arm.

I can't choke it!

He let go and slid his arm over the devil's wings and under its arm pits, trying to keep his limbs out of its reach. He looked up to Galen for instruction.

Aaron had worked his way out from his corner. The bleeding from his shoulder didn't look bad. The cut on his brow had reopened as well, but so far it hadn't bled into his eyes.

Galen attacked Aaron's Icanitzu from behind, taking a jump step forward as he threw a low round kick. Arturus had never seen anything kicked that hard in his life. Galen's shin impacted with the Icanitzu's thigh, spinning the beast away from Aaron, buckling its leg. Arturus heard the smack of the kick over the Kyle's gunshot. Aaron and Galen swarmed the thing with punches.

"Too many!" Avery shouted.

Arturus looked back down to his enemy. It was starting to regain some of its wits.

Galen, help! I can't fight an Icanitzu.

He had to choke it, soon. Or break its neck, or something.

But its claws.

He dropped a couple of elbows onto the back of the thing's neck to keep it stunned and then reached out to grab one of its hands. He gripped its forefinger, pushing against the back of its hand with the heel of his palm for leverage. The resistance was more than he expected. He pushed down with his hips which had the effect of forcing his body weight forward. This flattened out the Icanitzu even farther while increasing the pressure on its digit. Its finger popped out of socket with a loud snap.

It can still claw me. I can't choke it yet.

So he moved on to the second finger.

Snap.

And then the third.

Snap.

The thing let out a high pitched howl.

He let his body relax after each break before pushing down again with his hips, rocking forward each time as he grabbed a finger, and rocking back as he pulled to break it.

And the fourth.

Snap.

He couldn't remember Galen's instructions on how to break thumbs, so he moved on to its other hand.

Snap.

"Too many!" Avery shouted again.

"Turi, disengage," Galen shouted. "Avery, get the AK ready. Everyone else run."

Drip.

"Run!"

Arturus leapt up from his Icanitzu. It stood up behind him but quickly fell over. The devil tried to catch itself as it fell, its fingers splaying out at odd angles when its hands hit the stone. It wailed again.

Arturus followed the hunters in their dash out of the room. He hadn't realized how smoky the air had become while he'd been fighting on the floor. The haze was thick enough to water his eyes and stick in his throat.

Avery's AK 47 went off behind him on full auto. The muzzle

flashes lit up the haze around him, almost blinding him.

"Run Run Run Run!" Aaron was shouting.

They sprinted through the dark rooms beyond, dyitzu fire swarming at their backs and sometimes lighting their way. Johnny ran straight into a wall, unable to see it as they turned a corner. He stopped, stunned, his nose broken. Duncan grabbed him by the collar and dragged him onward. After a few stumbles, Johnny regained his wits.

"Through here!" Aaron shouted. "Avery, another clip."

The reports sounded off at a breakneck tempo.

"Go!" Duncan shouted as Arturus passed him.

They were no longer beneath the river, Arturus could tell. The rooms were just as dark, but as they neared the islands of light he could tell that the stone had returned to the deep shades of purple.

"I don't see them," Avery said as he caught up.

"Keep moving," Aaron replied. "We haven't got much of a lead on them."

Arturus hadn't realized how hard he was breathing. He felt light headed.

Keep it together.

The passages blurred by as they ran, dots of distant light appearing and receding.

"Down here," Aaron ordered, taking them down a dark side passage.

They might run on past us.

They raced into the blackness.

Or we might run into a dead end.

The passage took them right, then left, and then right again. It was so dark that Arturus couldn't quite see the people in front of him. They slowed down as a group, stumbling forward as fast as they dared go.

Someone finally stopped. Arturus and the rest of the hunters halted around him.

"Fuck," Wistan said.

The hunter was slapping at himself.

"You okay?" Aaron asked.

"Yeah, fine."

Arturus was glad for the break and tried to catch his breath. He heard something in the distance.

That's not coming from behind us, that's ahead. Is it water?

It didn't sound like water. He couldn't place it.

The claws of the dyitzu that are chasing us, perhaps? Did they somehow get in front of us?

"Fuck," Wistan repeated. "Something's on me. Mabe, get your lighter."

Arturus heard the hunter rustling through his pack.

"We need to keep moving," Aaron said.

"How's your arm?" Galen asked.

"Fine. Bleeding, but not much. I'm not light headed or anything."

"We don't have much time," Duncan's voice came out between his gasps for breath.

The sound was more like the dropping of pins, Arturus noticed. Thousands and thousands of tiny pins.

"Quiet," Aaron chided. "I'm trying to listen for the dyitzu."

Mabe's shuffling in his pack stopped. "Got it."

I don't know if I can run much farther. I'm exhausted.

He tried to remember what had tired him out so much. Was it the fight with the Icanitzu? It must have been. And the adrenaline.

I fought it. Will Galen be proud? Or mad that I didn't kill it? Is it still coming?

He bit his lip as if the pain would wash away his fear.

He couldn't feel any pain.

Too much adrenaline.

He heard the flicking of Mabe's lighter and saw the sparks. After the third try, a single finger of flame shot up from the lighter. He held it up towards Wistan. "You okay, man?"

Is the sound getting louder?

"Oh shit, what's that?" Mabe said.

Arturus and the rest of the hunters gathered around Wistan. On his arm, illuminated by the lighter, was a small spider. It was maybe a half inch tall.

"Poisonous?" Wistan asked, his voice shaking.

"Nothing in Hell is poisonous," Aaron answered.

Galen grunted his agreement.

"Shit, I've got one on me too," Johnny's voice was strangely nasal.

Arturus caught a glimpse of him in the lighter's light. Johnny's nose was horribly disfigured and swollen. Arturus could see the dip where the septum had broken. Johnny slapped at his shoulder.

The lighter went out for a second, but Mabe quickly relit it.

The spider on Wistan's arm was oddly reflective. Arturus got even closer to focus on it. Its legs appeared to be made of metal and were catching the light. He saw as it moved that there was a miniscule spur near the bottom of each of its legs. It moved a few inches across the hunter's arm, perhaps scared by how close Arturus had gotten, its spurs burying themselves into Wistan's flesh. The man's skin raised just slightly before popping back down as each leg freed itself. Behind the spider, welling up from its footprints in the skin, were small beads of blood.

The sound is definitely getting louder.

"Silverleg spider," Aaron whispered as he flicked the thing

off of Wistan's arm.

"Light a torch," Galen ordered, his words as urgent as Arturus could ever remember them being.

Arturus then heard the howl of an Icanitzu echoing through the corridors behind them.

Mabe returned to his pack.

"Quickly, Mabe," Galen said.

The rain of pin drops was loud enough that Galen's voice didn't drown the sound out.

Mabe's torch sprang to life. Arturus looked down the corridor.

Spiders were coming around the bend. A few had come ahead, but behind them, where they were thickest, he couldn't even see the floor beneath them. Many were marching along the walls. The corridor was lit with countless points of light as the torches caught the thousands upon thousands of silver legs. The myriad lights spun in circles, pouring down the corridor, dancing over Arturus' head and across his body.

"More torches," Galen ordered. "They're swarming."

Two more sprang into life, and then another, each one multiplying the amount of tiny lights.

The spiders feared the flames.

Some, perhaps blinded or confused, fled towards the torches. They popped in quick conflagrations as the hunters brought their fire low. Most of the spiders pulled away, however, and fled to the edges and corners of the corridor.

The four men with torches, Mabe, Wistan, Johnny and Avery, moved to the front. The spiders fled farther away, their sudden movement sounding like a shower of pins.

"Should we go back?" Mabe asked.

Aaron shook his head, slowly, from side to side.

"Two torches in front, two in back," Galen said. "How many extras do we have?"

Arturus didn't dare take his gaze away from the spiders. He heard the hunters answer his father, though he wasn't paying enough attention to know who was saying what.

"I've got two."

"One left."

"Two."

The ten of them huddled together. The four men with torches moved to the corners, their backs to the group.

Arturus heard the pops of the braver silverlegs as the torches caught them.

As quickly as they could, they pushed forward through the pops and the thousands of points of reflected torchlight. The spiders climbed the walls en masse, scurrying away from the fire to the tune of a hundred thousand needles dropping.

The spiders did not thin as they rounded the bend.

How many can there be?

— 30 —

Arturus could not see well from the center of the huddle. The hunters around him were warm and sweaty. It was hard for him to keep his balance as they were constantly pushing him from all sides. Johnny did lose his balance, but stopped himself from falling by reaching out and touching the wall. Arturus caught a glimpse of his spider covered hand.

"Fuck." Johnny shook them off. "Fuck, fuck."

Arturus caught a glimpse of Johnny's hand again between Aaron and Duncan. It was a bloody mess.

"How do they keep getting on me?" Kyle asked.

Galen pointed up.

Arturus looked but wished he hadn't. Some of the silverlegs had managed to cling to the ceiling. They dropped off from time to time.

The torches scare them and they lose their footing.

"Jesus," Kyle muttered. "Which way, left or right?"

"Right." Aaron replied.

They crept down the corridor. The smell was awful, like food after a corpse had gotten into it.

"Will they come after us?" Wistan asked.

"Dyitzu probably won't," Galen answered. "They'd have to burn their way through, or the spiders would rip them to pieces. The Icanitzu might, though."

I couldn't fight one here, amidst the spiders.

The right side of the passage opened up. Beyond it was a wall of rotting flesh and spider eggs.

"Oh God." Arturus wasn't sure who said it.

"Keep moving." That was Aaron.

"My torch is getting low," Wistan warned.

"Get him a replacement," Aaron ordered. "Wistan, don't light it until you've used that one up, you got me?"

"Yes, sir."

A spider dropped onto Avery's shoulder. Arturus reached

to flick it off of him. One of the legs caught in his fingernail. He had to swat the thing off with his other hand. It left an odd dent in his nail, right above the cuticle.

"Left or right?"

"Right."

Arturus heard a sudden rush of flame. The popping became louder and more consistent. The rain of pins got louder as well. He stood on his toes and craned his neck to try and see what was going on around him but was pushed back down as the group kept going.

"Switched torches," Wistan reported over a sudden rush of fire.

Arturus stepped on a silverleg. He felt the slightest tingle in his big toe.

One of its legs is stuck in my boot.

He felt the tingle with each step. He lifted his foot to try and work out the needle but had to put it down to catch his balance. The tingle became a tiny shout of pain.

Can't do anything about it now.

"Right or left?" Arturus was losing track of who was saying what.

"Right," Aaron answered.

"We'll go in circles."

"I said right."

The corridor wound on, turning back on itself in places. Arturus wished he was on the edge of the huddle rather than being stuffed, practically blind, in its middle.

"My torch is low."

"Mine too," that was Johnny's voice.

We'll have to use two more torches soon.

"Look, a crawlway! It might be our way out."

"That thing is full of spiders."

"We are *not* going in there."

"There has to be a better way," Aaron said. "Keep going."

Arturus did his best not to imagine what would happen when the torches went out. They would be trapped in the darkness. Then the spiders would walk all over them. He bit his lip.

This time it hurt.

Be like Galen. Galen's not afraid of anything.

But his heart wasn't like Galen's. His heart was like Rick's. He wore it on his sleeve sometimes so that Massan could see it. So that Alice knew that he loved her. So that Ellen knew that he didn't.

They can't keep coming.

But this was the Carrion and the spiders *could* keep coming. They could run out of torches and still have miles of silverlegs left to wade through.

"Left or right?"

"Left."

"Why not right?"

"We've already been right."

"How the fuck can you know?"

"Because there's God damn burnt spiders to the right. Go left."

A spider ran across his boot. He didn't bother to try and get rid of it. It ran off of his foot on its own, scurrying as quickly as it could into the shadows.

It's not your fault the devil gave you silver legs.

Kyle ran into Arturus from behind, hard, pushing him into Mabe.

"Jesus," Mabe said, but just kept on walking.

Arturus' right ear was ringing now, and he couldn't hear anything from it. For some reason, hearing the rain of needles only on his left side gave him a sense of vertigo.

Don't you dare fall.

His ear was throbbing.

Kyle was shooting right next to me. And my rifle was on that side, too.

One silverleg in particular caught his eye as it moved across the wall. It was as large as his fist.

The swirl of lights around him added to his sense of vertigo.

Blood was still dripping from Johnny's hand.

"Right or left?" Someone asked.

"Fuck," Aaron shouted.

"We haven't been left," that voice was Patrick's.

"That goes back to the original fork and then to the dyitzu," Galen said.

"Well, that's the way we have to go."

"We may not have enough fire."

"I'm low," Avery said. "Need another torch."

"Turn around," Galen ordered. "To the crawlway."

Please don't.

"Agreed," Aaron shouted. "Turn around."

Arturus heard another torch come to life.

"Fuck, burnt my finger."

One extra.

"As fast as you can," Aaron ordered.

"The spiders."

"Leave a few!"

"Jesus fucking Christ."

They retreated back through the corridor. Arturus saw the burnt corpses of the silverlegs as they walked over them.

"Straight or left?"

"Straight."

"Left," Galen said.
"Left," Aaron agreed.
"Why the fuck are we going to the crawlway?"
The ringing in Arturus' ear increased in intensity, making it even more difficult for him to be sure of which one of the hunters was speaking. He tried to stay steady. His world was beginning to spin.
"Because we'll only need two torches there." Galen said.
Oh God. In the crawlway I'll be first.
"My torch is low."
"We've only got one extra."
"I don't care, it's low."
"Let it burn your God damn hand."
Arturus saw the crawlway. It was circular and had a slight upslope.
"Turi, you first," Galen said. "Give him your fresh torch, Avery. Put out the others, except for Wistan's. Quickly, boy. Wistan you're last."
Arturus waved the torch around the lip of the hole. The spiders either popped, consumed by the fire, or fled. He climbed in and moved forward. He could hear the hunters piling in after him.
"Fuck! They're on me. Turi, be more careful."
"No time," Galen said. "Keep going, Turi."
He crawled as fast as he could. The passage narrowed until, even on his hands and knees, his back touched the ceiling. Some of the spiders seemed not to know which way to run. The ones that popped left their legs behind. Some of the needles rolled down the passage. Some caught in his clothing. He could hear that not all of the hunters had made it into the passage.
Please, no narrower.
Screams echoed up the tunnel.
"Wistan's fucked, they're all over him."
"Get the torch, Kyle," Galen shouted.
"I can't, he's fucking dying."
It was Wistan who was screaming.
"Get the torch."
"I can't. I'm not getting back out of this tunnel."
"Grab it with your feet."
Arturus waved his own torch back and forth frantically, trying to clear the spiders faster. Without a torch in the back the spiders would catch up to him.
"I got it! I fucking got it!"
"Go!"
"They're on my legs!" Kyle yelled. "They're all over my legs!"
"Who's got the spare torch?"
"Wistan did."

"Fuck."

"I've got one, it's mostly burnt down."

"Is that you, Johnny."

"Yeah." Johnny sounded like he was pretty near the front.

"Anyone else?"

"Faster, Turi," Galen said.

Kyle's screams of pain intensified.

"Keep going, Kyle," Aaron shouted.

"He's not moving! Kyle's not moving!"

"Listen to me, Kyle," Galen's voice boomed in the tunnel. "I will carry you to safety, but if you lose that torch, we'll all die. You get me? I don't care how much it hurts, you keep crawling."

Smoke was in Arturus' eyes. He could barely see enough to make sure to keep the silverlegs away. He felt one as it marched across his head and down his neck. He was initially relieved when it came to his shirt, until he felt it going down his collar. The passage narrowed further, forcing him to crawl from his belly.

What if it gets too tight?

"They're all over me!"

"I don't want to die like this."

"Kyle, you with me?"

"Kyle? Kyle?"

"Kyle?"

"Fuck!" Kyle responded. "I lost the torch."

"Go back."

"I won't go back."

"Now!"

"I can't feel my legs."

"Get him Johnny's torch."

"Johnny, pass it back!" Aaron shouted above the din.

Arturus tried to look back. The afterimage of his own torch blinded him. He could vaguely see the reflected light of Kyle's abandoned torch along the top of the passageway, but that was all he could make out. He turned back to the spiders.

Please end. Please end.

"It's only a stub."

"Kyle doesn't have a lighter," Galen shouted. "Mabe's got to light it."

"The lighter is in my pack."

"Faster, Turi," Galen said.

"Get it out."

Turi felt the heat of his own torch on his hand. It was almost too much to bear.

"Mine's low," his voice sounded high, and he could only hear it in his left ear.

"I've got it lit!" Mabe said.

"Pass it back."

"Kyle?"

"I'm alive. Pass it back."

Someone screamed, but it sounded too hoarse to be human.

"Fuck."

"What happened?" Aaron asked.

"Patrick, he got the fire in his face."

"Get me the torch."

"Kyle you okay?"

"I've got it. I've got it."

"Patrick, move. Move, Patrick."

"He ain't breathing right."

"Patrick, if you don't move, I will climb over your ass."

"Grab onto my feet, Patrick. I'll pull you. Come on, Patrick. Push him, Duncan."

"Oh fuck! He ain't right."

"He breathed some of the fire!"

"What's going on back there?" Aaron's voice cracked.

"He ain't right man. He ain't breathing right."

"Keep him calm." That was Galen's voice. "Keep him moving."

The pain in Arturus' hand was more than he could stand.

"I'm almost out!" Arturus shouted.

"Light your shirt on fire," Galen ordered.

Arturus pushed his torch ahead. It was little more than a burning stump. He caught sight of his hand. Blisters were bubbling up from blackened skin. He struggled to get his shirt over his head. His sweat made the cloth cling to his body. He pulled as hard as he could, feeling a sharp pain in his shoulder. The shirt ripped. He tossed it over the torch. Everything went dark.

Oh no, I smothered the fire.

The shirt lit, his sweat hissing as the flames spread.

Thank you.

He pushed the burning pile forward with his rifle.

"Your pack too, Turi," Galen said, "Anything you can burn. Hunters, pass your clothing up front."

"Good idea," Aaron shouted.

"Kyle, leave a burning pack behind you. Kyle? Kyle?"

"He's still moving, but he ain't talking."

Arturus felt clothing land on his ankle. He reached back and grabbed it. Another few shirts followed.

His own shirt was burning quickly. He tossed an article of one of the hunter's clothing forward as his own burnt out.

"This won't last," Arturus shouted.

"Turi," Galen's voice echoed, "if your light goes out, run as far as you can, as fast as you can."

Arturus began coughing with every breath. He was

crawling over the ashes of burnt clothing, much of it still very hot.

"I don't want to die like this."

"Kyle, you alive?"

"He's fine, keep moving."

"Fuck what's that noise?"

"Patrick's vomiting."

"Keep going."

With his shirt gone, the spiders were walking all over his skin. He wasn't able to tell whether the liquid pouring down his back was sweat or blood.

"I can't breathe."

"Light!" Arturus screamed. "There's light."

"Move, boy."

Did I tell them wrong?

He feared it was just the afterimage of the torch, but after a few more feet he knew the light was real... but it was also dim.

He ignored the spiders, letting them crawl as they wished, and pushed the flaming clothing through the tunnel as fast as he could.

"Kyle?"

"Patrick ain't moving."

"Grab on, Patrick."

"Push him."

We're going to make it.

The dim light grew larger, drawing him forward.

Suddenly he was there, at the end.

"We're here!" Arturus added another shirt to the burning pile before him and pushed it through the exit.

"Duncan, push him!"

Arturus slipped out from the crawlway. He kicked the burning clothes away from the wall and dropped his pack onto it. The circle of light kept the spiders at bay.

Oh no, my ammo.

The hunters piled out, one by one. They were a bloody mess.

Galen emerged lithely, a flare gun in hand. He discharged round after round into the chamber.

The room was huge. Nearly a hundred yards wide and filled with spiders. The vermin spread away from the flares like ripples in water.

"They thin towards the back wall," Aaron shouted.

"There's the exit," Galen said, pointing.

Galen turned back and helped Patrick out of the tunnel. The man was covered in vomit. Half of his face had been burnt off. He had no hair or eyebrows. Duncan came next, and then Kyle.

Kyle was pale. His legs had been flayed. Galen pulled strips of cloth from his own pack as the light from his flares began dying away, one by one. Some of the strips he added to Arturus' pile. He used two of them to tourniquet Kyle's legs, using a rifle barrel and a cleaning rod to twist them tight.

The other hunters added what they could to the fire. Johnny cut off his pants and threw them in. The first of the rounds in Arturus' pack went off. Galen gave him a look as he hoisted Kyle onto his shoulders. He fired off another flare towards the exit. The spiders were waiting at the edge of the light.

"Run for it," Galen shouted. "Follow the flare's path, or you'll die."

Johnny took two steps and screamed, looking down at his feet.

"Don't fall," Aaron shouted. "Run where they're thinnest!"

Patrick looked unsteady, but he managed to move. His breathing came in gasps. Blood trickled from his mouth.

Arturus began his run towards the exit. Needles began shooting into his feet as he crushed the spiders. Another flare went off over his head.

He felt the pain in his feet more strongly than he had felt anything else in his life. His legs began to wobble, going weak. He felt his body fighting him. It did not want to run. It did not want to let him put any more weight on his legs.

He dared to look behind him. He watched Mabe fall down. The man did not get back up. The spiders covered him over.

Fear pushed Arturus onwards. He looked down, trying to make sure he didn't stumble. Someone had caught up with him. He couldn't see who it was out of the corner of his eye. Tears welled up.

I can't. I can just die. Lay down like Mabe.

He couldn't breathe. He'd inhaled too much smoke in the tunnel. Hell weighed down on his shoulders.

I'm sorry, I can't.

He wondered about the next life. It would be terrible, he knew, but at least he would be able to breathe. The needles in his feet became daggers. He couldn't say how many there were.

He looked to his right. Galen was beside him, running with Kyle on his shoulders. Running with all that extra weight, plus his pack and body armor.

If I fall, he'll have to carry me.

That seemed horribly unfair. Arturus had never felt pain like this before, and he couldn't imagine what the needles in Galen's feet must feel like with the weight of an extra person on his back. Arturus didn't want to add to Galen's burden, and somehow that mattered more to him than anything else. He looked up and saw the exit through the light of a dying flare. They ran towards it. The spiders thinned out more.

Arturus made it through the exit. A corridor veered off to the right, and he took it. Odd symbols, looking like moons and stars, had been carved into the side walls. Then he saw a shadow in the darkness before him.

Is that a person?

It was only a boulder, perhaps waist high, with a Star of David carved into it. Beyond it was a dead end.

"Go back!" Galen shouted.

Some of the silverlegs had followed them into the corridor.

Galen fired a flare over the heads of the hunters to help scatter the spiders and they made it back around the corner.

"This way." Galen led them, flare gun in hand.

They came to a river in the next chamber. Beyond it there were no silverlegs. The river was ten feet wide. Galen sprinted forward and leapt it, even with Kyle on his shoulders. The hunters jumped into the water, some too tired to even keep their rifles over their heads.

"Keep your weapons dry," Aaron ordered.

Those that could, obeyed. Galen dragged the hunters out of the river as they made it to the far side. Many stayed on their knees.

"Come on," Galen told them. "The place is thick with devils. There will be no safety at the river."

Arturus managed to follow him through the passages. Sometimes he and the hunters were moving on all fours. He could not guess at how long they traveled. If Galen told him it was five minutes, he would have believed it. He would also have believed it had been five days.

Eventually Galen led them to some steps. Arturus could no longer walk, so he crawled up the stairs. The room Galen had taken them too was cold, with a single entrance and a ceiling that was only five feet tall. The hunters followed in, leaving behind them a trail of blood and water.

I should crawl to the corner. Make space for the others.

Arturus passed out.

When he awoke, Galen was gone.

"Where's Galen?" Arturus asked.

Aaron was the only one that stirred. "He's out. We left a trail. He's gone to mop it up."

Arturus took stock of the hunters. Some had taken off their shoes and boots. Their feet were horribly swollen. It appeared that none of them could walk. Kyle's legs might have to be amputated. Patrick's breathing was quick and tortured. He might not live. None of them looked ready for a fight.

One dyitzu and we might all be doomed.

Consciousness came and went. He fought to keep it, because he wanted to stand guard. Galen would be proud of that. Eventually he managed to sit, feeling the cold stone against his shirtless back. He heard footsteps. They were booted, which was a good sign. He didn't know what he'd do if it was a Carrion man. Surrender, perhaps?

"Galen," the voice reported.

"Turi."

His father entered and grunted.

He's proud that I was able to keep watch. He probably doesn't know that I was asleep for most of it.

Galen looked across the room at the wounded hunters.

"We can't move," Arturus said.

Galen nodded.

"We're going to be late," Arturus said.

"They will seal the entrance, certainly, before we have a chance to return."

Arturus' gaze fell to his own boots. He saw silver needles sticking out of them in many places.

They're going to wall us in. We'll be buried in the Carrion.

"Rick will be sad," Arturus said.

Galen nodded. "Get some sleep, Turi. You need to heal."

Arturus imagined Rick's face. He imagined Rick all alone in the battery room. Cooking breakfast by himself. His brow would be furrowed. He would cut the hound liver quickly, and fiercely, as if that would somehow help him vent his anger. He would talk to himself and sleep poorly. He would become surly and snappy, except there wouldn't be anyone there for him to snap at.

If we never come back...

Rick would cry. The thought hurt Arturus like the needles in his feet never could.

I'll come home, Rick. Just wait. It'll be like that time when Galen was missing for a year. You'll see.

He heard some noise in the corner and looked over to Aaron. The hunter had stirred. He had something in his hands. It looked like braided hair.

He's a good leader.

He thought of Alice. That was probably her hair. He imagined her too, in the hovel with the dreamcatcher. She, also, would be waiting for them to return. He felt a sharp pang in his throat. No, she would be waiting for Aaron to return. He hoped that the dreamcatcher could stop all the nightmares she might have for them.

It's just a symbol, silly.

He remembered how the beads would rattle when someone knocked on her door blanket. He remembered her smile.

But the last thing that he thought of before he drifted off was Ellen. Of how warm his cheek had felt when she had kissed it. Of how angry she had been when she threw the knowledge fruit at him. Of how she had thought that he must be the black knight, since he was in Hell.

The black knight looked better anyway.

And then sleep took him.

Part III
The Squire of the Deep

From the Book of the Infidels, Gehennic Law: The Golden Net

In all of Olympus there was no goddess more beautiful than Aphrodite. She was married, however, to the hideous and deformed hunchback Hephaestus. Though Hephaestus was the most skilled craftsmen in all of Gaia, Aphrodite was not always satisfied with his love. Soon she sought another. She was the epitome of femininity, and was thus drawn to Ares, who was excellent at all things masculine.

Aphrodite's mother-in-law, Hera, became angered at the mistreatment of her son Hephaestus, so she told the Craftsmen God that his wife had not been faithful. Furious, the hunchbacked God then forged a golden net so strong that it had the power to ensnare even a divinity. He laid it on his own bed, and, when Ares came to his wife, he sprung his trap. He then hung the unfaithful pair in the Agora of Olympus for all to see."

Zeus and Apollo came upon them in the morning, seeing also that all the other gods were staring at the trapped pair.

"Look at Ares there," Apollo said, "naked, helpless and trapped in that golden net with Aphrodite."

"I know," Almighty Zeus replied while admiring Aphrodite's form. "That lucky bastard."

From Neostoicism: Philosophia

"Men often find the whys of the Universe to be opaque: If God is Love, why Polio? But I've found that the greatest of our philosophical questions are not difficult at all. They only appeared so, since we had always supposed that it was we who were the answer."

—Endymion

"Don't shit where you eat."

—Ares

Benson, where's he gone?

Carlisle's wound bled freely. It had sapped his strength, and he had fallen—so now he crawled.

I have been dying for years.

His mind, unguarded, began remembering truths he had long denied.

He collapsed completely.

It hadn't always been this way. He hadn't always been damned. He used to have angels over his head. He remembered lying like this next to Anna McNamara in an Alabama cornfield. They weren't married, and she needed to stay a virgin, so he sodomized her. He didn't know what he was doing, not really. He was just a kid. No one had ever sat him down and told him in Bible school what sodomy was.

Except he knew.

He knew damn well he shouldn't have been doing it. He didn't even need the Good Book to tell him that. And it wasn't like he stopped it there.

Stay awake. The Infidel is close behind me. I must keep going.

He caught his breath, shook his head to clear his memories and conscience, and then continued to crawl.

He looked back and saw his trail, left like a slug behind him, stretching back the five thousand or so feet to where he had first fallen, to where the Infidel had stabbed him.

Impossible.

"Can you hear me?" The woman's voice was deep and sultry, the accent unrecognizable. "Can you hear me?"

Anna?

He meant to call it off with Anna McNamara, but he was going to make sure he did it the right way. He invited her over to his father's farm and took her for a walk, right by that cornfield where he'd penetrated her and dirtied his manhood. He told her his mind, then. He told her exactly what God wanted for them.

She understood.

She told him how right he was, how strong he was. How she wished she could fight the sins of the flesh like he could. He was going to teach her. He was going to help save her soul. He meant to. He really did.

That time he took her in the cunt.

She bled a muddy river, just like the one he was bleeding now.

He clutched at the stone as he tried to drag himself forward. He felt the grain of the stone slide beneath his slick fingertips.

No, Anna. You did it to yourself. You shouldn't have tricked me into fucking you.

The Infidel was coming. Of course the Infidel was coming.

Carlisle hadn't stabbed himself in the side. But it was a woman, a shade, who approached instead. She stood over him for a few moments before finally kneeling next to him. She reached out and touched his shoulder. He found her touch comforting.

"I need you to remember for me, Carlisle." The low feminine voice invaded his dreams. "I need for you to let me know what happened. Nod if you can hear me."

He'd betrayed himself back then, and he knew it. Any fool could see that. It wasn't too long before all the fools did. He was a fornicator. His father was furious when he found out. The man beat Carlisle's ass good, too, wailing on him long through the night.

"My boy wants to knock some girl up, that's fine," his father said. "He wants to knock some girl up *and* sit down. That shit ain't happening."

Carlisle saw their eyes on him at church. Saw how the mothers hovered near their daughters when he was close. Saw how Meghan Thomson, the pretty little thing from his youth group, looked at him as if he was some kind of trash. Good girls wouldn't talk to him anymore. Only the sluts wanted anything to do with him.

Sluts like Anna McNamara, and she wanted him something fierce. She called him all the time. Saying she was sorry. Saying that they would wait until they got married to do it again. But he knew what that *slut* wanted. He wasn't falling for that shit again.

You can't ever get that back, Joe Carlisle. Once you give that away to some no good whore you can't ever give it to your wife. You can be a born again Christian, but there ain't no such thing as a born again virgin. You do it once, and you're a fornicator. A good for nothing, dirty-ass-motherfuckin'-fornicator.

Fornicator? Was that even a bad thing?

He hadn't cared, right? Fuck them. He didn't need them. He needed Jesus. He prayed all night. He prayed all day. He came to Pastor Burnak and laid it all out for him, stripping his soul as bare as babe at baptism. He didn't hold no punches. He was a sinner. He was fallen. He was of the flesh. But oh my, sweet Lord on high, Jesus Christ, he was going to get better. He was going to reform. He was going to pray and repent. He was going to give God his whole heart and beg his righteous forgiveness.

But it wasn't like everyone else could see that. They couldn't know that he'd been the receptacle of divine mercy.

To them he was still a fornicator.

He'd halfway made it to redemption when Anna came to him. She'd been missing her period, she said. She'd been to the doctors, she said. It was dangerous for her to have the child, she said. They were going to give her an abortion.

An abortion?

She was going to go inside that body of hers to her godless womb and destroy that poor innocent soul that lay helpless within her? That kid hadn't asked for its father to sin. Abortion? Hell no. Not if he had anything to say about it. If God hadn't wanted that child to be born, he wouldn't have had that child made. It was a sin to kill. She was going to be a murderer. If she died with that baby, then she died. That's the way God wanted it, right? The doctors, they knew all about science and evolution and all that bullshit, but they didn't have a God damn clue about the important things. About how God had a plan for them all. About how He was going to take care of Anna McNamara if she trusted Him. About how this world was nothing. This world was shit. Hell, they were all nothing. They might as well all be good for nothing, dirty-ass-motherfuckin'-fornicators. They had all fallen. Didn't those doctors know that?

"They can be real book smart," his preacher told him, "but they don't have no common sense."

Abortion? *Abortion!* You sinful no good *slut*. How dare you? She was going to have that child. She'd convinced him to do that dirty deed as surely as Eve had convinced Adam. She'd made him the object of hate and teasing at Lewis County High. He was through with sinning. They weren't going to be murderers. He'd given himself to Jesus-motherfuckin'-Christ, didn't she know? She was going to have that baby. She sure as hell was. She was going to have it just like God wanted her to.

They kept her at his father's farm because Anna's mother hadn't wanted to hear any of it. She wanted to follow the doctor's advice. She was just like them doctors. She knew a shit ton of shit but didn't know a goddamned thing about common sense. Eternity was forever, motherfucker. Even a good for nothing *fornicator* knew that. She'd sent the police, but the Lewis county police department knew better. They weren't going to take part of killing no baby.

They'd done the right thing. He knew that. They'd made the good choice. Even she knew it by the end. He knew she did. She didn't regret it one bit. Not even as she was screaming on the operating table while the blood gushed out from between her legs in muddy rivers. Not even as the doctors swarmed all over her, trying to save her life. He'd seen the baby that came out of her, all three pounds of dead and soulless flesh.

He'd done the right thing, right? He'd followed the Bible, right? Them doctors didn't know shit.

He could look into the eyes of Anna's mother. He wasn't wrong. He hadn't killed her daughter. It was just Anna's time to go. God had taken her. Better her daughter's life than her daughter's soul, right?

He could say that. He could go home and sleep at night.

Sure he could.

He wasn't going to Hell, because Jesus owned his soul. He didn't have anything to worry about. He'd read the Good Book.

Except he had gone to Hell.

He hadn't paid enough attention, he knew now. He'd missed the couple of things that you could not do. He didn't know what they were then, but he'd found out after he died.

"You can't deny Christ," Maab had told him. "After you've accepted Him, you can't let Him go, or he's gone forever. You can't write blasphemy, either. Do it and you are forever damned."

Says so, right in the God damned Book.

He'd known it, or should have known it. It was his fault for not paying enough attention in Sunday school.

He'd broken both rules with a single sentence that he'd doodled in his senior year English book while studying on the porch by his father's cornfield.

Does God exist?

But for all the bullshit that field in Alabama had held for him it had everything that he wanted now. After all, he hadn't stabbed himself in the God damned side.

He'd vowed it would be different in Hell. He wouldn't be godless here. He'd do right, finally.

He couldn't let himself die. Not again. Not when Maab had given him a task. Had given him someone to rescue. He only hoped the Infidel hadn't gotten to the rest of Maab's men, too.

Nod if you can hear me.

He'd fallen unconscious, he realized. He felt his own cold blood on his cheek. He nodded.

"Maab?" he asked weakly.

"My name is Lilith, Carlisle. I'm here to help you."

She was circling him slowly, step by step. He fought to keep looking at her, but lifting his head from the endless pools of his own blood was too much for him.

"Christ, too," he mumbled into the muddy liquid. "He was stabbed in the side."

"Yes he was, my sweet."

"I can't stand."

"Yes you can, my sweet. You need to come to me. Can't you hear me singing?"

"The boy," Carlisle said. "I need to save the boy."

"Come find me, Carlisle."

"How?"

"This place isn't real, remember. You died again. We're in the same room, but we're not close enough yet. Listen to me. Listen to me sing."

I've heard this song.

Carlisle pushed himself to his feet, ignoring the blood that trailed out of his side.

I've known this song! I heard it on the wind! The boy's mother! The song of angels!

He followed the music.

— 31 —

"I hate waiting," Ellen said.

She sat alone with Rick, staring down at her plate. She felt guilty for not eating her helping of the dyitzu meat. Rick had seared it on the battery powered hotplates and added a powdered spice he said came from ground down hound bones. It had been garnished with hungerleaves and soaked in knowledge fruit vinegar. Her devilwheat meal had been sweetened with honey and spiced with some powder that was unknown to her. It tasted spectacular, it really did.

She just wasn't hungry.

Her eyes wandered across the table to Rick.

His wooden spoon was working his own devilwheat meal, but there were long pauses between his bites. Most of his meat was untouched. He had cut some of it into peculiarly small pieces.

"It's worse this time," he said.

It must be worse for him. I barely know them. Galen and Turi are his entire life.

"Because they're in the Carrion?"

"Morbid girl, why would you ask me such questions?"

She looked back down at her plate. "I'm sorry."

"Don't be," he said shortly. "Yes. It's worse because they're in the Carrion. Turi would tell you that I don't sleep well when Galen's gone. Even when it's just for a couple of days. Even when Hell is all but empty of devils. It's stupid of me to worry about things I can't control."

He let his spoon go. It clattered against the marble plate, its head still buried in the meal.

Ellen smiled. "Galen told you that it was stupid to worry, didn't he?"

Rick laughed and leaned back in his chair. "How did you know?"

"Sounds like him, not you," she said. "And because he told

me the same thing."

Rick massaged the bridge of his nose with his thumb and forefinger. She watched him intently for a moment and then tried to finish her food. Chewing took forever. She managed to swallow a few more bites.

This is hopeless, I'll never finish it all.

"Does Galen hate me?" she asked.

"No," he said suddenly. "Why would you think that?"

"He seems so, well, mean, I guess."

Rick shook his head and smiled. "He just hates women, is all. He likes you more than most. When he talks to Turi about you, it's always in a good way."

I think I love that boy.

It occurred to her that she was just being stupid. She was a lost, lonely little girl, who, after being thrust into Hell, fell in love with the first young man that she'd run across. But feelings were feelings, she knew. She had them, and there was no use denying them.

"Why does Galen hate women? Did he love one?"

Rick laughed aloud. "Galen could be impressed by a woman, or want a woman. But I can't imagine him respecting a girl enough to love her. It's something I try very hard to protect Turi against. Galen is always filling his head with misogynistic bullshit, even though we both agreed that wasn't the way we wanted to raise him."

"But why?" she asked. "Why does he feel that way? There must be some reason."

"We were all raised at different times, and in different places. People don't age in Hell, and Galen is very, very old. He doesn't have much use for women as partners. Doesn't have much use for me, either, come to think of it. His world is a cold, emotionless place, full of duty. One time, when Turi was very young, I asked him not to go out hunting. I asked him what I was supposed to do if he didn't come back."

Ellen leaned forward. "Well, what did he say?"

"He told me that when my favorite pot has broken, to remember that it was just a pot."

"What's that supposed to mean? What a cruel thing to say, that people are only as important pots."

"It's just how Galen thinks. People and things have purposes. His purpose was to hunt and gather food. To protect and feed Turi. If he died, I was supposed to go and find another hunter. Another protector for the boy."

And you would have, too. You would have found someone else to help raise Turi. But now, if they don't come back, you won't have anyone to raise.

"They're supposed to be back by now, aren't they?"

Rick nodded. "But Galen can take care of himself. It's

always him that's out. He's such a good fighter, Ellen. You have no idea. I know when he's gone that I'm probably more likely to die at home than he is in the wilds. I know it, but I don't feel it. This time it's different, because he's in the Carrion. This time he really can die. And worse. This time Turi's out there with him."

He got up, as slowly as an old man might, and moved over towards the wall. He pulled a lever, and the battery began to hum. Ellen watched the moving gears. Slowly, bit by bit, the battery stone began to rise.

He sat back down at the table and looked at his food. She reached out and touched his hand.

"They are coming back, right?" she asked.

"They might be unscathed. Maybe they have seen a mighty devil, or a lot of them, and are lying low. Maybe someone's injured. They might have to wait for him to heal before they return. There are traps in the Carrion. A passage may have closed behind them, and they may have to work their way back."

She shook her head. "I'm sorry, I have to ask this. I just don't know. Is any of that likely? I mean, are they dead?"

"Who knows? It's not fair," Rick managed. "Turi shouldn't have gone out there with him."

Rick will be all alone.

"Would you move into Harpsborough?" she asked.

The idea seemed silly to her as soon as she said it. She couldn't imagine Rick, or Galen, or even Turi, living in Harpsborough. They were free people. It wouldn't be right for the Citizens to order them around, or take their goods, or keep them out of the Fore.

Not to mention those Citizens won't let anyone join them now anyway.

But surely they'd let Rick in.

He shook his head. "I couldn't live there. Better to be alone."

This really is Hell.

"I'll stay with you, Rick."

He smiled. "Thank you, you're a sweetheart. I'd be happy to have you."

She took careful stock of the tortured man before her. He was in many ways the opposite of Galen. Galen was built for this place. Galen did not care who lived and who died. Galen could watch his son die in the most gruesome way and fail to blink. Why would he blink? That's just one more instant where he'd be vulnerable to an attack.

Rick's brow was furrowed, his eyes red. He cut the dyitzu meat into a few more small pieces. He was able to chew one and swallow it.

I'm feeling what you're feeling. I know how it is.

"Are you okay?" she asked.

"No. I can't even use Galen's stupid philosophy. Turi was the point, he was the duty. Why get another pot if I've lost the thing it was supposed to hold?"

He shoved his fork back down into the tray.

"What would Galen do if you and Turi had died?" Ellen asked.

Rick thought about this for a second, his face horribly serious.

"He'd try and find another boy. You see, Turi is supposed to do something. Something very important."

"I'll help you," Ellen said suddenly. "We'll have a child, if you want. I'll help you raise another Turi."

Oh God, what did I just say?

She hadn't meant to offer herself as a wife, or a lover. Or to replace the man's son. She looked at him worriedly, waiting for him to get angry.

But Rick just nodded.

Didn't he hear what I said?

"It's useless to try and eat this," Rick said.

He got up from the table, picked up his tray and walked over to the counter. "What do you know?" he asked, fishing around in the supply closet. "A pot."

He started spooning his food into the urn.

Isn't he going to say anything?

"You finished?" he asked her.

"Yeah," she stood up and handed him her plate.

Of course he won't get angry. He took my words as they were meant.

This was Hell, and because of that Ellen decided that Galen must in some way be right. Without a purpose, or a duty, you would just go mad. The trick was finding a duty worthy of all this suffering.

But I don't have to worry about finding that. They already have the duty picked out for me. I just have to trust this family and trust that their goal is a worthy one. I just have to make their cause my own.

She didn't know if the thoughts actually made her feel better or not. There was still this vast empty pit in her chest that opened up whenever she thought of Turi.

But now it's different. It hurts just as much, but now I can still move. I can still do things. There is a reason for me to breathe.

Rick's shoulders were hunched. He seemed to have been exhausted from the short chore of packing away their food.

And I have to keep breathing, that way Hell can go on hurting me.

Chelsea sat as one of the four wealthiest Citizens. They

had taken down the pulpit and installed instead a table for the main judges to sit at. The forty-five remaining members of the Fore filled out the Citizen pews. The Infidel Friend stood defiant in the central aisle, surrounded by his hecklers, looking up at his judges. The shadow of one of Father Klein's crosses fell over his head. Chelsea couldn't help but have a little bit of respect for this man.

Oh, what a waste. If only the Infidel hadn't got you.

To her right was Father Klein. To her left was the empty chair where Michael would soon be seated. Beyond that, Mancini and Copperfield. She and the others, it had been agreed, were the ones who were to ask questions. Then the entire Fore would vote on his guilt or innocence.

It would be Michael, alone, who would then decide the depth of the punishment.

As if it would be any vote but guilty. As if I don't already know what Michael will do to him.

But she tried to keep an open mind. She tried to convince herself to be a fair questioner.

The Father is afraid that his death will bring more. He says the Infidel Friend are both numerous and resilient.

But Michael would be the one to make the punishment. They could always say to the Infidel's men that they had voted him guilty, expecting some lesser sentence. Michael would be the one the Citizens would blame, but who knew if the Infidel's men would buy that excuse? Who knew if they'd even care?

Michael emerged from the chambers where Father Klein slept. From the chambers where the spider corpse and eggs were kept.

The spider that Michael killed. Could he fight an Infidel Friend? Is he gambling that he can?

The First Citizen wore his best poker face. She watched him descend into his seat. In his right hand he held a stone orb made of marble. He slammed it down against the table.

Silence.

"You seem fearless," Michael commented to the man.

His words had been not been spoken loudly, but they were quite audible in the quiet room.

The Infidel Friend's response also rang out clearly. "Most honored judge, I fear you greatly."

Lip service. If he's afraid, then Aaron's in love with me.

"I warn you," Michael said, "don't be insolent. This is no game. Your manners here may well determine whether you live or die."

"Of this I am aware, most honored judge."

Then act like it.

Chelsea watched Michael purse his lips. He absently rolled the stone ball about on the table before continuing. "I have questions which I must ask you in order to make sure that the safety of this village is maintained. Are you willing to answer such questions?"

"It would be a privilege to give you information that might help your brave people, most honored judge."

Is he deliberately trying to goad Michael?

"Why did you travel to Harpsborough?"

"I must protest the question, your honor. I had no intention of traveling here. I was dragged here while terribly wounded. My arrival was not a matter of my choice."

"Don't fill my ears with shit, Infidel Friend—"

"Cris."

"What?"

"My name is Cris. No 'h,' lest it cause confusion."

"You know damn well what I was asking."

"If it pleases you, most honored judge, I'd ask that you clarify the question so that I might answer it in a manner more towards your choosing."

He's trying to piss us off. Why?

"What were you doing in the general area?"

"I was sent in the name of the Infidel to scout nearby. I came closer to discover the extent of the settling. Then, if it were to endanger any group of people, I was going to warn them to leave."

"You are a liar, Infidel Friend," Michael responded, lines of worry forming on his forehead. "Altruism is not something your kind have. You are godless."

"I will not disagree with you if you were to say that my altruism in this case was paired with some other motive. Nonetheless, helping you was my intention."

"Are there others of you?"

"No, I was sent alone."

Chelsea couldn't tell if the whispers that came from the Citizen pews were of relief or disbelief.

"How were you wounded?" Michael asked, his poker face again in place.

"I was tricked. An unfriendly hermit shared food with me and said he would lead me to some cracks formed in Hell. Instead he led me to a pit of demons. I escaped, but only after he shot me."

"And what happened to this hermit?"

"I find it unlikely that he survived my own bullet."

"Murderer," she whispered into Michael's ear.

"You admit murder?" Michael asked.

"Had I not shot him, he would have finished me. He fired first. Have you no self-defense clause in your laws?"

Mancini leaned forward. "We only have your word that he fired first."

"True," the Infidel Friend responded. "But it is also true

that you only have my word that I fired at all. Still, if it pleases you, I have definitive proof that he fired first."

"Do tell."

The Infidel Friend pointed to the wound in his shoulder.

"I hardly call that definitive," Mancini said.

"Give me a gun. I'll show you how rarely I miss."

There were angry mutters about the pews. Michael slammed his stone against the table.

He's so arrogant.

"We are not here to try you for murder, Infidel Friend," Michael said loudly.

"Cris."

"Cris, then."

"Thank you, most honored judge. I would ask you, what is it exactly that I am being charged with?"

Michael leaned back in his chair. The infidel's posture had not changed. He had actually moved slightly closer. The shadow of the cross which had darkened his hair now fell onto the floor behind him.

For being an Infidel Friend. Is there anything worse?

"For denying God his rightful love," Michael said. "For engaging in acts which are harmful to the souls of Hell. For cavorting with devils. For mutilating and desecrating the Body of God—"

"I'm sorry, if I may so humbly interrupt your honor in this litany," the infidel said, seeming genuinely baffled, "but could you run that last one by me again?"

"Mutilation and desecration of the Body of God."

The infidel smirked. "Far be it for me to disagree with any of these charges, most honored judge. And please bear in mind, as I give you this question, that by it I in no way mean to doubt the veracity of this allegation—but how did I manage to affect the Body of God?"

"Your tattoo—"

"Scarification."

"Whatever. Your body is a sacred thing, and defacing it—"

"Like, for instance, chopping Martin's hand off?"

How the hell does he know about that? Has everyone been gossiping to him the entire time he's been in prison?

"That's different," Michael rubbed the back of his head with his hands. "Your body is a sacred thing, given to you by God—"

"Was not."

"Whether or not you deny your Creator, infidel, it does not change the fact that your body is His."

"While I must disagree with you there also, I would point out that my original point of contention was not on the philosophical nature of free will and ownership. It was a factual disagreement."

He must know his pretentiousness is going to get him killed.

"Surely you don't doubt that God made your body," Michael seemed incredulous.

"The body God furnished me with would not," Cris replied, "let's say, regrow my hand were it chopped off. I will, however, agree to the factual nature of your charge if you change the verbiage in this trivial way. Let us say that I am guilty of mutilating and desecrating the Body of Satan."

Chelsea covered her mouth to hide her laughter. Michael gave her a dark look.

He's playing Michael, not me.

Father Klein jumped in. "Your body is a copy of that one made by God, and therefore bound by the same restrictions."

"Oh, I very much doubt you believe that."

"If you did not heed the Word of God in your last life," Klein said, "it is insufferable that you do not do so now."

"In addition to showing you that your claim is fatuous, I would to also point out that you have an error in the consistency of your jurisdiction."

"I rule this city," Michael said, "and I rule the surrounding wilds."

"Let's say that Hidalgo fellow came into town, perhaps sporting a tattoo."

How does he know who Hidalgo is, or that he tattoos himself? Do they tell him everything? What kind of prison guards do we have?

Then it struck Chelsea that Aaron's first attempt to get information out of the infidel was to send Molly in to talk to him.

He probably knows what I eat for breakfast.

"Hidalgo's business with us is his business," Michael shot back. "It is not yours."

"Perhaps, unless I were inclined to feel that my fair treatment was my business. But strangely enough, I agree with you here. Maybe it could be said for Hidalgo that it would be odd were he held, as an outsider, to such tenuous theological grounding? And even if it were sound, God's law has been completed. Mayhaps only Man's law should hold now? In all of recorded history, your God, Yahweh, Father of Jesus, hasn't been able to convince more than a third of the world to believe that He even exists. Maybe we could forgive Hidalgo for not wanting to follow a God that failed?"

Michael's mask crumbled. He didn't seem angry, just shocked.

Did he just say that? Is he trying to die?

"God has not failed!" Klein burst out, standing as he spoke. "Fool! How self-deluded. What kind of man are you? That you think you can. . . come in here, *in God's own house,* and say that kind of blasphemy? What arrogance? What selfishness? What. . . If most men on Earth didn't believe Him, then that's how He wanted it."

"Great," the infidel said. "So He's not incompetent. He's just evil."

"God *made* evil," Michael broke in. "He determines what it is. Who are you to question the morality of God?"

"A recipient of his injustice."

Klein's mouth hung open for a moment. "How much arrogance can you have? You realize that you are talking about a God? A mortal cannot know His mind. It is beyond us."

"Assuming we cannot know Him, then whether he is good or evil would be beyond us as well, would it not?"

"No!" the Father shouted. "He has told us that He is good. He made good and evil."

"Maybe. Maybe morality isn't an accident of power. But who's to say that, since he created both, and can act with one, that he cannot act with the other."

"God says."

"And you believe him?"

"Yes."

"On what grounds?"

"Faith."

"Very well. If God's goodness is the premise behind you exercising God's law in this place, and I might add, this place where He doesn't exist, then I accept that your punishment of me is based on no good reason."

"No good reason?" Michael asked.

"Faith is belief in the absence of evidence."

"Faith is the only reason."

"No, most honored judge, it might actually be the only exception."

The sudden absurdity of the argument struck Chelsea. If God were a human, then it would be idiotic to trust that he didn't lie about himself being truthful. If God were only human, then his idea of morality would only be an opinion, like anyone else's.

But God is not human. And we had plenty of proof on Earth that He was the benevolent master that He claimed to be. But reason isn't enough. Reason is corruptible. Here, so close to Satan, faith is all that we have. We have no other choice but to blindly follow His will, because the devil will make sure our souls rot with every exception we make.

"You would know differently if you had ever felt God in your heart," Klein said. "His words were backed up by the facts on Earth. A pity you missed them."

"A pity," the Infidel Friend agreed. "A pity that we all did, for we are all here. Does the Book not say, 'let he who has not sinned cast the first stone?'"

"It does," said Father Klein. "It also points out that the Devil quotes scripture."

"You got me there," the Infidel Friend admitted, "but you got yourself equally. We all chose to be devils, by action or inaction. I find it difficult to justify myself hurting anyone for that. Let me go my way, and I'll not harm you. You go yours, and unless you try to hurt me, I won't stop you."

He's trying to do what Mancini warned. He's trying to talk circles around us. But he's too abrasive. Instead he's making us all hate him.

But his effect on Michael was startling.

No one's stood up to him in years. Michael respects that kind of thing.

"It is imperative that all men try to correct their mistakes," Michael said, as if quoting one of Father Klein's sermons. "We came here as wolves. Let us leave as sheep. If you do not try and follow God's way, here, after all has been made clear to you, then you are truly evil. More than that, you are willfully evil. At least on Earth you could have claimed to not know what was going on. After seeing proof of His will all around you, after finding out that you failed the One who loved you more than any other, after all that, you chose to deny Him. I offer you mercy, infidel. Forgive God, here and now. Admit that it was *you* who failed. If you do this, I will be merciful in my judgment should the Citizens find you guilty."

"Mercy is the suspension of justice," Cris said. "You kidnap me, against my will, for the purpose of charging me for the crime of being who I am—as if that were not an honor. Then, after falsely declaring me guilty, you dangle mercy before me. All I must do is love your God. Is that not the same horrible farce of justice your God played on you?"

"God cannot be unjust! God is—"

"Were we not all created sick, and ordered to be well? Were we not all damned for being what we were made to be? Were we not all told that if we loved God, we would be redeemed? Is there anything in your lives, any of your lives," Cris turned and motioned to all the Citizens, "for which you actually deserve *eternal* torture? Have any of the scars you've caused actually been *infinitely* deep? If you hold me to this, then you are truly Yahweh's children."

"We are sinners! We do the best we can," Michael said. "We follow His laws as we can. We are only human. This is all we can do. I'm sorry that you find that an inconvenience. Is that all you had to say in your defense?"

The Infidel Friend shook his head. He began walking forward. Klein, Copperfield and Mancini ran from the table.

Michael came to his feet, drawing his pistol and leveling it at the man. Chelsea slid her chair back. Michael did not budge.

He's stared into the eyes of the Minotaur. What has he left to fear?

The Infidel Friend marched up the steps of the church and stopped just inches from the judge's table. Chelsea dared not move.

Will Michael shoot?

Cris looked Michael Baker in the eye and spoke in an earnest whisper.

"I have this to say in my defense, sir. You support a village of many people. They are well fed and well armed. I can only say that I am very proud to see human beings doing so well here. It is thanks to you that they can stave off the true tortures of Hell. Because of that, sir, if I were to see you in the wilds of Hell, and you were besought by devils, I would save you. I wouldn't care of your creed. I wouldn't care of your race. I wouldn't care of your God or your Devil. I would only care that you were a good man. Now you stand there, sir, and you look me in the eye and tell me that if, in the wilds, you saw a devil throwing fire at me, that you wouldn't do the same."

Michael met his gaze. "I would watch you die."

You're lying, Mike.

There was a catch in her throat. It hurt for her to swallow.

He's a good man, Mike. Can't you see that? He's just different.

"You godless bastard," Michael said. "I would watch you die."

Michael, please be lying.

The Infidel Friend nodded and stepped down from the dais. He regained his arrogant and defiant posture in the center of the pews of hecklers.

"Have you anything else to say?" Michael asked, holstering his sidearm.

Chelsea could see only apathy on the infidel's face. "I have nothing to say to you."

She could tell that the words cut Michael to the quick. The First Citizen sat back in his chair, his face a mask of worry.

You hurt him, Cris. For whatever that's worth.

"Then we shall vote," Michael said, and then cleared his throat. "All who say he is guilty?"

This wasn't the first time that Chelsea had ever seen Michael's Fore give a unanimous vote, but it certainly didn't happen often.

"All who say he is innocent?"

The Infidel Friend raised his hand.

Chelsea covered her face again, struggling to smother her laughter. Michael shot her another dark look.

"All abstaining."

There was no one left.

"Very well," said Michael Baker, the First Citizen of Harpsborough. "You are guilty. You mock us, and blaspheme in our very church. Such behavior is inexcusable. Luckily for you, however, we are not as heartless as your peers. We struggle to be the children of God, bastard children though we may be. When possible, we love our enemy. We love you today. To prove this, and that we are as merciful as our Lord of the old world wants us to be, I shall not have you executed. Rather, you shall be exiled through the Golden Door. Know that no one who has ever gone through the Golden Door has returned. Know that it is not thought that this path leads to certain doom, but rather, that its tunnels take you to another part of Hell so distant that it would be impossible for you to find your way back.

"So rules this court."

Thank you Mike. Thank you.

The First Citizen slammed the stone on the desk as punctuation.

There was buzzing about the hall. Chelsea wondered how many approved of the decision. If an Infidel Friend did come spying on them, then they could truly say that they did not kill the man. They had merely sent him away.

The Infidel Friend nodded, and then turned on his heel. His escort of hunters had to jog to catch up with him in order to take him back to custody.

Outside the village erupted at the news. It was a hollow and empty buzz.

Chelsea could not say if they were pleased or displeased.

That in itself probably means that we have enough time to exile him before they start forming a lynch mob.

— 32 —

Arturus rolled over onto his shoulder. The Carrion stone was cool beneath his body. He saw where his breath had condensed against the wall.

Either that or I've been drooling.

Someone, probably Galen, had left a small black t-shirt beside him. He struggled into it.

Avery and Duncan lay in one corner, blood seeping through the bottom of their boots. They were coming in and out of consciousness. Too tired from the fight and the run to stay awake for long, Arturus guessed, but the needles in their feet were probably too painful to sleep through.

How long have we lain here?

He saw a small silverleg spider climbing the wall. Arturus wondered if it had ridden in on his back. He sat up, working at his boot with his un-burnt hand. Pain lanced up his leg and into his stomach. His vision blurred.

He let go of his boot and waited for his eyes to stop watering.

Aaron was sleeping peacefully. The cut over his eye looked fine. The wound at his shoulder had bled out into a puddle where he slept. The blood there had thickened in the air so that Aaron's rhythmic breathing barely disturbed it.

Patrick's wheezing breaths came in short, quick gasps. He looked blue in the face. At times he would pass out, and his breathing would deepen. The pain would wake him, though, and he would try to scream. Fortunately it came out as a hoarse gurgle.

We would muzzle him, if it wouldn't kill him.

Johnny Huang had given up both his pants and his shirt, and lay wearing only boots and boxers. His face had swollen up around his nose. He looked ghastly, his bruising having spread across his cheeks. His mouth hung open, perhaps to allow him to breathe. Tiny scabs covered his right hand.

Kyle's legs were a bloody mess. He was as pale as death. Arturus was worried that he might already be dead.

"Galen," his father's voice announced.

"Turi," he responded.

When did he leave again? Why?

Aaron also stirred and used his arms to push himself back up against a wall. He looked about to his fellow hunters, without an expression of worry or remorse. He looked lost, though.

Galen ducked into the room. He stepped over Arturus and knelt between Aaron and Kyle, taking stock of the man's flayed legs.

"Does he need amputation?" Aaron's voice sounded almost as hoarse as Patrick's mock screams.

Galen lifted a flap of the man's tattered pants. Blood oozed out from where he'd lifted the cloth. The warrior grimaced. "He might die from it. Probably has better chances as it is."

"He can regrow all that?"

"I had a friend who was crushed by a stone from the pelvis on down. He didn't die, though, because the stone had twisted his body in a way that kept his wounds shut. We pulled him back an inch a week until he was whole."

"Jesus."

"Kyle's will seems strong. He could well live."

"And Patrick?" Aaron asked.

"Hopefully the pain becomes manageable before he's able to shout again," Galen said. "If not, he'll kill us all."

"You've been scouting?"

Galen nodded.

Aaron lowered his voice, but Arturus could still hear him. "What's it like out there?"

"Thick. More dyitzu than I'd thought possible. There are hounds about, too. Enough of them to make lying in puddles of our own blood pretty dangerous. Not much chance of getting back without another fight. Besides, other than through the spiders, I haven't found a good way out of here, yet."

"How much longer can we afford to lie here?"

"Not long." Galen shrugged his shoulders and looked back to the room's exit. "But we haven't much choice."

"If it comes to it, we may have to leave some behind."

"Won't matter now," Galen said. "Till I find a way back, we've no recourse. But I saw something else, while I was out scouting."

"What?"

"A marker stone. No healing on it, so I know it was placed recently. When I was in the Carrion last, that meant that there was an upcoming meeting to be had amongst the people here. A ritual to their God, Mithra. The tribes all stay hidden in sealed cubbyholes, sending only their strongest out to hunt and gather. They join together only for this."

"Is there a possibility of getting any help from them?"

"I doubt it very greatly," Galen said, "but at such a gathering I might see some of the friends I used to keep amongst the enemy. When I was working with your village founders, before they escaped slavery and came to Harpsborough, they served me well. It may be that one of them can give us some aid. Or perhaps lead us back."

"Will you be safe?"

"As much as you, at least."

Galen stood. There was no mark on him, though his clothing was tattered.

His soles were tough enough that the silverlegs didn't hurt him.

Galen drew a knife and bent down to inspect Arturus' boots. "Are your feet swollen?"

"Yes, sir."

Galen nodded. "We'll have to cut these boots away. Angling your foot out would cause too much damage with the spider legs still in you. We need to pull the boot straight back."

"We can just lace it back together, right?" Arturus asked.

Galen smiled. "Yes, or you'll go barefoot."

Galen began cutting a line from the top-front of the boot, straight down along Arturus' instep, and on towards his toes. The pain came back as the knife worked away at the leather. Arturus eyes watered again. His nose began to run.

"It hurts," Arturus managed.

Galen eased him back against the stone. The man's touch was practiced. Arturus trusted his ministrations even more than Rick's.

"It hurts," Arturus repeated.

"I know, son."

Galen stopped after he had cut to the sole, which he left intact. He rummaged through his pack until he found some bandages and then, to Arturus' dismay, a pair of tong-like tweezers.

"I'm not ready," Arturus said.

"Be offensive. Attack the pain."

"I can't. It hurts."

"Face it. Look at your feet. Watch."

Arturus did as he was ordered. Galen pulled at his boot. The needles in his foot moved, loosened by Galen's efforts. Explosions went off in his brain. He let out an involuntary gasp.

"Quiet, boy."

Arturus squeezed his eyes shut and nodded.

"I asked you to watch," Galen said.

Arturus did. He couldn't understand how all those tiny

needles could hurt so badly. A few Galen removed immediately, pulling them out with his tweezers through the sole of Arturus' shoe. The needles were covered in his blood. Each one had a tiny spur on its end, curved back so as to catch in the skin.

For some reason those spurs made Arturus angry.

"Hell has entered your body, son. You must face this pain while I purify you. Those who wish to be well heal faster. Do you want this pain?"

"I do."

After the some of the needles had been removed, Galen began working the sole away from his foot. He felt the tug against his flesh as the remaining silver legs were being pulled out of him. He gasped.

Tears were coming down from his eyes and snot was pouring out of his nose. His stomach was clenched so hard that he had to sputter to breathe.

At last the boot was removed.

He finally managed to inhale. His chest rose and fell as his vision cleared. He wiped the snot away and tried to shake his head clear.

I did it. I'm here. The agony did not destroy me.

Galen rested Arturus' foot on his own thigh and used a cloth to stop the bleeding. The pain brought by the dry cloth brushing against his freshly opened wounds was considerable, but it was nothing compared with what he had just experienced. Galen worked quickly to bind the foot, wrapping the gauzelike strips of cloth quickly. The wrap was firm.

Arturus held up his foot and looked at it. A bit of red seeped through the bandages.

We'll have to redress it soon.

But that wasn't so bad. Exhausted, Arturus let himself crumple back against the stone.

"Good," Galen said. "Now let's get to work on your other foot."

Ellen had heard of the Golden Doors, but she had never seen them. The doors were doubled, like the ones that led into Father Klein's church, but these were much larger. They looked obscenely heavy and had beautiful pictures inlaid upon them. On the right door was a hunchbacked smith with a mighty hammer. On the left was a half nude woman, covered only from the waist down. She was young, but not slender, and had one arm across her chest. She looked blankly at those who stood before her.

The Citizens of Harpsborough who had dared come down these long hallways spread out about the infidel in a half circle. Four of the Harpsborough hunters stood before the door, their guns raised and pointed at it. Two more covered the Infidel

Friend.

"What's behind there?" Ellen asked Rick.

Rick frowned. "A tunnel."

"Where does it lead?"

"No one knows, Ellen."

Two of the hunters brought the Infidel Friend at gunpoint to the door.

"On your knees," one said. "Hands behind your back."

The infidel complied.

He looked at the door and then towards the girl called Molly.

Ellen didn't know why, but Molly looked away as if she were terribly ashamed.

"Worry not," the Infidel Friend said to the First Citizen. "The Infidel's men will seek no revenge upon you for my treatment. Your clemency is notable."

Michael produced a long, slender, golden key and passed it to one of the hunters.

They were talking about something, but Ellen couldn't hear their words. She could hear the Infidel Friend's reply, however.

"You still have people in the Carrion," he was saying. "You send me through here and you won't have anyone left to get them out."

"Quiet," Michael ordered. "Graham, open the door."

The hunter called Graham walked up to the door and inserted the key. The lock turned with a long series of clicks. Graham took the woman's golden handle, while his friend took the smith's. Together they opened the doors, revealing a steel grate.

The passage beyond was long, dark and deep. One hunter held up two woodstone torches. Another tried to light them with heavy strikes of firerock and hellstone. The sparks showered down upon the torches, each flash of light sending bursts of illumination down the dark corridor beyond.

Ellen could feel the cool air pouring out of the place. The chill, and perhaps her own fear, caused goose-bumps to rise on her flesh. The hairs on the back of her neck rose as well. She could hear the hum of the waiting Harpsborough people, the creaking hinge of the golden door, and one thing more. Something very distant. Down the corridor, she thought she heard a woman singing.

The torches came to life with a pair of roars, and the hunters held them up beneath the golden archway to clear the darkness. The Harpsborough people shuffled about, many of them trying to get a better view of what lay beyond.

The Infidel Friend would be walking down that tunnel, weaponless as he was now and naked, as he would soon be.

Satisfied with their search of the corridor, Graham and his

friend put their torches through the grate and dropped them. Together they moved towards the chain. They pulled it, alternating heaves. Matching their efforts, the grate lifted in small jerks. It reminded Ellen of the maw of some great shark that was slowly opening to accept the Infidel Friend.

"Strip," one of the hunters ordered.

He did so without modesty.

"It's as if they never ate the apple," Ellen overheard Father Klein whisper. "They have no idea that their nude bodies are shameful."

The man's scars and wounds were fresh, some not even covered over. A bit of blood was even seeping from the man's leg where the hound bite had partially re-opened. He seemed as oblivious of the wounds as he was of his own nakedness.

He's so beautiful.

The grate neared his shoulder level.

He has nothing to be ashamed of.

"Go on through," one of the Hunters said when the grate was high enough.

Ellen turned her head away. She felt Rick's hand grip her shoulder. Molly started to cry.

Some of the villagers called out to him, "Go on through! You heard him! You won't last long!"

Can he survive in there?

The Infidel Friend looked towards Michael.

Alone?

"It seems you've caught me in your golden net," he said.

And then, without waiting for anyone's answer, he walked into the corridor. He bent down and picked up the two lit woodstone torches. He extinguished one against the rock and then used the other to light his way.

"That was a message," Ellen realized aloud, touching Rick's arm. "The golden net. He was speaking to someone."

"Quiet, girl," Rick said.

Ellen held her peace, but she felt as if there was something inside her, waiting to explode. Those words, they meant something. If that were true, then one of these villagers, Ellen knew, must therefore be in league with the Infidel Friend and his men.

The hunters began lowering the grate. It came down much faster than they had raised it, and, as if in a hurry, fell the last three feet to hit the stone with a metallic crash. If there were any enemies down that dark and deep passage, they certainly would have heard the noise.

Graham and his friend began to close the golden doors. Ellen tried to watch the Infidel Friend as long as she could. The man was walking down the corridor, his lit torch surrounding him with a bubble of light.

Again she thought he heard the woman sing, but perhaps it was just the breeze.

The door closed and the woman's voice was silenced. Graham locked it and then handed the key back to Michael.

"It's a message," Ellen said to Rick again.

"I said hush, girl. We'll talk about it later."

Of course. I'm so stupid. If someone knew the message and they heard me...

Molly walked up and touched the door, her hands running along the hunched shoulders of the smith.

"I hate this place," Ellen said. "I hate it."

Rick nodded, his jaw set, his eyes angry.

The sound of a thud against stone brought Arturus back to consciousness. He looked about quickly, his hand on his pistol, but no one else seemed alarmed.

"Got the fucker," Duncan said.

He was holding his rifle upside down. On the stock was the crushed remains of a spider, its silver legs still twitching.

"Keep it quiet," Aaron warned.

"Good, I'd been watching that bastard," Avery's voice was strained.

Galen was working on Avery's foot now. Beads of sweat were dripping down the hunter's forehead.

Johnny Huang woke up long enough to give Arturus some dyitzu meat. Galen must have brought it for them to eat. It wasn't cooked. He ate it raw and drained his canteen.

"Fuck you, Satan," Avery was saying, his face contorted with pain. "If I ever get my hands on your scrawny little neck..."

Galen had a pile of little silverleg spider needles at his side. Some were very small, only a half inch long or so. Some were three or four inches. Arturus was very glad that one of those hadn't pierced his feet.

"This will be the worst one," Galen warned. "It worked its way into your foot while you were running. I'm going to have to fish it out of there."

Avery nodded and bit his lip. To his credit, he made no noise while Galen's tweezers made their way into the hole in his skin. Galen worked, searching the insides of the man's foot for the needle. Avery's face turned red, and he exhaled suddenly. The hunter squeezed his eyes shut and beat the floor with his fist.

Galen must have found it.

Arturus turned away. He didn't want to watch anymore. Even so, he could not ignore Avery's suffering, and each time the man took in a quick breath Arturus could not help but wince.

When Galen finished, he returned to his pack. He added

Avery's spider legs to a growing pile.

"Are we going to keep those?" Arturus asked.

Galen shrugged. "Perhaps. Waste not, want not. Then again, we are also told not to run with scissors."

Arturus didn't get the joke.

He looked towards the exit. He thought of how long it might take them to get home.

"Have you found the way back yet?"

Galen shook his head. "I didn't leave the room while you were sleeping."

Arturus tried putting a little weight on his foot. His head swam from the pain.

Not ready yet.

"Are we going to make it home?"

Galen ignored the question.

"Are we?"

"It depends on how this meeting goes. If we can get help from the Carrion people, we might have a shot. This is a very dangerous place, boy."

Galen pulled his blanket out of his pack. He cut it into long strips with his knife.

Not enough bandages for all of us.

"Will they help us?" Arturus asked. "The Carrion people?"

"Maybe. Perhaps the few men I knew would try. We'll find out at the ritual."

Galen's deft fingers rolled up the strips of blanket. Arturus could see he needed more, so he offered up his own.

Galen grunted thankfully and started cutting that one as well.

Wait, when did I get that? I burnt my pack.

Perhaps Galen had placed it over him while he slept. The act seemed too tender for the warrior, however, so he might have received it from one of the other hunters.

"What kind of ritual." Arturus asked.

"I don't know. Much may have changed. They worshiped a God called Mithras."

Arturus frowned. "How? How could they worship some false God? Don't they know where they are?"

Galen gave a sad smile. "No one stopped us on the way to Hell and told us what was going on, Turi. Many people believed in one hell or another before they died, so they just go on believing what they did when they were living."

Arturus frowned harder. He found the idea disturbing.

"Aaron, are you ready to walk?" Galen asked.

Aaron looked dismally at his feet.

"No, but we've got to start getting the blood off of us soon. We're lucky no hound has found us yet."

Galen nodded. "Who's got Mabe's silencer?"

"I do," Avery said.

The man didn't protest as Galen took it out of his holster. Galen then turned to Aaron. "Arturus and you will be the first ones."

Me?

Aaron crawled over to a wall and placed his hands upon it. He pushed himself up, grimacing as he stood. Arturus got up as Galen had taught him, posting up one leg and one arm in order to let his other leg swing under him. The blood rushed away from his head, so for a second the pain in his feet seemed distant. As he regained his senses the agony came crashing back in. He felt his legs wobble.

Aaron edged along the wall towards him with timid steps.

"My left foot is better than my right," Aaron told him.

"My right is better."

The two supported each other, arms over shoulders. Arturus felt the hunter's weight pressing upon him. He looked up towards Aaron, who was looking down at him. Aaron nodded seriously, his eyes squinting.

We need each other.

They took their first few steps. Arturus felt blood oozing through the bandages on his feet, but it was better this way. His right foot could take the weight. Galen moved in front of them. He had to hunch in order to avoid the tight ceiling. Arturus and Aaron were already bent over.

Each step was a nightmare. Together they made their way past Kyle and through the room's exit. Before them was a long series of stairs that led down. Arturus could already hear the river.

We're so close to the water.

Dangerous, but it would make it harder for a hound to scent them.

Aaron took the first step down with his left foot. Arturus followed.

"This isn't going to work," Aaron said.

Arturus nodded and sat down. He used his hands to help himself, sitting on each stair before moving again. Aaron followed suit. Galen was ahead of them, his MP5 raised to the level of his eyes. His steps were slow and sure, keeping his weapon steady.

When they made it to the floor, Arturus and Aaron again reached out to each other for support. Their progress was hideously slow. Arturus did his best to remember the caverns they walked through, but the pain was ruining his concentration.

"Hold here," Galen whispered. "I'll check the river room."

Arturus had never felt as close to anyone as he did to Aaron now. They clung to one another, afraid to let go, unsure if they could even stand on their own. Unsure if they would even be able to fight if a devil were to come at them now. Arturus found himself not caring about who ended up with Alice.

If he gets her, so what?

Aaron deserved a woman like that. A woman like that deserved Aaron. How petty his jealousy seemed now while their very lives were on the line.

Galen leaned back into their room. "All clear, come along."

They followed him.

The river room was cold, shrouded entirely in darkness except for a single yellow light that winked down at them from a small cubbyhole. Arturus could see one exit across from the river, but there could have been more hidden in the dark corners. The light from the cubbyhole illuminated the surface of the running water, giving Arturus the impression that it was opaque, as if it were a river of flowing obsidian.

Galen trained his gun first towards the exit Arturus could see, and then towards one of the black corners. Arturus sat down and drew his pistol. He pointed it towards the visible exit.

Galen dropped a bundle of wraps at Aaron's feet.

"Get yourself cleaned up. Wring all the blood out of your clothes. Let me know when you're done."

Aaron nodded, stripping down. He had to do so while sitting because of his injured feet. His shirt clung to him as he struggled to get it off. Arturus watched as some of the skin on Aaron's wounded shoulder came off with the shirt. Seeing the Lead Hunter naked reminded Arturus of when they had watched the Infidel Friend bathe, except that Aaron did have body shame. He covered himself for a second and tried to stand. He gave up trying to regain his feet after a moment and scooted himself towards the river.

Galen knelt next to where Arturus sat, his eyes still on the darkened exit.

"Why is the Carrion so bad?" Arturus asked him softly.

"I can't say that I know for sure," Galen whispered, "but there was a man called Saint Wretch, who retreated into the Carrion many years ago. Before Michael or Father Klein were ever damned. He was said to have dealt with a devil and that he had been made invincible. You could not shoot him, so in that way he was like an Icanitzu. But you couldn't hit him with Hell stuff either. The rock, your fists, it didn't matter. He was a charismatic man, and many devils and men fought for him. He fought the Infidel and was said to have retreated through the Carrion after he was defeated."

"How could he have lost, if he was invincible?"

"The people at the Pole have a story about that. They say that the Infidel wounded Saint Wretch's devil. Wretch was afraid that if the devil died, he would become vulnerable, so he carried the devil away."

The darkness beyond the river seemed less inviting. He heard Aaron lower himself into the water.

"How are we going to find our way home?" Arturus asked. "What if they wall us in?"

"We can always dig through the barrier," Galen said. "But we'd probably make too much noise. We'll have to find some other way. Remember, you can never block out an entire region."

Arturus nodded.

"But, boy, listen to me very carefully," Galen said, looking into his eyes. "If I'm gone you should know how to find your way back."

"How could I know the way?"

"Do you recognize this river, son?"

Arturus looked at it. He could see almost nothing of the chamber at all, except for where the light poured out of the cubbyhole. The light illuminated some of the stones above it. They were set in a bricklike pattern that arched up towards the ceiling.

"The Thames?"

"That's right boy, or close enough to it. The river keeps its own house. Of course, it's warped by the Carrion, and it's joined up with another offshoot of the Kingsriver. But still, it's enough."

"Enough to find a way home."

This was the Thames. The water that flowed down it was the same water that had passed under the bridge by his home. The same water that must have passed by Rick as he filled the clay pitcher.

I miss you.

Arturus reminded himself to keep watching the exit. The blackness beyond seemed menacing. Shadows danced in the darkness there, but he was almost positive they were his imagination.

"What if we find him?" Arturus asked. "Saint Wretch, I mean?"

"It's not likely. That was so long ago it is remembered only as a story, and stories are rarely true. But I hope we do find him."

"Why?"

"I've not fought an immortal," Galen said.

Arturus glanced over towards Aaron. He was wringing out his clothes into the water. The droplets falling from the cloth sparkled, lonely points of light in the darkness. He was surprised by how muscular Aaron's shoulders looked.

Alice would probably like that.

Aaron emerged from the water. Arturus could not help but

compare himself to the hunter.

Alice could never pick me over him.

Aaron covered himself with his wet clothes while Galen bent to wrap his wounds.

"Quickly, Turi."

"But no one will be watching the exits."

"Safer to spend less time, I think."

Arturus crawled over to the river and took off his clothes. He decided he'd wring them out first to give them some time to dry. He felt nervous.

Aaron will know how boyish my body looks.

He bit his lip.

Devils can come at any second. Look at the exits.

The water was cold. His punctured feet ached as he dipped them in. Then he quickly submerged his whole body. The shock was anything but refreshing. He had to kick his feet to keep from being taken by the current, but the movement hurt terribly. He clung to the stone to keep from drifting away. Holding the wall, he dipped his head beneath the water. He felt the cool water on his eyelids. He wanted to stay like this forever, held by this terrible river.

He came up for breath, feeling the stings of a half dozen other puncture wounds along his arms and shoulders where the spiders had walked across him.

He pulled himself out of the water and sat on the bank. His shirt was wet, so he had to struggle to get it on.

Galen had finished wrapping Aaron's feet and was working on the Lead Hunter's shoulder.

"I'm just going to bleed right back into it," Aaron said, shaking his head.

Galen nodded. "To a hound, the smell of your wounds now would just be a whisper. No need for us all to go on shouting."

Galen wrapped up Arturus while Aaron watched the exits. The bandages didn't take long to finish.

It seemed easier to walk on the way back, he noticed as he and Aaron supported each other. Aaron also seemed to be moving better, though they both readied themselves to crawl when they saw the stairs. They heard a half shout. The voice was loud only for a second before being silenced.

"Patrick," Galen said. "He's starting to regain his voice. We're going to have to find some way to keep him quiet."

Arturus' wraps were a bit wet already, so he couldn't be sure how much of the liquid was water, or how much was his own blood. Still, he could not deny that the dip had proved invigorating.

At least while we were in the river room, we weren't sitting around just waiting to die.

"Turi," he announced as he stood up at the top of the

stairs.

He had to duck just the slightest bit as he entered the chamber. Slowly, he and Aaron separated and sat down.

"Duncan, you're next," Galen said.

Which is what I get to do now.

— 33 —

Alice felt out of place in the Fore without Aaron to escort her. Copperfield looked a bit aloof as she passed him on the stairwell. She knew the building well, a claim that very few villagers could make. With Aaron courting her, many of the Harpsborough people had taken to asking her about the Fore's interior. They used to ask Molly, but no one really believed what she said.

Poor girl.

Graham, the hunter who had let her in, was walking up behind her. Only John, the serving boy, gave her a sweet smile. He also blushed. Alice shook her head.

A few Citizens were spread about the parlor room, talking and laughing. Staunten was eating some hound cheese. Hell knew where he had found it. The man ruled the stores, she supposed, so he could get about anything he wanted. Massan had probably brought it in from the Pole.

They live with all this, while I live below.

Worse, Aaron had been helping her stay alive. If he never returned, she would have to spend far more time in the wilds trying to find food.

Michael Baker was leaning over the chess board, his hand absently rubbing the back of his head. Mancini was sitting back in his chair, relaxed, drinking some of his own bloodwater.

Turi made that board.

On the board was a pair of crystal cups. At first she thought it was odd that they would put their drinks there, but then she realized that they must be standing in for pieces.

He never finished.

The thought made her feel horribly sad, because now he might not ever get the chance.

"You wanted to talk to me?" Michael said, not looking up from the board.

"I came about Aaron,"

The conversation in the room stopped. Michael made his next move in silence. Mancini hovered over the board, his face suddenly worried. Then he looked up at the ceiling, as if thinking about something.

The Citizens were all looking at Michael. He gave one of them a nod, and they began to pile out of the room. Only Mancini stayed.

Of all the people not to go.

"Go on, Alice." Michael said.

"You're going to wall him in."

Michael didn't look up from the board. "You're damn right I am."

She felt her blood rising. The back of her neck felt warm.

"Why?" the harshness of her voice surprised her, so she composed herself and repeated it more softly. "Why?"

"That was the understanding. They had five days. Now they've two."

"If they're not back by now—"

"Yes, you're right. And I have been strongly counseled to wall up the Carrion early. If some have been captured, then even a single day is a long time for them to hold out against torture. Some of them might lead the enemies back to us. Then again, they could be dead already."

"Or they could be in need of our help. You know the Carrion. Take some hunters and go save them."

Mancini looked over to her.

Michael stood, bumping the board and jostling the pieces. Mancini reached out and stabilized one of the wine glasses to prevent it from falling.

Oh God, I've crossed some kind of line.

"Aaron volunteered to go." Michael pointed a finger at her. "He knew he might not be coming back, and he knew no one was coming after him. Now I know why you're mad, woman. I'm sorry, you'll have to find some other Citizen who will help you weasel your way into the Fore."

How could he?

"How dare you. I love him, Mike."

"Yeah?"

"Yes."

"Then go in there and save him yourself. I've lost almost everyone I've ever known to the Carrion, and I'm not about to lose anyone else. Let alone myself. Now you can get the fuck out of the Fore or I'll have Graham drag you out."

I'll kill him. Molly was right.

"You're scared," she said suddenly. "You're afraid of the Carrion. That's why you won't go, because Molly's right. You're just scared."

"Graham, get her out of here."

She felt Graham's touch on her shoulder, but she shook him off.

"Sir?" Graham's voice was pleading.

"You're intimidated by Aaron," Alice said. "You're probably glad that he's gone. You were afraid he would replace you. Well, there's going to be another Lead Hunter soon, and you'll be afraid of him replacing you too. But you can get rid of him just as easy, right?"

Michael shook his head. "Now, Graham."

"Sir, I can't just grab her."

"Now!"

Graham grabbed her.

"No! Graham, let go. Let go!" She shook herself free and turned her back on Michael. "I can walk myself out."

Father Klein was a little shocked by the condition of Molly's hovel. She didn't have many possessions with which to make a mess, but what little she did have was strewn about for maximum effect.

"I know why you're here," Molly said.

Her eyes were black and puffy. Either she'd managed to get a man to beat her, or she'd been crying.

"Oh?"

"You're here because I gave the infidel all that information. Well, I'm sorry."

"Molly, I'm here because we're worried about you."

"Please."

"You've been cooped up in this place awhile," Klein said. "Almost the entire time since you spoke to the infidel. What time you haven't spent in here you've spent in the wilds. Higgins said he saw you as far out as Riverbend. Are you trying to get yourself killed?"

Molly wouldn't look at him. She scratched one of her breasts, so he looked away.

"I'm just trying to find some food. Make sure I'll be okay when your stores run out."

He put his hand on her shoulder. He could feel wetness on the front of her shirt, probably from her tears.

"I think you're just trying to protect yourself," he said. "You're trying to stay away from the village. You're afraid we think badly of you. But this is dangerous, Molly. You can't keep going that deep."

"Why not? Who's going to care?"

"Well, we are, Molly. There's no shame in getting tricked by that Infidel Friend. No shame at all. Sure, he fooled you into giving away secrets, and of course it was tough for you to go in there and try and do what you did, but you were brave, Molly. Brave. You tried to help."

"Aaron was just using me. Like everybody else has."

"Not everybody."

"Yes everybody. Especially Aaron. I thought we were lovers. He just wanted a lay. He was just using me one more time. I'm glad it didn't work out for him."

Klein knelt down behind her. "I don't think you're mad at him. I think you're afraid for him. I think you're worried that he might be dead."

"Go back to your church, Father."

"What's wrong, child. What did the infidel say to you?"

"Nothing, alright? He didn't tell me a damn thing. I just went in there at the wrong time. Just had a breakdown." She was crying again. "Damn," she said, wiping snot away.

"It's okay, Molly. They're vile people. I don't know how he did it, but he managed to hurt you very deeply. You may be afraid, or even ashamed, to tell me what happened in there, but that's part of his trap. Whenever you're ready, you can come to the church, and tell me. I've been in Hell a long time, child. I know how to take out the barbs that an infidel's tongue leave in the souls of the faithful."

"Fuck off, Father."

"God bless you, child."

He had lain down next to Johnny. The man had to be rolled over every once and a while because he had a tendency to snore. The noise was more than they were willing to risk. Johnny didn't seem to mind too much. Arturus found that if he could keep the hunter off of his back, the chances of him snoring were smaller.

Patrick's breathing was erratic. Sometimes it seemed as if he was holding his breath. His face would darken, but then he would pass out and start breathing again. It seemed like Galen and Duncan were taking a long time, but was it too long?

Arturus used the top corner of his straight razor to bore holes into his boots, lining them up on both sides of the incisions Galen had made. Then he laced the boots up with a few strips of cloth that had been too thin to use for bandages.

There.

He started to put one foot into a boot, but after feeling a moment of pain, thought better of it.

"Lucky bastard, your father," Johnny said.

Arturus jumped, having thought them man was asleep. "How do you mean?"

"No spikes through his feet."

"His boots," Arturus said, holding one of his own up. "I wish mine were as tough."

"You would have thought I would have been okay, too."

"Oh, why?"

"I'm so close to the ground. Could see the spiders better."

Arturus chuckled softly again. "But you're about an inch taller than me."

Johnny didn't say anything back. He snored instead.

Arturus shook his head and then rolled the man over.

"Were we gone this long?" Arturus asked Avery.

He nodded. "Sure were. Should be back soon, though."

If they don't come back?

He tried not to think too much about that.

Patrick's breathing became intense again. He was trying to scream. For a second he managed to, but his voice quickly became horse again.

"Quiet," Avery said. "You'll bring the devils down on us. Be a man Patrick."

Patrick seemed to be getting worse, though. His chest was heaving up and down. His eyes were wide and wild.

"Get him quiet," Johnny said.

Avery crawled over to him. "Patrick, you can't do this, man. You can't keep shouting."

Arturus leaned back against the stone, trying to ignore the noise.

In the distance, he heard a hound howl. He shot up straight, hand on his gun.

"They heard him," Johnny said.

Kyle was beginning to stir. His eyes looked cloudy.

"So help me God, Patrick," Avery was saying, "you had better keep your mouth shut. That hound will come in and kill us all. You have got to stay quiet."

"He's panicking, man," Johnny said.

Patrick broke down into a fit of coughs. Blood mixed with burnt flesh came pouring out of his mouth. Arturus couldn't imagine the extent of the man's pain. It was intense enough to knock him back unconscious, but Patrick didn't stay out long. He awoke quickly, breathing faster and faster. He arched his back and tried to scream.

"Keep him quiet!" Johnny sounded panicked himself.

Avery tried to smother him with a blanket.

Arturus stood on his weakened feet, faced the exit and drew his pistol.

Won't be much against a hound. I'll have to empty the clip straight into its head.

Johnny had made it to his knees and was checking to make sure his rifle was loaded.

It has to be alone.

The room wasn't very defensible. Nothing to hide behind, but at least there was only one way in.

Nowhere to run to, though.

He could hear the hound again.

"Was that closer?" Johnny asked.

"Quiet," Avery said. "You have got to stay quiet."

Patrick arched up again. Avery shoved him back down and then let out a yelp. Patrick had bit his fingers.

"You'll kill us all Patrick! Keep your damn self silent."

Patrick tried to scream again.

Johnny was shaking his head. "You've got to stop him, man."

Patrick began thrashing against Avery, maddened by the pain. Arturus had never seen a man's eyes look so much like a hound's. Arturus turned away. Somehow, through all the blood and burns, Patrick found his voice.

This time the shout was silenced with a gurgle.

Arturus looked back.

Avery had slit the man's throat.

Arturus bit his lip fiercely. He didn't want to be here in the Carrion. He should never have let himself come. Did he think he was going to be a hero? Had he truly let himself fantasize about returning home, the hunters singing his praises? Did he really think that Alice was going to look at him differently after this?

Home. I want to go home.

He tasted blood in his mouth, and stopped biting his lip. Galen wouldn't approve of that, he knew. It was just giving the hound one more drop to smell.

— 34 —

Galen's gaze narrowed when he saw Patrick's corpse. He looked at Arturus accusingly.

As if I was in charge. As if I could have stopped it.

"We're going to have to leave here soon," Galen said.

"How?" Johnny asked. "Most of us can't even walk. Kyle's hopeless."

"It doesn't matter. A hound heard us."

"We could move downstream," Arturus suggested.

"Nope," Duncan answered. "That's where the hound is."

Galen nodded. "I went looking for it, but I didn't spend too much time. I couldn't find it."

"Upstream then," Aaron said. "That's our only chance."

Galen shook his head. "That current's swift. If we were healthy we could do it, but as we are..."

Arturus struggled to find a plan. There didn't seem to be one. "Anywhere we go, we'll leave a trail."

Galen nodded.

"What are we going to do?" Johnny asked. "Hold our asses and pray?"

"I'll carry Kyle," Galen said. "There's another room like this one nearby."

"And what about us?" Johnny looked angry.

Aaron struggled to his feet. "You crawl."

"Come," Galen said. "I'll show you the place. It's not far."

Galen collected some of their remaining shirts in order to wrap Kyle's legs. He reset the wounded hunter's tourniquets, too. Kyle passed out, either from the pain, the lack of blood, or both.

"I hope he doesn't start screaming," Avery said.

He better not.

Arturus tied his boots' laces together and hung them around his neck.

Better to be barefoot for now.

Arturus and Aaron leaned on each other for support again after they had made it down the stairs. Behind them, the rest crawled.

"Try not to bleed too much," Galen warned.

Avery gave him an angry look, but Galen had moved on.

The purple walls passed by, and again Arturus couldn't hold them in his mind. He tried to remember at least one room in five so that he might find his way back. The attempt was futile.

I'm lost.

After about ten minutes, Galen laid down Kyle and let them rest. The shirts on the wounded hunter's legs were soaked with blood.

Aaron and Arturus sank to the ground together. Aaron produced the blonde braid and ran his fingers over it. They were all out of breath.

Galen moved to watch the exits.

Arturus looked to him. His father seemed different somehow. Arturus had always taken him for granted. Now he felt he could see the man as the hunters might. He was comforted by how Galen was so well respected. Part of him had always felt that Galen was the greatest fighter in all Hell, but he had always assumed that was his own bias. It felt good to have the notion confirmed.

Everything he taught me is right. Everything he taught me is precious. I want to be like him.

He heard the hound's howl again, though it was very distant. When the last of the howl had passed, Arturus shuddered.

"Is that Alice's?" he asked Aaron.

Aaron looked up from the braid. "Yeah. You like her, don't you?"

The question seemed abnormally bold, as if they were supposed to know such things, but not say them. "Of course, she's the prettiest girl in Harpsborough," Arturus answered. "It's a shame I'm too young for her."

Let him think I'm mature. Let him think I don't dream about her every night. Let him think that it won't break my heart and soul when he takes her.

Aaron nodded. "She made me promise to take care of you."

"Really?"

"She did. But you carry your own weight."

"We carry each other's."

As they were sitting shoulder to shoulder, Arturus felt his silent laugh.

"That's really true," Aaron said.

Arturus gave his own silent chuckle.

Literally.

The hound burst into the room.

Arturus found himself standing, his gun in his hand. Galen was already firing Mabe's silenced pistol. He dropped it after it was unloaded. There had only been four bullets left. The hound leapt at him. Galen pivoted away on his left foot, batting at the hound's paws with his arm. As the hound landed, Galen gave it a soccer style kick to its ribs. The impact was enough to lift the monstrous animal.

It struck out again, leaping at him and snapping with its jaws. Galen kept his hands high and stopped the beast's momentum by slamming both of his arms into its right shoulder. With his right hand, the warrior grabbed the thing's ear and used that as leverage to push his forearm into its neck. The hound tried uselessly to bite at him. Galen overhooked its foreleg with his left arm. The hound must have weighed nearly four hundred pounds, but Galen was able to keep it half standing.

Galen turned to the side suddenly, as if he were going to try one of the hip throws he had taught Arturus, but instead he planted his leg next to the hound's and dropped. They tumbled to the ground, Galen's momentum rolling the thing as he kept a hold of its foreleg and ear.

A suicide throw. He showed me that. Everything he taught me works.

The hound struggled, feet clawing at the air, coming up on its side. It tried to regain its footing, but the throw had landed it next to the chamber's wall. Galen kept the thing's back legs from clawing him by putting his knee on its belly. He let go of the hellhound's ear and clutched for the knife at his belt. The hound bit at him, but the warrior's blade slashed its throat. Galen held it there, pinned against the stone, as it bled out.

Arturus holstered his weapon.

Aaron's mouth hung open. "How?"

"The Carrion," Galen said. "It was my home."

"Who's winning?" Father Klein asked Michael and Davel as entered the parlor room.

"He is," Michael said. "He's always winning."

Mancini frowned. "You're getting better."

"No, you're getting drunk."

Mancini let out a laugh.

"Do you mind if I speak to you alone, First Citizen?" Klein asked.

Michael looked up from the board upon hearing the honorific. "Of course."

The Father did not often use his title.

Mancini started to stand, but Klein stopped him. "Please stay. Mike, would you mind having this discussion in the church?"

Michael shrugged. "Of course not, Father, lead on."

The First Citizen stood up and walked with Klein out of the parlor room.

"Did you get a chance to speak with Molly?" Michael asked as they walked down the stairs.

"Sure did, but she wouldn't say much. I think you're right, she did give the Infidel Friend the information. Aaron said he gave a little too, but he was probably just being too hard on himself."

"Probably," Michael said. "He's a little misguided at times, but he's not foolish enough to do too much harm. Did she tell you why she opened up to him?"

Father Klein pushed his way through the door curtain that separated the stairway from the first floor waiting room. He held it open for Michael. "At first I feared that she might be a traitor. You know, maybe she was the one who put corpsedust down Ole' Bense's throat. But she's locked herself up in that hovel like a hermit since. She's been crying herself to sleep each night. She wandered pretty far into the wilds the other day. As far as Riverbend."

"Jesus."

"I know. Even the hunters don't always go out that deep."

They passed through the next door blanket. The aroma of the Fore, perfumed with burning incense, did a lot to protect Michael's nostrils from the stink that had clung to the town since the death of the giant spider. Michael gave out a dry heave as the smell of Harpsborough hit him head on.

"You all right?" Father Klein asked.

"Sure, sure," Michael responded. "Must've had too much dyitzu. You think she's found something out there?"

Michael stepped over one of the sleeping villagers. A couple more people scattered out of their way as they walked towards the church. Kylie's Kiln was lit, so the air was smoky. That, at least, was a smell that the First Citizen had come to love. Kylie may not have been the best looking woman in Harpsborough, but she was certainly one of the most giving. The pottery smoke reminded him of the soft times they'd spend together in the mornings. It was more appealing than the coppery odor of Mancini's still or Copperfield's scent of woodstone dust—and a hell of a lot nicer than sweat and spider guts.

"Can't imagine it," Father Klein was saying. "I think she might be wandering. Hoping to get lost or killed."

One of the younger villagers nearly ran into them. Michael caught the young man and steadied him before passing on. He heard the mixed shouts of victory and defeat from the gamblers behind him.

"That bad? You think she's suicidal."

"Could be, Mike. Could be."

"How? What could he have said?"

"I don't know. I think maybe she fell in love with him."

Michael stopped dead in his tracks. It took Klein a few steps before he noticed and turned around.

"Love?" Michael asked. "After one conversation?"

"They're tricky things, those Infidel Friend. He might have picked up on how weak she was. She thinks everyone hates her, uses her."

"She might be right."

"Could be." Father Klein shrugged. "Maybe it didn't take much. He probably just showed her a little respect. Perhaps he politely declined a sexual advance while complimenting her. Probably did it deliberately, that unfaithful bastard. Broke her down just to get her to spill the goods."

"Well, I'm sure her head will clear up in a few days. She's probably too pussy to get herself into too much trouble. Not many demons about. Still, I'd like her followed on one trip. Just to make sure she's not found another Infidel Friend."

"I'd like her followed more often than that," Klein said as they started moving again.

"Why? You think she's a traitor?"

"No, I think she might really get herself hurt."

"She's many things, but she's not suicidal."

Father Klein shook his head as he mounted the church steps. "I beg to differ. Remember, everyone talks to a priest. From what I hear I think she might be suicidal."

"Why do you think that?"

"Because that's how she died, Mike."

Their new chamber was even smaller than the last, the ceiling even lower. Arturus tossed his boots into one corner and looked down at his feet. He could only see his toes around the wrappings, but they felt fairly good.

He was very tired, though.

"I'll need to leave soon, to make sure I get to the ritual," Galen told Aaron.

The Lead Hunter nodded, out of breath, as he lay down against the stone.

Galen knelt, carefully lowering Kyle. The man seemed as light in Galen's arms as a baby. This, and Galen hadn't slept since they'd been in the Carrion. And he'd fought. And he'd scouted. And he'd carried the man for at least fifteen minutes.

"I'm going to mop up our trail," Galen said.

Arturus watched him leave.

"Is he human, Turi?" Johnny asked.

Arturus laughed at first, but stopped when he saw the man's question was in earnest.

"Yes."

"Have you ever seen him tired?"

"Yes. He gets tired."

He's tired now. He's just being proud.

Michael followed Father Klein into the church. The place was as busy as the rest of Harpsborough. Men and women sat together, chatting in the pews. Some were even on the floor. Only a couple were praying. Michael and Klein were greeted by everyone as they walked down the aisle.

Michael watched the shadows of the crosses slide down Klein's back as they moved towards the front of the church and made their way to the side door that led to Klein's private room.

Klein again held the door blanket open for Michael.

The room was sparsely furnished. The cot was finer than anything a villager might sleep on, but less lavish than any Citizens' bed—except for maybe Aaron's. That bastard would sleep on anything.

Past this room were the church's stores. Klein led Michael to them.

Dust had settled on many things here. Most striking were the statues of the pagan gods which had been in the church's archways when Mike and Klein had first settled Harpsborough. The Father opened one of the chests. At the bottom was a thin layer of spider eggs.

"This is all that's left?" Michael said.

Klein nodded.

It wasn't much.

Michael gave out a long whistle and shook his head. "How much longer?"

"A couple days. Maybe less."

"Damn."

Klein let the lid of the chest fall shut. "Julian's food is gone. Our best hunters have chased after it into the Carrion. There are fewer devils than ever. Without Aaron, the hunters have almost no chance of finding any food."

"They're fine."

"They haven't caught a single devil since he left. Not one."

"It's only been a few days."

"Wouldn't have happened while Aaron was here."

"They'll learn."

"Well, while they're learning, the people will be starving. Even if they bring in twice what Aaron did, it won't matter."

Michael took a deep breath and exhaled slowly. He sat down on the chest.

"Unless you can get out there and catch another spider," Father Klein said.

"No."

"You could give it another shot."

"I knew where it was, Klein."

Klein took a step back, running into one of the pagan statues. "What?"

"The expedition was a farce. I knew where the spider was. I led them there. I had found its lair when I was still Lead Hunter."

Klein sat down next to him. "Then you've got to change things, Mike. You've got to convince the Fore to give food to the villagers. Even so, it might be tight."

Mike rubbed the back of his head and frowned. "The Fore's had a promise. Once they earn Citizenship, they're never to be endangered again."

"That was Charlie's promise, not yours."

"I told them I'd keep it, after I killed Charlie."

"It's not right for some to have so much, while others die."

"I'll see what I can do."

Father Klein stood up and moved to exit. He held the curtain open, as if dismissing the First Citizen. "You had better try, and try hard. God is not here to disapprove of your actions, Mike, but your conscience is."

Those words haunted Michael as he walked back to the Fore. He went up the stairs in a daze and fell into his favorite chair. He blinked when he saw the chess game. He had forgotten it. Mancini had left, but not before making a damn good move. Michael searched the board to try and find a good reply, but without any luck.

The game seemed as hopeless as the city.

— 35 —

Arturus awakened when he heard Galen mention his name. He looked up to see his father speaking with Aaron.

"How long has it been?" Aaron was asking.

"Four days, about. Maybe six since Julian's been gone."

"Damn. What did you find?"

"There was another stone marker. That means the ritual will begin shortly."

"Sure," was Aaron's response. "Take him, then."

Avery sat up quickly. "You can't let him take the boy. He'll have no reason to come back."

I'm going somewhere? To the ritual? What did I miss?

Aaron looked tired, pale. Maybe the wound on his shoulder had been deeper than he'd let on. "No, Avery. Arturus is Galen's son. He has every right to take him along, and we have no right to keep him."

"I don't want to be abandoned here. None of *us* can walk."

"Believe me," Galen broke in, "if we don't return, it will be because we are dead. Our only chance is for one of us to make it back in time to warn Harpsborough not to fill in the entrance. If I can get there and let them know that we're here waiting to recover, then we can make it."

Johnny nodded his head. "He's right, Avery."

Avery didn't seem convinced. "Even if Galen comes back, I guarantee you the boy won't be coming back with him."

"And would you begrudge him that?" Aaron asked.

Avery thought about it and sat back. He crossed his arms and looked away.

"No," Arturus said.

Galen looked at him oddly for a moment.

"No, you won't go?" Aaron asked.

"No, I won't leave you," Arturus said. "This is the first important thing I've done in my life. I don't want it to be marked by cowardice."

Galen grunted.

"You're a fool, then," Avery said.

Arturus bit his lip. Avery was almost certainly right. Would he kill himself pretending at an honor that he did not have?

"We are what we repeatedly do," Arturus said, quoting a lesson Galen had taught him years ago. "If I act a coward, then I am a coward."

"Go, Turi," Aaron said. "Those are Galen's words that come spilling out of your mouth. Or your heart. You two will be back. I know it."

Galen stood and walked to Arturus' side. "Can you stand?"

Arturus did and was surprised at how little pain there was in his feet.

"Does it hurt?" Galen asked.

"Not badly."

"Good. Get your boots on and follow me."

They moved quickly through the Carrion's wilds. Galen had never held him to a higher standard than he did now, chiding mistakes so small that Arturus often didn't even know that he'd made them. With the ambient noise of the other hunters gone, Arturus began to recognize the signs of the devils. He could hear echoes of breathing, oddly amplified through the dark chambers. Footsteps, marked with the sounds of clawed feet scraping across hellstone, and then the ever so distant hound's howl, also reached his ears. They were lucky they even survived the crawl from their old chamber to their new one, he realized. He had never imagined that there could be so many demons in one place.

Galen increased the pace, and Arturus started to feel the wounds reopening in his feet. He dared not complain. A fight now would surely be beyond him. There was no way that he could run.

They ducked low below an overhang, and Galen brought them into a small circular chamber.

"Are you okay?" Galen whispered.

Arturus nodded.

"Your feet?"

"Okay, maybe bleeding a little."

Galen nodded, and handed him his canteen.

"I didn't get to clean my weapons," Arturus told him. "My pack is gone."

"It's fine. We'll get to them later."

"How can there be so many devils?"

"The Minotaur I sought," Galen said. "He's here. I looked all through the labyrinth to find him, and he's been in the Carrion. He's been here the entire time."

No wonder there were so few devils around our home. The

Minotaur is calling them here.

Galen led him down a shoot. The warrior scooted along on his buttocks. It was almost as narrow as the tunnel they had crawled through to try and escape the silverlegs. They emerged into a series of rooms with black crystal walls.

Not black. I can see through them. They just look black because everything is so dark.

Galen took him carefully through a maze of passages. The crystal walls stayed with them. Arturus found it difficult to remember to keep looking through them. Objects on the far sides of the wall were visible, but distorted by the crystal's imperfections.

Galen raised a hand and crouched low.

Did he see something? Hear something?

Arturus stopped at the edge of a crystal wall. He peered through it and around it, but could see nothing. All was quiet. Galen hadn't moved, though, so Arturus didn't dare to do more than breathe.

Then he saw them, but they made no sound.

They are as quiet as death. As quiet as me, or Galen, or Julian. They have to be. They live here.

The mass of them, at least two score, rippled in Arturus' vision as he watched them through the crystal.

They'll see me if they only look.

But Galen had stopped them in darkness.

It's lighter where they are, so I can see through and they can't.

When they moved past the wall their forms coalesced into solid shapes. The first two moved in tandem, their padded boots touching the stone without disturbing the silence. Both had shotguns at the ready, held up near their chests. They were dressed the same way, with well fitted dark clothes that helped them blend in against the Carrion's background. They each had pistols holstered at their belts.

They are in uniform. They are part of an army.

The men that followed wore lighter grey cloaks, much more easily seen than the two in front of them. They were decrepit things. Some were tall enough that their ankles, thin and knotty, could be seen beneath their cloaks. They were all bent at the shoulder, their right hands placed on the backs of the man in front of them. Their wrists also looked terribly thin. They moved as one, in step with each other.

Slaves.

They were arranged in ranks of four, sixteen deep. He could hear their cloaks swishing, just barely, with their every synchronized step. Two more of the warrior types came after them. They were so hard to spot when compared with the slaves that he had almost missed them.

Another shadow, blacker than the rest, and therefore just

slightly more visible, came out from behind the crystal. It was a slender man, perhaps even an adolescent, moving gracefully within a velvet or silken black robe. The cloth clung to the man's chest, which seemed oddly full.

A woman.

For some reason Arturus feared her more than the rest. He felt his breath quicken and his heart beat faster. She was as quiet as the warriors but walked with her shoulders held erect. Two more soldiers followed after her, equipped the same as the other four. The group seemed dangerous. Far more dangerous than the Harpsborough hunters.

As dangerous as Galen. Carrion born. Was Galen once one of these men?

He could no longer hear the slaves, either because they had moved farther on or because the beating of his heart was drowning them out.

The procession passed behind another crystal wall, and Arturus watched their shapes bend and distort before they finally disappeared. He waited for some time before Galen moved again.

I wish I were home.

They had not traveled far before Galen led him under another low stone overhang and into a small square room.

A narrow alcove came down from the ceiling of the chamber. It was so narrow that Galen could barely fit in it. He climbed it easily, putting his back to one wall and his feet on the other. Arturus peered upwards, but he couldn't see any gap in the stones above.

Galen proved him wrong. The warrior steadied himself after he had climbed as far upwards as he could and pushed up against the ceiling. The rock there moved. Galen disappeared into the darkness. Casting a nervous glance behind him, Arturus followed.

The room he crawled into had no light at all. Galen, his face illuminated from below, was all that he could see—and even he disappeared after the stone was replaced.

"Rest for a moment," Galen ordered.

Arturus searched blindly for a wall, his hands outstretched. He found one, and leaned against it. He wiggled his toes. His feet were feeling good. Better than he'd expected after climbing up the alcove.

"Are you tired?" he asked his father.

"I am," Galen's disembodied voice replied.

"Why don't you show it? One of the hunters doubts you're human."

"It is not pride that makes a leader stoic, Turi."

But you're not the leader, Aaron is.

But Galen was right, if Aaron and he gave conflicting

orders during a fight, the hunters would obey Galen.

"Why then?" Arturus asked.

"When hellhounds travel in packs they are vicious things. They will attack large groups of men, even when the hopes of winning are small. They will fight fiercely and to the death so long as their pack leader is strong. So it is with men."

Arturus felt the sweat cooling on his body. His breathing had returned to normal. He had never felt so relaxed as he did now, wounded and blind, lost in the Carrion.

"People are different," Arturus said.

"When there are no guns or arrows, entire armies will stop their fighting to watch their leaders duel. They wait to see whose champion will be victorious. To see whose hearts will be broken."

It dawned on Arturus that it was for this reason that Galen was who he was. Why he never showed happiness and sadness in great degrees. He was too busy being a leader.

I don't want that life.

But he had it already. Even as the hunters would follow Galen's orders in battle, Arturus realized, they would follow him in peace—particularly if Galen and Aaron were gone.

Patrick died.

He realized now why the man's death had made him so sick. He could have stopped it. It had been his responsibility to find a way to quiet the man.

But I sat back, instead, waiting for someone else to find the solution. Looking to another for strength.

"I could have saved Patrick," Arturus admitted aloud.

"Feel no guilt for that," Galen told him. "Only make sure that you learn from your mistake. Are you rested?"

"I am."

"Then follow me."

Arturus crawled towards where Galen's voice had been. He reached up above himself to see if there was room to stand.

There wasn't.

He could hear Galen's body armor shifting ahead of him. He followed the sound.

"Watch out. Wall," Galen warned.

Arturus searched with his arm until he found the stone. "How far?"

"We are very close, it is best now that you be very quiet."

"Stop here." Came Galen's whisper.

Arturus could feel strange vibrations through the rock. They were oddly rhythmic. A series of lesser tremors followed by two final deep thrums. He could almost hear them now, having felt them with his finger tips. He laid down his ear to the stone and listened.

Drums.

"Put this on," Galen's voice said.

Cloth hit Arturus' shoulder.

He heard the sounds of Galen unbuckling his body armor. Arturus took off his own clothes. With his fingers, he inspected what Galen had passed him. He identified by touch a pair of rough pants, a shirt, and some sort of robe.

"Leave your weapons here," Galen said. "I'll have some on me, but they probably won't fire, so try and keep out of trouble."

"What's happening?"

"We're going to go down into the ritual. We may be a little late. I can hear the drums already. Slaves aren't held to any specific order, though they usually pack together with the clan they came with. There are many clans. Keep out of trouble and wait for me to make contact. I'll wave you out once I've found a friend, and we'll come back up this way. If I show you my thumb, follow me. We may have to exit through a different passage. You're dressed as a slave, so do anything anybody else tells you to. Try and keep out of notice. You'll stand out a bit, though, since you're healthier than the average slave. I'd dress you as a warrior, if you weren't too young for it, and I'd leave you here if I was sure we could come back this way.

"Are you ready?"

"Almost." Arturus said, pulling on his shirt.

The cloth was surprisingly cold. He put on the pants next, and then the robe. "Ready."

Light poured up into the chamber as Galen removed a block from the floor. The warrior looked down into the room below. Arturus could see his father's clothes, which were dark like the ones worn by the Carrion soldiers. He caught sight of his own, which were colored grey, like the ones worn by the slaves.

Galen seemed satisfied that no one was looking and motioned Arturus down.

Arturus lowered himself through the hole. The drop was nearly one hundred feet. He was in an alcove, very similar to the one he had climbed up before, only much higher. The room itself was perhaps fifty feet wide and had hundreds of alcoves running up its sides.

Arturus put his back against one wall, his feet and hands against the other, and let himself slide slowly down. Galen followed from above, placing the stone back into the ceiling.

I better remember which one of these to climb back up.

The color of the room was a rich, dark purple. The ambient light was soft. Low compared to the wilds around his home, but far brighter than the rest of the Carrion.

He could hear the drumming more clearly now. Some chanting accompanied the percussion—a low single monotone which stopped just in time for the sound of two deep and final drum beats. The pattern repeated again and again.

"How can they make so much noise?" Arturus asked.

"Because of rooms like this," Galen answered. "Their ritual chamber, and all these buffer chambers, are sealed off but for a single entranceway which they control... and ours, of course."

Galen was no longer whispering. Arturus could see now that he had a shotgun strapped across his back, and a pistol at his belt.

The same as the other warriors.

Arturus came down to the ground and got out of the way. Galen dropped the last few feet and started walking towards an exit. He stopped for a moment and made a chip in the rock wall with the butt of his gun.

"Remember that," he said.

That chip is where our exit is.

The drumming became louder as they moved through the next few rooms. Those rooms were wide, tall and full of alcoves. Many side passages broke off from each chamber, but the main path seemed to be spiraling in towards a central point. It wasn't long before they ran into other people. A few of the slaves bowed in deference towards Galen, but the soldiers ignored him. There were more men in the next room, and more still in the room after that.

The drum music was even louder, and the chanting alone was almost able to drown out Galen's voice. "Keep your head on straight," Galen said, shouting over the clamor. "These rituals can sometimes be... barbaric."

They made their way into the final room. The wave of body heat was a shock to Arturus since the rest of the Carrion had been so cold.

He pushed his way through a crowd of adults, a sea of angry faces and grey robes. Many of them were gaunt, so poorly fed that their clothes appeared to be hung on sticks, not shoulders. Others, the soldiers, looked different. Their pale faces were calm and cruel. There was no spare fat on them, surely, but they weren't malnourished either.

Arturus broke through into an open space in the room so he might take stock of it. This chamber was shorter than the rest, only thirty feet tall or so, and its purple walls were lined with black pillars. Topping the pillars were a series of black arches. Carved into the center of each arch was the torso of a man, half encased in stone. Spidery letters were etched into the stone, long, thin, and silver.

He felt Galen's form as his father came up behind him.

"It's amazing," Arturus said.

"What?" Galen shouted back.

"Amazing!"

Galen nodded.

Galen forced his way deeper into the room. The Carrion people, seeing his soldier costume, made way for him. Arturus had difficulty following him. Often the crowd would close in behind his father, so he was forced to fight to keep up. They stopped beneath one of the black arches. Another young man in a grey robe had managed to climb up the side of one of the pillars. Though the lip around the base of the pillar was thin, Arturus managed to copy him.

He was able to see almost the entire room from his perch.

The Carrion people were gathered around a raised central stage of flat, polished granite. Towards the back of the stage was a hellstone throne. It had strange steel rings protruding from its arms and legs.

Who are these people?

The chanting grew louder, as did the double beat of the punctuating drums. Arturus could feel the beats in the hollow of his chest. The sweat of the Carrion people was starting to make him nauseous. Much of their perspiration had soaked into his robe.

Pillars of fire erupted from the corners of the stage. The heat grew even more intense, and the air became even harder to breathe. The smoke from the fires drifted towards the ceiling before coming back down upon them, leaving a haze thick enough to obscure the far walls. Arturus found it difficult to keep his balance, so he leaned on Galen.

His father looked up at him for a second.

There were screams, and at first Arturus feared that devils had somehow found their way into these sacred chambers, but they were not screams of fear or pain—they were screams of rapture.

The men around the entrance of the chamber began to stir. Arturus tried to see what was going on, but though he was high enough, the entranceway was on the same wall as he, and the pillars blocked his view. All he could see coming in was a tight pack of darkly clad warriors, standing shoulder to shoulder, struggling to clear a path into the crowd.

High pitched and ecstatic screams filled the air, sometimes drowning out the low chanting. The men nearby the warriors began to jump up and down, waving their arms with abandon. Arturus saw a grey cloaked head disappear, as if the commotion had caused him to faint. The head did not reemerge.

The Carrion soldiers were making progress now, shouldering the common people out of the way. The drumming's pace increased, catching up with the rhythm of Arturus' heart.

Behind the soldiers, walking gracefully into the space that had been cleared, were two priestesses. They wore the black cloaks which Arturus had seen before, but their hoods were thrown back. They alone, in this sea of madness, seemed calm. Their faces, pitiless and beautiful, were harshly angular. Their hair, both a dirty blonde, was worn identically, pulled back behind their heads and falling in layers behind their shoulders. Braided in with their locks were black feathers.

At the sight of the priestesses, the Carrion men seemed to lose all control. They fought in earnest against the black wall of warriors. They reached out longingly over that human barrier, trying to touch one of the two women. These men, so hopeless and so underfed, seemed to have found some strange energy within them. There was something coming up behind these priestesses too, and it was being carried forward, but Arturus couldn't clearly see what it was yet.

Waves of euphoria swept through the Carrion people. They stopped pushing against the soldiers, but let themselves be swept away. Many more fainted.

"Gagaev!" some shouted.

"Gorgon!" yelled others.

Six soldiers, arrayed in two single file lines, followed the priestesses into the room, bearing the front of a giant litter on their shoulders. The screaming became so intense that Arturus could no longer hear the drums, he could only feel their vibrations in his chest.

Their litter was wide enough to carry two men. Chained to it was a Minotaur. Arturus felt Galen shift beneath him.

The Bullman had been chained face up, and its nose was bleeding into its brown fur. Arturus could see its one exposed wild eye. At its neck, the fur gave way to dark brown hairless skin. Its shoulders were more muscular than Arturus had seen on any man. They were broad, and black veins stood out amongst its rippling muscles as it fought, perhaps mindlessly, against the chains. Where its torso ended, the fur picked up again. Its legs, stocky and well muscled, ended in thick black hooves. At the back of the litter were six more soldiers, and following them were two more priestesses carrying a black trough. Slaves and soldiers alike scrambled to get out of the litter's way.

The procession moved easily through the room now.

Arturus looked down towards Galen, but he could only see the back of his head. He swallowed deeply, his eyes watering from the smoke, his ears throbbing with the music.

Sweat poured down his body.

The Carrion people screamed still louder. Something else was coming in through the chamber. Something that must be even more terrible that even the Minotaur.

"Maab! Maab! Maab!"

Those nearest the entrance fell together to the ground. Some of them had fainted straight away. Others had fallen to their hands and knees. A woman emerged from behind the pillars. At first Arturus could only see her head over the crowd, but as more and more succumbed to her and fell to their knees, he could see her from head to toe. She was clad in a dark satin sheet which clung to her figure. Her hair was full, spread back from her face like a lion's mane. It was golden blonde, and where her priestesses had black feathers braided in, she had white. Her hairline was covered with a shimmering white band. Her eyes and eyelashes were painted over with a dark black paint. A light blue shade shadowed her eyes and continued along the sides of her face to her temples. She was imperious, and voluptuous in a way which Alice could never hope to match. It was as if someone had taken all of Molly's attributes and managed to fit them on Alice's slender frame.

But for all this, she walked like a man.

There was no sway in her hips, no real grace to her movements.

Galen was shouting at him, but though he was only inches away, Arturus couldn't hear his father at all. Reluctantly, he looked away from the woman and leaned even closer.

Galen shouted in his ear.

"What?" Arturus yelled back.

"My friend. I've seen him."

Arturus nodded.

"Head on straight."

Arturus nodded again.

"I'm sorry that—" Galen's voice was lost in the crowd's noise for a moment. "—first time you see this. I'd wanted it to be different for you."

"What to be different?" Arturus shouted back, as loud as he could, but he couldn't even hear himself.

"I'm sorry." Galen moved away, leaving Arturus clinging to the pillar.

Don't leave me.

His eyes returned to the woman. She had come to the foot of the stage.

"Maab! Maab! Maab!"

The Minotaur had already been taken up on the granite platform. For a moment, even though it was bound tightly in its chains, it was able to stand. The Bullman was perhaps eight feet tall. Soldiers swarmed all over it. The thing struggled, but its arms and legs had no room to move. It toppled. The darkly dressed warriors struggled to lift the beast. It took nearly a score of them to force the thing onto the obsidian throne. They ran its chains through the rings at its hands and hooves.

The slaves' screaming did not die away or lessen at all—it was the chanting that became louder. More soldiers entered the chamber, carrying huge stone bowls in their hands. They offered these up before themselves, looking down at the ground as if the sight of what they carried was too glorious for them to behold. The four priestesses at the foot of the stage disrobed as the bowls neared.

The sight of their flesh nearly caused Arturus to fall from the pillar. He had never seen a naked woman before. He looked towards the main woman, but she still wore her black satin. The priestesses turned and dipped their slender white arms into the bowls, covering themselves up to the elbow in whatever liquid they contained. The smoke was thick in the air, and it played tricks with Arturus' vision. The light from the pillars of fire swirled in the haze, clinging to the nude bodies of the young women. With their arms covered with a slick and dark brown substance, the four of them made their way up the stage's stairs towards the Minotaur.

Arturus felt the wrongness in his heart.

The women moved towards the bull's genitals. Arturus looked away. He searched the crowd for Galen. Most were on their hands and knees, but others stood together in packs around the edges of the room, screaming as loud as they could. Galen had to be in one of those packs.

Why? Why are they doing this?

He glanced back at the Bullman and was horrified. He had never seen anyone touched like that. He could not imagine what insanity must have a hold of them, what demons had planted lies into their souls to make them do such a thing. Instinctively, he was revolted, the image of the demonic bestiality bringing bile into the back of his throat.

This is wrong.

He could not find Galen, and now nearly half of the room was blotted out by the smoke.

"Maab! Maab! Maab!"

The woman ascended to the stage.

"Maab! Maab! Maab!"

That's her name. That's Queen Maab.

She disrobed at the top step.

Arturus could not take his eyes off of her.

She approached the bull.

No.

The priestesses had the thing ready.

Arturus looked away, staring at the faces of the men that still stood around him.

There is lust in their hearts. But how? How could they lust while watching this?

He dared one more glance. Maab was standing on the Minotaur's knees, her back to the seated thing. Slowly she squatted down and lowered herself onto it. The chanting and screaming grew still louder. The Carrion people who had fallen to their knees reached their hands up towards the ceiling. The beats of the drum came in a steady stream, shaking Arturus to the quick. He let himself fall from the pillar and leaned back against the walls. He had hoped they would be cool, but they had taken in the heat of the room.

This is wrong.

He was the only one not watching. Those around him were crazed madmen, shouting as loud as they could, so full of emotion that they were shaking.

Then he saw someone else not facing the stage. The man was searching the crowd instead.

Not the only one.

For a second he thought it was Galen, but nothing could have been further from the truth. That soldier was as filled with malice as those around him were with lust. His pale skin was stretched tightly across his spiteful face. His hair was cut short, almost clean shaven. His armor was an odd, greyish color.

Icanitzu skin.

Arturus moved so that a group of standing Carrion slaves stood between himself and that dangerous figure. He continued to look for Galen through the haze. He saw one black, shaved head of a young boy amongst the rest.

Julian.

The drumming grew faster and faster, incessantly pounding against Arturus' senses until it drowned all else out. His ears were ringing badly. He put his hands up to cover them and was surprised with how drenched with sweat his hair was. He stepped over and around a few of the kneeling bodies.

For half of one of Arturus' breaths, there was silence, and all that he could hear was the ringing in his ears. Then the shouts and screams of the Carrion men came to a climax as the drums beat on. Arturus looked to the stage.

Maab had broken the bull.

She stood up slowly, letting the thing's broken organ slide out of her. The Minotaur was twitching, as if in seizure. Maab stepped down from the throne and moved to the edge of the stage. Everyone stood as one and rushed towards her, reaching out to touch their goddess. They groped at her, but she, without having to avoid them, always seemed to be just inches away from their fingers. Her voice was high and strong, easily heard against the low pitched howls of her followers.

"Who protects you?"

"Maab!"

"Who feeds you?"

"Maab!"

"Who breaks the bull?"

"Maab!"

"Who loves you?"

"Maab!"

"Who holds the darkness of Ahriman at bay?"

"Maab!"

"Who sings to the fates at night to save your bodies?"

"Maab!"

"Who calls to the great Mithras, born of Rock, for the salvation of your blood?"

"Maab!"

"Who pulls from the bull its essence, that it might strengthen your warriors?"

"Maab!"

"Who chips away at the stone, that Mithras might come again?"

"Maab!"

The soldiers swarmed back onto the stage. This time the Bullman offered no resistance, unable to even clutch at its ruined masculinity. They dragged it upwards, as if to get it standing, but the best the beast could manage was to hold itself up on its hands and knees. One warrior, the one in Icanitzu skin, grabbed the thing's massive right arm and twisted it behind its back, exposing its belly to the crowd. Hell healed all wounds, Arturus knew, but there were scars along the Minotaur's abdomen. Either it had suffered those wounds very recently, or it had been cut with something treated with rustrock.

"Maab! Maab! Maab!"

Maab accepted a black dagger from one of her priestesses. It shined in the firelight.

She placed her fingers in the Minotaur's nostrils and pulled its head back. She slit the thing open, from its neck to the ruined organ at its pelvis. The blood spilled out from its belly into the bowls. The priestesses, their nude bodies covered in blood, moved quickly to empty the bowls into a black trough.

Arturus forced himself to look away.

Julian. He's one of their slaves!

Arturus tried to cut across the middle of the room but found that the people there were so closely packed together that he couldn't make any headway. They treated him as an annoyance, shifting back and forth to try and keep him back.

If I can get to him, I can lead him to our escape route.

Arturus gave up on the center of the room and moved as quickly as he could towards one of the walls.

"Bring forth the babies."

Arturus made it to the wall, and fearing for the lives of infants, again climbed a pillar. There were no babies, however. Naked men were being brought to the stage. Arturus was struck with the idea that they might also be forced onto the throne, and that Maab might break them, too. He was relieved when they were lined up before her.

He climbed down and continued around the room.

Julian. Come on. Where'd you go?

He could only see the tops of the men's shoulders on the stage now that he was back on the floor. Maab's voice came and went, sounding almost like one of the Latin prayers that Father Klein would give. Only her voice was higher, sweeter, more powerful, and infinitely more despicable.

Her servants poured the Minotaur's blood across the shoulders of those young men.

"Blessed is the Baptism of Mithras. Blessed are his warriors. You are the gleam in the eye of the great Ahuramazda. You too, now, have been carved from stone. Your flesh, made weak by the mothers who bore you, has been made strong with the blood of the Gorgon. Your will, which was made vulnerable by the teachings of your fathers, has been made invincible by the will of Ahuramazda. Your soul, which was made to be tortured and victimized by servants of Ahriman, has been steeled against their wishes and wants. You are the light in the darkness. You are the gleam in eternity. It is your hand which turns the keys of damnation. It is your wish which calls out to Sol for his light, for his love, for all that you are and all that you will be."

Arturus spotted him. He was standing behind a group of soldiers and slaves. He was looking towards the stage. Arturus climbed up and around one pillar to clear a clot of people that he couldn't pass otherwise. He was nearly to Julian. If it were not for the drums and the chanting and the insane screams of Maab's followers, Arturus could have shouted out to him.

Julian turned, making eye contact with Arturus. His mouth lulled open.

The men about Arturus surged towards the stage.

"Pick me! Pick me!" one man jeered.

The renewed press of bodies dragged him towards the site of the ritual. Arturus did his best to keep his bearings and to keep Julian's head in sight. Both he and Julian were shorter than the average Carrion man, so it was easy for Arturus to lose him. Still, the men about him were thin and frail, and though they possessed of the wiry strength of madmen, Arturus was able to shove his way through them.

They parted before him now, his strength giving him license to bully them away.

"Me! Me!" another was screaming.

They were all asking to be picked, stretching their arms towards the stage. Arturus suddenly saw Maab clearly. Saw her breasts swinging as she pointed out one man in the crowd.

"You!" Came her high voice.

She looked again through the mass of her flock and picked out another.

"You!"

For a moment, Arturus had the blinding fear that *he* might be picked, for certainly she seemed to favor the better fed of the slaves for whatever lottery it was they were playing. However, the age of those she chose seemed always to be about the same.

I'm too young.

He received an elbow to his jaw. He turned suddenly, twisting against the crowd. The man who had hit him was struggling like all the rest, looking only towards the stage. Maddened further by the blow, Arturus gave even less care to those around him. He brought himself low, as Galen had shown him for wrestling, and brutally pushed himself through the spindly limbs of the worshipers.

"You!"

The slave she had picked was close to Arturus, which caused the men there to move out of his way as he fought towards Julian. Arturus seized the opportunity to jump up a little.

There he is!

Julian had been pulled along with the crowd, just as he had, but had been taken a little closer to the stage. Arturus pressed straight towards his mark, shouldering the grey slaves aside. He caught a glimpse the boy's black skin through the bodies.

"You!"

Maab's voice was distant now. He saw she was picking men on the other side.

Galen!

Arturus' heart leapt as he saw his father in the haze at the far edge of his vision. His father was leaning close to another soldier, shouting in his ear.

What if she picks Galen?

But she couldn't. She was only picking the slaves.

"You!"

Her shout shifted the crowd, and Arturus lost sight of his father. When he looked back towards Julian, the boy seemed farther away.

Is he running from me?

The thought struck him suddenly. What if Julian hadn't been stealing these people's devilwheat? What if he had been a member of their tribe this whole time? What if his disappearance wasn't a kidnapping? What if he had chosen to live with his people?

No.

Arturus felt that he knew Julian too well for that. The boy would never turn his back on Harpsborough. Particularly not for a group of people who practiced such perversions.

Julian was being dragged by the crowd, Arturus decided. The men, all wishing to be picked, were trying to force their way to the far side.

"You!"

Maab's voice was even more distant, but the crowd could

run no farther. Arturus' world swam with his fatigue. The air had been somewhat better along the walls. Here, in the press of people, he could hardly breathe at all. Someone stepped on his robe. If he hadn't been enclosed by so many of the slaves, he would have toppled over, but he was kept from falling by those around him. Arturus grabbed his cloak and forced it back out from under the other man's foot.

"You!"

Julian was only a few feet away. The crowd was buzzing again, pushing away, but Arturus didn't care what new turn their ritual was taking. He lunged forward, covering the last few feet, and caught Julian's arm.

Julian turned to face him, eyes wide with shock.

He didn't recognize me before. Not really. He thought he saw me, but I was wearing the cloak.

"Turi?" Julian mouthed.

Arturus nodded.

"We're here to save you," he shouted.

"You!"

Julian was nodding, as if trying to process it all.

He can't hear me.

Arturus leaned in close. Julian came forward as well, putting his ear next to Arturus' mouth.

"We're here to save you!"

Arturus straightened, keeping his tight grip on Julian's wrist so that they would not be separated.

Julian's mouth was still open, but he nodded dumbly, as if only now comprehending. Arturus leaned back in and shouted more. His voice felt hoarse, but he didn't care.

"Aaron and Galen and I. There's a way out. We can get you home."

He straightened again. He had expected Julian to look relieved, but the boy seemed to be more shocked than anything else, as if he was horrified by what Arturus was saying.

"You!"

Arturus bent in once more, noticing that the press of bodies was suddenly easing. He rejoiced in the sudden breath of air. He was about to shout in Julian's ear, to reassure him that all would be well, that they were going to make it back to Harpsborough, that he wasn't going to be left alone as a slave in the hands of some demonic blood cult—but he stopped. He had the sudden feeling that everyone was looking at him.

He turned away from Julian. All of the grey robed slaves, all of the soldiers, even priestesses, were staring at him. There, on the stage, stood the most beautiful and cruel woman Arturus had ever seen, her finger set level with his heart.

The men parted in front of him, clearing a way to the stage. There was a surge behind him as the gleeful grey robed slaves helped propel him forward. Arturus glanced back to Julian, who stood still behind the grey wave which dragged him away.

He searched about himself desperately for a chance to escape, to find some way to avoid this fate. He saw Galen, there, in the crowd. The man's face was a mask of horror.

Me.

— 36 —

Arturus lay uneasily against the stone, his mind racing. He had been brought to this room and locked in with the other eleven slaves that had won Maab's lottery. Arturus had no idea how he could have drawn her eye. None of those picked before or after him had been as young as he.

Maybe she was picking someone else nearby me?

These men were not nearly as gaunt as the other slaves. There was more meat on their bones, surely. Their wrists were thicker, and their shoulders filled out their robes more fully.

We're all well fed.

Arturus shifted suddenly when he noticed that one of the men was staring at him. He met the man's gaze. The man looked down, but not away. He smiled.

"Are you a sweetie?" the man asked.

"Huh?"

"Are you a sweetie, or are you fresh? You look a little young to be wrestling about at Heaven time. For a second I thought you were one of the Little Ladies." The man laughed. "Bet some Kruk took you in under his wing. Kept his little birdie safe."

Heaven time? Little Ladies? Kruk?

The man had an odd look to him, like he was hungry.

Lust.

The realization sent a shiver up Arturus' spine.

The man had friends. Two of the other slaves sat very nearby him. Arturus didn't think he was the group's leader, though. If he had to guess, it would be the broadest of the three, who was watching on with a look of amusement.

"Bullies are the loneliest of creatures," Galen had told him. "Fight one, and you will find you have made a friend."

"Sure, I'm a sweetie," Arturus said. "Whatever you want to think."

The trio of men laughed.

"I thought I could tell that," the man went on. "Everyone in the room is a pitcher, and you're a catcher. Might make you a bit nervous?"

Pitcher? Catcher?

"Shaking in my boots," Arturus responded.

The leader shifted and spoke. "Careful Samson, little tiger has teeth. Wouldn't want to get bit before you see Queen Maab. . ." His face cracked into a broad smile. "In the flesh."

"You're a lucky one, sweetie," the lustful man said, and settled back against the stone.

He did not, Arturus noticed, stop staring.

The door opened.

Two soldiers stood there. One held a tray of food bowls.

"Heaven time," said the one without the trays, leveling his shotgun, "and Maab says there's to be no fighting. Equal shares. She doesn't want any of you to spoil your good looks."

The trio in the corner stood up, but stopped suddenly when the shotgun was pointed their way.

"No need to rise, buttercups," the soldier said. "Just stay where you are. The tray will be by."

Arturus felt his stomach growl.

They were given two bowls apiece, one of devilwheat, another of water. Arturus had never seen people eat so quickly. To catch up, Arturus mixed the two bowls together and drank it all down. The meal only made him more hungry.

When had I eaten last?

The soldiers came by and took the bowls. The bowls were counted to verify that all been returned.

"Sleep well. Maab will see you shortly."

The door closed.

The man was still staring at him.

Graham hadn't liked the idea of following Molly for a handful of reasons. First was that this mission was sanctioned secretly by the Fore. If Molly caught him, she would go around town telling everyone that he was a creep. He wouldn't be able to blame it on his orders because the mission was secret, so everyone would think he was some sort of sick stalker. Secondly, it wasn't terribly easy to follow someone through the wilds of Hell. The chambers were arranged like a maze, and it was pretty damn difficult to track someone over solid stone. Lastly, the crazy bitch might shoot him. He would have to follow her closely to make sure he didn't lose her. No easy task while she was on the lookout for demons. It was very possible Molly would sense that she was being followed and ambush him. He would like to think that the woman would keep her weapon safetied, and that she'd notice he was a hunter before she fired, but that was a lot of trust to put in someone. Molly wasn't renowned for either her caution or her altruism, so Graham was left feeling rather vulnerable. He'd have felt safer chasing Duncan.

Still, it was difficult to say no to Michael. Graham might have declined anyway, except that if Aaron never returned they'd be looking for a new Lead Hunter. It was probably going to be between himself, Martin, or Crispen, and he didn't want to hurt his chances by turning down missions. The other reason he had accepted, Graham was able to admit to himself, was that Molly had an ass like a golden caboose. He'd had more than one fantasy about sleeping with the woman, and when Michael had asked him if he'd follow the girl, he'd imagined that at some point she would find a pool of water, strip down, and bathe in it.

He was beginning to realize that this was never going to happen. If Molly was going to bathe, it was going to be in the river room with Alice or Kara standing guard to make sure that no one came in while she was doing it. She wasn't going to leave herself weaponless and naked in the wilds where some dyitzu could come tear her to pieces.

He caught sight of Molly as he came around a bend in the corridor. He dropped back slowly and peered around the corner.

She was walking, her hand trailing against the right wall.

Graham realized that she'd been moving in this way for the last hour. She'd always been taking right turns.

If she kept that up, he was going to have a much easier time following her. Sure enough, her next three turns were all to the right.

Graham found it odd that they hadn't yet traveled in a circle. Usually following a wall like that would lead one into a loop. He guessed they must be up against a barrier of some sort.

She's looking for something.

He spotted her again, having paused in a room. She was inspecting the right wall very closely. Her fingers were running up and down it. She reached up along the rock to inspect the some of the higher stones. Graham watched as she stood on her toes. Her breasts were shoved into the stone and her butt stuck out as she reached higher.

Whatever she was looking for, she didn't find it.

She collapsed to the floor in a heap and cried.

Graham had seen Molly cry before. There had always been an element of insincerity with her tears, and they always seemed to come with an agenda. She'd tried to turn the entire village on Aaron, for instance, after they'd broken up. Of course, after all the mean things she'd said about First Citizen Mike, nobody listened to her. These tears, however, were much different. They seemed very genuine. She seemed desperate, at the end of her means.

Graham's heart went out to her in a way that surprised him. He'd always thought of her as a slut. As a bitch. As a dangerous woman who didn't have feelings. He'd never thought that he'd want to protect her.

She stood suddenly, and Graham darted for the shadows.

Still crying, she turned around and stormed back the way she'd come.

If they saw her last time at Riverbend, then she's probably picking up where she leaves off each time. But why? What could she think is out here?

He was worried about her, certainly. In her current state a one legged corpse singing Dixie could sneak up on her. But he had been hunting in these halls at least twice in these last few weeks. It wasn't easy to find any devils here. He trusted that she would be safe.

He also turned about, his fingers trailing along the wall which Molly had been following.

What in Hell is she looking for?

He used the wall to backtrack where she had come from. He knew the area well, and he wasn't interested in finding secret passages in the stone, so he was able to travel a good bit faster than Molly had been.

What does she know that we don't? Did Julian somehow give us the slip? Was the boy's wheat really in here? Or maybe his sinfruit?

Whatever it was, he decided it had to be important. The woman wouldn't be looking so hard for something this deep into the wilds unless it was worth the risk. Most of the Harpsborough people wouldn't travel this far out even if they were starving.

After a while, he passed the curve in the river which the Harpsborough people had named Riverbend.

He recognized the next few chambers and shook his head.

There's nothing out this way.

Or maybe she wasn't looking for anything at all. Maybe she was just following the wall because it helped her find her way back. Maybe she just wanted to get away from it all.

But then why was she looking so closely for passages or markers in the stone?

It just didn't add up. He'd report to Mike, of course, and maybe the First Citizen would be able to put two and two together.

I can go just a little farther.

The next few rooms looked very familiar.

I've been here recently. But for what?

He jogged along the wall, his heart quickening.

He stopped when he came upon the Golden Door. Suddenly her motivations became clear.

She's looking for the Infidel Friend.

Arturus had been able to catch a little bit of sleep, but he doubted it had been much more than an hour. The man was still staring at him. Arturus wondered if that was what had awakened him. He had a vague memory of a dream where he was being watched.

Many of the others were sleeping as well.

The door opened.

"Alright, serfs, on your feet," the soldier ordered.

"I've got to shit," said the staring man.

"That's where we're taking you," the soldier assured him.

"And after that?" asked the trio's leader.

"Maab."

— 37 —

Queen Maab lay, reclined in her bathing pool, her breasts protruding through the surface of the water like mountains. Two soldiers stood silently along the back wall, almost disappearing against the dark purple stone. Two of her priestesses sat on a stone bench that was by the pool, the hoods of their satin cloaks thrown back to reveal their sharp and beautiful faces. Two young girls attended her in the pool. They looked to be ten or eleven, and already their eyes were devoid of innocence. A young man was also in the room, perhaps Arturus' own age, or just slightly younger. He was nude.

The room was lit with a pair of torches and perhaps a hundred candles. Arturus couldn't imagine even Michael Baker burning so many at one time. The waste of it all shocked him.

Her resources must be endless.

Maab raised one of her slender arms and waved.

The young man responded, coming to her.

"Toband, fetch me the sylvium tea." Her voice sounded whimsical. "And some more hot water."

The candles were made, at least in part, with fat, giving the room the odor of a man's flesh burning. Arturus felt bile come up in the back of his throat.

Maab's arm returned beneath the water. He fought not to stare at her nudity and averted his eyes. The rest of the slaves were doing no such thing. They looked at her with equal parts fear and lust. Fear, as if she were that Minotaur which she had broken. Lust, as if she were some goddess.

In a way she is.

Arturus shook his head to clear his thoughts. The smell of the candles and the feelings that Maab's naked flesh stirred within him made the effort useless.

The boy she had called Toband returned, a stone mug on a tray. Behind him were two more naked men, carrying between them a pot of steaming water. Slowly and carefully, they poured it into Maab's bath. The steam filled the room, drowning out some small part of the candles' aroma.

Arturus found himself watching Maab as she sat up to drink the tea. Her breasts met the water at her nipples, which were wide, pink, and relaxed. She sipped at her drink, delicately. Arturus looked away again.

The tea's odor was even more pungent than the candles'. It smelled of rotting mint.

Arturus stood with the other eleven silent and awestruck slaves as Maab continued to bathe. She stood up from the water. Arturus watched the liquid pour down the curves of her body. Watched it flow down from her hair and run across her chest. Watched as her nipples hardened in the cool Carrion air.

He swallowed.

The young girls stood beside her, each with a washcloth. Maab walked up the steps that led into her bathing pool and stood ankle deep in the water.

She's barely taller than me.

The girls cleaned her gently, paying special attention to her breasts, buttocks and womanhood. Arturus could feel that the slave on his right was shaking. He was stuck shoulder to shoulder with the man, and there was not enough room for him to distance himself without stepping forward or back.

Arturus swallowed again.

The man's shaking became more violent, and Arturus looked at him in alarm. The slave's eyes were opened unnaturally wide. Froth was collecting at the corners of his mouth. Around him, the other slaves weren't fairing much better.

What's wrong with them?

Maab shifted her weight from one foot to the other as the young girls switched from the washclothes to drying towels. Her legs were long and slender. The hair between them was also blonde, but a slightly darker variety.

Arturus noticed that he was also shaking.

What's wrong with me?

Maab had been fully dried. Arturus looked forward to the moment where she would put some clothes on, as her body disturbed him deeply. She stepped down from the lip of the bathing pool and walked towards the slaves. At first they flinched back, all except Arturus. Then, finding their courage, they moved back in line, some even being brave enough to step forward.

"So many," Maab said. "Surely, after taking the bull, I could only want desert."

They blanched in fear, and those that had been brave enough to move forward stepped back. Arturus tried again to look away from her, but that seemed to be impossible. It was as if she filled the room.

"Still, I'll want him to last a *little* while, at least," she mused, placing a finger on her chin. "Which one of you, do you suppose, is the strongest?"

All the slaves raised their hands. Arturus did too, trying to make sure that he didn't stand out, but he was a little later than the rest.

"That's nice." She smiled. "All of you are. Well, Little Ladies, do you suppose you could take these big men back there and find the toughest of them?"

The young girls nodded.

"Follow the Little Ladies, serfs," she ordered.

The young girls walked towards one of the exits and the men began to follow. Arturus fell in line.

"Except you."

Arturus stopped.

"You can stay here."

She knows. She knows I don't belong.

The slaves laughed uncomfortably, perhaps unsure of whether they should be jealous, or if one of their competitors had been eliminated from the lottery. They filed out.

Maab's deep blue eyes rested on Arturus.

He felt a catch in his throat and fought not to swallow. He failed as she stepped forward and looked him up and down. Maab turned back to her priestesses.

"See to the gathering. Make sure everyone is ready to leave when I'm done."

They nodded as one, bowing a little as they did so, and left the room. Maab then turned to her soldiers.

"Get Kayla and send her in. You may leave after that."

They nodded as well, and followed after the priestesses. For the moment, at least, Arturus found himself alone with the Queen.

She walked back to the pool. She crouched down beside it, her knees together, and dipped one finger into the water. She leaned back, sitting along the lip of the stone and let her feet down into the water. "What's your name?"

Arturus had to fight for his voice. "Turi."

"Good. Come here, Turi, and wash my feet."

Her feet?

He began to walk forward. He heard a scream of pain from one of the slaves in the room beyond and then a giggle from one of the young girls. He almost stumbled.

What's happening to them? What's happening to me?

"Turi, are you dense?"

Arturus stopped, unsure as to what he had done wrong.

"How are you going to wash my feet without a washcloth?"

He nodded, and walked over to pick up one of the ones that the Little Ladies had discarded.

"Not a dirty one, Turi. One of the fresh ones over there."

Arturus spied the fresh cloths by a few of the burning candles. He walked over to them. It felt uncomfortable to walk with Maab's gaze on his back. He looked back towards her, but she wasn't actually watching. She was holding her foot out of the water and appraising it.

Without looking away she spoke to him again. "There's a bowl over there too, Turi. Bring it."

His legs were still shaking.

He picked up the bowl and the washcloth. He moved back towards her. His heart was beating fiercely in his chest. He didn't know what she was going to do to him, or how, but he was terrified. He dipped the bowl into the water and removed it. He placed the washcloth into the water with both hands, and wrung it.

"Slowly, Turi. You're going to wash your goddess' feet. Not the dishes."

Arturus nodded. He looked for a moment into her eyes. She was the most beautiful woman he had ever seen. Beside her, Alice would seem plain. He looked down quickly. His heart was forming feelings that he knew he could not afford.

"Sit, Turi."

He did so. Some of the water from the bath had spilled out onto the stone floor. He felt the warm liquid soaking through his robe and into his pants. She placed one of her feet on his leg.

"You may begin," she said.

Arturus nodded. Her toes were well manicured. The nails seemed shiny. She didn't even have cuticles. Her foot was smooth, devoid of any calluses. He started at the toes. He watched the water drip down between her big and middle toe in a small river that spilled off of her ankle and on to his pants. She stretched her arms, her pointed nipples rising and falling with her movement. He fought to keep his hands steady.

She noticed his shaking and smiled.

He continued washing as best he could, running the rag along the bottom of her foot. He felt the ball of her foot beneath the cloth, which seemed a little dry. He dipped it in the bowl again.

What if I'm doing this wrong?

Would she have him killed? What if she found out he was an outsider? What if she knew already?

"Who is your priestess, Turi?"

Arturus was stunned. He didn't know how to answer. He didn't know any of their names. Surely he would be discovered. "I have no priestess. There is only you."

She laughed. "Are you a virgin, Turi?"

Arturus looked down.

"I mean with women of course. I know you serfs sodomize each other. Oh, don't worry. I'll not stone you for it. It's to be expected, I must guess. Men have such terrible appetites."

Arturus didn't answer. He began to run the cloth over her heel.

"You are, aren't you? You've never been with a woman."

Arturus felt shamed.

"I saw you at the ritual. At first I thought you were just fresh. Maybe you are. But then I saw you bull your way through the crowd. Jealousy, it must have been, that propelled you? You are young to be a Kruk, but that's something to be proud of I suppose. Has your priestess ever recommended you for baptism?"

Arturus shook his head no. He moved the cloth over to the top of her foot and then ran it along her ankle. She lifted the foot away, over his head, and placed it to his left. He found himself staring at her from between her legs. Warmth spread through his groin. There were tears in his eyes.

I want to go home.

She placed her other foot in his lap. He bit his lip and dipped the rag back into the bowl.

I don't care what happens to me. I just want to go home.

He began again at her toes.

This isn't how it's supposed to be. I'm supposed to be sitting next to Alice. I'm supposed to love her. I'm supposed to be able to look into her eyes.

I could love Maab.

But there could be no loving a woman like this. There could be fear. There could be obeisance.

And hatred.

He looked at her again, meeting her eyes.

It struck him that hate was a thing very close to love. So close that he didn't know if he would be able to tell the difference between the two when one came, or if there even was a difference at all.

"Compliment me," Maab said.

He had no words. His feelings seemed to block them out. The weight of her expectation fell heavily on his shoulders. He searched desperately for something to say. For the greatest compliment that he had ever heard.

"Speak, Turi."

He found his voice and looked into her eyes. "Yours is the face that launched a thousand ships and burnt the topless towers of Illium. Sweet Maab, make me immortal with a kiss. Suck forth my soul, and see where it flies. Please, give me my soul. Here I will dwell, for heaven is in those lips. All is dross, that is not thee."

Her slap sounded as a crack. He felt the warmth of it on his face, the sting where her hand had touched him. He felt sad for having somehow insulted such a creature.

"Helen is half mortal, Turi. You may not compare me to her." Her voice was cool and loving, and she leaned forward, kissing him on his cheek. The warmth there multiplied. His whole face felt warm. "But those are sweet words, Turi. Uttered as they were from the mouth of a damned man, they are quite touching. The first kiss was for the attempt, Turi. Stand, and I will redeem you."

Arturus stood unsteadily.

She moved down into the pool, onto the first step, so that she was just slightly shorter than he. "Have you ever kissed a girl before?"

Arturus shook his head.

"Relax, Turi. You learn this one by doing. Kiss me."

He leaned forward slowly, unsure of himself. He felt her wet breasts pushing into the clothing at his chest. He opened his mouth, just a little at first, and then wider from her coaxing. He was unsure of how to move his tongue. He pushed his forward, but she kept it back, and he made sure not to push it so far again. He felt her tongue moving inside his mouth, or rather, he realized, inside the space their mouths created together. He kept pace with her. It was a slow thing, the kiss. And as the motion became second nature, he felt his blood surge. His world had collapsed into that tiny space they shared.

He was breathing heavily, he realized, through his nose. She felt so small beneath him. So exquisite. So soft.

The feeling did not last.

She came out of the water and was suddenly taller than him. He had to lean his head back to keep kissing her. His neck felt horribly vulnerable. She seemed stronger than him, too, pushing him back across the stone floor. He hit a stone wall and could go back no farther. She was all about him, protecting him—loving him or hating him. He couldn't tell which and didn't care either.

He felt safe. She wouldn't let anything happen to him. Maab would keep him safe.

She stopped, suddenly, their lips still touching for one last moment, and then drew back.

He was out of breath.

She filled his vision.

Whoever I kiss, ever again. I will always think of her. I will never be rid of her.

Someone else entered the room. Screams of pain were coming from that direction. The slaves there were in terrible agony. More laughter, too, from the Little Ladies. It all seemed so distant.

Maab leaned down and kissed him again. Her touch was so soft, so gentle. He felt like he was a delicate thing in her arms. Of course she had to be gentle. She would break him otherwise. This time she finished by sucking his lower lip.

"Have you been toughened at all?" Maab's voice was a whisper.

Arturus shook his head, unsure as to what that meant, but harboring a terrible suspicion.

"Not even a little?"

He shook his head again.

"A shame," she smiled. "I'll spare you."

She turned to the person who had entered the room.

"Kayla, I like this one. Mark him as mine and return him to his priestess. Maybe we'll have him baptized in the next few years."

The priestess bowed low. "This way, serf."

Arturus fought not to look back as he followed the dark priestess out of the chamber.

He failed.

Maab was sitting down on the stone bench, looking towards her upraised foot.

— 38 —

Kayla led him down a corridor, passing the room where they had imprisoned him previously. There were two soldiers standing there.

"I'll be done with him in a second," she said. "I've got to mark him and then take him back to the serfs."

The soldiers nodded.

She brought him in and removed a black dagger from her cloak. "Take off your shirt, serf."

Arturus did as he was told.

"Hmm." She smiled. "Strong little fellow. No wonder she likes you."

The priestess stepped forward, dagger raised. Arturus had the terrible fear that it had been treated with rustrock.

What's she going to do?

"Don't flex your arm, it will take longer to heal. I don't want you bleeding any more than you have already. Look at you! You've left blood everywhere."

Arturus looked at the ground where they had walked. The wounds on one of his feet must have re-opened and they'd been leaking through his sewn up boot. She began carving a symbol into his arm. The pain was nothing compared to having the legs of the spiders removed from his feet.

"You take pain well little fellow," she said. "That's good in one of Mithra. Definitely necessary if you are to be worthy of a priestesses."

She likes me.

Suddenly the entire society seemed backwards. Like Harpsborough, except that the girls were the way the boys were supposed to be, and the boys were the way that girls were supposed to be.

Just in case I can't escape, I better be ready.

He imagined Alice, or Molly, and thought of what they might do in his position.

What does this woman want to hear?

"I think you're the prettiest priestess," he said, quickly, as if on impulse.

The look of pleased shock on the girl's face encouraged him, so he continued.

"I might never be worthy of you."

She shook her head and looked him up and down. "In a few years, you better. You think you can do that for me?"

He nodded.

"I promise I'll be gentle on you," she said, half distracted by the work she was doing on his shoulder. "I have a mean reputation, but I'm kind to the sweet ones. I only break them who ask for it."

Arturus swallowed.

She stood back from his arm and dabbed at it with a cloth. "Looks good." She cleaned her dagger and sheathed it in her cloak.

She wrapped up his arm with a cloth strip and tied it off. "And," she said, whispering into his ear, "Maab's city is very close to mine. She has taken three of my mates for her own, and regularly borrows from my lot. So see that you qualify for me. Of course, she breaks her men every time."

Arturus could not disguise the shudder that ran down his spine, so he did his best to pretend it was one of desire, not of horror.

"Get your shirt back on, young man."

Arturus did as he was told, being careful not to move the bandage on his shoulder as he pulled his shirt sleeve over it. He put his grey cloak back on, too, which was wet in places from Maab's bath water.

"Here you are, soldiers," Kayla said, leading Arturus back out of the room. "Keep him safe."

She smoothed his cloak and ruffled his hair.

"Good for you," one of the soldiers said, "you've been marked. A few years and you might be one of us."

Arturus nodded seriously.

It had better not take me that long to escape.

He wondered, though, if he could even survive out there in the wilds of the Carrion. Galen had told him that he could follow the river home, but the river was the most dangerous part of the Carrion. There were devils crawling all over it.

I have to try.

The soldiers led him back out into the room where the ritual had taken place.

"Where do you belong?" one soldier asked him.

Arturus looked around, and saw Julian's face. He did not see Galen's.

"Over there," he said, pointing to Julian.

"Ah, one of Selena's," a soldier replied. "That Maab mark may be the only thing that saves you, friend."

They brought him to where Julian sat on the stage. Julian did not meet Arturus' gaze, but left, moving to sit as far away from him as possible without leaving his group. One of the men touched Julian on the cheek, an oddly sexual gesture that suggested ownership.

Arturus thought he understood Julian's reaction better this time. Julian was trying not to get killed, or worse. He wanted to escape, surely, it's just that the cost for failure would be too high.

For him, but not for me.

He leaned back against the stone stage and listened.

I'm so close to the alcove. I could escape out there. I just have to break away.

He looked to see if the soldiers were still looking at him. One was, and the man smiled at Arturus.

I'll have to wait until they leave. In the meantime, let's hear what they have to say.

The two soldiers were talkative. Arturus caught his breath when he saw the sadist soldier in Icanitzu hide. He was put off enough by the man at a distance. When close up, the soldier was terrifying. His dark grey Icanitzu armor seemed to glitter in the firelight.

The soldiers stopped speaking until the man was out of sight.

"Where's he going?"

"Who?"

"La'Ferve, you idiot, I thought he was going to be leading Maab's forces back."

La'Ferve.

"No, he's going out to find the traitor."

Galen. They're chasing Galen.

"Who's leading Maab's priestesses back?"

"Gilgamesh."

"But she's got the Minotaur. You know Gilgamesh hates having his hounds near that thing."

"Well, we get to be by those fuckers as we go."

"Can't get used to that, traveling with hellhounds."

"Me neither. Gilgamesh's conditioning broke off of one a year ago, ate three serfs before they shot him down. Was right by Lethe, too, so they had to scatter the serfs and run for it. That's why they pull their teeth these days."

"It isn't worth it."

"Sure isn't."

Arturus saw the first set of troops marching out.

"Normally I feel safer traveling with Maab's guard. Maybe we can convince Kayla to break off early."

"Unlikely, we'll probably go in to visit."

"What was it like?"

"What?"

"Being with Maab, when she chose you last year. What was it like?"

"I don't like to talk about it."

"Tell me."

"She had ten of us in a row. We didn't last ten minutes."

"Ahriman incarnate."

"Don't swear."

"Sorry. Maybe that's why she likes La'Ferve so much? He can stand up to her?"

"No way."

"No way?"

"Nope. She likes him because he can kill. Nothing can stand up to her."

Kayla motioned to her group, and the two men moved to join her. She moved out with a dozen or so soldiers and nearly a hundred serfs. Two other priestesses accompanied her. Following that, came Maab's men. Maab had her headdress and paint back on. Arturus felt an ache in his stomach as he looked at her.

A man moved to talk to her. He was also dressed out of the norm, and more heavily armed. He had a coat made out of the fur of a hellhound. He was wearing jeans, but they had been split along the legs. A sawed-off double-barreled shotgun was holstered at his side, and the man had what looked to be a revolver strapped to his chest.

Gilgamesh?

The man spoke with Maab for a few moments, making wide gestures with his hands. No, not Gilgamesh. This man was familiar.

Pyle! The Betrayer!

He was in the Carrion? Perhaps he was the one who captured Julian.

What if he sees me?

But Pyle already had seen him. Arturus waited to be pointed out, but Pyle did no such thing.

He winked at Arturus.

Keep your head on. Stay calm. You'll find a way to slip out of the crowd.

Arturus felt someone touch his shoulder, so he turned to see who it was.

Julian was sitting down next to him, nonchalantly, not even looking at him. It was as if Julian didn't know him at all. Arturus could see where the sweaty touch of one of the slaves had wiped away some of the dust that clung to the young boy's face. Beneath that ashy layer, Julian's skin tone was darker. It was the color Arturus remembered.

Julian's under there, safe, hidden from these people by that layer of grey.

"We came to save you," Arturus said softly. "Galen and Aaron are with me. They're in the labyrinth beyond."

Julian nodded, almost imperceptibly. "Stay quiet a bit," he whispered, his lips barely moving. "I'll tell you when it's safe to speak."

— 39 —

"It's safe now," Julian told him.

"There's a way out of this chamber," Arturus said. "We only need to get to it."

Julian gave a barely perceptible nod. "Who's your priestess?"

"Priestess? No one is my priestess, we snuck in here."

"Turi, you're marked now. I know you think you've got to get out, I know, but for your own sake, I should tell you. . ." Julian broke off speaking for a moment while he waited for a pair of soldiers to walk by. "I should tell you what the punishment is for trying."

Arturus watched another group of slaves stand up, soldiers at their corners. They began marching out of the ritual chamber.

More are leaving!

It was only one group, however, and no one else seemed like they were getting ready to depart.

"What's the punishment?" Arturus asked.

"They chain you to a block, face down and naked. They cover your eyes so that all the other serfs can get at you. You've got no chance for revenge. Consider yourself lucky if your friend comes and rips off your nuts in the beginning. That way the rest of the Kruks can't torture you. You're on the block for three days."

"But we won't get caught. We'll make it to Harpsborough."

"Tried once, already, Turi."

Arturus turned to look at his friend. Julian's face was expressionless. His chin was raised slightly.

"This time you have help," Arturus whispered.

"Three days. I had tried to escape with a friend. We got caught together. We were chained side by side, just like you and me will be, if I go with you."

"You have to come."

"Three days. My friend got the stilling on the second. He abandoned me."

"We won't get caught."

"They kept taking him anyway. I could hear the sound as they pushed him back and forth. Back and forth. No one ripped my balls off Turi."

Julian cocked his head to one side, looking across the room at something. He seemed as carefree as anyone here.

Maybe Julian's close. Maybe he'll get the stilling soon.

"Okay. You want to stay here?"

"I'm not going with you. Listen to me, Turi. Listen very carefully. I wish I could make you stay, but I know you won't. You'll have to watch out. The hounds obey them. They have a trainer, Gilgamesh, and he has found a way to bend them to his will—"

"Galen's there, he'll make sure—"

"Shut up, Turi. We don't have much time. Now you listen to me. I was taken here by that one to the right. The one in split jeans. He's called the Lamb, because he's Christian. He's not the one you have to worry about. He's only as strong as a person is. The rest of them drink from the Bullman. It makes them stronger. It makes them harder to kill. La'Ferve is the scary one. He wears devil skins for his clothes. He's the one that caught the Minotaur, and they say he's had so much of the bull's blood that he's hardly human. He was shot in the head once and survived it. He can smell like a hound, track you all on his own. His protégé, Hale, was the one who caught me the second time. You've been marked, though. They may send La'Ferve after you."

Another group got up to leave. Arturus dared to glance at the man in Icanitzu skins.

La'Ferve. Can you really smell like a hound?

"Don't go back to Aaron and Galen," Julian went on, staring intensely into Arturus' eyes. "You'll only bring Maab's men to them. They'll be slaughtered. Don't go back to Harpsborough either. I've seen them hunt and track, Turi. Each of their men is worth three of ours. They're as silent as me. They survive here, in the Carrion. And if you shoot them they don't always die. The bull's blood has made them strong."

I have to see Galen.

"Julian, I—"

"Quiet," Julian said harshly. "I'll tell you this, and then I'm gone. There are serfs over there watching me talk to you. There are Kruks among them. I'm risking a lot just to warn you."

"Okay."

"When they capture you they're going to chain you down. They'll leave you there for three days. But you'll be blind. You'll have no way to measure the time. You have to try and smell their breath. If you can smell the devilwheat you know it's just been meal time. You have to survive six of those. Then they'll let you go."

Tears were streaming down Julian's cheeks, leaving little lines of dark skin in their wake.

"Julian."

"It hurts the most in the beginning, until you're ripped all the way. Then the blood helps some. To survive you'll have to think of something, some woman in Harpsborough, maybe. Maybe your mother. Something. Whatever is dearest to you. Hold it close. Don't let it go. You'll have to keep it because you'll start to *like* it. You can't let that happen. I'm sure that's what gave the man the stilling, Turi. You start to *like* it."

Julian wiped the tears off his cheeks with his robe. It smeared the grey off of his face.

That's his shield. With the dust gone they'll be able to see the real Julian.

There were a thousand things Arturus knew he should ask, but only one question came to his mind.

"Who did you think of? What helped you survive?"

"Honey."

Honey?

Julian got up and moved away. Arturus didn't dare follow him.

Soon they'll leave. I'll hide here. No one knows to count me. Then I can try. Three days.

— 40 —

Arturus stood up slowly from his hiding place behind the stage and looked about the empty ritual chamber. The room, once so full of people, was intensely empty. A grey hem, ripped from the cloak of its owner at some point during the ceremony, lay by the entrance. Pools of sweat had formed puddles at low points in the floor. Pools of blood and other liquids did the same on the stage. Over where the torches had burned, and on the ceiling above the stage where the Carrion people had used whatever pyrotechnic substance they owned, black stains of smoke clung to the ceilings and walls. A few extra torches still lay in a pile on the edge of the stage.

Whatever dark magic this place once possessed had been dispelled. Now it was just another empty chamber. It was hard for Arturus to imagine that this was the room in which Maab had held her blasphemer's ceremony.

There was the sound of a footstep. Arturus ducked back behind the stage, crouching low.

"All clear in the Holy Room!" a soldier shouted.

Of course they're looking. Other slaves might also choose the Carrion over their masters, no matter what the punishment.

Arturus tried to imagine what the man was doing. Was he walking around the stage and heading towards the exit?

Did he dare peek, or would the man discover him?

He waited, and then looked.

The soldier's back was facing him. The man moved out of the ritual chamber, looking about in the next room.

Safe.

After a few minutes passed, Arturus stood up again took in a deep breath. He saw Pyle out of the corner of his eye. It was a split second before Pyle impacted with him, sending him reeling back across the stones. Arturus' feet slipped in sweat, and the man caught him up in a bear hug. Arturus struggled to get out of his grip, managing to twist his back towards the man. Pyle's hands, however, were firmly clasped, and Arturus could not get away.

"Another Harpsborough rat," Pyle whispered in his ear. "If you see one, there's another two in the bulwarks."

Arturus fought desperately to free himself. He worked at the man's fingers, but Pyle's grip was too strong. He tried again, pushing against the man's wrists and elbows. He remembered Galen's teaching and tried to grab at Pyle's legs by bending low and reaching between his own. Pyle was quick, strong and moved easily, almost instinctively, out of the way. Fighting panic as much as his foe, Arturus struck out, trying to stomp with his right heel on the instep of Pyle's foot. Pain lanced upwards into his body from his wounded foot as the blow landed. Pyle wrestled him into the stage, slamming his face into the stone. Blood poured down over Arturus' eye from where his brow had met with the rock. The liquid blurred the vision of his left eye, so he closed it. Arturus tried to strike with his heel again, this time trying to kick backwards and catch Pyle in the groin. Pinned as he was against the stage, the attempt was futile.

"I've caught one," Pyle shouted aloud.

Hopeless.

But he hadn't tried everything that Galen had taught him. Arturus studied Pyle's grip with his open eye. The man's right hand was over his left. Arturus wormed his thumb down near the base of the grip. Pyle's fingers were too tightly clenched for him to dislodge them, but that wasn't Arturus' aim. Arturus worked his fingernail under Pyle's. He kept his finger carefully bent, so that his first knuckle joint would support his nail. He jerked his arm back with all his might.

Pyle let out a shriek as his nail tore off. A little bit of it still hung on to his forefinger, dangling as if by a thread. The man still hadn't let go, so Arturus went for the man's second finger. This nail ripped off halfway, diagonally and down to the cuticle. Pyle shouted again, and finally released him. Arturus ran, wincing in pain each time his right foot impacted with the ground. He made it to the lip of the stage.

Pyle was close behind him. Arturus picked up a woodstone torch from the stage and swung it as hard as he could. The crack of the torch's impact was as loud as a man's shout. Pyle collapsed to the ground, holding his head in his hands. Arturus made a mad dash for the exit.

Pyle stood, one eye shut, with the help of two Carrion soldiers. He put a hand to the swelling on his forehead. It was a hard knot, nearly the size of a baby's fist. A sudden unexpected pain shot through him, powerful enough to send him back to his knees.

It was coming from his fingers.

He held the offending digits in front of his eyes.

"Did you catch him?" Pyle asked, looking up at the blur beyond his hand.

"He's nowhere to be found, Pyle."

"Well, do you have the exit guarded?"

"Yes. Securely, and we've swept through. We can't find him. There's only a few of us left though. Most everyone else has gone already."

One of Pyle's ruined fingernails was still attached, hanging uselessly. He gritted his teeth, and gripped his bloody fingernail firmly with the thumb and forefinger of his left hand. He shouted as he ripped it off.

He batted the soldier's hands away with his left arm and stood on his own.

"We need Gilgamesh," Pyle said, surprised by how much the pain colored his voice.

"He's to escort Maab home, he's no time to track a serf."

Pyle fought this time to control his voice. "Get one of his hounds then, and Hale."

The soldier shoved him a little. "I don't take orders from you, Lamb."

A female voice quieted them all.

"Was it the young male? Picked by the Queen at the c eremony? The well fed one?"

Pyle nodded, unwilling to trust his voice to stay firm in the face of the pain coming from his head and fingers. He recognized the voice of the priestess, but he didn't remember which one she was. The pitch of her speech was unusually high, though. He tried to look in her direction, but his vision of her was unclear. All he could see was a black blur. He fought back the urge to vomit.

"Then yes, men, by all means," she was saying. "Fetch Hale, and one of Gilgamesh's hounds. And be quick. Maab had him marked this very day."

"Jesus Christ," Pyle managed.

"Watch your tongue, Lamb," the priestess said. "Don't mention your foul Yahweh in this place of Mithras. I'll lead the hunt."

Pyle looked at her again and tried for a second time to focus on her. She was shorter than most, and had brown hair.

God damn—Sinna. A Little Lady. This fucking hunt's going to be run by an eleven-year-old.

Pyle had regained his bearings and most of his vision by the time Hale arrived. Harnessed beside him, and held by two wary Carrion warriors, was the hound. It was just a little thing, about three feet tall. Its mouth was muzzled shut, and its claws and first knuckles had been removed from each of its four feet. Its eyes were wide and confused, evidence of Gilgamesh's drugs. Practically the only thing Maab's men had left the hound with was its sense of smell. Somehow, the plight of this creature, even though it was a devil, moved him.

It and I are much the same. Castrated by Maab, blackmailed by her magic, doing whatever we can to avoid the pain she gives us in her disappointment.

Hale wore his hair in a ponytail, almost like Harpsborough man might, but his face was clean shaven. Maab would allow no less.

"It won't work," Hale said. "Too many people have been through here. No way to scent the hound."

"No one has seen him but the Lamb," a soldier mentioned. "Perhaps this Lamb is lying?"

Pyle sneered. "You think I hit myself in the head with a God damned torch?"

"Watch your tongue," Sinna said. "I will not warn you again. Still, your point is well taken."

The Little Lady walked slowly about the ritual room, her satin robes swishing around her ankles. "Is this all your blood, here?"

"No," Pyle answered, pointing to the stage. "The blood there is from him."

Don't forget how smart the Little Ladies are.

Hale motioned to his men. The hunters dragged the hellhound forward. They lifted the thing up to the blood and pointed.

"Scent," Hale said harshly. "Scent!"

The hound barked.

"We have him by blood, now," said Hale. "Until his wounds close, he is ours."

— 41 —

Arturus clenched his jaw as he pulled off his boot. He squeezed his eyes shut, and the bright lights that squeezing created were all he could see. He ran his fingers along the bandage on his right foot. The blood had soaked all the way through.

And that used to be my good foot, too.

He struggled until he got his other boot off as well. The dressing there was much cleaner. He took off his grey cloak and began ripping it into strips.

The sound of the ripping worried him, but he doubted that anyone could hear him. He rewrapped both of his feet. He checked the wound on his forehead. His eyebrow had been cut seriously, and was still bleeding. He tied one strip as a headband around it, as tightly as he dared, and hoped that the blood would not get back into his still stinging eyes.

He felt about in the darkness for his discarded boots, and having finally found them both, braced himself to put them back on. Despite his greatest attempt at fortitude, he gave out a whimper as he put on the right one. He tied the remains of his robe together, making a satchel to carry the torch he'd brained Pyle with. He knotted it together securely with a few more strips and slung it over his shoulder.

There.

He did his best to remember the way out, but there were no visual cues for him to follow. He ran his fingers along the floor around the trap door which led back down into the Carrion tribe's chambers. A lip had been dug into the stone, presumably treated with rustrock, to make it easier to lift. Confident that he would recognize the feel of the trapdoor he wanted, he moved in a spiral around the room, hoping that his clothes and his weapons would still be here.

They weren't.

Galen must have taken them.

There was another possibility as well, Arturus knew. Maab's men might know of these trap doors, and have searched them already after finding out about Galen. If that were the case, all his efforts were sure to be in vain.

He still had the torch he'd used to brain Pyle with, but he had no access to fire.

If they catch me, three days.

He moved into the next chamber and followed the right wall until he had an idea of the shape of the room.

He heard the bark of a hound echoing up from below.

No. There can't be hounds down there. Galen, please come save me.

"He's still in here," Hale reported. "The hound couldn't smell him at the exit. You sure you checked through Maab's chambers thoroughly?"

"Yeah," Pyle said. "Can't hurt to try with the dog, though."

"No." The Little Lady contradicted him. "Now that we know he has yet to escape we are free to search him out in here. He is undoubtedly hidden in one of the buffer rooms. Take the hound back to the Ceremony Chamber, we'll just follow his scent from there."

Pyle didn't like the tone of her voice.

I'm going to kill that little shit.

They didn't make it all the way back. In one of the buffer chambers, the hound let out a whine and led them to the wall. It began clawing, as if trying to climb up one of the alcoves.

"Look," Hale said. "Blood, on the wall."

Boy's good.

"He must have climbed up and down here," Hale was saying. "He knew to confuse the hound. See, there's blood on both sides."

Sinna looked at the wall and cocked her head.

"Why would he change sides when he got to the top?" she asked.

That is odd.

"Maybe the blood is dripping from his head to his feet," Pyle mused.

Sinna chuckled.

I'm not sure which of these children I want to kill more.

Pyle moved into the alcove and looked up. He put his hands and feet on the wall and started to climb.

"Keep looking," Hale ordered.

"No." The high voice responded from beneath him. "Stay put."

Pyle began climbing the chamber wall, aware that Sinna was watching him intently. At one point he slipped on the boy's blood, almost falling.

Maybe I'd land on that little whore.

He made it up to the ceiling and looked about. On a sudden impulse, he pushed upwards. The stone moved. The shock of it almost sent him tumbling again.

"He came through here!" Pyle shouted down. "There's no light, but we should be able to follow him."

"No," Sinna countermanded. "It's too dangerous to chase him through the dark. I think I know where that might lead out. We'll pick him up in the wilds."

"He's unarmed," Pyle shouted back. "We may never find his scent out there. We should chase him here."

"Unarmed?" Sinna giggled. "Pardon me if that doesn't ease my mind, those words coming as they do from a bludgeoned lamb."

Her face would turn red if I strangled her, then blue. If I get her away from those soldiers, I'll show her what it feels like to be as helpless as I am.

The hound led them quickly through the tunnels. It stumbled from time to time, perhaps because of Gilgamesh's potions, or perhaps because its ruined feet were harder to balance on. They had taken six soldiers with them, including the two who held the hound's harness.

Enough, in Pyle's estimation, to kill most things in the wilds. They had no serfs to scatter in case they ran into a large pack of dyitzu, though, so the hunt could get bloody.

Boy won't be able to stay ahead of us for long. I'll be back with Maab soon enough.

The hound growled as it approached a bend.

"This way," Hale said, leading them into a room.

"Check the ceiling," Sinna ordered.

She gives orders just like Maab.

Pyle climbed one wall while a soldier tried the other.

It wasn't nearly the climb that he'd performed in the previous chamber, but Pyle's head throbbed each time his heart beat, and his legs felt weak.

"Here it is," the soldier reported.

"No visible blood," Hale said, kneeling to the ground. "He may have had time to treat his wounds."

The hound was already struggling to leave the room.

"Still enough scent in the air," Hale said.

He pointed back out of the chamber, and the soldiers let the hound continue its hunt.

They stopped suddenly at Hale's order.

"He must be getting desperate," the man said.

Pyle caught up to him and looked ahead into the room that had disturbed Hale enough to bring him to a halt. Pyle's back straightened when he saw the large domed chamber roof, pitted with man sized holes.

Harpies.

"He wouldn't have dared come through here," Sinna's high voice intoned.

"Must be no harpies," Pyle observed, "or we'd see his body."

"Either he's suicidal or he's fresh to Hell," Hale said. "Though I can't imagine even someone damned yesterday being dumb enough to run into a harpy nest."

Pyle knew why they were confused. Turi wasn't from the Carrion, so he'd never seen or been warned about harpies before. Hale seemed reticent to enter the room.

If I'm ever going to get a chance to repay that little shit for my fingernails, I'm going to have to let them know where he's from.

"He's never seen a harpy," Pyle said. "He's from Harpsborough."

"Like the darkie?" Sinna asked.

Pyle nodded.

"Oh the wonderful gifts you keep bringing us."

"He moves quickly," Hale said. "But he's moving differently now than he was earlier. Ever since we passed the black crystal. He's spotted this hellstone vein, and he's following it. I think now he must know where he's going."

"Maybe he's headed home then," Sinna mused. "Hale, is this the way to the barrier? Is this the way out of the Carrion?"

"I'm not overly familiar with this area, but I don't think so."

The hound tugged feverishly against its harness. The thing was eager to leap into the harpy den.

"It's not," Pyle answered. "I roam around here all the time. He'd need to travel down with the crystal if he were trying to get to Harpsborough. This vein dead ends after a day or so."

"Well, he's headed towards something," Hale assured them. "I can feel it."

"He may not be alone," Pyle warned. "He might be trying to get back to a friend. Maybe friends."

He watched Sinna consider that. Pyle had long ago learned to stop being shocked by how smart the Little Ladies were. It was better just to pretend they were adults.

"Then we must find him quickly," she said. "He may also be alone, and be trying to get to a gun. Either way, we should brave this room. Are we sure that nest is empty?"

"Yes," said Hale. "The hound wouldn't want to go in so badly."

"Keep your shotguns up," her high voice warned. "Just in case."

"He stopped here," Hale informed them as the hound sniffed about the room.

One wall was made of small, black bricks, almost the color of obsidian.

Firerock.

"Will we catch him soon?" Sinna asked.

Finally, something that little slut doesn't know.

Hale shook his head and undid the tie that held his hair. He placed the tie in his mouth and spoke around it while he worked his hair back into a ponytail.

"He's still bleeding. He'll either tire, or get himself killed shortly."

"Look at this, sir," one of the soldiers manning the harness reported. "A brick is missing. Now how did he do that?"

Pyle looked curiously at the wall. "Look here. He jammed something in between these bricks. It lessens the load on the other ones. If nothing is binding the bricks together you can pull one out that way. An old Harpsborough trick."

"Well, I'll trust my shotgun against his brick any day," Hale said.

"Fool," Sinna said, rolling her eyes, "that's firerock. He just wants something to light his torch."

Pyle imagined her face burning. The hair going up in a sudden blaze while her flesh dripped off of her steaming skull.

"How long, Hale," Sinna asked.

"This blood hasn't even clotted. He must be tiring, or the wounds are getting to him. Hopefully another hour. Less, if he tries to rest."

They moved quickly out of the room, jogging behind the slow lope of the hound. It wasn't stumbling at all now, Pyle noticed. The exercise must have helped to clear its system of Gilgamesh's potions. He hoped that Hale had more of those in his pack.

— 42 —

Dust filled the chamber next to the Carrion barrier, causing Ellen to cough.

Martin said so many people had arrived to help fill the barrier because a hunter's share of dyitzu had been offered by the Fore as compensation. Not all of them were actually helping, however. Alice, the one that Turi liked, was just watching. Hoping, maybe, that Aaron would come and start shouting from the other side of the barrier before it was finished. Hoping, just like Ellen was, that they would have to undo all the work they were doing to let the men back in.

The villagers came armed with wheelbarrows of gravel, mined from a nearby chamber. They would spill the gravel into a pile by the barrier where two hunters would shovel it into Julian's hole. It was this shoveling that filled the chamber with dust.

The corridor had been cooler, originally. Rick had told her it was because the Carrion was such a cold place. Now the hallway was warm, heated by the bodies of so many men working.

Ellen brushed the dust off of her shoulders. If Turi were to come back and they were to dig him out, she wouldn't want to look a mess.

I'm deceiving myself. He's not coming back.

"That should be good," Rick said to the hunters. "Pack that in as best you can, and we'll brick it over."

The dust began to clear now that more wasn't constantly being flung into the air. Rick and the hunters started laying the bricks, pouring some sort of paste over them as they went. Ellen walked by Alice and tried to give the girl a smile.

The woman looked terrible. Her blue skirt looked to be grey from the dust which covered her face as well. Tears had cleared away some of the dirt on her cheeks, making her attempt at stoicism a fairly transparent lie.

Alice did her best to smile back at her, but she just couldn't hold the expression. Ellen knew how she felt.

By the time Ellen made it to Rick, he was taking a break. She offered him her canteen.

He smiled and drank from it.

She sat down beside him.

"This is important stuff," he told her, holding up a handful of the paste. "It's ground hellstone. The water helps keep it even. When the water dries out, it will heal those bricks together. It will be as strong as any wall in Hell."

Ellen didn't want the wall to be strong. She wanted it to be easy to break through. Who cared if the demons came? Who cared if Turi was probably dead already? If they were alive, didn't they want them to have the best chance of coming back?

The hunters got their second wind, and Rick went back to directing them. Ellen watched the wall grow higher and higher, layer by layer. It didn't have to be too high, just high enough to block the stone that the boy Julian had managed to lever open. As if the gravel wasn't enough on its own. As if Rick hadn't already built a wall on the far side as well.

When the work was done, the Harpsborough people left quickly. Their promised lot of food was waiting for them back in the village, after all. Ellen felt more comfortable now that they were alone again.

Rick didn't get up right away. He leaned back against the wall and poured water over his head and shoulders. "It was tough work. I'm pretty hungry."

He said so, but he didn't stand.

Ellen nodded.

Rick wiped some of the water off of his brow. "Yeah, I'll look forward to eating tonight. You've got enough fruit for us?"

"Yes." Ellen's voice sounded distant to her own ears.

"It's good to see all these people working together." Rick was looking anywhere but towards the wall. "Builds spirit. The villagers feel better. I like working with them, too."

"Of course."

"It's a good thing, showing them how to build the walls. They've seen it before, of course, but it helps them just the same. They'd be able to make their own, I think."

"Yeah."

Rick breathed in through his nose and looked up to the ceiling for a second.

"I'll show you how to make a pie out of that fruit," he went on. "You'll probably pick it up pretty quickly. Pretty quickly. It's tricky making dough out of devilwheat. You have to be really careful about what you put into it. What you put in. And cooking it is a chore. It'll come apart really easily if you cook it too much. It dries out too much. Then you don't really have a pie. You know. It dries out too much."

He blinked a few more times before speaking again. "We did a really good job—"

Ellen reached out and took his hand. She held it for a second, and then she hugged him.

Rick covered his face and cried.

— 43 —

"You've got to be fucking kidding me!" one of the Carrion warriors shouted over the cacophony of water.

Pyle peered into the chamber. It was a purely natural cavern, perhaps a mile in length. Its left and right walls were ragged and sheer. Possible to scale but it would require an expert climber to do so. Water streamed down in places along the sides of the cavern and fell freely from cracks all along the five hundred foot tall ceiling. A particularly tremendous waterfall, wider than any Pyle had ever seen, flowed out of the far end.

Hale said something, but Pyle couldn't hear him over the torrents.

"What?" Pyle yelled.

"Giant's Tunnel," Hale shouted.

"Bullshit." One of the warriors disagreed. "Giant's Tunnel ain't got water."

"The settling," Sinna's high pitch could be heard easily. "You can see its cracks all over the place. It must have let some river in."

Pyle walked in and took full stock of the place. "Would have to be under a major offshoot of the Kingsriver or Lethe. Too much water for anything else."

"Lethe." Hales eyes narrowed as he peered across the cavern. "You can tell because Hell's architect hasn't touched the place. Completely natural."

Turi had lucked out, Pyle surmised. If he had tried this escape just a month ago, this place would have been one long easy run. As it was, the boy might end up gaining some ground by the end of it. It was hard even to see through the chamber. The waterfalls pouring down the rock and free falling from the ceiling filled the air with mist. That mist clung to the walls, too, making them dangerously slippery.

Who knows, one of us might even fall to our death?

Pyle looked down from the ledge.

Jesus.

The cavern remained sheer as it hit the water level. The water itself was a churning mass, running as fast as any rapid. In places it was being drained away, creating huge whirlpools. Jagged rocks thrust themselves up out of the churning abyss, seeming almost to bob in the tremendous currents, fading in and out of view as the mists moved. There would be no swimming in that sea, Pyle knew, and any fall was likely to be deadly.

"Let's race across," Pyle yelled. "Leave the dog."

"No!" Came Sinna's response.

"We'll need it if he makes it to the far side." Hale agreed with her, of course. "There's an exit to Giant's tunnel over there, just left of that waterfall. If he makes it, we'll need to be able to track him."

"Well, I'm not carrying him," Pyle shouted back.

"Of course not."

Hale lowered his pack and took out a stone jar. Two of the Carrion soldiers grabbed the hound by its legs and forced it on its back. Hale knelt on the hound's throat and grabbed its jaws. The hellhound's eyes were wild, and the beast gnawed uselessly at Hale's hands.

Hale poured the liquid into its mouth, shifting his knee along the thing's throat. Some of the potion was sputtered out, but some had to have been swallowed. Hale worked quickly to bind the hound.

Pyle walked around the ledge which they stood upon, checking the walls. He found some of Turi's blood on the left side.

"Here he was," Pyle reported. "It looks like he climbed straight up from here."

"Why would he do that?" A Carrion soldier asked.

"Waterline," Pyle answered. "Look up there. As you get higher you get drier. Easier climbing that way."

Hale had managed to attach the hound to his back. The man's pack had been designed with that purpose in mind.

Brilliant bastards, Maab's men.

"There he is!" Sinna ran forward, pointing along the wall.

One of the Carrion soldiers lifted his shotgun.

An excellent weapon for the labyrinth, but it won't do you much good here. Boy's out of range.

The man didn't even get off a shot. The boy had disappeared from view, hiding in a crevasse.

But the blood was on the left?

The boy must have climbed up and over the entrance. If they hadn't just spotted him, Pyle would have led them the long way around.

Smart little bastard.

The cavern turned too, just slightly towards the right, as it went on. That bend in the wall was going to protect Turi as he made his way down Giant's Tunnel.

"We have a plan?" Sinna's voice squeaked.

"He picked the correct route, and he's about an hour ahead of us," Hale pointed out. "We're not going to have a good shot at him until he makes it to the back. I remember there being a ledge over there. It's right at the bend. If the settling hasn't made it crumble, we can set up there and get a clear shot at him as he tries to get out."

Pyle spat over the ledge. "The settling may have made more exits."

His spit disappeared into the mists.

"Let's hope not." Hale cinched a rope around his waist tightly enough to make the half-comatose hound on his back yelp. "We'll have him trapped unless it has."

Sinna said something to the man, but Pyle couldn't hear it over the water.

Hale turned back to Pyle and the Carrion men. "The water will cover the noise of our guns, so we don't have to worry about a quick retreat after we fire."

Sinna paced back and forth. "It's better if we capture him."

Hale nodded in agreement. "If we get to the ledge fast enough, he'll have to climb across our field of fire to make it out. We can shoot in front of him to try and get him to come on back. If not, or if he doesn't respond, then he dies."

"Let's hope he doesn't," Sinna yelled. "He's been marked by Maab. And he's pissed me off enough that I have half a mind to strap on a cock and be the first to greet him on the stone bed. The Kruks will have to wait in line for me."

Pyle imagined her slipping, falling along the wall. The rocks would break her bones as she hit them. Maybe one jagged outcropping would pierce her skin, punching through the ribs at her chest and letting blood spill into her lungs. She would tumble farther down, bones shattering and bruises accumulating until she hit the bottom, tainting the water with the froth of her blood before the suction pulled her under and bashed her to death upon the cavern floor.

Bitch.

Hale took to the wall, climbing as if he weren't weighed down by a hundred pound hellhound.

Fucker's drank too much of the Minotaur blood.

Hale looked down at them. "Our plan only works if we make it to the ledge before he gets to the exit."

Sinna walked behind Pyle and pushed him forward. "You're next," she said, her delicate mouth pulled up into a smile.

She smiles like my sister.

"Galen," the warrior announced just moments before he stormed into the room.

Aaron had never seen the man so angry.

Jesus, where's Turi?

Avery sat up, bending to try and see behind Galen. "Tell me you took him home." Avery's eyes were suddenly clouded over with passion.

Galen shook his head.

Avery slammed his fist into the stone.

Aaron hadn't realized how much the boy had meant to Avery. Johnny Huang was also sitting up now, and like Avery, he made no attempt at stoicism.

"What happened?" Huang asked, "Is he—"

"Maab's got him." Galen tossed his pack into the wall and then knelt before it.

Duncan was awake now as well, looking confused. Only Kyle remained unconscious, and he had every right to.

Maab. Klein was once one of her slaves.

"What happened?" Aaron asked.

"I got in there and met my friend." Galen loaded a few rounds into his Heckler and Koch clip. "I thought Arturus would be safe. I'd put him in a back corner while the ritual was going on. He spotted Julian in the crowd. He did the right thing, I feel, and tried to rescue him. It didn't work out."

Aaron noticed that Galen's hands were shaking.

Is it anger that makes him shake, or fatigue? Has he slept since we got here? He must have, it's probably been five days.

"Has it been five days since we left Harpsborough?" Aaron asked aloud.

Galen nodded. "We're probably already bricked in. If not, it will happen shortly."

Aaron felt the breath go out of the room.

Avery struggled to his knees. "We get the boy first. Then we worry about getting home."

Galen stopped rustling through his pack and looked at the hunter.

Aaron saw that Johnny was nodding. Duncan at first looked unsure, but his expression hardened, and then his head began to nod as well.

"That's right," Aaron said. "We can't leave him behind, but Avery, you can't walk. As far as I know only I can."

Johnny Huang stood up. He grimaced, but the effect was convincing.

"Okay," Aaron conceded. "Johnny, you're good too."

Galen loaded the clip back into his MP5.

"Do we have a plan?" Aaron asked the warrior.

“Yes. The Carrion people are breaking up from their ritual. They’re heading back into their separate hiding holes. We hit one of the groups, kill everyone but their leader and find out where he is.”

Aaron joined Johnny in flanking Galen as they left the chamber.

“We’ll be back soon boys,” Aaron assured them. “Don’t you worry.”

“Hey!” Avery called.

They stopped in the doorway.

“Yeah, what’s up?” Aaron asked.

“Good hunting.”

— 44 —

The six Carrion warriors were spread out on the rocks around him. Sinna was a bit higher than the rest. Pyle hadn't expected her to be such a good climber. If she wanted, she could have outdistanced them all. Maybe not Hale, if he was unencumbered, but as it was he had a hundred or so pounds of dead weight strapped to his back. As Pyle watched, one of the hound's legs twitched.

Almost dead weight, anyway.

Pyle couldn't blame Hale for choosing the lower route. It had certainly looked promising. Even with the trouble they were having, they would still probably save time crossing the cavern's bend. If Hale was right, and the settling hadn't taken out the ledge he spoke of, they should be able to rest in just a few minutes. The stone here was slippery, however, and Pyle would be surprised if they all made it across Giant's Tunnel alive. For the first few hundred feet his fear had masked the pain. Now he was too tired to be afraid.

He had to be careful when he looked for handholds using his right hand. Two of his nails were missing, and the pain would blind him if the tops of his fingertips touched the stone. Sometimes he didn't even have a choice. The swelling on his forehead throbbed mercilessly, giving him a pounding headache and making the world swim around him.

He saw the hound kick again.

It's starting to wake up.

Hale was looking over his shoulder in alarm. The hound was enough of a burden asleep. Awake, its unbalancing movements could well cost the Carrion man his life.

"We're coming around the bend," Hale shouted. "Keep your eyes sharp."

The man wasn't lying. Pyle could see more and more of Giant Tunnel's back wall as they climbed. It would not be long before Turi would be exposed.

"I see the ledge!" Sinna's shriek sent spasms of pain pulsing through Pyle's head. "The settling didn't take it."

Hale shouted something else, but a waterfall was streaming down from the ceiling right next to him, so his voice was lost in the din.

Pyle did his best to use the same handholds Hale had. The settling and the water had weakened the rock enough that some of the more promising outcroppings couldn't hold his weight.

The ones that can handle Hale and the hound should be fine for me.

Pyle stopped. The next section of stone was particularly smooth, and a small stream, perhaps three feet across, made sure that it would be slick as well.

Now how did Hale make it across that?

He took a deep breath and looked out across the cavern.

He could see the right corner of the back wall now, and the ledge wasn't too far away either. Pyle looked back the way he'd come. It certainly wasn't any distance at all compared to how far they'd climbed already. He glanced down to the churning sea below him.

Jesus.

"I see him!" One of the soldiers shouted.

"Where?" Hale had found a solid foothold and was leaning back to get a better view.

"Near the corner, about a hundred feet over."

Pyle saw the young boy for just a second, moving across the stones.

He's almost at the bottom.

Turi was in trouble now. He was going to have to climb up nearly an eighth of a mile, climb sideways nearly twice as far, and then cross the tremendous waterfall before he could make it to the exit. And all of that had to be done while nominally within the range of the Carrion shooters.

We've got you boy.

He turned his attention back to the climb. Hale must have used a handhold on the other side of the stream. Pyle gritted his teeth and shoved his right hand deep into a crevasse. His arm shook with his agony as his unprotected fingertips were pressed into the sharp rock. Tears formed in his eyes. Pyle shook his head to clear it, reaching out with his left hand to try and find something to grip across the water.

He tried one prospect, but the stone was slick, and at a bad angle. If he were to put all his weight on that stone, he would surely fall. Blood trickled down his forearm, coming from his fingertips and collecting in the crease by his elbow.

Whatever pain I feel, Turi is feeling it worse. He's got bleeding feet, no food, no chance for sleep, and he's all alone.

The sound of a stone skittering across the wall caught Pyle's attention. Pyle blinked away the tears from his eyes. At first he thought the rock had come from above him, from one of the Carrion soldiers, but a second rock flew in. It was definitely coming from out there in the cavern. Pyle looked across to the far wall. He couldn't see much because much of his vision was blocked by the waterfall which had drowned out Hale's speech earlier.

Then he saw another stone, coming from the back right corner of Giant's Tunnel, sailing through the air at them. It got caught in the falling water and disappeared.

"Is that coming from the boy?" Sinna shouted.

"Yeah," Pyle answered.

"Kid's got one hell of an arm," one of the soldiers noted.

Fucking idiot.

"Kid's got a sling," Pyle shouted back.

"Where'd he get a sling?"

"His robe, maybe." Pyle watched the next rock.

It wasn't aimed for them. Turi was firing at the far wall.

"Can he hurt us with it?" the soldier asked.

"He's got pebbles, not sling bullets," Pyle squinted his eyes, trying to focus his blurry vision on the far wall. "His aim's going to be bad. And the air will take the speed out of his throws anyway."

"Well, why's he throwing them?"

If you'd shut the fuck up for a minute I might be able to figure it out.

He saw another of Turi's slingstones. He watched it travel through a maze of falling water to impact again with the far wall. Pyle searched around that area. He saw something move.

Dyitzu.

There were two of them, traveling along a ledge across from them. Pyle could tell that they weren't sure where the sling stones were coming from.

Turi's next shot was back towards Pyle's direction. The dyitzu watched the rock fly.

That little shit.

"Move!" Pyle shouted.

He searched fervently for another handhold with his left hand. He didn't find anything promising. He reached out with his foot, trying to find a crevasse he could jam it into.

The first few dyitzu's fireballs were already coming. One buried itself in the waterfall, but another just clipped it. Half extinguished, the remaining ball of dyitzu fire spun out of control until it slammed into the side of the cavern.

"Use the water for cover," Hale ordered.

More of the fire came shooting in, missing by a wide margin. The next set was closer, though, and one fireball landed right above Pyle.

Fuck.

Pyle reached into the stream itself and found a handhold. He pulled his body into the water. His left foot found some support, and he used it to let go with his left hand and search for another handhold.

There, that's what Hale must have found.

He tried to get a good grip, but his fingers, now slippery, couldn't cling to it. More fire came in, impacting above him. Some of the fire was mixing with the water there and began streaming down towards him.

Pyle tried another hold, but the stones fell away. Steaming water and dyitzu fire poured over his right hand, singeing his unprotected fingertips. A scream escaped from Pyle, but he dared not let go. He remembered burning his face off.

The fire is your friend.

He reached back to the last handhold he'd tried, not caring how tenuous it was. He clung to it with all his might and moved through the stream. The water poured over his body. His left hand slipped, and he reached out with his right, slamming it down on a jagged rock. The stone cut into his palm, but he didn't care. He lifted himself, letting the sharp stone edge cut deeper into his hand until it caught on his bones and tendons. Finally he found another solid handhold. Shortly thereafter he was able to find a place for his feet as well.

I'm alive, but my right hand may be useless soon.

He made his way as quickly as possible behind the cover of the falling water. That brought him nose to nose with the groggy hellhound.

Well hey, fucker.

Hale turned and gave him a grim smile.

"What now?" Pyle shouted.

"There's no way we can make it to the ledge with the dyitzu there," Hale answered. "And what's worse, we can't make it back, either."

God damn.

More rocks slid down next to Pyle. At first he thought it was Arturus at work again, but they were coming from Sinna as she scaled cliffs above them.

She came to a point where she must have been in the dyitzu's line of fire. She drew her Beretta pistol.

"They're out of range," Pyle shouted up to her. "You're just wasting bullets."

She fired anyway. Pyle couldn't see how well she did because of the waterfall, but one of the Carrion soldiers whistled. She fired off another round. And another.

Wait, she's not aiming at the dyitzu.

Her bullets were landing near where they had last seen Arturus. One the dyitzu ventured a fireball out that way.

"Go on," she ordered, and Pyle could hear her smile in her

voice. "I'll cover you."

Aaron and Johnny stood guard while Galen finished hogtying the dyitzu.

"We've got to get you some pants," Aaron told the near naked hunter.

Johnny smiled and nodded, adjusting his ammunition belt over his boxers.

The dyitzu was still breathing but certainly not conscious. After braining the thing with the back of his rifle, Galen has made an incision in its throat. Aaron guessed he had cut its vocal cords.

"They'll scatter their slaves at the first sign of trouble," Galen was saying. "That keeps the roving bands of dyitzu off of their trail. Confuses the local hounds, too. Good news is that will work for us. Don't shoot any of them. Trust me, they won't attack. The only thing they'll be interested in is finding a different priestess to protect them."

"What's the dyitzu for?" Huang asked.

Galen ignored the question. He tightened the knots around the dyitzu's wrists enough that it was brought back to consciousness. It tried to scream, but only a slight gurgling came out of its throat.

"It's harder to kill a Carrion Born than it is to kill one of us," Galen said. "Now don't ask me why, because I won't tell you. It is enough that you know this is true. Make sure you fire multiple shots into each target if you haven't got them in the head. They're armed with shotguns and pistols and that makes them strong in the close tunnels. We're better in the big ones, but in the Carrion, we can't afford fighting there. Try to keep your distance, nonetheless. Almost all of their shotgun rounds are going to be buckshot, so the farther back you are, the more time their volleys have to spread."

"Yeah but the dyitzu—"

"Whatever you do," Galen again ignored the hunter, "don't shoot the priestess, or we'll find ourselves doing this all over again. Any questions?"

"The dyitzu?" Johnny asked, both eyebrows raised.

Aaron answered for Galen. "It's the first sign of trouble."

The hound had awakened. It growled constantly and fought against the ropes that bound it. Hale paid it no attention, his eyes fixed on the back wall. Pyle had deliberately set himself up on the ledge to be as far away from the beast as possible. Even drugged and toothless, as the hound now was, fighting with a four legged animal on a slippery stone precipice didn't seem very promising.

He wasn't sure what had happened to the dyitzu. Perhaps

Turi had managed to kill them, or maybe Sinna had just scared them away. Pyle didn't care which so long as they didn't come back with some friends. He felt extremely exposed on this ridge.

"He's been down there a while," one of the Carrion soldiers shouted over the rush of the water. "Maybe we should offer him surrender. He might be willing to take it."

"Hell," Pyle answered, "stay in this cavern too much longer, and I'll be willing to surrender to him."

"Quiet," Hale ordered.

"We should send two of us out there," Pyle suggested, ignoring the order. "Maybe we can flush him out."

Sinna sat perched on one of the ledge's rocks, her knees held to her chest, arms folded over top of them.

"I see him," she said.

"Where?" Pyle didn't see any movement.

"There, that bit of grey. Near the corner. About thirty feet over from the thin waterfall."

Pyle searched and searched, but his eyes had difficulty focusing. The Carrion soldiers all moved towards the edge to see.

"Hah!" said Hale. "I think that's a bit of his robe sticking out."

"Shoot beside it," Sinna ordered. "Then we'll ask for his surrender."

We've got you now, boy. Pinned down, nowhere to go. Will you be brave enough to kill yourself, or fool enough to surrender?

The range was bad. Turi could probably hold out there until they got closer. But there was absolutely no chance of him getting to the exit. . .

Pyle blinked, refocusing his eyes.

There Turi was, at the exit.

How in the hell?

Sinna must just be looking at a piece of his robe.

Pyle drew his pistol and tried to get off a shot, but the boy had made it into the tunnel already.

"What are you doing?" Sinna screeched.

Pyle pushed his way past the Carrion soldiers, taking special care as he stepped over the hound.

"He just made it out," he shouted. "You're looking at a distraction."

"Impossible." Hale kept one hand on the hound to keep it down.

"Did anyone else see it?" Sinna demanded.

They hadn't.

Pyle pointed towards the exit. "I'm telling you, I saw him."

"He couldn't have gotten over there and climbed up without us noticing." Hale's tone, however, sounded unsure.

Sinna stood up on her rock. "He could have. He could have

climbed up behind the big waterfall.

"But he would have had to get over that far," Hale insisted. "How would he have done that?"

"He must have swam it." Sinna was visibly frustrated. "Damn. It's like chasing a fucking Infidel Friend. Let's move it. He may gain a little time, but not much. Besides, he's had to spend much more energy than us. He'll tire soon."

— 45 —

Aaron shifted in his cubbyhole, looking down into the barely lit chamber below. Still no sign of the Carrion men, though Galen had sworn they would be coming this way. On the other hand, Galen and the dyitzu were also below, somewhere in that chamber, and Aaron hadn't seen them either.

There were two entrances, each marked with a violet keystone topped archway. Galen hadn't specified through which one the enemy would be coming. Aaron looked over to Johnny, who was breathing heavily through his broken nose. He looked particularly foreign with the swelling.

I hate waiting.

His thoughts wandered to the lock of hair he'd left behind with Kyle, Avery and Duncan.

Johnny breathed in suddenly and turned off his safety. Aaron did likewise

The Carrion men moved in complete silence. The first pair were soldiers in dark clothes, shotguns drawn. Grey robed figures followed them, entering the chamber in two single file lines.

These are the slaves Galen warned about.

There were twenty or so of the slaves. Behind them came two more pairs of soldiers and the priestess. The priestess was the hardest to see, her black robe working as camouflage in this dark Carrion room.

The dyitzu stumbled into view. Aaron took aim at one of the soldier's heads. The slaves broke and ran, just as Galen had said they would, but none of the Carrion soldiers fired.

They're too well disciplined. They'll hold their fire until the last second. No need to give away their position with gunfire unless they have to.

The dyitzu fell to its knees. The Carrion soldier Aaron was aiming at dropped into a crouch, his shotgun raised. Aaron kept his sights on the man's head, lining up the shot over the dyitzu's shoulder.

"One," he said.

Johnny Huang shifted, getting his rifle set. "Ready."

"Two."

The priestess peered around one of her soldiers, looking at the bound dyitzu.

"Three."

Aaron fired, his gunshot followed almost instantaneously by Johnny's.

Aaron's bullet took the Carrion man full in the face. Johnny's shot was also a hit. Aaron pulled another round into his rifle's chamber and fired again, hitting one in the leg. Johnny put a second bullet into his first target.

The Carrion group ran, covering their priestess and firing back at them. One of their men supported the soldier Aaron had wounded, helping him retreat through the entrance. Aaron was surprised to see such humanity among such monsters.

They're brothers too, just like me and the hunters.

A soldier came back around the corner suddenly, firing his shotgun. Aaron heard buckshot as it ricocheted about in their cubbyhole.

Johnny cursed.

Aaron fired again, just missing the next Carrion soldier brave enough to peek around the wall.

"You okay, Johnny?" Aaron asked.

"Just a little buckshot, nothing serious."

The next time a soldier turned the corner, Johnny got him in the shoulder.

"They're running!" Johnny shouted, dropping down from his perch.

Where's Galen?

Aaron followed him, hoping like hell Johnny was right about their enemy's retreat. Johnny made it to the corner and took a quick look. He jerked his head back, but no buckshot followed.

"They're behind a couple of stone mounds back there, take a look."

Aaron edged up to the entranceway.

This is going to get me killed.

He dared only a quick glance.

He spotted two of the soldiers over the top of their cover. Lying against one of the stone mounds was a grey robed slave that had been shot in the crossfire. Aaron guessed that the remaining soldier and priestess were tending to the soldier he'd hit in the leg. Of course, they would have paid no attention to the wounded slave.

Wait a minute, we didn't shoot any slaves, did we? They didn't shoot any slaves...

He peeked around the corner again. The slave was sitting up now, an MP5 in his hands.

Galen!

At the first report of the Heckler and Koch, Aaron burst through the archway, Johnny in tow. Galen shot a second man down while Aaron took aim. The Carrion soldiers had turned towards Galen. Aaron's bullet took one of them in the side of the head. Galen came to his feet, the MP5 blazing. The last of the soldiers dropped, still twitching, to the Carrion floor.

The priestess had a pistol drawn, but she wasn't fast enough. Galen slammed the stock of his rifle into her face. Her gun fired as she collapsed back against the stone wall. Aaron heard her bullet skipping down the corridor.

Galen dropped his MP5 and caught the priestess' slender wrist with his left hand, overhooking that captured limb with his right. With a sudden twist he sent the priestess to the ground, her arm twisted at an odd angle behind her, her pistol skittering across the stones. Galen let go of her arm and gave her a front kick, sending her body away from her dropped weapon. He drew a pistol from his belt, and pointed it towards Aaron. Aaron instinctively ducked away. Galen fired, the bullet whizzing between him and Johnny. Aaron looked behind him and saw the bound dyitzu drop.

The priestess had regained some of her composure and used the wall behind her to help her stand. She drew a knife, which seemed a pitiful defense against the man before her. She threw it at Galen and then tried to kick at his groin. Galen ignored the knife, which bounced harmlessly off of his body armor, and blocked her kick with his own shin. Then, twisting his hips, he slammed that same shin into her midsection. He had kicked her every bit as hard as he had kicked the Icanizu, and the crack from his blow sounded out like a gunshot. The woman doubled over, vomiting. She screamed in pain after each retching, clutching at her ribs. Aaron thought they must be cracked.

Galen caught her by the hair and dragged her still vomiting form back into the chamber. He tossed her beside the fallen dyitzu and placed his pistol against her cheek. Even with vomit in the corner of her mouth, Aaron had never seen a woman more beautiful, more statuesque—more vulnerable or terrified.

"Where's my boy?" Galen shouted.

The pistol he held was shaking. Whether from rage, adrenaline, or from having stayed awake for several straight days, Aaron couldn't guess.

"Boy?" the girl's voice was slight and sultry.

She's prettier than Alice.

"The youngest picked by Maab at the ritual." Galen leaned forward, getting inches away from her vomit flecked face.

The girl's wide frightened eyes narrowed suddenly. "You. . . I know you," she whispered. "You've come back."

"The boy." Galen's voice was ice. "Or you die."

Aaron could tell the she was in awe of the warrior.

"He was marked, by Maab," she said, "but then he escaped. Since he's marked, no one will take him in. He'll have to make it to Calimay, and even she might not take him."

Galen leaned back away from her and looked to be considering something. "Calimay has turned against Maab?"

"She has."

"Where did he run too? Where are you searching for him?"

"I don't know." She swallowed. "Don't kill me, I don't know. I only know that Hale was sent after him."

"Hale?" Johnny asked.

The priestess nodded. "La'Ferve's apprentice."

Galen cursed, but Aaron didn't recognize in what language.

"He's got the Lamb with him," the priestess offered.

Aaron and Johnny shared a look. Aaron shrugged his shoulders.

"Lamb's are Christians enslaved by Maab," Galen explained. "She means that he's being chased by Pyle."

"The Betrayer?" Aaron asked.

Galen nodded.

How? How is that man still alive?

"Get her back to the others," Galen ordered.

Aaron shook his head and stood his ground. "You don't have the slightest idea of where to look for the boy. There's no God here. You'll have no miracle."

Galen nodded. "I'm not staying behind to find Turi. With this group missing, the Carrion hunters will try and find us. They have hounds. I have to stay and make sure that they can't pick up our trail here."

"You'll fight them by yourself?" Johnny asked.

Galen knelt on the ground and helped the priestess to her feet. She couldn't keep her posture, and stayed bent over even when he got her standing.

"No," Galen said. "When they come I'll draw the dyitzu."

Aaron took the priestess and passed her over to Johnny. "Then what? You're planning to stay and look for the boy when you've led the Carrion men astray, aren't you."

Galen nodded.

"You know you have no chance," Aaron pressed.

"I don't."

Aaron reached out and grabbed his shoulder. "You need to sleep. You may well end up killed."

"I still have a few hours before the hallucinations set in."

Johnny was shaking his head. Aaron saw where the buckshot had hit him. The hunter had some blood seeping out from his right shoulder. He was bleeding from his hand too. He had opened up some of the scabs there during the fight.

"You'll get yourself killed," Johnny Huang warned Galen.

Galen paid him no heed and retrieved his MP5. He didn't look back as he continued walking down that corridor.

Johnny shook his head. "If we lose him, we're dead."

Aaron frowned. "We're dead already." He put one of the priestess's arms over his shoulder to help her walk. "Come on princess. We'll tend to your wounds when we get back to the others. I don't want any fighting out of you."

She nodded dumbly. Her hair had clumped around the vomit in it, and some of the substance rubbed off against Aaron's shoulder.

"Can you walk?" he asked her.

She didn't seem to have heard his question but was looking to where Galen had left.

"Miss?"

The boom of Hale's shotgun died away.

"Another fucking dyitzu," he said.

Sinna looked at the twitching devil corpse with disinterest.

"They're thick around here. Real thick," Pyle said.

Sinna laughed melodically, though the noise sounded similar enough to a banshee's call to make Pyle's teeth hurt.

"He's leading them into us," she said.

Pyle considered the possibility.

She may be right.

"There's a river coming up soon," Hale said. "He could find a pack large enough for us to be in trouble."

Pyle's head throbbed mercilessly, and his right hand was swelling badly around the wound he had taken in Giant's Tunnel.

Sinna's little eyebrows were furrowed. She was considering the danger.

"Keep on," she said.

"But Priestess—" Hale was disturbed.

"Look, he's bleeding very badly from his feet. His pace is much slower now. He's paying for the swim and the climb in Giant's Tunnel. If he leads us into a pack of dyitzu, it will be the last thing he does."

"Yeah," Pyle said. "But what about us?"

"Don't worry." Came Sinna's high pitched reply. "We'll have him captured in less than half an hour."

She pointed towards a puddle of blood in one corner.

She's right, he rested there.

Pyle bent down and inspected the blood. It hadn't even had time to clot.

And he can't afford to rest.

— 46 —

Arturus heard the boom of the shotgun in the distance.

Closer still.

They were moving much faster than he was now. He could barely walk, and his right foot had swollen so badly that the laces which held his boot together had spread open. He could see the grey wrapping he'd placed around that foot through the torn boot.

He forced himself forward into the river room, his unlit woodstone torch held up as a club. No enemies.

He considered drifting away with the current. How long could he just float? How long until he passed through a room full of dyitzu and they doused him with flames, or leapt into the waters and tore him to pieces. Or until he came to a waterfall and fell to his death?

The Infidel Friend had done such a thing, drifting away, counting on luck to save him.

But this was the Carrion.

There would be no Ellen to pull him out. The current would just pull him deeper in.

"Galen!" he shouted. "Galen."

His voice echoed in the river chamber.

He tossed his firestone brick across the river and watched it clatter in a series of sparks on the far bank. He slung satchel, torch and all, after it before he dropped into the water. The current was swift enough to make him fight to get to the other side. He made it just in time to avoid being swept into the next room. Water poured off of his clothes and spilled out of his open shoes as he made his way out of the river.

He tried to stand, but only managed to get up to his hands and knees. He was out of breath.

I need to keep going.

He was so tired.

I have to go now, or they'll find me here.

His heart was beating too quickly, and his vision was shaky. Blood started coming down from the cloth at his forehead, dripping into his right eye.

Somehow he managed to stand, and then he limped across the chamber. The hobble made Arturus feel like he was a corpse.

He picked back up his brick and torch, pressing on as fast as he could. He was leaving a trail of water behind him, but what did it matter? They had a hound. They could follow him even if he left no trail at all.

"Check the far side of the river," Sinna ordered. "Quickly. That was him shouting."

"It's getting time to drug the hound again," Hale reported.

"What's he going to do, bite you?" Sinna asked. "Get him across."

Pyle waited with her on the near bank as the soldiers forded the waters.

She's probably afraid to get her robe wet.

"What are you staring at, Lamb?" Sinna challenged him.

"You. If your soldiers all die, I might rape you."

She giggled, girlishly. "You'd have to grow a dick first."

"Maab will let me have it back soon enough. In the mean time I might settle for a fist," he said.

"I'd break your hand." Sinna's smile was malicious. "Then where would you be? You think Maab would ever let you grow your cock back after you had tried to desecrate a priestess?"

He glared at her. He imagined feeding her to the hound. It would chomp at her wildly with its toothless maw, trying to eat her. It wouldn't be able to cut her, of course. Its saliva would tangle her hair. The strength of its jaws would break her nose. She would scream in her high pitched voice. He could almost hear it. And then he would feel bad for the hellhound. They'd been castrated by Maab together. They owed each other something. He'd cut bits of her flesh off with his dagger, piece by piece, and feed them to the hound. That's the least of the revenge that poor beast deserved after all it had been through.

He realized he was still staring at her. She hadn't flinched.

"How much did Maab leave you with?" Sinna asked him. "An inch, a quarter?"

He turned away suddenly.

"Don't be worried." She moved closer, reaching one of her slender hands behind his head and touching his cheek in an intensely sexual way with the other. "If we return Maab's property to her she'll be happy. And I'll plead with her to give you your dick back."

She drew him in, turning his head back towards her, and kissed him. She sucked his top lip into her tiny mouth, biting him hard enough that it blocked out the dull throbbing from the bruise Arturus had left on his forehead.

"And then," she whispered softly in his ear, her tongue flicking his earlobe, "when you're a man again—then I want yours to be the first cock I break."

Pyle looked away, his whole body shaking.

Hale was saying something, shouting at them from across the river.

"What?" Sinna asked, though Pyle could tell that her eyes had not left him.

"He's got to be exhausted now. He should have used the river to try and break the hound's scent, but he didn't. He just ran straight through."

Sinna disrobed and wrapped up her Beretta in the cloak. She tossed the bundle over to Hale and jumped, nearly nude, into the water.

Pyle's mouth filled with saliva at the sight of her pre-adolescent body. He felt blood rushing to what was left of his organ.

He absently scratched at his groin.

I'll kill her.

He held his gun and ammo belt over his head and jumped in, surprised by the swift current. With one hand upraised to keep his weapon and bullets dry, he kicked his way across.

I may just fucking shoot her. Maybe if I kill them all Maab won't know.

But she'd know, and he knew better. He just had to bide his time.

Wait. If I was the first man Sinna broke, I'd be her lieutenant. Did that little cunt just ask me out?

He emerged on the far side. Sinna was putting her robe back on. The hound was struggling mightily against the soldiers. They were having trouble keeping it still and were leaning back against its pull. The thing wanted to continue the hunt.

Sinna smiled at him.

"I should drug it," Hale said.

"We're almost there," Sinna chided. "Just don't let your soldiers free him, is all."

They jogged again through the wilds. Water was dripping off of their bodies, but Pyle was heartened. He could see in the dim light the river water that Turi had left behind him as well. It didn't last long, but when the water was gone, he noticed something else. The hound did too.

"He's bleeding very badly," Pyle said with satisfaction. "He doesn't have much time left."

"He's only just ahead of us." Hale's eyes were wide with adrenaline. "I can feel him."

At least I'll get to tear this one to pieces.

They followed the hound. The tunnel dimmed, almost getting too dark to see.

"If only we had torches," a soldier muttered.

"It's okay, he'll dare not light his. If he did, we'd see him," Sinna answered.

Bitch's ears are as sharp as the hound's.

He struggled to keep up with the pace of the hunters, but he wasn't about to let little Sinna outpace him. The priestess was running along quickly beside them, barely even breathing hard.

"Here!" Hale said. "He took a left here. He's not going straight anymore. He's hopeless."

They trotted down the dark corridor. The stone was black in some places, a deep purple in others. There was enough ambient light to see but only for a few yards. Odd symbols, looking like moons and stars, had been carved into the sides of the corridor.

Pyle saw a shadow ahead.

There he is!

But it was just rock. The passage dead ended. There was a symbol carved into the stone. To make it out, Pyle had to get within a few inches of it. It was star made out of two triangles.

A Star of David.

"Dead end," Hale said.

"He may have run here deliberately," Sinna said. "Check. Maybe there's a passage."

The hound was confused. The thing was letting out a low whine, and its ears were flicking back and forth. After a moment, it dropped low to its belly.

The hell?

"What's that sound?" Sinna asked.

Everyone quieted, except for the hellhound, which kept whining. Sinna kicked it, and the thing finally shut up.

Have I heard that before?

"Wind chimes?" one soldier asked.

"It sounds like pins dropping," Hale said, bemused.

It did sound like pins dropping. Thousands and thousands of pins.

Oh, God in heaven. Silverlegs.

"Torchlight coming!" Hale shouted. "Look!"

But it was more than torchlight. Millions of little reflections, dancing like frenzied fireflies, filled the corridor's distant entrance.

Nowhere to run.

Sinna's face looked terrified. For the first time in Pyle's memory, she looked like a little girl. She backed up against the wall as her men stared ahead in confusion. She looked towards Pyle and clutched at his swollen hand. Her fingers brushed one of his broken nails, but he didn't care. He bent down to listen to her.

"I'm afraid of death," she whispered into his ear.

He could hardly hear her over the sound of the spiders. "Of course."

"Will you hold me as we die?"

She seemed so vulnerable. So much like his sister, and so unlike Maab. He was suddenly aware that she truly was just a little girl. "Of course, my lady."

The silverlegs came pouring down the passage, covering the floor from wall to wall.

They're swarming. How can there be so many?

Hale and his men fired their shotguns at them.

Fools.

Pyle clung to Sinna and waited. She burrowed her head into his chest. He sat down slowly, leaning back against the wall and sliding down it. She climbed into his lap, curling up into a fetal position. She rested her head on his shoulder, and he rocked her back and forth.

"Sing to me," she said. "Won't you?"

He nodded.

The booms of the soldiers' shotguns became more rapid. One soldier was shouting for ammo, another was crying out in pain. A third made a break for it, charging headlong into the spiders, but the silverlegs were too thick. He toppled over after a few strides, and the spiders covered him over. The hound was howling now, a terrible, terrified high pitched howl.

"Summertime," Pyle began, *"and the livin' is easy."*

The hound's howl turned into a short whine. The sounds of the shotguns were replaced by the screams of the soldiers.

"Fish are jumpin', and the cotton is high."

He felt the first sensations on his boots. It seemed more like tingling, really, than anything else. That tingling began spreading up his legs. The successive spiders began ripping through his clothing, and then he felt them digging in into his skin as they marched across his shin bone. He was being flayed, slowly. He clutched the weeping Sinna to his chest and tried to cover her with his body.

"Your daddy's rich, and your mother's good lookin'."

The tingling became a burning as the tide of spiders rose. He saw their little spurs catch on the now exposed flesh of his legs with each of their eight legged steps. His skin would rise just a little bit until it ripped off of the spur. The shrieking of the still dying Carrion soldiers let him know that his own death would not come quickly. He tried to fight the spiders, to keep them off of the girl, but the swatting at them did no good. The millions of little wounds on his body screamed in pain. The lacerations stayed silent only so long as he kept perfectly still.

"So hush now little baby—"

They were creeping across his chest and over his neck. A source of light was coming towards him, sending the silverlegs into a panic. He covered his eyes with his arm.

He felt the flesh melting off of him. One of the spiders was crawling across his ear, the same ear that Sinna had whispered into. He imagined the silverlegs swarming all over the girl, imagined their tiny legs as they tore the flesh from her bones, imagined that she must be feeling the same pain that he was feeling now. He reached up with his free arm and covered her eyes. The spider on his earlobe entered his ear.

No!

He could feel it crawling up towards his brain. The blood in his ear was drowning it, he knew. He could feel its death throes against his eardrum. Pyle had never imagined such pain was possible. The blow from the torch, the moment when he burned off his own face. . . castration—they were nothing. Desperately he cupped a hand over Sinna's exposed ear. The motion left his eyes unprotected, but he couldn't bear the thought of her experiencing such agony. He pushed her head down to his chest, keeping her other ear safe against his own body. Something was coming. He looked up with his eyes, because he could no longer move his head. He saw torchlight approaching, illuminating the corridor as it came, scattering the spiders before it. One spider crawled down the bridge of his nose and across his cheek, a giant silhouette against the coming storm of swirling lights.

He's been driving them towards us.

The limping form of Turi approached. The boy bent down waving his torch over one of the still writhing soldiers, clearing most of the spiders away. He stood again, this time armed with a pistol he'd taken. He brushed the spiders off of it with the butt of his torch.

One silverleg made it onto Pyle's eyelid. He felt the little legs pierce through the skin and catch on the surface of his eyeball. He blinked suddenly and felt the razor legs cutting through his eyelid. He opened his mouth to cry out, letting spiders in there as well.

"Mercy," he shouted, and tried to say more, but all he could manage was "her."

He couldn't see anymore. He wasn't sure if he could even move. He heard a single report, and the writhing form of the girl in his arms suddenly stopped moving.

There was no second shot.

— 47 —

Graham walked across the empty village. The smell Harpsborough had achieved during its brief period of prosperity still clung to it. The stench was perhaps even worse now, as there was no smoke from the still or Kylie's Kiln to mask it. Alice was here, leaning against her hut, eyes opened and unblinking. She looked almost as if she had the stilling. She twitched though, and scratched her nose, so he felt it was safe to leave her be. Martin was here as well, leaning against the Fore next to Benson and muttering to himself. Graham could hear the snores of some off duty hunters, and there were a few Citizens about.

Other than that, the village was deserted. With the spider food exhausted this morning, everyone had suddenly returned to the wilds. Graham paused at the Fore's door blanket. He felt like he could run through there without permission.

With Aaron gone, I belong in the Fore.

He pushed against the blanket but then lost his courage. He popped his hand against it a few times. Chelsea answered, pushing the tapestry aside. Her hair had fallen in front of her face, but Graham could still see the dark circles beneath her eyes. She was mourning somebody. Probably Aaron.

"I'm here to see Mike," Graham said.

Chelsea nodded and motioned him in.

"John," she called. "John, go and tell Michael that Graham's here to see him."

He entered the Fore, and Chelsea let the door blanket fall behind him. John's sandals clapped loudly against the Fore's stairs as he ran up them. Chelsea didn't bother him with any questions, returning instead to a card game she was playing on the Fore's waiting room table.

Solitaire.

John's sandal claps returned as he came back down the stairs. "He says to head on up. He's in his chair."

Even most of the Citizens are in their rooms. Harpsborough feels so empty.

Graham marched up to the third story and entered the parlor room. Michael was sitting in his chair, looking at the chess set.

"I think I've got him," Michael said.

"Who, sir?"

"Mancini. You see, he's attacking me here, but after I move my knight here. . ."

Graham looked blankly at the pieces. He wasn't sure how they moved, but it did seem like Mancini had a few more of them than Mike did.

"Sir, I've more news on Molly."

The First Citizen nodded and leaned back away from the chess pieces.

"I was thinking about that," he said. "We might want to take her into the church, have a mock trial or something. Scare her out of this. She's liable to kill herself."

"She may have found something, sir. She may have found an alternate way to get behind the Golden Door."

"Impossible."

"Hell's a big place, sir."

"I had twelve hunters with me when we went up and down the surroundings of the Golden Door. There's no way in."

"She's bought some torches, sir, and she's gone pretty deep. She's found some tunnels that lead up and is exploring them. I think they go to the great bridge."

Michael's hand came up and covered his mouth. "She's going that far out?"

"Yes, sir. That's why I didn't come back yesterday."

Michael stood up and walked stiffly about the room. He stopped for a moment in front of the ancient mauser rifle which hung on the wall. He ran his finger along it, removing some dust. "We'll bring her in, definitely." He stared at the dust on his finger. "I'm not too worried. It's not like she's likely to find the Infidel Friend, even if she did somehow find a way in. It's been days since he was sent in there."

"I wasn't worried about Molly, sir." Graham stepped forward, feeling the soft carpet beneath his boots.

The motion caught Mike's attention, and he looked up from his dusty finger. "Oh?"

"This isn't some common man you threw through the Golden Door, sir. This is an Infidel Friend. If there's a way out, then he's going to find it."

Michael nodded, rubbing the dust off of his finger.

"That's assuming, of course," Graham went on, "that he hasn't found it already."

Arturus' shoulders were hunched from fatigue. His steps were slow and deliberate, and he favored his right foot heavily. He didn't even bother to look through the black crystal as he passed them. He should have been more careful, but he couldn't find the energy to do much more than walk.

He was not surprised when he heard the growl of the hound behind him. The hound was a four footer and broader than it was tall. Arturus was too tired to feel much fear.

If it kills me, it kills me.

He clutched at one of the grey bags he'd made from his cloak and emptied its contents on the floor. The bent silver legs sounded like pins as they scattered about.

"You want me?" he asked the beast.

It moved forward, sniffing at the objects. Arturus could see it measuring the distance. Perhaps it could jump far enough to clear the makeshift caltrops. Maybe it couldn't. It tested the ground with one paw before yelping and pulling back. Arturus raised his pistol and took aim. The thing turned and ran.

It might find a way around.

He continued walking. At times he almost felt as if he was wandering, but the many of the Carrion rooms looked familiar. Galen had taken him to the ritual along this route. As long as he could follow it backwards, he would be able to find the hunters.

If they haven't moved.

The corridors blended together. Sometimes he wondered if he was just tricking himself into thinking that he knew where he was. Maybe all of the rooms of the Carrion looked similar. Maybe he was wandering deeper into the wilds, farther and farther away from his friends. Farther and farther away from Harpsborough, and Alice, and Ellen. . . and Rick.

The thought of his other father brought a catch to his throat.

Would they have filled in the wall yet? Would they make Rick do the building? What a cruel thing that would be.

What he wanted right now more than anything else in the entirety of damnation was a piece of Rick's burnt flatbread.

The next room gave him pause.

Is this it? Have I finally made it?

He cleared his throat. "It's Turi," he reported.

He entered the passageway slowly and followed its turn. They were all there.

I'm safe.

He felt as if he had been struck dumb.

"Turi!" Aaron shouted.

Johnny Huang caught him up in a hug that was so tight that it hurt. Avery's laughter was as loud as Aaron's shout, and Duncan had to shush them before they made enough noise to draw demons.

"I knew you'd make it back!" Avery said, grabbing at Arturus shoulder.

He saw Kyle, leaning up against a stone wall. He looked pale, but he was awake. The man gave him a wan smile and a thumbs up. Aaron reached over and tousled Arturus' hair.

Arturus sighed and laughed.

I'm safe.

He could breathe easily for the first time since he had entered the Carrion. Aaron was beaming, and when Johnny finally released him, Aaron hugged him as well.

They were all around him, struggling to keep their voices down. He saw his father, asleep in one corner. In another, he saw the captured priestess.

"Don't worry about her," Aaron said as Arturus looked at her. "We captured her to try and find you. She's no trouble."

"You made it!" Avery congratulated him, "Galen told us you'd been captured! You gave them the slip, huh?"

"Yeah," Arturus laughed. "I gave them the slip."

Arturus had no idea that they would have been so happy to see him. He hadn't really thought that he was that important to them at all. But they did care. They loved him as if he was one of their own. As if he was one of the villagers of Harpsborough.

And I love them right back, as if they slept in the chamber next to mine. As if they ate in the battery room with me each morning.

Still, for all their celebration, a part of Arturus felt empty. He looked over towards Galen, who was now eying him from where he lay near the wall.

"He was looking for you all day yesterday," Aaron said, whispering into his ear. "Man hadn't slept for more than an hour since we'd entered the Carrion, but he still went out looking for you. He finally had to come back."

He's disappointed in me. I was supposed to stay still. I was supposed to keep my head on. But I was sure they wouldn't pick me, and I saw Julian. I thought it was the right thing to do.

Fatigue swept over Arturus. He moved beside Galen and lay down.

Galen looked at him through squinted eyes. His father smiled, grunted, and then rolled back over to sleep.

Arturus' heart swelled in his chest.

"I'm proud of you boy," Galen said, his voice sounding muffled since he was speaking towards the wall. "Would have taken a lot of skill to escape from them and make it all the way here. I'm proud of you."

"I thought maybe they had caught you," Arturus said.

But Galen had already fallen asleep. Arturus shrugged, fatigue was also taking him. He placed his remaining pouch of silverlegs down carefully. He spotted his clothes lying next to Galen. Arturus took them and bundled them up to use as a pillow. When he laid his head down, however, he felt something metal in one of the pockets. He reached in to find out what it was.

It was his razor.

He smiled.

His eyes closed, almost of their own accord. It was not long until he was dreaming peacefully of the battery room, and of Rick, who had burned his flatbread.

— 48 —

Galen stood guard while Arturus knelt by the river.

"Is this safe?" Arturus asked.

"As safe as anywhere in the Carrion. There's only this entrance, and a dyitzu would have to climb to make it."

Arturus eagerly took off the blood-soaked grey pants and torn shirt he'd been wearing. He dipped himself quickly into the river. The water carried away the blood and sweat which had clung to his skin.

He pulled himself back out quickly and began dressing his wounds. His right foot didn't look any better than it had before he and Galen had gone to the ritual, but his left had almost healed completely. Neither foot stung when he wrapped them with fresh bandages. He walked about for a moment, feeling the cool Carrion air on his skin, waiting to dry a little.

His old clothes felt so much more comfortable than the serf's garb, even the newer black shirt, and he felt much more like himself when he put them on. It was as if all those things that had happened to him, watching the Minotaur and kissing Maab, had happened to some other boy. Some poor boy who wore a grey robe.

He smiled at the idea of it.

"You have a whetstone?" Arturus asked, his voice sounding quiet above the rushing of the water.

Galen searched through his pack with his hands, his eyes still on the exit. He tossed a small stone over to Arturus.

This is the same water that flows through the Thames. Rick might have watched it flow by.

Arturus knelt by the river. He felt the vibrations of the bone-handled straight razor as he ran it over the whetstone. After a few quick strokes he tested the blade's edge on the hairs of his chin. Satisfied with the result, he tossed the whetstone back to Galen.

The man caught it with his left hand without breaking his

vigil and put it back in his pack.

Arturus began by shaving down on the right side of his face with quick and even strokes.

Galen moved closer to him and spoke while he shaved. "I made a successful meeting with my old friend." Galen's voice was just loud enough to be heard over the river. "We're waiting another day or so, letting all of Maab's priestesses clear out before we meet. He's agreed to try and lead us back to Harpsborough."

Arturus nodded, dipping the razor into the river. The room was too dark for him to have a proper reflection, but he could see a shadow on the water where his head was. He was careful to place the blade to the right of it so that he didn't feel like he was stabbing himself.

"Maab's people are being pushed by something, he told me," Galen went on. "The devils are thick here, terribly so, but they're even thicker as you get deeper into the Carrion. Maab's people have many devilwheat troves like the one Julian found, but now they're not able to get to the farthest of them. That's probably why they kidnapped Julian when they did. They didn't mind losing a little grain in the beginning, but it became more precious to them when they stopped being able to get to their other sources."

Arturus started shaving his neck, paying special attention to where it met his jaw.

"At first I thought that the Minotaur she used in the ritual was the cause of all her woes, but my friend let me know that she's had that thing captured for years. There's something else out there, deep in the Carrion, gathering strength. If he's right, then it's not just a Minotaur. Maybe it's a few Minotaurs together, or a council of Nephilim. Who knows?"

Arturus tested his jaw with his thumb. He seemed to have gotten everything. He washed off the blade one last time, again careful not to disturb the shadow of his face, and dried the straight razor on his pants before folding it into its bone handle.

"We'll have to pay careful attention," Galen was saying. "If we're able to get back home, that is. As the pressure builds, Maab's people might try to cross over. They may want to take Harpsborough. Of course, whatever devils dwell deep in the Carrion won't be far behind them."

"If?" Arturus asked.

"If," Galen said. "I'm not sure how well versed our guide will be with the area. We may have to just gather enough woodstone torches to make it back through the silverlegs."

Arturus frowned when he thought of the spiders. "Unpleasant."

"Unpleasant indeed. More than that, I'm not entirely sure that my old friend is still loyal. He may try to lead us astray."

"They have control of hounds," Arturus said. "They used one to chase me. I had no gun, just a torch, so I led them towards the silverlegs. I used the torch to drive the spiders into Maab's hunters."

"Smart move." Galen approved.

"They had a little girl with them. I recognized her, I think. One of Maab's. I don't want to leave without Julian."

"Unwise."

"They are doing terrible things to him."

"I am aware. Do you know where they are keeping him?"

"With Selena."

"We could, if we planned it well, raid Selena's clan. If we rescue Julian, it will take us some time to get him back to Harpsborough. However, the war we start between Harpsborough and Maab's clans would be immediate. It would be improper to start that war without letting Harpsborough decide for themselves if that was what they wanted. In all likelihood, we'd return to find the village destroyed."

"I understand."

Galen nodded and moved back towards their chamber. Arturus stood, but remained by the river, watching it flow by. Galen stopped and waited.

I've learned something. Something important. Something to do with myself. I need to talk this out.

"You were here, years ago," Arturus said.

"I was."

"Was I born here?"

"Yes, Turi. Yes you were."

"So in a way, I've come home."

"In a way."

"My blood mother and blood father, are they still here?"

"No."

"The Carrion makes Maab evil, doesn't it."

"Partly. In Hell, as it was on Earth, the only things of any real value are the ones we've fought for and won on our own. Both places are so inhospitable to us, so inamicable to our condition, that we have to twist those creations against themselves to find enough time and space to breathe and love. Dyitzu or polio. Hounds or cancer. Minotaurs and droughts and earthquakes and settlings and small pox. It's all the same. Perhaps Maab would have been a nicer woman if she had been faced with a less formidable adversary than the Carrion."

"What am I, then, if I was born of such a place?"

"Whatever you make yourself."

Arturus knelt again, looking at his shadow in the water. He had the sudden urge to stab it.

"But how can I know how to make myself?" he asked. "Maybe Maab has the right of it? Didn't the Devil make Hell?

Doesn't He decide what is right and wrong?"

"Morality is very different for you and me than it is for a dyitzu. Different for a lion than it is for a gazelle. Satan, the Fore, God, at some point they made all their rules up. You can too. I choose, because of who I am, to spend my life fighting Hell, fighting for people, fighting to raise you the best that I can. I made those rules up, made up that morality. Others—Satan, the Fore, Maab, God—make up different ones, and it makes no difference to me. I get along with them when I can and defeat them when I can't."

"But couldn't I just decide that my rules are only for me? Couldn't I hurt everyone but me?"

"You could. The way you asked that question, though, seems to belie the fact that you don't want to make that rule up for yourself. You might find that by following that type of rule you will tear apart the groups of people who support you. You might find that you hate the man you create by following it. Like Maab hates herself, and in some way, like Michael hates himself."

"But, still, I can't just decide what I think is right?" Arturus said. "Satan's going to judge me, won't he? When I die here, won't there be a Reckoning? Won't he decide if he likes what I've done, or hates it?"

"You really give a damn what that bloke thinks?"

Arturus considered the question. His shadow rippled with the water. He imagined the different faces that he could put there.

I am my own Reckoning.

"No," Arturus said, standing. "No I suppose I don't."

He found that he liked that shadow, oscillating with the water beneath him, and as he thought about it, he found that he liked the person who was casting it, too.

— EPILOGUE —

Carlisle lay dying on the cold stones of Hell. He watched his black blood as it crept across the floor, a muddy river fed by the wellspring in his side. The half-congealed liquid was marked with his own footprints, his lifeblood depressed in the pattern of his treaded boots. He felt a malevolence closing in on him—black wings on the edge of his vision. He half sat up from the blood he was lying in and looked all about himself. He couldn't see very far, but he knew it was out there. A devil, a sentience, a thing that hated him even more than he hated himself. A thing that was coming to kill him.

"Infidel!" Carlisle called.

The evil seemed to recede as if forced away by the word.

How many times has this happened?

"You found me, Carlisle," Lilith said.

God let his only begotten son be tortured and crucified.

"Save me," He begged.

"Oh, it's far too late for that."

"The Infidel, he's coming for me."

The black wings pulled back again, even farther.

"Who?" her voice sounded playful.

"The Infidel."

She bent down beside him. He remembered her from before, except last time she'd been little more than a shadow. Now she seemed real. "Oh," her low voice crooned, "say that name again. I love it when you say it."

"Infidel."

"Yes, do you see him, standing there? He keeps the devils at bay, my sweet."

The devils at bay? A blessing.

It hadn't always been like this.

He crawled up to his hands and knees. He saw the Infidel, silent, only a shade, but oh so very real. While he was near, the black wings could close no farther.

"Save me!" The pain blurred Carlisle's vision, and he had to fight to breathe.

"The best I can do is give you ways to fight the Devil," Lilith said.

"I don't want the Devil, I want the boy."

"Tsk, tsk. You want the angel's get, I know. But you're not headed that way. You have to take a look at the big picture. Do you remember why you were looking for him?"

Because Maab said so. Because. . . I hate Maab. She took my cock. I hate her. I hate her. Why did I want to do anything for her?

"I've forgotten," he admitted.

"Redemption, wasn't it, my sweet?"

Yes. Redemption. I failed God. I was sent to Hell for my sins. I wanted to help God. So I had to serve Maab. I had to save the one thing that was pure in this entire place. The child of the angel.

"I remember. I needed to do good."

"That's very noble of you, my sweet. You're making the devil who calls himself Mephistopheles angry, though. Can you feel him, the blackness clawing to get in?"

"I feel him."

"Roll on your back."

Carlisle did as he was told. Lilith descended upon him, straddling him. Her shoulders and arms were strong. Too strong to look feminine. Her face had a sharp angle to it. A girl's face, certainly, but her jaw was very muscular.

"So we need to fight the Devil, don't we?" Lilith asked.

"Yes! I hate Him."

He felt his own sick blood soaking through his clothes. He felt almost like he was drowning in it. "Tell me how to fight Him!" He shouted the words too strongly, and the pain became more than he could bear.

The dark circle was closing quickly around him. Lilith seemed to lose some of her substance. He could almost see through her.

"Who killed you?" she asked.

She's trying to make me say his name. I won't do it. Benson warned me. He told me not to say his name.

"No, witch! I'll not fall for your tricks." He sat up suddenly and reached out, taking hold of her neck. "Tell me! How do I fight the Devil?"

He was grabbing her throat as hard as he could. Her eyes looked sad. She leaned forward and held him as if he were her very own son. His grip about her throat slackened, and she lowered him into the blood. She kissed him gently on the lips.

Tears welled up in his eyes.

"Faith, child," she said. "You must give up your Faith."

She's trying to trick me!

"Never. That's what keeps me close to God. If I'd had enough Faith I wouldn't even be here."

She seemed even less solid. He *could* see through her. Beyond her was a tide, a flood, a maelstrom of black water—or black blood.

She kissed him again, so softly he could barely feel it. "I'll explain why, will you listen?"

"Yes."

She hummed for a few moments, the song of angels, and then she kissed him again—this time a bit more forcefully. "The Devil needs you to have Faith, because with Faith you can forgive anyone anything. You gave your Faith to God, once, remember? The Devil knows that if you've given it once, you'll give it again. He's going to come asking for it."

"You're wrong, woman, I'd never trust the Devil."

"You say that, my love," she whispered into his ear, "but you know that hasn't always been true. You've made mistakes before. I mean, how else were you sent to Hell?"

He nodded.

"Let's say you were reading the Bible," she continued, "and God ordered that genocide be committed. What would you think?"

"God would do no such thing!"

"Of course He wouldn't, but what if He did order it? Let's say He told Moses to kill some tribe to the last man. Imagine He ordered only their virgins be spared so that His men could have them. Imagine you had read it on Earth, what would you think?"

She's bedeviling me.

But a part of his mind wanted to know. A part of him that had grown to fruition during his schooling. The part of him that had scribbled blasphemy into his senior year English textbook. He imagined reading what she had described in the Bible.

"God would only order such a thing if it were just, so the people He ordered killed must all be evil."

Her kiss was so faint, like a butterfly landing on his lips. He could see the tide of black water rising beyond her.

"You see, you gave your Faith to God, once, when He came asking for it, and now you'll forgive Him anything." She was whispering so softly that he had to fight to hear her. "You'll give your Faith to the Devil, soon, and He'll take it, and you'll forever be His."

Maab. This woman is worse than Maab. Maab at least wanted to save the angel's child.

Carlisle gathered his will to resist her. "Never, I'd never give my Faith to the Devil. I will always give it to God. No matter how many times he asks me."

"Fool! He'll take your memories. You'll know nothing,"

Lilith said as the black tide swept over them.

"It won't matter."

"You'll know as little as a babe. You'll know nothing of God or Satan. You'll know nothing of the universe, or of good and evil. And Carlisle, do you know what will happen this time? Do you know the one difference between your future life and your past one?"

"No."

"This time the Devil will ask you first."

The black wave swept his blood away, swept Lilith away. He felt a resonance building in her absence, powered by a low masculine voice that slowly overtook his soul.

"Now," said Mephistopheles, "you need to get your dirty hands on that child, don't you?"

Carlisle breathed in the dark ocean water. It felt cool against his lungs, as if it was extinguishing some fire that had been burning there. "I do."

"Good, then let's see if we can work something out. If I were to tell you how to get back to the boy, what would that be worth to you?"

Hellsong continues in Book II: Knight of Gehenna

Want to be notified when the sequel is released?
Register as a Citizen at hellsongseries.com

Need to look up a term?
Check out the Gehennic Encyclopedia as a free download on Kindle or view at our website:
hellsongseries.com/encyclopedia

Submit your Fan Fiction to contact@ehhknovel.com for possible inclusion into an upcoming magazine.
Details at ehhknovel.com/submissions

Shaun McCoy lives in South Carolina. He is an accomplished Pianist, Cage Fighter, Chess Player and Writer. You can check out his fan page at: www.facebook.com/shaunomccoy

www.ingramcontent.com/pod-product-compliance
Lightning Source LLC
LaVergne TN
LVHW041105080826
845145LV00007B/1693